Jessica F... ...began in
the worlds of th... ...she has written
screenplays and two non-fiction books. Her previous three
nove... ...
...about Jessica, visit her website www.jessicaruston.com.

Praise for Jessica Ruston:

'Deeply moving and emotional' *Heat*

'A fantastic debut' *Company*

'A tight, compelling study of love, obsession and breakdown.
I couldn't stop reading' Jojo Moyes

'Wonderful ... Ruston is staggeringly assured' *Sunday Express*

'A real page turner' *Woman* magazine

'It's the sort of book you want never to end. Intriguing,
atmospheric and utterly mesmerising' Penny Vincenzi

'A story to get lost in' *Grazia*

'Twists and turns and everything you need to keep you glued'
Adele Geras

'Littered with exciting twists ... utterly thrilling' *Closer*

# JESSICA
# RUSTON
# THE LIES YOU
# TOLD ME

**headline**
review

First published in 2013 by HEADLINE REVIEW
An imprint of HEADLINE PUBLISHING GROUP

1

Cataloguing in Publication Data is available from the British Library

ISBN 978 0 7553 8364 1

Typeset in Sabon by Avon DataSet Ltd,
Bidford-on-Avon, Warwickshire

Printed and bound by CPI Group (UK) Ltd, Croydon, CR0 4YY

Headline's policy is to use papers that are natural, renewable and
recyclable products and made from wood grown in sustainable forests.
The logging and manufacturing processes are expected to conform to
the environmental regulations of the country of origin.

For LGHR, who grew alongside this book.

# Acknowledgements

Great thanks to everyone at Headline Review, in particular Sherise Hobbs and Lucy Foley for unparalleled editorial support of many and various kinds. To Joan Deitch, fo her eagle eyes and dexterity in detangling timelines. To Simon Trewin, for combining sounding board, cheerleader and strategist in one charming package. To my family and friends for their lack of resemblance to the horrors I populate my books with. And to Jack, for everything and forever.

# Chapter One

That morning I received a key in the post. It was in a small Jiffy bag, my name and address on the front, written in a hand that I didn't recognise. I could tell it contained a key without opening it. Standing by the front door I squeezed it without thinking, as I did with every parcel, like a child on Christmas Eve, and felt its small, hard outline. There was a card or note in there as well – I could feel its ridge. Such a small thing. How could I ever have known how great its impact would be?

Or maybe some unconscious part of me *did* know, because I hid it. I don't know. It was a strange thing to do, but then we all do strange things sometimes, don't we? There's nothing odd about that. We all have our little quirks. Some of us pretend to be TV chefs when we're cooking dinner. Some of us count the cracks in the pavement and group our steps into patterns of five, ten, fifteen. Some of us can't sleep until we've mentally gone through the list of everyone we know, checking them off, as though by doing so we will keep them safe throughout the night. Some of us.

Anyhow, I hid the package, sliding it into the pocket of the cardigan I wore in the mornings, separating it from the pile of post: a gas bill, something for Mark from his practice, a cardboard package from Amazon, which I knew contained a work book I had ordered – and decided that I would not open or look at the small brown envelope again until Mark had left, would not even acknowledge that it was there, in case thinking about it somehow gave the secret away.

I carried the post through to the kitchen and left it in the usual place on the corner of the island while I went to fill the kettle. Mark would be down in a minute, in his usual morning flurry of aftershave and undone buttons, and I would kiss him and then he would be gone, out of the door and off to work, with a 'goodbye' and a 'see you later' and a 'have a good day'.

When Mark had gone I poured another cup of coffee and sat down at the kitchen table. I don't have to leave till half nine – I'm a university lecturer and don't do early starts – whereas he's usually out of the door by eight, and I relish that time when the house feels as though it is mine and mine alone and I can enjoy the silence of it settling around me, like an old jacket that has become used to every inch of your body. My morning ritual gives me the space to reclaim the house after Mark's departure. That makes me sound awful, doesn't it? As though every day I wait for my husband to leave, almost pushing him out of the door in order to get 'my' house to myself for a while. It's not like that, not really. I just like the space and feeling of calm descending over the house, like a dog turning around and around in its bed after its owner has walked it.

Usually I just sit for a while, five minutes or so, picking at my cuticles or watching one of next door's cats prowl around the garden and thinking that I really should do something about that tree we've always said we would prune back. I don't read the paper, I have it sitting in front of me, making me feel guilty that I'm not as interested in what's happening in the latest war zone as I should be. Sometimes I make lists. Shopping lists, lists of jobs that need doing around the house, lists of things I need to do at work, lists of films I want to watch. I've always made lists. They calm me.

Today though, I didn't just sit, and I didn't make any lists. Today I removed the envelope from the pocket of my cardigan and put it on the table in front of me.

*Klara Mortimer, 57 Hamilton Road, London, SW17 2DG.* I definitely didn't recognise the handwriting. It's one of the things for which I have a good memory. Mark finds it strange, but to me, seeing someone's handwriting is just like seeing their face. Letters make up words which make up images and take on life. The way people shape their 'e' or join an 's' and a 't' is as individual as their fingerprint. You can get a sense of a person without knowing them, simply from the way they form their letters.

What could I tell about the writer of this missive by the letters they had formed? I ran my fingers over them, tracing their shape. They were neither particularly rounded nor were they spidery, they were not formed with flair and panache but nor were they cramped and uncomfortable-looking. They were even, well-formed, polite-looking letters. Well-mannered, not pushing themselves forward, yet not meek. Not the incomprehensible scrawl of a medic or the angular letters of an architect, self-conscious as a pair of designer glasses with blank lenses. They were clear, with no sense of hesitation about their tails. Their creator was well-educated, I thought. Confident. I could tell by the varying width of the strokes that they had been written with a fountain pen, not a biro or fineliner, so I guessed their creator was someone older. And that was all I could fathom.

I turned the Jiffy bag over. There was no return address. I didn't expect there to be. The postmark was from Central London. Nothing to indicate who it might be from. Nothing on the outside, anyhow.

I waited for another minute, and then without thinking about it any longer, I slid my thumb under the edge of the Jiffy bag and tipped it up so its contents fell out onto the table: a single key, as I had guessed, and a thick sheet of writing paper, folded in two. I opened the note, and began to read.

And that was the start of it all.

*Dear Klara,*

*This note will probably come as something of a surprise. I hope that it does not dredge up too many difficult memories, but I have put off writing it for a long time. Long enough.*

*I do not know exactly what you have been told about your mother – why she was not around while you were growing up, where she went and why – but I do know that it could not have been the truth.*

*And I cannot be the one to tell you. Over the years I have been tempted, so many times, to simply find you and tell you what I know. But it would have been wrong, it would not have been what she would have wanted. And I do not even know the whole story myself, not all of it. But I know enough to believe that you must be told, you must discover for yourself the woman she really was. And I think that now is the time.*

*So, I am sending you this key. I have kept it safe, as I promised her I would, for more than twenty-five years. I'm sure she didn't expect it to be that long. But then, she didn't expect a lot of things that happened to her. None of us do.*

*She loved you, Klara, so much. She told me when you were born that it was as if the sun had come out at night-time, lighting her life in the most surprising way.*

*You must never think that anything that happened was because she did not care about you, did not try to put you first, always. She would have done anything for you – if she had had the chance. It is her tragedy, and yours, that she did not.*

*I'm in danger of saying too much. So I will sign off.*

*The key is for number 17, 31 Founthill Way, London SW21 3NG.*

*I hope so much that you will find what you need.*

N.R.

I let the key sit in the palm of my hand, feeling its weight. It was small, made of brass, worn-looking. It hung from a single spiral of metal. No key fob, nothing giving away the location of its home. It felt – furtive. As though its owner had kept it concealed, not wanting to risk giving away any clues to its application. Where had it lived, until now? In the bottom of a drawer, covered with papers? Tucked inside a wallet, in someone's pocket? Hung from a hook in a kitchen? It had a history, this key. A story to tell me. One that I had been waiting to hear all my life. One that I had yearned to be told. One that I was going to have to unlock.

Suddenly, and entirely without warning, I burst into tears.

The key sat easily in the pocket of my jeans, leaving no visible outline. I could feel its presence though. Its weight. Really I should have just told Mark as soon as he got home. That would have been the normal thing to do, the straightforward, honest course of action. I knew that. He would have sat at the table with me and read the letter, would have puzzled over its meaning for a little while, but not let me start to obsess about it; would have talked the possibilities over calmly and logically before accompanying me to the address and finding out what was there. There would have been no subterfuge, no secrets, no space in my brain for the story to grow and take on a life of its own. For the questions to start lining up in formation, filing themselves in the cabinet of my mind.

But there was no time to do that, I told myself; we were due at his parents' house for dinner, and we couldn't be late, and this couldn't be rushed. He'd want to go to Founthill Way immediately, and I knew we couldn't squeeze it in, and – I just needed more time. That was all. There was nothing sinister or suspicious about what I was doing. I wasn't hiding anything. I just wasn't ready to show him yet.

And anyhow, we had to leave in a hurry, picking up a card on the way there. It was Mark's father's birthday and the whole family was gathering, and I had been tasked with providing pudding. So I made brownies and allowed myself the space to let the note sink in, telling myself that I would talk to Mark on the way home. The mayhem of Gironde Road was always a distraction. It was impossible to dwell on things once you were through the purple front door of the ramshackle house; it was always too full of people and noise and laughter, and other, less commonplace adjuncts to family life – unicycles and kites and, one time, a woman having a baby in a birthing pool in the dining room.

It had taken ages for Mark to introduce me to his family, when we were first together. He was scared, I think, that their eccentricities would scare me off. He knew that I was used to quiet family dinners that involved serious discussions and long pauses, not the mess and mayhem of his family home. But he was quite wrong. By the time I met the Olivers, nothing could have put me off Mark. And they provided the context for him, the backdrop for who he was, explained why convention and rules and doing things the right way was so important to him. Ever since I had met him I had wondered where some of his little rituals came from, but hadn't found the way to ask: why he had to check that the back door was locked three times before he could come to bed, why he could not bear tinned soup, to the point of turning his head away when he walked past it in the supermarket, why he threw food out before it had reached its best-before date and could frequently be found standing in front of the fridge patrolling it for rogue items that might be nearing the end of their shelf-life.

He told me that first night, in bed. I hadn't had to ask in the end, he just opened his mouth and started talking. 'It was weirder than you can imagine. They're practically suburban these days, compared to how they were then.' He rested his head on his hand, his elbow lying out to the side, and I shifted closer, enjoying the scent and feel of his nearness. He radiated warmth and safety.

'How was it?'

A long pause. 'Lonely,' he said eventually, and I could have wept, his voice was so small and quiet. It was the last thing I was expecting him to say. 'I know,' he continued, 'sounds strange, doesn't it? The house is so busy, so full, there are people everywhere.'

'Was that not the case then?'

'Sometimes it was. It's slightly more ordered now.'

That was hard to imagine.

'But then . . . people would be there, but I'd never know who they were. There's no feeling in the world like coming home from school to find your house full of strangers, and not a single member of your family to be seen.'

'Frightening.'

'You get used to it, that's the sad thing. I stopped expecting anyone to be there. To give a shit.'

'That *is* sad.' My family had been odd, and small, no doubt about it, but I had never felt that no one cared where I was. 'Is that why medicine appealed, do you think?' I went on. 'Something you could control, some way of helping people?'

'Maybe. Not that I feel in control much at work. I shouldn't complain, should I though? I had two parents.'

I shrugged. 'Sort of. At least the one I had was there most of the time, unlike yours.'

'Maisie was on "a journey".'

'She had four children. She should have been at home.'

'She believed that we had to find our own way in the world. That it was our responsibility, not hers. All that crap.'

'Are you angry?'

His shoulder shrugged underneath my head. 'I used to be. I'm not any more. What's the point? Are you?'

I *was* angry – but on his behalf, not my own. I was angry about the things I had learned. That the reason he always checked the locks was because one day, when he was five, he had woken up to find all of the doors of his house open and a strange man standing over his bed, half-naked. His parents had held a party, things had gone the way they always did, they had wandered off to the Common to commune with trees, and he had been forgotten about. That his hatred of tinned soup was because he had lived off it for years, feeding his younger brothers and sisters. 'It was the only thing I knew how to make. It was the only thing that I could trust wouldn't poison us.' The fridge had been full of rotting food, and strange poultices that his father Barney had made to heal the ailments that could so easily have been cured by a trip to the pharmacy that the family did not believe in. Mark used to clear it out surreptitiously, throwing things away when he could, and trying to prevent his siblings from opening it and

eating what they found in there. 'Serri did onc̵
told me. 'She was sick for days.'

'It was child abuse really. You do know that,
twirled my fingers in his chest hair and he shi̵
underneath my touch.

'Not abuse. There was no intent to harm.' A
medic.

'Neglect, then. What would you do if you tho̵
same was going on in the home of one of your patien̵

'It was a different time. They were different people̵
turned out all right, didn't I?'

I sighed, and kissed his neck. 'More than all right. ̵
makes me sad to think of you like that. All by yourself.' ̵
to stop because a lump had formed in my throat, thinkin̵
it. I loved Mark fiercely, protectively, possessively.

'What about the name?' I asked, letting a smile conceal my
tears.

'Ha, the name. Mark was the most sensible name I could
think of when I was little. It was the name of a man who lived
down the street, who worked at the bank. And it had the same
initial as my real name, so before I could change it officially I
could sort of pretend that it was mine. If people wrote to me
as M. Oliver I could pretend it stood for Mark and no one
would know that it was really Moonbeam.'

I let my eyes close. And the sadness I felt was tinged wi̵
pleasure, that he had allowed me in like this, that I had worl̵
my way between the clamped-shut edges of his life like a b̵
sliding into an oyster.

# Chapter Two

I hardly slept. All night I lay next to Mark, listening to him breathe in and out, slowly and evenly. Thinking. Wondering. Who was N.R.? Why had they written to me, and why now? What was I going to discover about my mother?

Sadie left us when I was six. Just walked out of the door one day, or so I imagine. I was too small to remember. All I know is that one day she was there, tall and slim with billows of fudge-coloured hair and long, elegant fingers, smelling of spice and musk, and then suddenly she wasn't and I went from being a normal little girl (well, quite normal; I was always quiet, always lived in my own head) to 'the girl whose mother left'. Because it's not normal, is it, for your mother to leave you? Fathers, yes, they melt away all the time, going off with other women or in search of something or just because the drudgery gets too much, and no one bats an eyelid, no one looks sideways at the ones they left behind and wonders, Was it them? Was it something they did, to make him unable to bear it any longer? But when it's the woman who goes . . . people whisper.

They stopped once she was dead, on the whole. That was few years later. She had gone to America to work, Daddy ld me, and that was where she died. She was a model, my other – a beautiful, incandescent woman who lit up every

room she entered. Was that what killed her? Her beauty, the burning flame of it? Or was it something prosaic, like lung cancer or a stroke or taking a corner too fast? I didn't know. That's strange, isn't it? Not to know how your own mother died. But Daddy got so upset when I asked, he became so distressed and started to breathe hard, so I stopped asking – and then it became one of those things that you haven't talked about for so long that mentioning it seems . . . indelicate. Like when you forget someone's name soon after meeting them and then it's too late to ask and you have to call them 'mate' or 'darling' for evermore.

So, we had just bumbled along, Daddy and me. I had tried to find things out about her, of course, secretly, as I got older. Had Googled her, but her career seemed to have fizzled out, or maybe she had started doing something else when she was in America, because there was little mention of her as a model, just some articles and lists of people from the Seventies. But then she had been working before the Internet was invented, long before, and she hadn't been famous, not really. I looked up my family on one of those genealogy sites as well, inputting what information I had into the family tree programme, and found nothing. I didn't have enough details for the thing to work properly, and again, I couldn't ask Daddy, so I left it, and just kept on wondering. It didn't matter, I told myself. I had Daddy, who was the best father in the world, and he told me stories about her sometimes, and she wasn't coming back anyway, whatever I did, so I might as well just get on with it. I still wondered though.

Eventually, at around four o'clock in the morning, I slid out from between the sheets, shut the bedroom door quietly behind me and went downstairs. I sat up for the rest of the night, watching old movies that I had seen hundreds of times before. I knew all the lines, so my lips moved silently as I sat on the sofa in the reflected half-light, surrounded by a battalion of cushions and covered with blankets like a mountain. Doing this stopped me thinking, stopped my brain from racketing along like a pram flying down a hill, during those nights when everything in my mind rose up to meet me. So I sat and watched, while the sky slowly lifted its lids and shrugged off that darkest, thickest part of the night, and became morning.

And then Mark was up, blinking and showering and breakfasting, and I kissed him goodbye and waved him off to work just like yesterday, like the good wife that I wished I could be, the one that he deserved, the one who did not keep anything from him, all the while counting down the hours until the working day was over and I could leave the university and head to the address in the note. I had already sent Mark an email telling him I had a meeting and so would be late. It wasn't a lie.

Founthill Way was one of those meandering, twisty roads in a bit of South-West London that was neither one place nor another, somewhere between Tooting and Wimbledon and Morden. I'd lost track some miles before, and had been thankful for my Sat Nav for at least three postcodes' worth of road.

There was a pub on the corner of the street, and I wondered about going in and getting something to eat until I saw a woman coming out of the front door, shuffling in greying sweatpants that dragged on to the ground, her cheeks sunken and her hair lank. The sort of woman you saw on the six o'clock news, dead in a doorway and no one to care. I decided I'd stop and pick up a burger on the way home instead. I was just putting off the moment, anyhow; it was like meeting a blind date and suddenly losing my nerve. The woman looked up and caught me staring at her, and her eyes turned darker still. I turned the wheel quickly and headed down the road and away from her.

Founthill Way was a strange place; it consisted of part housing, part industrial units, part wasteland. On the left-hand side of the road was a bingo hall, a plastic banner above its doors proclaiming a winner every night and hot food. The large car park in front had signs on the railings advertising weekly car-boot sales. It made sense. This was just the sort of place where you'd come to get rid of your junk.

Or acquire someone else's.

Numbers 7, 9, 11, 13 Founthill Way were a row of houses, one step up from pre-fabs, small rectangles of front garden full of trampolines and broken bicycles. Number 15 didn't seem to exist, nor did 17; 19 to 25 were more caravans. A man stood in front of one wearing an old jumper that sagged over his potbelly; he was silent, smoking, observing me as I drove slowly past. I took care not to meet his eye. Then there was a section of industrial units, big slabs of corrugated metal with vans parked in front. *27 Founthill Way*, said the sign at the entrance, and then there was a list of the businesses with units there: a window company, a wine merchants, a commercial bakery. I drove on.

And then I rounded a corner and found myself in front of an open driveway at the end of the road. There was no number on it, but something made me turn in. It was 31, I was sure of it. It had to be. I'd reached the end of Founthill Way, so if it wasn't here, it wasn't anywhere.

I stopped the car, but I didn't get out. Not straight away. Instead, I took the note that had come with the key out of my bag and stared at it, as though it might help, as though something would suddenly become obvious upon what must be the fifty-third reading; some clue would make itself known to me.

*I have put off writing it for a long time and cannot do so any longer*. Why? What had happened to make N. R., whoever they were, write now? What had changed in their circumstances that meant they could no longer put off the writing of this cryptic note? And why *had* they put it off for so long, come to that? It wasn't as though they were revealing anything of themselves. Far from it.

*I do not know exactly what you have been told about your mother – why she was not around while you were growing up, where she went and why – but I do know that it could not have been the truth*. Why could I not have been told the truth? Why such certainty that there was so much that must have been kept from me? *Why she was not around while you were growing up*. The line was so unclear. Did the author of the note mean *before* she left, when she was simply away in London a lot, or after she had gone for good?

*And I cannot be the one to tell you*. Once more I asked myself, why? I had no idea who this 'I' person was, where they lived, what their relationship was or had been to my mother. I didn't even know whether they were male or female. What possible reason could there be for such secrecy? What possible harm could it do, for them to simply tell me what they knew, rather than leading me along this path with breadcrumbs, enticing me with mysterious notes and anonymous sign-offs, presumably so that they might ease their own conscience without actually putting themselves at risk. But at risk of *what*?

'Oh, just go in and find out, for fuck's sake,' I told myself crossly, shoving the note back into my bag and getting out of the car all in one movement.

31 Founthill Way turned out to be a collection of low buildings, arranged around the yard in which I was parked. To my left was a white-painted building, not a house, maybe

a mews block, with a stable door, and next to it, a small metal sign saying *1*. A light was on inside. In front of me were four workshops, wooden with corrugated-iron roofs. The doors to three of them were shut, but the last one lay open, and I walked towards it.

It was full of furniture, stacked from floor to ceiling; book-shelves and sets of apothecary drawers and coffee tables, all periods and in all states of repair, and it smelled of wood and sawdust and polish and paint, the last from a large dresser that was in the process of being covered in one of those trendy putty-coloured shades that always slightly reminded me of zombie movies. They were called things like 'Shrew's Tail', but 'Rotting Flesh Number Nine' would have been more appropriate.

'Help you?'

I turned, embarrassed to be caught snooping.

'Sorry, I—'

'You here for the chest of drawers?' The voice belonged to a tall man in paint-splattered overalls, who emerged from behind a tower of furniture at the back of the space, wiping a brush on a cloth in his hands. He had a thinning hatch of straw-coloured hair, fine, long fingers and pale blue eyes.

'No, sorry, I'm not looking for . . . Is this your place?'

'Well, it's not the Queen of Sheba's.'

'No. No, I mean the whole of number 31.'

'Oh. No.' He didn't elaborate.

I nodded, awkward. I knew I should explain myself, but I didn't want to tell this stranger what I was doing there. We stared at one another. He seemed to feel no need to fill the silence, whereas I felt more and more uncomfortable with every passing second. I had to say something, otherwise I was going to end up offering to buy a bloody chest of drawers simply to justify my presence here.

'I'm looking for number seventeen.' I didn't say anything else. Two could play at his game, I thought defiantly. But he didn't seem to care, just nodded and walked to the entrance.

'Over there,' he said, pointing to the right-hand side of the courtyard, at a row of lock-up garages. 'It's the one in the middle. You taken it over?'

I looked to where he was pointing. The garages were dilapidated, but looked reasonably secure. 'Yes,' I replied. 'I – it seems that I have.'

He gave me a strange look, but didn't ask any more questions, just shook his head and took his paintbrush back inside. I could hear him shuffling about in there, whistling faintly under his breath, as I walked towards the garages.

I had expected it to be rusty, or difficult to open, like something from a fairy-tale. The garage looked as though it hadn't been touched for decades, but someone seemed to have been keeping an eye on it, because the padlock was clean and oiled, and the key opened it easily.

Inside, the lock-up was cold and almost empty. I swallowed my disappointment. No teetering piles of furniture here. Instead, there was just one pile, sitting in the centre of the space, looking almost like some kind of installation in a modern art gallery – something my sister-in-law Serri could have created. *Travelling Light*, she might call it, and we would all be impressed and stand around drinking cheap white wine and talking about what it meant. A bare light bulb hung from the middle of the ceiling and I flicked a switch to turn it on. Someone had been paying the electricity bill, then. N.R.? Or someone else?

Below it were two large trunks, of the sort that one might have taken on a cruise in the days when travel took weeks rather than hours. Made of metal, heavy-looking and dusty, they sat on top of one of those low wooden crates of the type used to pack furniture, raising them slightly off the floor. To protect them from damp, I supposed. Again, someone had been paying attention, making sure the contents of the garage did not disintegrate over the years.

The trunks had padlocks on the front, but they were not locked. I flipped the hinges down and opened each trunk in turn.

Inside were four large cardboard boxes, two in the first trunk and two in the second. They were dark brown, with lids, and white rectangles on the side so that you could make a note of their contents. The rectangles were empty. The boxes looked old, and the dark brown was actually a sort of pattern, I realised, as I looked closer. They were dusty and the corners were worn. They reminded me a little of old photo albums, like the ones in which my father kept snaps of my childhood. Seventies' patterns. I touched the top of one of them.

Tentatively, I lifted the first box out of the trunk and raised its lid, and then immediately shut it again, as my eyes filled with tears and my hand rushed to my mouth. I had only caught a glimpse of what was inside the box – a flash of brightly coloured fabric, silken and fine – but it was not what I had seen that caused my reaction. It was what I had smelled.

I took a deep breath and shut my eyes. When I opened them I had to stop myself checking to see if she was standing there behind me, her presence was so strong. And for a moment – for that moment – it was as though she *was* there once more, as though I was not standing alone in a cold lock-up garage in the suburbs of south-west London, but back at home, in my childhood bedroom, being put to bed by her. It was her scent, faint and faded but unmistakable, that had risen up from the box, as though it had been waiting to meet me and I could almost feel her skin next to mine as she bundled me up in my duvet, she in her silk and stockings, me in my pyjamas, soap-clean and sleepy. 'Sleep tight, Puffin.' Her voice was a whisper, as faint as the echo of her scent, but I clung on to it as I wrapped my arms around myself and sobbed.

The drive home through Tooting was long and slow, and I spent every minute of it willing it to be over, and at the same time wanting it to continue forever. I could not imagine going through four boxes' worth of such powerful feelings. Though my logical brain knew that smell was the most evocative of the senses, that it connected directly to some near-primal section of our brain, and that the first glimpse of the contents would likely be the most shocking, most affecting, the rest of my mind whirred away creating scenario after scenario that played in my brain like an old home movie.

The boxes did contain what I had suspected they would, then – my mother's possessions, or some of them. I had guessed that this would be the case – hoped, even – but I had not counted on it, had not allowed myself to assume that it would turn out to be true. Now that I knew it was, a whole raft of questions rushed in, clamouring to be answered. Had she taken the storage unit on herself, and if so, when? If she had been the one to sign the contract originally, who had she passed it on to? Who had been paying for it since her disappearance and death? Why had she taken it on? If she *hadn't* been the lessee, then who had? Who had felt the need to store boxes of her belongings, and keep them safe?

And now they were uncovered, what else might I find that had been buried for so long in the past?

And as I wondered who the man or woman might be who had safeguarded my mother's things for so long, and why they had done so, a thought struck me. One that had been bubbling up in my mind since I first opened the envelope the morning before. One that I had been trying to keep pressed down, that had tugged at my imagination and my fears and memories. The thought that maybe the person 'safeguarding' my mother's things had not been doing that at all. Maybe their aim had never been to keep her things safe, but to keep them *secret*. And if that *was* the case, why – and what else might they have been hiding?

# Chapter Three

It had been a long time since I had consciously thought about my mother, but that night, after I had got home and lied to my husband about where I had been and what I had been doing – 'departmental meeting and we went out for drinks afterwards; I put the meeting in the diary,' I told him, making a mental note to add the evidence later to our shared calendar that hung on the fridge, retrospectively making my excuses – I said that I had some marking to do and went upstairs. With a mug of hot chocolate in my hand, I sat on the window seat that I had had built into the bay of the little back bedroom which I used as a study. I had covered it in cushions like a nest, and here, looking out over the rooftops, I dredged up my collection of memories.

Doing so was like diving for pearls. I kept them buried in the sandy recesses of my mind, carefully covered over with seaweed and rocks so that they could not float up at unexpected moments. I had learned that if I did not do this, they would ambush me. I would be walking along the street or giving a lecture at uni, and suddenly *she* would be there, her voice, or the flicker of her silk scarf, or just her scent. These fragments were so fragile that they dissolved into nothingness if I stared at them for too long, but they still had the power to stop me in my tracks.

Now though, I took them out, just as I had lifted the boxes out of the trunks in the lock-up garage earlier, and began to examine them. It was a fairly paltry hoard of memories by most people's standards, but she had gone when I was just a little girl, so what would you expect?

First, of course, came her scent. It floated up from the pile, just as it had done yesterday, causing a flood of emotion to engulf me. I rested my head on the window pane and remembered. It was Opium, heavy and spicy, with a promise of adult experiences that I could only begin to guess at. She wore it constantly, so all her clothes smelled of it, her hair and even her jewellery. It was as if her skin had become soaked with it. It entered the room before her and hung around, loitering in the corners after she had left. When I crawled into my parents' bed on a winter's night when I had woken with a nightmare, the sheets on her side were perfumed with it, and so was the pillow. I would bury my face in it, and fight against the fact that the scent gave me a headache and made my nose tickle as I breathed it in, hoping to also breathe in a little of her magic.

Their bedroom led me to the next memory, which sparkled and glinted in the light as I uncovered it: her jewellery. She was a magpie, my mother, always drawn to that which glittered. I learned early on that if I wanted to please her, all I had to do was ask Daddy to help me buy her a trinket – a brooch or a pair of earrings, it didn't matter to her as long as it dazzled and shone. Earrings were my favourite, because she would let me put them in, ever so carefully poking the post through the hole in her lobe in what seemed to me to be an almost surgical procedure, requiring great care and precision on my part, and immense and sacred trust on hers.

She treated all her jewellery with the same irreverence, driving my father mad when she chucked the diamond earrings he had bought her into the bottom of the leather case she kept it all in along with the cheap tat I had given her, and the stuff she picked up almost everywhere she went. It all lay, in an ever-increasing tangle of cut glass and pearls and amber and silver, until one day she would announce, 'That's it, I've had it with this mess! I can't see anything. Klara? I need your help. Bring me your nimble little fingers.'

And I would skip upstairs, thrilled to be needed so urgently for such an important task, and begin to carefully unknot the pile that she would dump in front of me on the bed. It would take ages, but I didn't care, because as long as I was doing it I was allowed to sit there, in her room, surrounded by all of her things, and feel special. Useful. And when I had finished I would be rewarded; she would let me put on anything I liked from the now tidy case. I have a photo that sits at the bottom of my own jewellery case, of me after one of these sessions. I am covered in jewels like a gypsy; huge ruby-red glass earrings suspended with loops of ribbon from my unpierced ears, rows and rows of beads and silver chains, brooches on my cardigan and in my hair. The whole look topped off with a slick of red lipstick. I look absurd, obviously, but I also look proud.

Proud. Of her.

Now I am led to the next link in the chain. She didn't meet me from school that often; quite a lot of the time it was Daddy. Later, of course, it was always Daddy. It was a good thing, I suppose, that I was already used to him being the one to meet me, his bearded face catching my eye when I came tumbling out of the gates in a flurry of lunchboxes and damp swimming costumes and stories about what naughty thing the twins had done in class today. It was one less place to miss her. I didn't mind that she couldn't often make it, I was proud of her. Proud to be able to say that my mother wouldn't be able to make a cake for the stall at the fete or be there for sports day because she was 'very busy, she's a model, she's got a very important job in town.' But that pride would swell into a tight balloon in my chest when I would roll out expecting Daddy and she would be there, infinitely exotic and glamorous, especially next to the other mums, whose grey faces and beige hair only served to provide a foil for her beauty. She knew it, and they knew it too, standing in tight huddles into which she was not invited, their eyes suspicious and their arms protective as they ushered their children towards them but more pertinently, away from her. To them, she was decadence, she was irresponsibility and cigarettes and frivolous behaviour, she was all the things that they had given up – if they had ever known them – she was everything they were afraid of and everything they longed to be all rolled into one fur-coated, stiletto-heeled package. Even as a small child I could see it. She was more interesting, more beautiful, more – simply *more* – than all of them put together, and I wore my pride like a cape, defensive and all-encompassing.

Another. The café in town that she used to take me to after school on the days she picked me up. It was run by an Italian man and it smelled of freshly ground coffee and sweet, sugary pastries. The owner was effusive and round-bellied, he would swoon over my mother and fuss over me, bringing me a cushion from the back so that I was better positioned at the white Formica table, bringing my mother her usual order without her asking for it, and an ashtray, and usually there was something else as well, a flower that would appear next to her place, as though from nowhere, or an extra little sweet treat for me, free refills of espresso for her. We would always have the same thing – she, an espresso and a coffee ice cream with butterscotch sauce, most of which I would end up eating, after I had finished my burger and chips. The man there made special child-size burgers, and served the chips in a little paper cone. Daddy took me there once, after she had gone, not knowing it was where we always used to go. It hadn't been a secret, not as such, but we never talked about it to him. It was our place. The owner grinned at me but kept quiet, not showing that he knew me, and Daddy ordered us both burgers, but I only ate half of mine. It felt wrong without her.

*Without her.* Whatever I did, that was the biggest memory I had of my mother, the one that, in the end, took over all the others. Her absence, not her presence; the space that she left. Her not being there for my birthdays, never being at another school play or ballet performance. Daddy sneaking in at the back, having rushed to get there from work. The slight pause that I would try to hide whenever someone asked me about her. The way I told stories or constructed certain sentences in order to avoid mention of mothers. Whatever I did, it would always be that way. She had missed so much of my life and I knew so little about her that often it felt as if she had never existed, as if the memories I thought I had were just a construction, a mirage. And now? Now she was here again, in my head.

Why had I locked these images away? I asked myself. Why had I always been so afraid to let them out into the light, to use them to keep her alive in some small way? People did this, people who had lost loved ones, I knew it. I had heard them speak of it, in documentaries and on radio programmes. 'We kept her memory alive for the children,' they said. 'It's important that they remember her as she used to be.' That was it though, that was the answer. My father had never wanted her memory kept alive, had never wanted her to remain with us, in the house, through her belongings and through photographs of her. Had never wanted her to drift into the realm of the normal, the much-loved but missing. She had become canonised in her absence, a mysterious figure of whom we did not speak, because doing so upset my father too much. And I had always thought that that was just what grief was – the inability to endure any reference to or trace of the lost and loved one. Had accepted it as true love, real loss. Because what else could it be? Now though, I wondered.

My hot chocolate had gone cold and grainy in the bottom of my mug. I stood up. The note and key that had arrived in the post had led me to the trunks, and as I unlocked those, my own memories had also been unlocked. And now I had to open the boxes themselves. They were still in the back of my car, covered with an old rug, not that Mark would go looking in there.

Tomorrow I would get them out, bring them inside and unpack them. And God only knew what I would find there. I had no way of knowing what I would be walking into. And the thought terrified me.

# Chapter Four

I stood outside my father's house – my old home – and paused for a second. In the cotton bag dangling from my elbow was a home-made ginger cake, his favourite, and a copy of the book chapter that I was currently working on and wanted his opinion on. One of the advantages of my job as a lecturer and archivist at City was the time they allowed me to publish my own books – this latest was on between-the-wars European cinema, a pet topic of mine. At the bottom of the bag was the note. I hadn't quite decided whether I was going to show it to him yet, or whether I would even tell him about it. It felt treacherous to talk to him about it before telling Mark, but at the same time, right. It concerned his wife, after all. No one that Mark knew. Still, though. It's little justifications like that that make up a big lie, isn't it? You never start out meaning to deceive – I didn't, at least. But one untold fragment leads to another hidden letter or concealed conversation, and before you know it you're carrying this great big weight of untruth around with you everywhere you go. That is what happened with Mark. It's not that I can't trust him – I trust him with everything. It's just that once you start telling lies, it becomes a habit. The envelope was small and light, and if you'd looked in the bag you might not even have noticed it. But its presence both there and on my mind was weighty.

'I'm going to Budapest next week,' my father said as he measured the coffee out into the pot with a wooden spoon. The small kitchen was warm and full of the smell of soup. He had become a good cook over the years, if a frantically untidy one. He had had to learn, I suppose. He never baked though. For someone who was able to juggle the most complex of concepts with ease and dexterity, he found the precision required by baking surprisingly frustrating and baffling. He liked to be able to chuck handfuls of stuff into pots and see what happened after a couple of hours of simmering, not to have to weigh out exact amounts and add them in a particular order. So I brought cakes round and he gave them marks out of ten, in three different categories, recorded in a special notebook – flavour, texture and presentation.

'What for? A conference?' I asked. He was always giving lectures at gatherings of the great and good, fellow specialists in linguistics.

'Mm. Just for a couple of nights. I'd have asked if you wanted to come with, but I'm hardly getting any time off.' He sounded disgruntled. I accompanied him on his trips sometimes, not to attend the lectures themselves – our fields of expertise were far from overlapping – but just for fun. It was a tradition that had started when I was eleven or twelve and deemed old enough, firstly to amuse myself for a couple of hours or be left with a colleague while he fulfilled his work obligations, and secondly, to be able to appreciate the programmes of cultural enrichment that he planned for such trips. He took pride in winkling out the most obscure sights and curiosities to take me to. No dull old Louvre or Colosseum for us; we went to the Parisian sewer museum beneath the Quai d'Orsay, and a tomb in Rome that was lined and decorated with the bones of long-dead monks, their femurs forming ghoulishly beautiful arches in the gloom. I saw shrunken heads at the Pitt Rivers Museum in Oxford, wizened like long-forgotten and dried-out apples on racks. At the Museum of Bad Art in Massachusetts, we pretended to be critics, glaring at the works through imaginary monocles and assessing their relative weaknesses.

As an educator, and as a parent, my father was generous and inventive. Nothing was too much trouble or too difficult to explain – he would always find a way. As I got older, I realised that I had probably been a sort of project to him, a blank genetic canvas onto which he could attempt to imprint – what? A version of himself? No, he had never been a vain man. A version of my mother? But he did not push me to be like her – the opposite, if anything. I don't know. I'm making it sound as if he experimented on me, and of course it wasn't like that. But he certainly derived huge satisfaction from seeing me learn, loved it when I expressed an interest in something new. Anything I asked about would be researched meticulously, involving trips to the library to unearth everything available on the subject of Vikings, or needlework, or hot air balloons He would then spend hours after I had gone to bed going through his finds, carefully locating and marking with Post-it notes the sections that he thought were the right combination of informative and entertaining enough not to be off-putting. And he never minded when, after varying but usually relatively short amounts of time, I tired of the current interest and moved onto the next.

So I grew up learning, and knowing there was no question that I could ask my father that he would not attempt to answer, finding out the necessary information if he did not already know it, seeing the expansion of my mind as a personal challenge and one that he relished.

No question, that is, apart from almost anything about my mother.

Of course he talked about her; it was not as though her name was *verboten*. But it was always on his terms. He had certain stories that he would tell, anecdotes that got wheeled out, and beyond that ... there was nothing. Whatever I asked, he returned to the same stories. I had never questioned this. Why would I? I had just listened, lapping up the tales he told me of her.

I would ask for them as bedtime stories, often, when I was little, and then less frequently as I got older. Maybe I got bored of hearing the same things over and over? No. I had never tired of it. Even now I recalled the feeling of comfort I got as I lay there, tucked into bed, listening. So why did I stop asking? Because of the look on his face when I asked, the flash of pain that passed behind his eyes, the frown that appeared above them. With growing awareness of others I began to see that it was my questions that caused those expressions, my selfish desire for comfort that hurt him. And so I stopped asking. I always remembered them though. Still did.

'She glittered when she came into a room,' he would tell me. 'Like a princess in a fairy-tale.'

'Like a fairy at the top of a Christmas tree?'

He nodded. 'Like the froth on a wave when it catches the sunshine at the seaside. She was all of those things and more.'

Our lines were as well-trodden and rehearsed as those from the fairy-tales that he read me.

*Go on.* I snuggled beneath the covers of my bed so that only the top half of my face was poking out and my chin was tucked under the quilt. My toes touched the hot water bottle at the end and curled themselves around its rubbery edge in anticipation of the tale that I knew was coming. There was the story about how they met, at a Christmas party. About how they fell in love, straight away. The story of their wedding. Another that I always loved, about him going to pick her up from a modelling job and waiting in the rain for hours while she finished shooting with a dog that kept on jumping up and covering her with muddy footprints, just so he could watch her, and so that she would know he was there waiting. That she was not alone.

But other than those tales, repeated until they were smooth and silky as pebbles on a beach, we did not talk of her. Did not mention her in casual conversation to others, smiled politely and changed the subject if others talked of her to us. I followed Daddy's lead, as children do, and it became a habit. It was just the way it was. Our stories were special, precious, practised – and contained.

So it took not a small amount of courage to stand in the kitchen that morning, cutting the ginger cake with an unsteady hand, blowing on my coffee to cool it, finding the right-sized plate for the cake, all of these little tasks simply ways of putting off the moment where I would open my mouth and break the silence that felt like a long-kept promise between us. Eventually though, I simply took a gulp of still-too-hot coffee and asked the question, trying to sound casual and failing, even to my own ears.

'Who were Mummy's friends?'

I had to ask. Ever since I had got the note and especially since I'd been to the unit and retrieved the boxes, my brain had been whirring with questions. Who might N.R. be? Who had he or she been to my mother? Why had they kept the unit so carefully – paid for it, I had to assume, for all these years – in order to store a collection of dusty rubbish that could have been stored anywhere? What were they trying to tell me? Had my father known them? Had he known about the lock-up? I couldn't ask him any of this straight out, but I could ask something. I had to ask something.

He didn't answer or say anything in response for a long time. Gave no indication that he had heard even, and I was beginning to wonder whether he was going to simply pretend that I hadn't said anything and, if so, what I would do. Would I have to repeat the question? Pluck up the courage to ask again on another occasion? I wasn't sure if I could. But I didn't have to. After standing in front of his cake, staring down at it, hands in fists on the edge of the kitchen island, his beard trembling slightly, the only sign of emotion from him, he spoke.

'Why do you ask?' His voice was careful, measured, as though he were trying not to give anything away. Or maybe I was reading too much into it. I do that, sometimes.

'Just . . . something made me think. Nothing important. Something Beth said about being a mother and suddenly everyone expecting you to be friends with women you have nothing in common with, other than the fact that you've both reproduced. I was wondering whether she found it easy to make friends with other mums.' I crossed my fingers behind my back as though it would erase the lie. I wasn't ready to tell him about the boxes, not quite yet. Something held me back.

'Well.' Another long pause. He was considering his answer. 'She didn't have lots of mum friends, not in that way, not really. She . . . she wasn't that type. The school-gate mum.' His voice was quiet, solemn. We both recognised that my asking the question, and him answering it, had changed something.

'No. She was never that sort of person, I suppose. But . . . what sort was she?'

He glanced up at me, a question in his eyes, and smiled. Oh, he knew me, my father. He knew there was more to my asking than a throwaway comment from my best friend.

'You know what sort of person she was. You remember.'

'Not exactly.' He hadn't answered the question, but had

31

deflected it back to me. Was it to become a stand-off, him refusing to say more until I gave in and told him what had really prompted my asking?

'I don't remember anything about her life. Who she saw, where she went. Just – fragments. She must have had friends. You both must have done.'

He shoved his hands into his trouser pockets and sighed. 'Yes, I suppose we did. It all seems like such a long time ago now.'

'It was a long time ago.'

'Another lifetime.'

'Yes.'

He carried his plate and mug over to the kitchen table, and I did the same, putting my crockery down on the red oilcloth that had been there for so long it was probably welded to the wood beneath it by now. When he was settled, he continued.

'We had separate friends, really. We weren't one of those couples who had lots of cosy dinner parties with other couples, all wearing lounge suits and drinking Campari or something, if that's what you're imagining.'

I realised that I didn't know what I had been imagining. I was so young when my mother left that I had no real concept of my parents as a couple, a romantic entity with a social life like mine and Mark's. Friends, dinners, picnics with the family. Outings to museums, shared school runs, trips to school fetes. These were things other people did.

'Mine were mostly work colleagues, hers were mostly in London. From before. We didn't mingle with them much.'

'Who were her friends though? Other models? Photographers? Artists?' As I spoke, it came to me that not only did I have no concept of my parents' joint social life, but that my knowledge of my mother's working life was based on a sketchy image of her getting the train to London to do vaguely glamorous things with an assortment of glamorous people, but with no real idea of what those things might be or who the people were with whom she did them. And I felt, for a moment, embarrassed by my ignorance, gauche and unworldly.

'Oh, that sort of thing, yes.' He was fudging, and we both knew it.

'What about from when she was at school? Did she keep in touch with people from then?' I pressed on.

'She was terrible at keeping in touch. She only saw people when they were right in front of her.' He smiled. 'But when she did, when she looked into your eyes? It was as though you were the only person in the whole world who mattered.'

I tried not to sigh. Yes, you've told me that, I thought. It's a line you've told me a hundred, a thousand times. And why do you insist on repeating it, on continuing this charade that we both know is false? What is it that you are shielding me from? *'I'm not a child any more,'* I wanted to shout. *'I don't need you to protect me. Just tell me the truth!'*

'When she looked straight at you, you felt so important; it was as though a light was shining down on the two of you, and no one else could break into your circle. Or that was what it was like for us, anyhow.'

The great romance, the great love. Suddenly I felt furious. Sick of hearing about this golden gaze that she bestowed on him, sick of how every question led back to the same stories, the same lines. They felt hollow now, hollow and meaningless. So what, if she had this power over you, this wonderful ability to make you feel important? That didn't help me – it didn't tell me anything about her, not anything real.

But of course I couldn't say it, any of it. We had been having this same conversation, or a version of it, for twenty-five years. It would not change now. *He* would not change now. And so I left the key and the letter in my bag, and I just smiled and patted his hand as if to comfort him, and he accepted it, and I sat and ate my ginger cake.

By the time I got home from work that evening, Mark was there, making dinner out of a pile of random bits and pieces that he had unearthed from the fridge – halloumi, sweet potato, Brussels sprouts, some leftover casserole, a courgette. I winced slightly as I saw the pan.

'Good day?' I asked, trying not to let my nose wrinkle, my fingers itching to take over.

'Busy enough. Uneventful enough. Eileen Addison died.'

'Oh, I'm sorry.' Mark always took the death of one of his patients more personally than some of his colleagues.

'Oh, it's fine. It was time. Anyhow. You?' He smiled at me to reassure and leaned over for a kiss.

'Yup. Went to see Daddy this morning.'

'How's he?'

'The usual. Off to Budapest, furious about some piece in the *Guardian*, about to be given his sixteenth honorary doctorate.'

Mark chuckled. 'Same old.'

'Exactly.'

I felt nervous, as though expecting a quizzing, but of course Mark wouldn't do that. As far as he was concerned, there was nothing to quiz me about. He was happy, contented, oblivious. I felt bad as I watched him, let my eyes run over the top of his head, over his hair which was going a bit grey at the sides, in a way that he hated and I rather liked. Felt that I should sit down with him now and tell him, just tell him, let him in. It would all have turned out very differently, if I had just done that. But I didn't.

# Chapter Five

Mark and I. We have been together for six years and married for three, and I can honestly say that I would not change a single second of those years. Nauseating, I know, but you see I never thought I would find love, not really. I was never one of those little girls who grew up dreaming of a wedding, or pretending I was a princess in a castle waiting for my Prince Charming, because I just assumed things like that happened to other people, to girls like Millie or Beth, pretty blonde girls who smiled and played nicely, not quiet, slightly odd ones like me. I had never had lots of boyfriends at school, had just tagged along on awkward double dates with Beth sometimes, before she had met Steve, whenever she had been with a boy who had a friend who could be persuaded to take me out as well. Bribed, sometimes, I suspect. At uni I slept with a couple of guys, mostly to shed my virginity and then to make sure that I hadn't been missing something the first time, and I got drunk and flirted with men who found me a bit embarrassing but acceptable for a one-night stand, and then I stopped that and just got on with my work and accepted that I wasn't cut out for love. Gave up on it, I suppose. And then there was Mark.

It was one of those stories that our friends urged us to tell, the story of How We Met, because it was romantic and a bit unusual. I was Christmas shopping in a desultory sort of a way, in the rain, trudging along Piccadilly from Fortnum's towards the tube station feeling sorry for myself. My feet were wet because my boots were leaking, and I was dragging my feet like a child, almost as though I hoped that someone would notice and take pity on me. I must have made a pathetic sight; hair stringy, face set in a pout, my coat frayed and damply doggy. I carried a single shopping bag containing the blow-your-head-off mustard that Daddy liked so much and which was the only gift I had bought so far. I reeked of self-pity.

I reached Hatchards and wasn't going to stop, because whenever I went in there I spent too much money on enticing-looking books for myself, and I had already done an Amazon order a few days previously. But the windows looked so Christmassy and welcoming, all glossy hardbacks and sprigs of holly and thick red ribbon, and I stopped to stare for a moment and imagine a life lived differently, one where I could sweep into all of these West End shops and buy whatever I wanted, all my purchases neatly boxed and bowed, and loaded into a waiting car that whisked me away. And for a moment my mind was full of images of that life, of a life that I might have had; of a different, better me – one who was happier and cleverer and funnier and more beautiful – and I felt light and warm and full of contentment. And then my eyes focused and I was looking straight into my reflection in the window, and I saw myself as I was then, at that moment, and it was not a gratifying sight. My eyes were wide and lost-looking, too deeply set, sad and lonely in the centre of my face, and my clothes were lacklustre; in fact, everything about me looked old and tired before its time.

I would have turned around and run to the tube right then, and almost did, but something caught my eye, something that distracted me from my morose wallowing and made me forget myself. A book-signing was taking place, as was often the case in the shop at this time of year, but this one looked different. The author was not sitting behind a small polished mahogany table, quietly inscribing his name, like usual, but standing, his arms waving in the air, animated and alive. On the table in front of him was a chemistry set, of the sort that children played with, all old-fashioned test tubes and coloured liquids. Something was smoking from one of them. Next to the set was a large plate, more of a platter really, covered in small portions of food. I could see some cheese, and what looked like a few squares of chocolate; there was a steak and various other things that I couldn't make out. I pushed open the door and walked over to the group of people listening to him.

He was compelling to watch. Wiry, with thin-rimmed round glasses and a pale blue shirt with dark sweat marks under the arms, he seemed to be in constant motion; he gesticulated and paced as he talked excitedly of vacuum chambers and spherification, viscosity and rotary evaporation. I was transfixed, as were the rest of the audience. Copies of his book were piled up and displayed on the shelves nearby, and I picked one up, knowing as soon as I did so that I would be leaving the shop with not just one but two copies, one to take home and pore over myself, one to wrap for my father, who would be as fascinated by it as I was. *The Art and Science of Molecular Gastronomy: A Journey Through Chemistry, Physics and Biology in Pursuit of the Perfect Bite* – a long title for a long book. It was over a thousand pages of dense type with colour plates, and would be a nightmare to lug home, but I didn't care. On a shit afternoon, in a shit week, I felt inexplicably cheered by this man and his evident passion for something so technical and relatively obscure. This was before Heston Blumenthal's snail porridge and bacon and egg ice creams were all over our Sunday supplements and Monday-night television screens.

'You'd never think he was the world expert in this stuff, would you? I'd have thought a molecular gastronomist would look much more like a mad scientist. Or like a chef.'

I turned to the voice at my shoulder, which appeared to belong to the man next to me, who was leaning towards me looking mischievous, like a schoolboy passing notes at the back of the classroom. He was tall, with thick dark hair that might have fallen into elegant waves had it been encouraged to do so; as it was, bits of it sprang up and out to the side rebelliously. He wore an ancient-looking checked shirt that was frayed at the collar, badly fitting jeans and a broad, appealing smile – and I immediately wondered why someone who looked so nice did not have anyone to encourage him to dress better.

'What does a mad scientist look like?' I asked. My neighbour raised his thick eyebrows at me, though not crossly, and whispered, 'Bearded, of course. Muttering under his breath.'

'His?'

'Oh yes, they're always male. Easily distracted, often wearing an unusual combination of clothes and glasses that tend to be either broken or lost the majority of the time.'

'You've just described my father.'

'I see. Well, everything I said was entirely complimentary. That list of attributes is one any man should be proud to possess.' His face asked, 'Have I got away with it?' and then he broke into a smile. 'Mark Oliver. Some people say you should never trust a man with two first names, but I entirely disagree.'

I let my hand extend to meet his. It was firm and warm. Reassuring.

'Sorry, I'm babbling. Are you a fan, then?' he continued.

'A fan? Oh, of . . .' I trailed off.

'Professor Cook's.'

I glanced again at the cover of the book. Ian Cook. 'Fortuitous name. Or is it, what's it called . . . ?'

'Nominative determinism – the theory that one's name influences one's career path? I've never bought into that, have you?'

'I've never given it much thought. But no, I don't see how it could be true.' I looked up. 'Anyhow, no, I'm not a fan. Or not yet, though I suspect I might become one. I was just – I was just curious.'

And that was that. I still have no idea why he started talking to me that day, what made him strike up a conversation with the bedraggled-looking creature next to him, what made him ask me to go for coffee with him, but I'll always be glad that he did, because it turned one of the most mundane days of my life into the most memorable – the one that changed everything.

What a cliché. But it did. *He* did. I'm not an especially sentimental sort of a person, not really. Don't read romantic novels, don't have boxes full of old love letters, don't send Valentine's cards. Never thought I'd be the type to say that one person, one meeting, changed my life. It sounds overblown, overly dramatic. Everything that happens to you changes your life, in a small, incremental way; it all builds up to create the patterns. To give one moment such import would throw everything out of kilter, would be to ignore all those other moments that gradually stack up to make your life what it is.

Or that's what I had always thought. But I was wrong. Of course I was wrong. The handful of extraordinary moments that send everything spinning off in a new direction don't negate all the other smaller moments. I suppose it had suited me, before, to tell myself that no one thing was going to make a difference to everything else. It helped me keep the illusion of control, meant that I didn't panic so much when something didn't go according to plan. It wasn't the end of the world, it wouldn't change much, didn't mean that I should just give up and hide.

Mark changed my life from the moment he walked into it. He made me feel as if I had come home; he made me feel as if I would always have somewhere to go, someone to turn to. He made me realise that I had found my family, and that it was him. Long before we were married I thought of us as inseparable, not in the cloying, pseudo-romantic way of couples who cling to one another like strands of seaweed to driftwood, but in a truer, more visceral sense. 'Let those whom God has joined together, let no man put asunder' – words that were proclaimed during our wedding ceremony and yet which felt almost superfluous by that point. We were already bound together; we had changed one another, and those changes could never be undone.

On the face of it, we had little in common. It's a good thing I've never been a believer in the importance of shared hobbies. You can have all the in-depth conversations about rambling or golf that you like, all the holidays taking in the wildlife of the Pyrenees you can stomach – but that's not what keeps you from turning your face towards someone in the middle of the night and wishing they would just disappear. If anything, those cosy little hobbies allow people to kid themselves that all is well when really they should have walked away years before. 'Oh, we rub along pretty well, and of course we're both such fans of the theatre.' '*We* could never run out of things to talk about. You're never short of conversation with bellringing in common!' It makes me shudder with despair.

Mark and I would never be like that, not a chance of it. He

was a medical student when we met, and a scientist in his soul. I was a linguist, a literature and cinema buff, working in those days at a small academic publisher. Mark was from a large family; my family consisted of myself and my father. He ran six miles, four times a week, and logged his progress in a special book. The most effort I had put into anything physical was getting out of playing netball at school. I liked nothing more than an afternoon on the sofa watching box sets of rare subtitled films; he couldn't see the point of having to read something at the same time as watching it. We both cooked, it was the only thing we had in common, really. On Guardian Soulmates we would have been a disaster. Good on paper we were not.

And yet, none of these things mattered. We understood one another, absolutely. He just made sense to me, in a way that no one else ever had, and vice versa: he was able to read me with no apparent effort whatsoever. I never had to think about what he might like, whether he would enjoy a particular play or book or not, I just knew (admittedly sometimes simply by deciding whether I would like it and working backwards from there). In turn, he knew without me having to say anything or even glance at him if I was uncomfortable somewhere, and exactly how to either put the situation right or extricate me. He could feel the rhythms of my body during sex better than I could myself. He needed none of the nuances and complexities of my family situation spelling out to him, he just got it.

If you've never experienced a relationship like this, then the best way I can describe it is that it's like as if you're two radios tuned into the same frequency, and everyone else is slightly fuzzy. God, that sounds like the line from a bad country song. Call myself a writer? But I never wrote a love story.

# Chapter Six

The restaurant where we had arranged to meet Beth and her husband Steve for dinner was one of mine and Mark's favourites, a little local Lebanese place where they made their own trays of tooth-searingly sweet baklava, dense with nuts and honey, and where you sat on long benches piled high with heavy kilim cushions. You used to be able to smoke hubbly-bubblys in there, until the smoking laws had come in, but they still kept them, displayed around the room on high shelves, emerald and ruby and sapphire, their filigree-gold bases glowing in the candlelight.

I was pleased to be there, with friends, with Mark, out of the house. Though much of me wanted to simply submerge myself in the boxes and ferret through them, a larger part of me knew that it would be a bad idea. I was going to have to talk to Mark about it all, soon; tell him what I had been sent and what I had found. It was all right that I hadn't told him up until this point; it had happened quickly, there had been no big decisions to be made, no actions taken that he would not have gone along with.

'It's busy tonight,' Steve remarked as they sat down opposite us, looking around the room, and I sighed inside. He was going to be like that, then. He was affable enough, Steve, half of the time, but he got into these moods where everything was wrong, no matter what, and it was impossible to shake him out of them. God knows, we had spent enough hours trying. Something had obviously happened to tip him into one of them tonight. Beth's eye-roll at me from next to him as she shrugged her jacket from her shoulders and sat down confirmed it.

'Always is here, isn't it?' Mark said calmly, evenly, and I squeezed his knee under the table. We had spent hours laughing at Steve in the past, at his childlike sulks, at his refusal to be coaxed out of them. Mark did quite a good imitation of his manner – Steve's pouting bottom lip, the way he eyed everyone around him as though they were a potential threat of some sort.

'How's my godson?' I asked. 'And Tillie and Ava?' Beth's eldest child, Tillie, was five, Arthur, my godson, was three, and Ava eighteen months. They were sweet children, and all entirely different from one another. Tillie was serious and ponderous, with dark curls and wide eyes, Arthur was boisterous and full of confidence, blond-haired and blue-eyed, and Ava was an English rose, her delicate porcelain skin and pink cheeks belying her extreme clumsiness. Every time I saw her she was sporting a new and gruesome-looking injury. 'Give me the rundown.'

Beth held out her glass as the waiter filled it with the salmon-pink rosé wine that we always ordered by the jug here. She ticked the children off on her fingers as she spoke, as though making sure she did not forget one.

'Tillie was awarded the prize for Most Thoughtful Child at the end of term. We are very proud.'

'Everyone gets a prize for something,' interjected Steve. 'Bloody ridiculous whining liberals, can't bear the idea that anyone might be better at something than anyone else. Everyone's a winner, according to them. Everyone can do anything they set their minds to. Load of rubbish. I thought school was meant to prepare children for the real world.'

'Misery. Like I said, we are very proud. She got a certificate and everything.'

'Aw, well done her.'

'Arthur is obsessed with *Toy Story* and thinks he's Buzz Lightyear. He's been wearing his costume for seventeen days straight now. We literally can't get him to wear anything else. I have to stealth-wash it overnight.'

'Oh God.'

'And Ava's got a black eye.'

'Of course she has. What was it this time?'

'A sudden attack by her cot, which viciously went for her by sitting in the same place it always does. I'm dreading having to move her into an actual bed. At least now she's relatively contained at night.'

'Well, physically she is. Vocally . . .' Steve winced.

'Oh yes.' Beth gulped at her wine. 'She has become quite loud. It's rather sweet.'

'It's excruciating.'

'Steve.' Beth frowned. 'She's only singing.'

'Ha. That's what you call it?'

'She's happy.'

'I'm not.'

'Clearly.'

There was a pause. I swallowed. I never knew what to say or do when things like this happened. Confrontation terrified me. I waited for Mark to crack the tension with a joke or a change of subject or a sledgehammer, anything. But he remained silent.

'You two have got it right,' said Steve eventually, his face dour. 'Only yourselves to worry about.'

Beth made a noise somewhere between a tut and a whimper.

I tried to catch her eye to smile at her in some kind of solidarity, but she was staring at her plate.

'Ready to order?'

All four of us looked up, relieved. But the interruption was short-lived and didn't do anything to move the conversation on.

'You don't know how lucky you are,' he continued once the waiter had gone.

Beth's glass hit the table with a thud. 'So what are you saying, Steve? That you wish we hadn't had the children?' Her voice was steely.

Steve shrugged. 'I didn't say that.'

'It sounds like that's what you mean.'

'Look, obviously I wouldn't change things now.'

'Is it obvious? I don't think it's that obvious. Is it obvious to you, Klara?'

I stared, eyes wide as a deer's. 'I . . .' I prayed for Mark to rescue me, pressing my leg against his in a plea for help, but he remained silent. Finally, I felt compelled to speak.

'Well. The grass is always greener, isn't it?'

Steve sat back in his chair and put his hands in his pockets. He looked cheerful for the first time since we had arrived at the restaurant. 'Ah,' he said, sounding pleased. 'Do I sense the yearning for the patter of tiny feet, treading shit into those nice cream carpets of yours?'

'Steve!'

'They do, there's no point denying it. Our house used to look nice. Smart, even – once. I remember it. Just.'

'Well, if Klara and Mark *were* thinking about it, you're doing a pretty good job of putting them off.'

'Oh, you remember what it's like. You can't put people off, not once they've got the baby fever. So, come on then. Have you caught the bug?' He raised his eyebrows at me.

'You're drunk, Steve.' Beth spoke quietly. 'I think we should go.'

'I've only had a couple of glasses of wine.'

'Here.'

He smirked. 'Ah, I see. No, I'm hungry. I want to eat.' He looked around for the waiter, waving a hand in the air as he did so. 'Any danger of our food over here?'

I cringed. And then cringed some more when his gaze returned to me.

'I'm not trying to put you off. You should go for it. You'll probably love it. Some people do, I've heard.'

Beth's eyes were full of tears now. I wanted to reach over to her, comfort her, but I was paralysed. 'Mark . . .'

'Let's not talk about it any more, eh?' he said, and I was grateful. Steve pushed though, shoving his shoulder against the door of our discomfort.

'You're keen, he's not. Well, it's normal. Was the same with us. She talked me into it in the end though. They all said I'd be glad that she had.' He snorted. 'People lie.'

'Everyone's different,' Mark replied stiffly.

'Yeah. Some people love it, don't they? They must do, I suppose. I'm sure I can think of one.' Steve raised his glass and pretended to think, theatrically. 'Yes, that bloke . . . His name's coming back to me – no, it's gone. Sorry.' He laughed. No one else did.

'It's complicated,' I said. 'There's more to it than—'

'Look, we don't really want to discuss it, mate, all right?' Mark rescued me, finally. And I thanked him, silently.

'Fucking hell!' Mark exploded as soon as we were out of ear-shot. 'That man's a wanker. What is Beth doing with him again?'

I shrugged. 'They've been together a long time. They've got three kids.'

'She'd be better off as a single mother.'

'Mark. They're our friends.'

He grunted. Steve had this effect on him. I didn't blame him. He was right, Steve *was* a wanker. But Beth was my best friend, and I wasn't going to let that friendship slide because she had made the unfortunate decision to marry a complete idiot. Mark wouldn't have done either, he was just letting off steam, and it was worse tonight because Steve had brought up the whole question of children, which we had been avoiding and skirting around for months. We were in our thirties, we had been married for three years, our friends were all reproducing . . . and we were not. There was nothing wrong, as far as we knew, but nothing was happening. We should have gone to have the tests, it wasn't as though we didn't know what we were doing. *Physician, heal thyself.* But Mark didn't want to. I couldn't get to the bottom of why. I couldn't understand it. But he was immovable. And so we drifted on, having sex at the right time of the month and pretending it was just coincidence that it was exactly then that I cooked a nice meal or took his hand and drew him up the stairs earlier than usual. And I went to acupuncture appointments in my lunch-hour and took folic acid and tried to encourage him not to drink too much, and waited. And waited.

I counted on my fingers in the back of the cab. Maybe we would make love tonight? There wasn't much point, it was too early, but you never knew. And I mustn't make our sex life all about that, though it was hard not to have it in the back of my mind as the days ticked away, as the months rolled relentlessly on. A family. I just wanted a family, of my own. The desire – no, the need – was all-consuming sometimes, overtaking everything, even the thoughts of the secret I was keeping, the boxes and N.R. and my mother and the strange storage unit; all of that was pushed to one side by the emptiness inside me.

And then we were home and the phone rang, and I was snapped out of my keening desire for a family by a member of Mark's.

It was Seraphina, again. As soon as I'd seen the shadow that appeared on Mark's face as he listened to the voice on the other end of the phone, high-pitched and urgent, I'd known who it would be. Had got up and followed him over to the bit of floor that he had chosen to stand and pace in. He never could take a phone call while sitting down, always had to be in motion. It drove me to distraction sometimes. I rested my hand on the small of his back for a moment, so that he knew I was there, with him, waiting. He glanced at me and gave me a small, grim smile in acknowledgement.

'Where?' I asked, when he came off the call.

He sighed. 'St Thomas's. You don't have to come.'

'Of course I'm coming.'

'Damn, I can't drive.'

'I'll call a cab.'

'Honestly, darling, I can go by myself. It's my mad family. We'll be there for hours.'

I looked at him sideways. 'What's yours is mine, remember?' I reached out and touched my wedding ring to his to show him. He nodded.

'Thanks.'

A&E was rammed. A middle-aged man sat slumped over a row of chairs, hand holding a blood-soaked bath towel to his head. It seemed to have been orange, at some point, though it was hard to tell. A teenage girl, sparrow-thin, slept against his shoulder. He muttered constantly, almost unintelligibly: 'Bastards . . . hard-working man . . . my dinner . . . course it ain't fair, course it ain't right . . .'

A large woman took up two whole seats at the far end of the row, dressed as though in her Sunday best. Handbag neatly balanced on her lap, feet in polished leather court shoes, pointing forwards. She sat quietly, staring straight ahead, not looking to either side. Nearby, a child played with a plastic fire engine, running it up and down the floor, a thick trail of snot hanging from one nostril as he chuntered and chattered to himself. I had to fight the urge to go and wipe his face with a tissue, since I doubted the couple watching him blankly would appreciate it.

'At least you're not likely to bump into any of your patients down here,' I whispered to Mark as we waited to speak to a receptionist.

'Small mercies.'

Due to his status as a doctor, even one not in the area, it meant that we were treated differently from the general public: we were immediately directed to Seraphina's cubicle.

'Ready?' I asked him softly, as we walked down the aisle of curtained-off treatment areas. You never knew what you were going to find with Seraphina. You had to be ready for anything.

'I suppose so,' he said, and he sounded so tired, I wanted to just turn around and take him home, pull him close under the duvet and wrap my legs around his to warm him.

Instead, we paused and listened for a moment outside the cubicle for clues. There were none.

'Elfie? Jesus Christ. What are *you* doing here? What happened?'

Seraphina was sitting next to the trolley on which her younger sister lay. Her head jerked up as she heard the curtain rattle back on its track and the sound of Mark's voice, and for a moment she looked far younger than her thirty years. Her eyes were wide and the circles under them heavy, and her face was as white as the sheets on the bed. She looked scared and guilty and relieved all at once, and within seconds she was up and clinging to Mark and sobbing, her thin back rising and falling as he held and shushed her and I patted her ineffectually on the shoulder.

I looked over at Elfie, who lay, motionless and quiet, gazing at us. She was deathly pale, and though I couldn't see any obvious injuries, she wore an oxygen mask over her face.

'Shh, shh. It's OK. We're here. Everyone's safe. It's all right.'

Eventually Seraphina's sobs calmed and she pulled away from Mark's arms, wiping her face with her sleeve, which hung long and ragged from her arm. I remembered doing the same thing when I had been a teenager, working away at the wool with my thumbnail until it wore down and I could hook my thumb through it.

'We were at the Serpentine,' Elfie started telling us eventually.

We had spoken to the doctor who had assured us that she would be fine, that they would keep her in overnight to be sure and to keep an eye on her, but that it really was just a precaution. 'She has had a very nasty scare indeed,' he said sternly, looking over at Elfie, 'but I think she's learned her lesson. No more playing in water.' Seraphina had nodded, her face grave, and a look had passed between the two sisters that showed that this story was far from told. 'You can have ten minutes, but don't exhaust her, all right? She's had a proper fright,' the doctor warned, nodding to Elfie that she could remove the mask, and propping the back of her bed up.

When the doctor had left, Mark sent Seraphina to get coffees, not looking her in the eye, his shoulder turned against her, and she had not dared argue.

Now he looked confused. 'The Serpentine gallery?' he asked Elfie.

'No, the lake. Though Serri chose it because it was near the gallery. She said it was good to be in water that was close to its positive energy.' Elfie and Mark shared a look. It was exactly the kind of thing that people in their family did say.

He nodded. 'OK. Go on. Why were you there?'

'She said she needed me to help her. She called me up yesterday and said that I had to go, that she was running out of time, and that there wasn't anyone else she could ask. I didn't really know what she meant.'

Of course she hadn't known what she meant! Much of the time *I* found it impossible to follow Seraphina's trains of thought – so how could a fifteen-year-old be expected to do so?

'So, I got the Tube over there.' And when Mark's brow furrowed: 'I know you don't like it, but I'm allowed.'

'You shouldn't be.' Mark was old-fashioned when it came to his little sister.

'Everyone else does.' One shoulder rose and fell, full of attitude, and for a second she was a normal teenager again, bolshie and pushing against the boundaries. Only in Elfie's case, when she was at home, there were no boundaries to push against.

'I've got an Oyster card.' She was trying to reassure him. As though that protected her.

'I know. Carry on.'

'When I got there, she was manic – I thought she might be spiralling.' Her casual use of the word almost made me weep. She shouldn't be so familiar with this world. She should be listening to Jessie J and poring over glittery nail varnishes and trying on unsuitable short skirts in Topshop, ones that she knew she'd never be able to get away with wearing, giggling with her friends and putting on too much lip balm and gazing at boys as if they were some strange species in a game park. She shouldn't be here.

'She wanted me to help her with her new collection. She said that if she didn't show it to the gallery soon, they might kill her off, that her slot might disappear and she'd be all sand and dust.' Elfie looked upset again now. 'I knew she didn't really mean kill her off, not actually. Not really.'

'But you were scared. You weren't sure.' It wasn't a question. It didn't need to be.

'She was going to get into the water first. It was going to be a self-portrait, and she was going to set it all up and use the timer on the camera. But then she said it would look better with me, because I was younger, more vulnerable-looking. She said it would all be fine. But it was really cold. And the dress was really long, and sort of floaty, and it got tangled up in the plants, and I was further out than I was meant to be.'

She said this last as though she was confessing, as though she was going to be in trouble. I took her hand. 'It sounds awfully frightening,' I said.

'It wasn't at first, because Serri said she'd done it before and it would all be fine, and it was quite exciting. I've always wanted to be in one of her projects.' A little colour came to the girl's cheeks then, a flush of shame at her vanity. 'But then she took ages to get the camera ready – it wasn't her fault, there was something wrong with it – and I sort of drifted out, and then when it all started to pull me under I panicked. I know I shouldn't have panicked, but I couldn't help it. And that made it worse, and she couldn't reach me – she tried, with sticks and things, but she couldn't. And . . . I don't remember much after that.'

Mark's fist was a ball of rage resting on the bedsheet.

'You didn't do anything wrong, Elfie,' I said, trying to reassure her and distract Mark from his anger all at once. 'No one's angry with you. You were trying to help your sister. I promise, you're not in any trouble.' Elfie was always worried about being in trouble. Not that she ever would have been, from her parents, at any rate. She could run away with a gang of drug-dealing Yardies for kicks and they'd smile and say she was expressing her need for more excitement in her life.

'Of course she's not in trouble,' Mark agreed gruffly.

'Thank goodness for that,' Seraphina said airily, appearing at the curtain opening. 'I was sure you were going to be furious. But no harm done, is there?' She smiled a little nervously, and held a brown plastic cup out to her brother. He ignored it.

'I was talking to Elfie. Go outside.'

Seraphina looked confused. 'But I want to—'

Mark turned. 'Go. GO.' And she did, still holding the other two cups, looking down at them as though she had only just realised that they were there.

He laughed, a short, bitter laugh. 'Of course, she assumes we're talking about her. No other possibility enters her head. It's all about Seraphina and her *art*, it's all about bloody Seraphina.'

'Don't be too angry with her,' Elfie said quietly. 'I am all right. The doctor said.'

But Mark was gone, opening the curtain with a flick, his footsteps striding down the corridor. I looked at Elfie and she nodded. 'Go on, I'm fine,' she said.

'What the fuck were you thinking, what the fucking hell did you think you were doing?' he raged, his breath emerging from his mouth in short, angry puffs, hanging in the air like poison. We were standing outside the entrance to A&E, by the smoking area. Seraphina had a cigarette dangling from her fingers but she hadn't dared light it yet.

'I was thinking about my *art*, Mark. I was thinking that I had to get it done or I'd be finished.' The words tumbled from her mouth, fast, like a stream of mice falling over one another in their rush to escape. 'I was thinking about her.'

'About her? Jesus fucking . . . I can't believe it. What exactly were you *thinking*?'

'She's always wanted to be in one of my pieces. She's said so. And she was perfect for this. I could see it all, in my mind.' She tapped her temple. 'So beautiful, so young, so vulnerable.'

'Yes. Exactly. So young, so vulnerable.'

Seraphina had the good grace to look a little ashamed at that.

'Were you ever going to get in yourself, or was that all bullshit? You planned for it to be her all along, didn't you? But you knew that if you rang her and said you wanted her to come and get in the lake in January, she might be a little reticent. So you came out with some crap about death and terrified the life out of her, so that she would come and help you.'

'No . . .'

'So that your fifteen-year-old sister would come and float around in a freezing cold lake, in the middle of winter, to be in one of your fucking stupid projects.'

Seraphina looked wounded. 'They're not stupid, Mark,' she said quietly. 'They're important.'

'Yes. More important than Elfie, clearly.'

'No, I didn't mean . . . I would never hurt her.'

'You already did, can't you see? She's in hospital, Ser. You already did hurt her.' He turned away in frustration, a hand rising into the air and punching it, walking off to try and calm himself, scuffing the ground with his shoes as he went. I watched his back, tall and stiff, and knew that he was best left.

She lit the cigarette now, and sucked deeply on it. 'She was Ophelia,' she said to me. I'd always shown an interest in

54

Seraphina's art, a genuine one. I believed that her talent was real. I just wasn't sure I believed that she would ever be able to harness it. 'It's part of a series.' The words were coming fast still, but she seemed a little calmer. Talking about her work gave her a focus. 'Iconic images of women. But all a bit – you know, different.'

Of course.

'I'm doing Dora Maar, *Whistler's Mother*, the *Madonna and Child*, the *Girl with a Pearl Earring*. Adele Bloch-Bauer – you know, the Klimt portrait.' I nodded. 'Ophelia's surrounded by flowers in the Millais original in the Tate, but I've got Elfie surrounded by Barbie dolls – well, parts of them. It took me ages to dismember enough.'

I was glad Mark wasn't here to listen to this. The thought of Elfie almost drowned to create a photo of her lying in water, surrounded by bits of plastic dolls would have been too much for him.

'She looks beautiful, Klara, she really does. It's going to be a big success, I'm sure of it.' Serri pulled her phone from her pocket and clicked to the photos. 'Look.'

The photo was striking. Elfie lay, floating languidly, looking almost beatific in the murky water. The dolls weren't obvious as such when you first looked, they could have been the flowers of the original. It was only when your eye focused in on them that you realised. It was just the kind of thing that trendy London galleries would go mad for. 'Imagine it blown up, huge, just that one image on a wall.' Her voice was excited, urgent. 'And then there are all the others. It's going to be—'

I put my hand on her arm, wanting to quieten her, calm her. 'Serri. It's brilliant. It is beautiful. But you do see, you must see . . .'

She nodded. 'I was stupid. I know, I can see that. I'm not mad, you know?'

I couldn't reply.

'I just . . . I just get caught up in my ideas,' she went on. 'And everything else starts to sort of fade away.'

Seraphina is a successful painter. I say successful – she is highly respected and her work sells well. But her output is sporadic at best. She's plagued by migraines, and frequently gripped by a conviction that everything she does is worthless, which often leads to her destroying months of work in a variety of creative ways. Last time she poured bleach over everything. Once she spent days cutting her large canvases up into tiny squares and scattering the pieces in the Thames, like ashes. Her methods of annihilation are one of the reasons I find it hard to take her semi-regular meltdowns that seriously – it all seems like another artwork. I'm sure I saw her photographing the bleach-drenched canvases, even though she quickly hid her phone.

But she's beautiful and charming and funny, Seraphina is, and so it's hard to stay annoyed with her. She has mad ideas and turns up with random gifts – when she has money, that is; it slips through her fingers like silk, due to all the inappropriately generous surprises that she springs on her loved ones when she's feeling flush. She hired a circus to come to the house for Elfie's birthday once, a full circus, clowns and acrobats and fire jugglers, the whole troupe of them. It was November, and they filed up Gironde Road, and all the neighbours came out in the street and stared. Elfie loved it, she still talks about it now. And who can blame her? I can't think of a more magical thing to happen when you're ten. And then Serri will disappear, working manically, obsessively, for months on end, and if you go round to see her she'll either not answer the door or do so after ages and stare at you as though she's never seen you before. She'll be wearing some strange T-shirt covered in paint, and she won't have eaten for days, or washed, and when you talk to her she'll look straight through you. I take her food sometimes when she's like that, though I know it gets wasted mostly, but at least I know it's there if she wants it. She reminds me of my mother sometimes.

The thing is, she doesn't need to work, none of the Oliver children do. They've all got whacking great trust funds from their grandparents. It's part of their problem, in my opinion. Apart from Mark, of course. He refuses to live off his. He used it to pay his medical school fees, though he had a job to pay for his living expenses, and he used a chunk·of it to buy our house, so it's mortgage free, and that's what enables me to do what I do, with its accompanying modest pay, but he would sooner work as a bin man than use it to pay his bills while he pursued some esoteric interest in the name of self-discovery. It's admirable. I'm not sure I'd be as principled, if it were me.

Elfie is fifteen now, and showing signs of being seriously bright. Mark's keen to get her to change schools, away from the place she's at now which encourages pupils to create their own timetables based on their interests, and send her somewhere properly academic like St Paul's or Westminster for Sixth form. He's offered to pay the fees himself, but no one seems too enthusiastic. I don't know if anyone's asked Elfie what *she* wants. She's a sweet girl. Grey eyes, skin so white it almost glows, too thin. Quiet, with an intense stare that, when it lands on you, is impossible to escape from. I can see her in a few years as one of those terrifying political journalists whose interviewing technique relies mainly on remaining silent until their subjects become so uncomfortable they can't stop talking.

I get on with her the best out of the siblings, perhaps because she and I are the most similar. We talk about books and ideas she's had and Angry Birds, the game we were both addicted to playing on our iPhones. She always seems slightly out of place, wherever she is, just a little disjointed from the rest of her surroundings. It's a feeling I am familiar with. Anyhow, she's no trouble, and she's good company, so after the Serpentine incident, when Mark suggested she come to stay with us, I was happy. We would put her in the third bedroom, I decided. We would look after her, we would give her some stability at last. And my heart lifted a little.

I was going to step in. I was going to be there for her, in a way Maisie never had been. I was going to— I stopped myself. I was *not* going to be her mother. You must not think like that, I told myself. You will be her friend, and then maybe, one day, you will be someone's mother. Maybe this is a trial run, to see if you're good enough – a test. I thought like that a lot, those days. Analysed what things meant, whether they might be a sign – that I was ready, and that it would happen this month, next month, the month after. It never did. But still, I kept hoping.

# Chapter Seven

By the time I got home from the hospital there was no escaping the sunlight, which had given up all pretence of creeping in around corners and glared in, cold and pale, through the windows. Mark had stayed at St Thomas's with Elfie, and I didn't have a class until the afternoon, so I undressed and crawled into bed, intending to sleep. Honestly. I did mean to. But too much had happened over the past few days, from visiting the storage unit, to dinner at the Olivers' and with Beth and Steve, to the hospital, to our decision to bring Elfie home with us when she was discharged . . . It all swirled around in my brain like water whooshing down the sink. And at the centre of the whirlpool were the questions. So many questions.

In the end I gave in. I got up and made a pot of tea, then wrapping a blanket around myself, I went into the study and pulled the boxes from their hiding-place in the cupboard, where I had secreted them behind some old picture-frames and my wedding dress.

I knew Mark would not be back for hours. *It's not as though you're doing anything wrong*, I told myself, but the words felt hollow. I might not be *doing* anything wrong, but I was not telling. I was keeping secrets tucked away like my mother's very belongings had sat tucked away for years. Guilt tickled the back of my neck. 'You are breaking your word,' it said. 'You cannot go back, once you have opened the boxes.'

I shoved the thought to one side as I pulled the first box towards me. I was going to tell Mark, just in my own good time, thanks very much. I needed to see what we were talking about first. Get it straight in my head. I had my laptop balanced on my knees, ready to note down the contents. I'd decided that this was how I would approach the problem – I would archive the boxes' contents. I'd opened a spread-sheet, ready. That was the way to keep things under control. Cataloguing. Nothing could be too terrifying once it was neatly logged in a spreadsheet. The cursor hovered over the header.

### My Mother's Belongings

I typed the words, and then deleted them. The sentence felt too personal, too comprehensive.

### Number 17, 31 Founthill Way – Contents

Yes, that was better. More official, more distant. Now I could assume the role of archivist in my head, curator rather than daughter. I knelt up and got ready to open the boxes. Four dusty lids, four sets of worn cardboard edges. Four small spaces in which whole worlds might reside.

As I took the lid from the first box I paused, closing my eyes for a moment, wanting to both prolong the moment and at the same time desperate to gobble it up all at once like a child with its stocking.

But when I opened the boxes, it was as though the stocking was full of balled-up newspaper and bits of coal, punishment for a bad child who deserved to be taught a lesson. My disappointment was almost overwhelming, so keenly did I feel it course through my chest. What had I been hoping for? The answer, I supposed. Or answers. The answers to all the questions I had never asked, the ones I knew needed to be asked and the ones I never even imagined needed asking: the answers to everything I was unsure of in my life, past, present and future, all neatly packaged up into four boxes. But it was just – stuff. One box of clothes, carefully packed. One of kitchen items again packed carefully but a random assortment of bits and pieces. There was a cheese-grater in there, for God's sake. A sodding cheese-grater. I felt like stamping my feet. The third box contained a pile of cardboard folders, magazine and newspaper cuttings – crammed and bulging with reminders of my mother's glory days. Another box contained just a large pink and white stuffed rabbit, a cheap-looking thing, tatty and a bit faded. The sort of prize you might win at a hoopla stand at the fair. Once more, I burst into tears. The frustration of it, the disappointment, the adrenaline followed by the let-down – it was all too much, and I knelt on the floor with my fists balled into my eyes and my face hot, sobbing.

Finally, I wiped my eyes and shoved the stupid rabbit away from me, pulling the final box towards me almost roughly. It was small and light and felt as though it could be empty, but as I jerked it across the floor, something slid across its base.

I didn't realise it was a diary at first. It wasn't marked as such on the outside, was just a plain black leather-bound book, with a gold-leaf border on the front cover. Only when I opened it did I see that's what it was, one of those five-year perpetual diaries, in which you wrote the day and month yourself. And on the front page, the words that made me gasp with shock and recognition – and a bittersweet sort of joy.

*Private property of Sadie Mortimer.* DO NOT READ.

The word *private* was underlined, twice. The original statement had been written in blue biro, but at some point the
surname had been crossed out and the name *Mortimer* written
beside it in black ink; by the same hand, but a more refined
version of it. A more adult version, but written by someone
still young enough to care what name was inscribed inside her
diary.

I turned the page.

# Chapter Eight

## 1 May 1970

This is my diary. Obviously. Well, that's what you're reading, isn't it? The diary of Mary Tomaszewski, though you know me as Sadie. That's who I am now, who I became before I started writing this. It's Sadie you are interested in, not Mary. I could write this as though it were going to remain secret, as most girls do: *Dear Diary, it's only you to whom I can confess my love for James Maitland from next door* . . . that kind of thing. Trusting that my secrets would remain kept within the pages, hiding them away in a box underneath my bed. But that's not why I'm writing this record. I'm not like other diary-keepers – you should know that from the start. This diary will be found, in the future, and it will be read by those interested in my life. I'll be famous by then. Maybe I'll be dead by the time they come to read it, maybe I'll simply be retired, writing my memoirs, sharing them with the world. Either way, people will want to know how it all started. How I got to where I know I am going to end up. Where I came from. And this will be what tells them. My story. Sadie's story.

I may only be seventeen, and I may live with my family in an unremarkable house in an unremarkable corner of the English countryside, living an as yet fairly unremarkable life (if you don't count the strangeness of my parents, but then I'm not sure that really counts, as everyone's parents are strange, aren't they?), but none of those things will be true of me for long. I will not be seventeen for ever – for only another two months, in fact. And when I am eighteen, my family may still be strange, in fact I'm 100 per cent sure they will be, but I will no longer live with them here in St Albans: I will live in London. And there I will make my mark, and will begin to live the life that I was meant to lead, with all the stories that I know are out there waiting for me to step inside. And I will record them here, because one day people will want to read them, and I will no longer be Mary Tomaszewski. I will be Sadie, and I will be remembered.

Here she had drawn a line, presumably to indicate that the entry was finished, and I looked up from the diary. She had always had a sense of drama, my mother, a predilection for the grand gesture. It was not something that she had had to cultivate as an adult: it was inbuilt, a part of her DNA. *I will be Sadie, and I will be remembered.* It might have been a line from a musical, one about a girl who runs away to find her fortune and becomes a star. End of Act One, curtain down, applause. Maybe that was exactly the kind of thing she had been imagining when she wrote it; that some day, the person ignoring her strict instruction not to read this secret diary would be a Hollywood film director or a biographer, checking over her life for details to better tell her story. Not her daughter, sitting up in bed on a cold January morning, feeling almost as though she were meeting her mother for the first time.

I shivered. It was the strangest feeling, reading her words, hearing her voice in my head. As though she had come back to life. I had not missed her for a long time, had put that feeling out of my head. But I missed her now. And I felt a rush of gratitude to the unknown N.R. for leading me to this, for giving me this gift.

I opened another document on my computer, and saved it in the same folder as the list of her belongings. I know, I know, I'm a cataloguer. It's not just part of my job, it's part of my personality. I have to know where things are, have to be able to keep track. There has to be a system. Otherwise everything falls apart.

So I needed to create a way of keeping track of all this new information that I was gathering about my mother – about Sadie, as I had known her to be, and about Mary, who I now knew she had been once. About this teenage girl on the cusp of adulthood who had had so many hopes and dreams that I knew would not all come true; a girl whom I should have known better than anyone, but whom I hardly knew at all. I had to try and pin her down, in the only way I knew how.

In a system. I created a new file on my computer and began to write down everything I knew. Everything I knew about my mother.

# Chapter Nine

In May 1970 my mother, Mary Tomaszewski, as she was then, had been seventeen, about to turn eighteen. So she had been born in 1952. I had known her birthday, of course, but I don't think I'd ever been sure of the year of her birth until now. *8 July 1952.* I deleted what I had just written and retyped it. It was too much like telling a story. This was an official document, or so it felt like.

*Date of birth: 8 July 1952*

That was better. More formal. As if I was creating her birth certificate or something. Marking her place in the world.

*Parents:?*

I realised I had no idea who her parents had been, who my grandparents had been. It was all part of the unspoken. Well, I knew now that her maiden name had been Tomaszewski, so she must have been Polish. Her blood resonated down through me in ways that I had never imagined, then; my name, my love for Eastern European cinema and culture had not come from nowhere, but from a genetic wellspring. And I had never had any idea. I started typing again.

*Parents: ? And ? Tomaszewski*

I went back to the top and added a heading. *Personal Details.* It was still spare. I added some more sub-headings, so I knew what gaps remained to be filled, as much as anything.

*Place of birth. Siblings. Home address/es.* All blank. But at least the document was beginning to take shape, beginning to look like something that I could grapple with. If there were spaces, then they could be filled.

Double return. New heading. *Personal history – 0–18.* And then, a little further down the page: *Personal history – 18–.* I left the end date blank. I didn't know what chunks her life would divide up into yet. How it would seem appropriate to record it. For now, I knew there was a life before eighteen, when she had planned to move to London, and when she had presumably done so, and then there would be her life afterwards. I could always change it if I discovered, when I continued to read, that she had not left home until later. But some instinct told me that she had. Something about the tone of that first entry had brooked no argument.

I wrote a few words under *Personal history – 0–18. Romantic ideals, dissatisfied with life at home, thought her family strange. Desperate to break out and move to London when 18.*

Under *Personal history – 18 –* I simply wrote *Modelling.*

There was something else to go in under *Personal Details*, I realised. This was not just about her life lived before my father and me. We were part of the story as well, though she had not known it when she had begun writing her diary. We had not even entered her consciousness then. But we were there.

*Marriages: Henry Mortimer, m.?*

This I knew, naturally, though I didn't know the date they had married. It was sometime before I was born, I assumed. Daddy had never marked it, and though they might have celebrated it when she was here, I had been too small to remember or know when it might have been.

*Children: Klara Louise Mortimer, b. 1979*

She had been twenty-seven when she had me. It sounds a little young now, when most twenty-seven year olds are still struggling in underpaid jobs, sharing rented houses with friends, living like students, dating and clubbing their way through life. But of course it would have been about average then. Normal.

I closed the book. Normal. It wasn't a word that had fitted with my memories of my mother before I found the diary, and it wasn't one that suited her any more now that I had begun to read. She had been aiming for an extraordinary life. One filled with glamour and passion and drama. One to be remarked upon by strangers. The girl who had written those pages, in the handwriting that I could tell she was still growing into, would not have envisaged marriage to an academic and a child at twenty-seven, I was sure of it.

What I was *not* sure of, was how it had ended up happening to her.

Now I began to fill in the gaps. The spaces between the facts. What did I know of her life growing up, of her childhood, so far? She had been a romantic. A dreamer, with big plans for her future. She had been dissatisfied with her life at home, whether for good reason or not. She had been determined to break out and make something big of her life, in London, away from everything she had grown up feeling so confined by. So no different to thousands of other teenage girls up and down the country, then. But she *had* been different. She had done it. Her single-minded ability to turn her back on everything she had known up until that point demanded respect, and I happily gave it.

I looked again at the screen. Here were the facts of her life, laid out as I knew them. It wasn't a great deal of information. The date she had died should be on there as well, but I didn't know it. It had been before I was a teenager, I thought, maybe twelve? But I couldn't be quite sure why I thought this. I bit the skin next to my thumbnail as I tried to remember. He had told me she had died, Daddy had. If I tried hard I could remember the conversation. It sounds strange, doesn't it, that hearing of your mother's death might be something you had to struggle to remember? Maybe I had blocked it out, or maybe by the time he told me that her absence was permanent I had already accepted it.

I had a feeling that it might have taken him a while to tell me, after it had happened. Yes. There had been a period of time when he had been distracted, more so than usual. I too was wrapped up in my own life, not yet at the age where I would realise that my father had his own worries and concerns outside of my immediate sphere or awareness, so had just assumed it was something to do with work, some problem that he was trying to solve, and had mentally brushed it off. Now though, it seemed more significant. How selfish I had been.

I closed my eyes. He had come into the kitchen when I was doing homework one evening, something to do with Latin verbs. The memory was obviously clearer than I had thought. He had sat down across the table from me and reached for my hands. I looked up, ready to be irritated by the disturbance, but something had stopped me.

'I have some sad news, Klara,' he said, and then he had taken his glasses off and laid them on the table. I looked at them in surprise. He never took his glasses off. They were part of his face.

I didn't speak. 'Your mother, Sadie . . .' and then he stopped. Her name was hard for him to say, I realised, with a sudden flash of empathy. 'Your mother will not be coming back.' The words were awkwardly formed; it was as though he had to turn them over in his mouth before he could allow them to emerge.

'I know, Daddy,' I said quietly, not yet understanding what he was saying. 'It's OK. We're fine, us two. We get along A-OK.' I grinned at him, trying to reassure.

'No.' There was a silence. 'I mean that she will *never* be coming back. Not here, and not anywhere.' He rubbed the webbing between my thumb and forefinger with his large thumb. 'She died, my darling. I'm very sorry. She died.'

I remember looking at him in surprise as a tear rolled down his cheek. I had never seen my father cry. Not when she left, and not since. I hadn't realised that it was a possibility.

'Oh Daddy,' I said, and almost got up and went to hug him but felt suddenly embarrassed to do so.

'I know,' he said, 'it's very sad. You must try to be strong. We must try to be strong.'

I nodded. And though I remember sitting at that table with him for what seemed like a long time, thinking we must give the moment time and space to expand and feel its import, I don't remember how I felt about her being dead. It's possible I didn't feel anything.

So. There was no date in my dossier to mark the end of her life. Not yet. No place of burial, either. I had asked him where she was, whether there was a grave that I could visit. It had been a few years later, when I was fourteen or so and interested in death in that romantic, stylised way that teenagers have. Not thinking of it as a reality, as something that would happen to me, but more as an interesting pose, a faintly glamorous abstract. I did not think of people who were now dead, people in history books, my ancestors, even my mother, as ever having really been alive, not in the way that I was. Not in a way that I could relate to, as people who had got up every day, cleaned their teeth, kissed their children, been afraid or excited or fretted about homework or the mortgage. They were – other.

Having no mother had, by that point, given me a certain kudos among my schoolfriends. There was a mystery surrounding me that everyone found a little bit fascinating. No mother. As well as the obvious tragedy of it that allowed me to look misty-eyed when Mother's Day was celebrated at school and gain sympathy when there was no mummy to watch me at ballet or in school plays, there were potential benefits of which my classmates were secretly a little jealous. No one to nag me about laddered tights or wearing badly applied make-up to school, no one to monitor my TV consumption or fret about whether I was eating enough fruit; no one with whom to have excruciating conversations about boyfriends. No one to ground me for being home later than I had promised, no one to say no, I could not go to that horror film because it would give me nightmares, no one to check my pockets for illicit lipstick and cigarettes. My father would never have thought to do any of these things, not because he didn't care, but because it would simply never have occurred to him that he might need to. The world of teenage girls was outside his experience.

So I quite fancied the idea of going to visit her. I liked the image of myself standing by a graveside, laying flowers down and talking softly to her as I had seen people do in movies. Touching the headstone before sadly, slowly, turning away. I saw myself dressed all in black, cutting a moving and elegant figure outside the church, which would be gothic and slightly crumbling.

When I asked Daddy though, he just shook his head.

'She's not buried here, my darling,' he said. 'She died abroad and she was buried there. In America.'

'Whereabouts?'

'California.' That was all he told me. He looked so sad.

Later, I asked him how she had died. It was when I was twenty, and away at uni. I had shunned all the London universities, despite them having some of the best courses, and being more convenient and far cheaper and generally more sensible options. I had also refused to apply to Oxbridge, which would have been Daddy's other preferred destination for me, claiming that it was because I didn't approve of their elitist applications policy and old boy network, but really because I was scared that I wouldn't get in. So, after the usual nail-biting rounds of UCAS forms and offers and exam results, I ended up at Bristol, which was far enough away to satisfy my urge to rebel by leaving home, but close enough for me to feel secure and able to get home within a couple of hours. My rebellion had clipped wings of my own making. I had never been the sort of girl to push the boundaries too far.

So Bristol it was. And it was big enough (coming from London, I didn't fancy being stuck in St Andrews or somewhere with two pubs and a golf course), and had a reassuringly eclectic mix of tea rooms and travellers, middle-aged women in tweed skirts and cashmere, and crusties with dogs on strings and rainbow dreadlocks. Again, just enough bohemia to allow me to feel as though I were stepping out on my own. I lived in halls for the first year and then in a shared house with three friends. My choice of course – History of Art and French – meant that most of the students I came into contact with during tutorials and study groups were from Surrey and called either Claire (sometimes with an 'i', sometimes without, but woe betide you should you get it wrong) or Sophie, and wore a lot of pink cashmere. I hadn't made many friends in my lectures. I was suspicious of all of them, and they thought I was strange and found me awkward. I had been to a London state school, I didn't ride or ski, and I was more interested in

Communist cinema and obscure European advertising logos than Monet and Degas. They didn't know what to do with me, nor I with them, so we simply nodded politely at one another and went our own way. They were nothing if not polite, the Claires and the Clares and the Sophies.

My housemates were Geraint, who had been my next-door neighbour in halls and with whom I had made friends on the first night over a pan of hash brownies. He was a literature student and had read a lot of the books I had, and was interesting and funny. Then there was Hayley. She was another Londoner, but that was really the only thing we had in common. She was tough, street-talking, hard-edged. She was everything that the Claires and the Clares and the Sophies weren't, and that was why I liked her. We'd met smoking cigarettes outside the Student Union and by the time we had finished smoking them we were firm friends in the way that you can become when you're young. Finally there was Jimmy. Jimmy was into fantasy novels and was studying electronics and was friends with Hayley for reasons that were unclear. I'd never have chosen to share a house with him, but he was quiet and pleasant enough and hardly ever left his room so I didn't mind. We must have made a bizarie foursome, looking back. The handsome, popular Geraint, the slightly scary Hayley, the weird Jimmy, and me. What was I? A bit of a swot, I suppose, terrified of not doing well, but also something of a poseur – I skulked around smoking Gitanes and wearing long thin scarves. I learned to juggle and took to carrying a set of balls with me everywhere I went.

Anyhow. That was us, that was me. We did the usual student stuff – argued about whose food was whose, stayed up too late and sat around in tracksuit bottoms eating cereal and watching *This Morning* for half the day, went to the pub too much, ate at all-you-can-eat places that gave us food poisoning, had one big party where the front door got kicked in and we spent the next three weeks finding fag ends in the soap and unspeakable things down the back of the sofa and vowed never again, drank cider by the river and argued about philosophy, slept with one another's friends (and, on one or two occasions, one another) and regretted it in the morning, sneaked into the cinema without tickets, saved up to go to festivals in the summer. And most of all, we pretended. Read Nietzsche and pretended we understood him, listened to trance and gabba and pretended that we liked it, went to parties and pretended we fitted in.

It was Geraint who suggested we play Truth or Dare. It started off typically enough, him asking Jimmy about anal sex and threesomes, Jimmy squirming and blushing and daring Hayley to eat a whole chilli raw, which she did without flinching, her eyes not even watering.

'Truth,' she said, when it was her next turn.

'Where do you actually come from?' Geraint asked her, his eyes dancing with mischief. 'I mean, I know you're from London. But I want to know if you're really the street urchin you like us all to think you are. I think you might be a nice girl, really.'

Hayley raised an eyebrow and I held my breath. The two of them often locked horns. 'So what's your actual question?' she said. 'You only get one.'

Geraint thought for a moment, his eyes never leaving her face. 'Have any of your relatives ever been to jail?' he asked eventually, looking pleased with himself.

Hayley threw her head back and laughed. 'Yes,' she said. 'Yeah, they have. My dad, and my brother. Oh, and my aunt.'

We were all quiet. We wore bravado as casually as our satin bomber jackets, but none of the rest of us would be able to answer such a question so casually, I was sure. Prison was something other; prison was serious.

'What for?' I whispered. But she shook her head.

'You'll have to wait your turn,' she said, grinning at me.

Geraint looked somehow disappointed with the answer he had received. I could tell he had been hoping to unmask Hayley as some kind of fraud. I knew he wouldn't though. Hayley was the real deal.

It was my turn next, and I answered, 'Truth,' as I almost always did. I was terrified of dares, of being made to do something stupid, some publicly humiliating thing, and I could see Geraint was in a dangerous mood, especially after his amateur detective skills had been thwarted. He was like that. I remembered that. I remembered everything. So I was relieved when Hayley asked the question.

'As we're on families, where's your Mum, Klara? You never mention her.' Her voice was gentle, and it took the edge off the surprise I felt at being asked the question at all. I'd got so used to fudging when people asked about my parents, and so few people asked outright, that it always took me by surprise when people did. 'Are your parents still together?' was a common one that people sometimes tentatively put forward, the bigger questions sitting unasked behind their eyes, and I'd just say that no, they weren't, and move the conversation on, and they usually left it at that.

But there was no such easy escape this time. The room went quiet. They knew there was a story here, some as-yet undiscovered fact about me, and they all wanted to hear it. And, for the first time in as long as I could remember, I wanted to tell them. Maybe it was the red wine, sitting sickly and oaky in my throat, maybe it was the atmosphere of conspiratorial togetherness, most likely it was a bit of both and something else as well, but I didn't want to fudge it any longer.

I wanted to tell. This must be what it felt like to be Catholic and feel the urge to confess, I remember thinking at the time.

'She's dead,' I said, and I watched their faces take it in. 'It's fine. It was a long time ago. She left when I was six. She went to America. And then she died when I was twelve or thirteen, I think. I'm not sure.' They were the facts as I knew them. I had answered the question. There was no need for me to say anything more. But I did.

'She's buried over there somewhere. In California. She was a model. I'm not sure whether that's what she went to do when she left. I never really . . . I was very young.'

They nodded, but their faces betrayed their incredulity. Hayley was the first to voice it.

'She just . . . she just left you? When you were *six*?'

'Yes.'

'And she never came back? Before she died, I mean?' That was from Geraint.

I shook my head.

'But she wrote and stuff, yeah? You know, you were in touch with her?' Jimmy spoke, and it was a bit of a surprise, as always. You sort of forgot that he could, sometimes.

'No.'

'What, never?'

'No.'

'But . . . why?'

I stared at Hayley. 'I don't know.' The truth of my words was a chasm in front of me and I gulped. I had never seen it before. How it must look from the outside. How strange it was, how unusual, how little I knew. How cold it must seem.

'I – my father told me she was away working. She had always gone away quite a lot. It didn't seem that strange, to start with. And then it turned into a long time, and I did ask,

I think, but I don't remember what he said. And then – then it just sort of became normal.'

'And then he told you that she was dead.' Geraint, again.

'Surely she sent postcards, or something. Letters.' Jimmy tried again. 'I mean, people do, don't they?'

I shrugged, trying to hide the child's hurt that had risen up in my throat. 'My mother wasn't people. She was – she was extraordinary.'

'I don't understand any of it, to be honest, Klar.' Geraint had arranged his face into a sympathetic, therapist sort of an expression, and it made me want to punch it.

'She was very unusual, my mother. Sadie.' I tried to sound authoritative, as though I knew her, when the reality was that I knew little more about her than anyone else in the room. 'She couldn't be hemmed in. And in the modelling world, sometimes you have to go where the work takes you. She made great sacrifices.'

Three furrowed brows were facing me. I didn't meet any of their eyes. I couldn't. There was a long silence. After a while, Hayley reached over and squeezed my arm.

'S'all right, Klar,' she said. 'My mum's fucking useless as well.'

And it was then that I started crying, because I wanted her so badly to be wrong about Sadie and because somewhere I knew that she wasn't; because all I wanted was to be able to say 'No, no, you don't see, this is how it was, this is what happened, let me explain, let me make you all understand.' But I couldn't. Because I didn't.

# Chapter Ten

'I've moved the chest of drawers from the spare room in here, and I found you a bookcase as well, for your school stuff. We can get you a desk at the weekend if you like. I want you to have somewhere where you can concentrate. Exams and everything.'

Elfie shook her head. 'I like to do my homework on my bed.'

'It's not very good for your back . . . OK. Whatever you prefer.' Mark held his hands up in surrender. 'I promise I won't be too much of a dad.'

Elfie grinned. 'Hardly. When has Barney ever worried about my back? I don't think he even knows if I have homework.'

'Probably not.'

I shuffled my feet a bit on the landing, making sure they were aware of my presence. They turned, and they both smiled. I breathed a silent sigh of relief. Mark was not bearing a grudge, then. He held his arm out to me.

'Hello, darling. We're getting Elfie all set up.'

'So I can see.' I leaned against the doorframe, wrapping my cardigan more tightly around myself. I would have to turn the heating up; the room was chilly. The little attic room had been transformed; Mark had been hard at work. The single bed had been covered with a floral bedspread that I didn't recognise, and the furniture that he had moved into the room had been freshly wiped down and polished. He'd put a water glass on the little bedside table and found a lamp from somewhere – the loft, I imagined – to go on it. 'Cosy. If I'd known he was this good a housewife I'd have taken advantage of it ages ago.'

Elfie giggled.

'They discharged you, then?' I went on. 'I thought they might want you to stay another night.'

'They did.' She looked over at Mark.

'I'm afraid I insisted she be allowed home,' he said.

'Ah, you pulled the doctor card.'

He looked shame-faced. 'Yes. I know. It's awful. But hospital's grim – you come out of it worse than you went in.'

'Hey, I wasn't criticising. Home's the best place to recover.'

Mark looked at me gratefully. 'Exactly. Home.'

Barney and Maisie hadn't made a fuss, when Mark had eventually managed to get hold of them. He had had to pass a message on to Maisie via three members of staff at the silent retreat she was taking part in. She hadn't felt it necessary to break her silence for this, but had written a short note that had been read out to him. *Take the path that you feel is right*, it had said, he told me later, when we were in bed, warming our feet on one another. Seeing my expression, he said, I know. She's in one of her Zen acceptance phases.'

'How about Barney?'

Mark glowered. '*He's* in one of his shag-anything-that-moves phases. When I spoke to him, I could hear a woman in the background – maybe two. It was hard to tell, he sounded completely stoned.'

'Hm. Well. Whatever works for them, I guess.'

'But it doesn't. I know it doesn't work for Maisie. She says she's fine with it, that she couldn't possibly chain him to her and that they have this wonderful sexual freedom, but surely if she was so fine with it, she'd be doing the same?'

'How do you know that she isn't?'

Mark rolled onto his elbow to face me. 'Darling. She's at a silent retreat. How much more do you need to know?'

I laughed. 'Point taken. How about Serri? When did she leave the hospital?'

'Oh, not long after you. She didn't exactly hang around like the concerned sister.'

I stroked his arm. 'I doubt you made it that easy for her, to be fair.'

He shrugged.

'Do you think we need to do anything?' I persevered. 'To help Serri, I mean – if Barney and Maisie aren't around. From what Elfie said, and from what we saw ourselves, she's pretty fragile right now. What about her doctor – should you speak to him?'

'Now that's something that really *isn't* our responsibility,' Mark said, and I bit my lip. 'Honestly,' he continued, 'there's no point. He can't tell me anything. I can explain what happened, and that's about it.'

'Well, I think you should do that, because I don't think she will.'

He sighed. 'OK. Yes, you're right, OK. I'll call him in the morning.'

'Promise? I'm worried that she's going to get worse.'

'I know. Me too.' His face was glum.

'And she is our responsibility really, isn't she? They all are.'

It would have been the perfect moment to tell him about the key, and the note, and the boxes that were piled up in my study and what was inside them, and the diary that lay, at that moment, in the chest of drawers right next to my head, slipped in beneath a pile of underwear. To read him the pages that I had read earlier, even, ask him what he thought. Ask him what he would do next. The house was quiet, we were alone, close, catching up with one another in the intimate way that binds couples together, seemingly small conversations the strands of which thread together like a schoolgirl's plait. It was the perfect opportunity. So why did I not take it? Because keeping secrets is addictive.

There are some things in my life that I have never doubted, never questioned. My father, for one. My relationship with Mark. His love for me. That sounds arrogant, doesn't it? Complacent. It's not. I never expected to feel like this. Never thought I deserved to. But the simple truth of it was there from the start, impossible to ignore. He loved me, whether I deserved it or not, and nothing I could do seemed to be able to change that. I behaved badly enough to test it, after all. Ignored phone calls, turned up late or not at all to dates, forgot anniversaries and burned dinners. Nothing I did made any difference. And so it became one of the simple facts of my life. I was Klara Mortimer, I was a lecturer at City University, I was loved by my husband, Mark.

Other things that were simply facts: I could rely on my father to answer any question I put to him, to find an answer for it if it was something that he did not know. Again, this was something that I had tested, again and again through my life. And he had never let me down yet.

I realised now though, that this might only be because I had never asked him a truly difficult question. Everything I had put to him so far had been something he could look up in a book or on the Internet, or ask a colleague about, or simply puzzle out himself, sitting quietly on the sofa until he had got the answer, his great brows wiggling as he thought.

So far.

And I realised then that I was afraid. Afraid because the questions I was going to ask him would demand much more of him than that, and I wasn't sure if he was going to be able to give it. They would require truth and honesty; they would require him to dig into his past and pull it into the present; they would require him to give me something of my mother's story and his own that I knew he wanted to keep for himself. Something that he had buried. And what if he couldn't, or wouldn't, find me the answers this time? What did that say about him, and me, and us – and everything else?

Other things I knew to be true. My best friend Beth was devoted to her family. Ever since I had known her, our meetings had fitted around school pick-ups and drop-offs, baby feeding times and toddler tantrums, outings to get new shoes and trips to the park, and only later had they graduated to the occasional evening meet-up, dinner and drinks, and even then the children were firmly in the forefront of conversation. I went to her house, not the other way around, because dragging three children into the car and to ours, where cupboards were treacherously unlocked and plug sockets were not covered with little plastic sheaths, was not practical. That was fine, I had accepted it as part of the deal if I wanted to be friends with her, which I did, because she was funny and sharp and could be shrewdly, satisfyingly bitchy in a way that made me feel as though I were part of a special gang, though she was never too unkind, never uncomfortably so. She told me stories of school-gate competitiveness that skewered the mums involved with perfect accuracy and made me dread the day they were part of my life, while also making me roar with laughter. She was a wise confidante and a fiercely loyal friend. And she was a mother, through and through.

So I had no qualms about asking her, as I stood in her kitchen eating biscuits and dropping crumbs on the island, what the biggest secret was that she had ever kept from Steve. I did it almost without thinking. She raised an eyebrow, as her hands cut brown bread Marmite sandwiches into crustless triangles. I had my answer ready for the question she hadn't yet asked. 'Nothing big,' I said. 'An email from – someone from the past. I don't know whether to tell Mark about it or not. He won't like it.'

It was sort of true, you see. And, more importantly, it was the kind of question that Beth could understand. She jumped to the obvious conclusion, that the missive had come from an old boyfriend, and thought no more of it. It was the type of thing that happened every day to married couples, and which caused no real ripples in their lives.

She shrugged, saying, 'Oh, I see,' and discarded the reason for the question easily.

Why had I asked her about her secret? For reassurance, I suppose. To be told that what I was doing was no big deal, even though she didn't know the full truth of it. To feel as though everyone kept secrets, everyone's lives contained a layer of untruth, running through their marriage like a fossilised starfish hidden silent inside a stone.

I got more than I had bargained for.

'Something much bigger than that,' she said, and her voice was quieter than I expected and there was a darkness to it.

I sensed that I had stepped onto dangerous ground but I kept going. I wish now that I hadn't, but it wouldn't have made a difference, for as soon as the words were out of my mouth it was too late.

'Oho,' I joked. 'Here we go. The dark heart of Beth Claybourne. Come on, what is it? A secret passion for Barry

Manilow? A midnight cheesecake-eating addiction? A double life writing Mills and Boon novels?'

'Ha ha. I know – I'm a dull housewife, you don't have to rub it in.'

She prickled, and I felt bad. I hadn't meant to mock her.

'Sorry, Beth. I didn't mean—'

'I know. I know.' She waved her hand in front of her face. 'Sorry. It wasn't a serious question, you didn't want a serious answer. It's just been one of those days.'

I didn't have a choice after that. 'Of course I wanted a serious answer. If there is one, I mean. I didn't think . . . You can tell me anything, Beth, you know that.'

She smiled weakly, then took a deep breath. 'OK. If you want to know. Sometimes I wish I'd never had children. Sometimes I wish I could just walk out of the door, without doing anyone else's coat up, or packing a bag full of snacks, or making sure I had enough nappies and wipes and little plastic bags, just me, and keep going, and never come back. Sometimes I envy . . .'

She looked up at me. 'Your mother,' she was going to say, I knew it, but she stopped herself. 'You,' she finished.

We both took a breath. What was unsaid weighed as heavily in the air as what she had said. 'Your freedom, your life, your marriage. The honesty in it. I can never tell Steve this. Because it would give him what he really wants. It would be the ultimate "I told you so". It's true, he always said it. "Children will tie us down, they'll come between us, they'll stop us doing things". And I said no, they wouldn't, I wouldn't let that happen. But . . .' She sighed. 'But that's not how life works.'

She turned away and started wiping down the polished wood surface of the island, and I could tell that she was crying, and I wished that I was a different sort of a person so that I could comfort her.

'Oh Beth,' I said in the end, and the words sounded paltry and pathetic in the face of her emotion.

'I'm sorry,' she said, and she wasn't apologising to me, but to her children for thinking those thoughts, to herself for letting them out in the air, to the world for failing. I could see it, but I didn't know how to fix it. 'Sorry. I love them, I'm grateful for them, I would never leave them.'

'I know,' I said quietly. 'Of course. Of course you wouldn't.'

And still it was there, in the room between us. *Not like your mother. Not like Sadie.*

I walked home from Beth's rather than get the bus. I needed the fresh air. And I needed the space to think, to absorb what she had told me. Her resentment, her dissatisfaction with a life that I had always thought of as rosily perfect had seeped into every corner of the kitchen while she had been talking; it had cloaked us like a sea fret, and it took me until I was nearly at the end of my street to shake it off. It had shocked me. How had I not seen it, until now? Had Beth hidden it so well, or had I just been too busy admiring the pink cheeks and glossy curls of her children to see the demands they placed on her, too focused on their happy cries to hear the need behind them? Too jealous of what she had, to see what she had given up to get it?

Had that been how Sadie had felt, I wondered. Suffocated, trapped in a domestic prison of her own making? Hemmed in by school pick-ups and bedtimes, unable to see herself any longer when she looked in the mirror, instead only seeing an amorphous figure of Mother, with Sadie herself lost somewhere behind the sensible clothes and over-full handbag?

Maybe. But even if that explained why she had left, it didn't answer the question of how she had died.

I had always assumed that Daddy was the only person who

could tell me that, and that as that avenue was closed to me, I would never get to know. But the key and letter from N.R. had changed all that. They had opened a door to Sadie's past. Brought up the possibility of friends, lovers, enemies. A whole life lived before I existed, a history that was just waiting to be told. I had her diary, I had her clothes. In my hands, I held the beginnings of the thread that would lead me to her. Now I just needed to follow it, and find out where it led – and to whom.

# Chapter Eleven

*8 July 1970*

So, here it begins. I am eighteen and from now on I will be known as Sadie. Not Sadie Tomaszewski, just Sadie. I'm sick of having to spell my surname to everyone, sick of them looking at me funny when I say it. I *want* people to look at me – just not like that.

I'm leaving today. This afternoon. This is the last day I'll spend in this room, the last day that I'll be Mary, daughter of Anne and Piotr Tomaszewski of 24 Laburnum Gardens, St Albans, Hertfordshire. The last day that I will ever be ordinary.

For posterity, then, I have decided to record something of my life up until now. It seems fitting somehow, to tell my story before I leave this place for ever.

The first thing they will say about my childhood, I imagine, is that I was adopted. It sounds terribly mysterious and almost glamorous, doesn't it? The truth is far more banal, far more suburban, I am sorry to say. My parents were old when they met, my mother already in her thirties, my father in his forties. I know, it's a bit disgusting, isn't it? You'd think they'd have accepted their lot by then. But apparently not. They wanted children desperately but couldn't have them. They tried, for years. I don't like to think about what 'trying' involved. Revolting. Anyhow, nothing worked, so they decided to adopt a baby.

Often it can take a long time, but in their case – and mine, I suppose – it was quite quick. There was a Polish girl who had got into trouble, and who couldn't keep her child, which was me, obviously, and because my father was Polish the adoption authorities gave me to them. The girl was happy because her baby was going to someone who would understand where it came from, or half of the couple would, at least, and my parents were happy because they had a baby.

My real mother was very young, younger even than I am now, I think, and her parents were furious when they found out that she was pregnant. They didn't find out until quite late on, apparently, because she kept it a secret. Kept *me* a secret. I think about her sometimes, and how scared she must have been. I don't know her name. My parents never told me. I'm not sure if they even remember. Sometimes people ask me whether I want to know more about her, know who she was. But I don't, not really. She doesn't seem that important.

My father works for a company that manufactures trucks and diggers, the sort of things that farmers use to turn their fields over and move things around. I don't know exactly what he does there. Something in an office, though I think maybe he used to work in the factory when I was younger. It's something dull, anyhow.

What else do you need to know about my father? He is strange – in fact, both my parents are. He's much older than my friends' fathers. He's old-fashioned, and he's strict. Far too strict. Every time I'm late home from school, or if my marks aren't as good as he thinks they should be, or if I just say something he doesn't like, he punishes me. Once he made me sit at the kitchen table all night long, writing out verses from the Bible, because he thought I had been day-dreaming in church. I kept on falling asleep on the page, and every time he'd pull me up by my shoulder and shove the pen back in my hand, and make me carry on. I had to go to school the next day and do an exam with my fingers rubbed red raw from holding the pen, but I still did it, because I knew that if I got anything less than an A, what happened next would be worse.

He can be crueller than that, as well. I had a pet once, just a goldfish, that I won at a fair. I didn't even like it much; it was quite boring, but it was mine, and I bought it a bowl and food out of the money that I earned on Saturdays at the newsagent, and I talked to it at night when I couldn't sleep. Talking to a goldfish, oh dear, I know, but I was so lonely, and it stared at me through the glass and made me feel as though I had a friend in the house.

Anyhow, after work on Saturday morning I went to the park instead of going straight home to help Mum, because Suzanne was going to meet two boys she knew, friends of her brothers, and she had begged and begged me to go with her. 'I can't go by myself!' she squealed. 'They'll think I'm awful, but I really like Paul. His friend Nigel's nice, as well – you could have him. He's posh and he's only got a few spots,' and she went on and on until I agreed.

So after work I got my bag and got changed quickly

in the toilet, shoving my scratchy blue uniform into the bottom of my bag and pulling on a tight striped sweater, and headed off to the park. I felt so free as I was walking there, I almost skipped. I had my wages in my pocket and it was sunny and I was going to meet my best friend and a boy, and it was so exciting!

I was almost there – I was just turning the corner into the park and waving at Suzanne and the boys who I could see on the swings waving back at me – and then I saw him. I think he must have followed me all the way there, waiting till I had seen my friends and they had seen me before letting me know that he was there. I didn't know how he had found out that I was planning on going to the park. Not until I got home, anyhow, and Mum wouldn't look at me, and then I knew that she must have been going through my things, and found the notes from Suzanne in my schoolbag. We had been passing them in maths, planning where to meet, and I had just shoved them in my book at the end of class. Stupid, stupid, stupid. I should have thrown them in the bin at school, or on my way home, or burned them or something. I should have known I couldn't relax, not even for a minute.

He killed the goldfish. I knew he would, as soon as we got into the house.

'You'll learn what happens when you lie, Mary,' he was saying as he went upstairs. 'When you lie, you let people down. And when you let people down, they lose something. You have taken something precious from them – their trust in you. It is not just yours, to be so careless with. So now *you* will lose something that is precious to *you*.'

My heart was in my mouth. And I knew what he was going to take from me.

He didn't flush it down the toilet, which is what I thought he would do. Instead, he simply reached into the bowl and caught my fish in his hand, and then, while it was flapping and wriggling in his palm, he took its tail with his other hand and held it out in front of my face. 'See what happens, Mary? This is what your mother and I feel like. As if we have had to watch something die right in front of us. Our trust in you. See how it feels to be so hurt?'

I nodded, and watched as the little fish bucked and gulped for a few more seconds before it died. Then he dropped it on the floor at my feet, and slapped me hard across the cheek. It burned hotter than my heart. 'Flush it down the toilet,' he instructed me as he left the room, my mother scurrying pathetically after him. And I reached down and picked it up, and stared at its small, dead black eyes.

It was that night that I started planning my escape. I listened as he sat downstairs, drinking and talking to himself in Polish, as he did when he got morose and pissed, and hating him. But it was really her that I hated more. My so-called mother. She was the one who had betrayed me. She was the one who was meant to understand me, to protect me. We were meant to keep secrets, confidences, together, mother and daughter, like other girls in my class did. We were meant to be on the same side. And she had gone through my things, my private things, and read my notes and gone running to him.

I cried that night, and hated myself for crying, but they were not tears of sadness or self-pity. They were tears of rage and righteous indignation, and with every tear I shed, I became more and more determined to do whatever I could to escape.

So you can see, can't you, why I have to leave?

Anyhow. That's my father. My mother, Anne Tomaszewski, is a housewife. What a terrible, suffocating thing to be called. Wife of the house, married to the house. Chained to it, more like, in her case. She is what people call 'houseproud'. Nothing makes her happier than a guest who offers to take their shoes off without having to be asked. She keeps things for 'best'. What's the point? They never get used, they just gather dust. Or they would in anyone else's house, but she dusts everything daily, wiping down every single surface of her three-bedroom semi with a yellow duster and a can of lavender-scented polish, so no dust ever dares settle, and no fresh air that might have seeped in is allowed to remain unfragranced. God forbid we should smell an actual flower, or catch a whiff of cut grass. No, the place is sealed shut and the air is regulated with fresheners and sprays. It makes me gag and choke.

I don't think she's ever had a job. I can't imagine anything worse than my mother's life, but I don't feel sorry for her. She chose it, and she seems to think it's worthy of respect. Who could respect *her*? What has *she* ever done? I despise her. I know it's an awful thing to say about your own mother, but if I can't be honest here, where can I be? It's the truth, so you should know it. One day this will be important.

I can't think what else there is to say about her. She's short and slim, she looks tiny next to my father, who is big and fleshy. I am taller than her, though not as tall as him. She has brown hair that she gets set every week at the hairdresser. She plays bridge. She is an active member of the Women's Institute. She goes to church every week and never misses a Saint's Day. She is Catholic, like my father, and she often holds coffee mornings on behalf of the priest, and encourages women with babies to come and eat her Victoria sponge and talk about their children's poos in our front room. She has, basically, a completely pointless life.

I'm an only child. They didn't adopt any more after me. I suppose they realised it wasn't as much fun as they had thought it would be. Or maybe there just weren't any more silly Polish girls around. I don't know, I've never asked them. I used to want a brother or sister when I was smaller, someone to play with, someone to boss around, but it never happened and so I stopped asking for it. Like lots of things.

Suzanne is the only one I'll miss. She's my only real friend at school. Oh, I talk to the other girls, but they're all stupid. All they want to do is get married to boys from round here and have babies, push prams up and down the street and get their hair done. Live lives like my mother's. Well, not exactly like hers, I don't suppose. They probably don't imagine getting beaten up on a Saturday night after their husband has come back from the pub, and having to wear long sleeves to church the next morning in the summer so no one sees the bruises. But it'll probably happen to them as well, or to some of them at least. Small, sad lives of no consequence.

Suzanne is different though. She wants something more, like me. She knows that this isn't all life can be. She's clever, Suzanne, she's going to be a journalist. She's always reading. People take the mickey out of her for it, but she doesn't care. Maybe when I'm a model and she's a journalist we'll be in the same magazine. Maybe she'll write a story about me. I'll give her an exclusive.

But she's staying here, for now. I asked her to come with me, but she wants to finish school and go to university. School doesn't quite know what to do about that. I don't think many girls have been to uni from our school recently. No one in her family has, and her dad's dead set against it, but she'll do it – she's determined. She just needs to get her exams and then she can apply, and it doesn't matter what they say then; she can get a grant from the government – she's found it all out from the library. I'll be proud of her.

So, I'll miss Suzanne, but our paths will cross again, I'm sure of it. In the meantime, I'm leaving – tonight, after my birthday tea. I thought I should stay for that. They won't realise I'm gone as quickly if I stay for that.

Before I go downstairs and pretend I'm happy to see all of my mother's stupid friends from church and their boring kids that she's asked round for my tea (at least I was allowed to ask Suzanne), I think I will copy the letter that started all of this off: the letter that is the key to my new life. It arrived a few weeks ago, and I had known it was going to, so I got it sent to Suzanne's house instead of here. The woman asked for my address so that she could get in touch and I thought quickly, thank God. She stopped me in the street, on my way to school. Suzanne and I were walking together, like we usually do; we meet at the end of her street which is two along from my street and walk arm-in-arm. Best friends. The woman was wearing hot pants, shorter than anything I'd ever seen before. They looked like they were made out of leather, and she had long legs and high platform boots. She wore a leather jacket like one a biker would wear, and she had big sunglasses and long, messy curls of dark brown hair. In between the fingers of her left hand, she held a black Sobranie cigarette. I knew that was what they were called, since I had seen them in magazines in the library. They were the only thing that made me want to smoke, and they suited her absolutely. She was the most beautiful person I'd ever seen in my life, and nothing like anyone I'd ever seen in St Albans before.

'You,' she said, pointing at me, walking quickly towards us as if she was in a hurry. 'Hello, what's your name? How old are you? I'm Coco,' she carried on, before I had a chance to answer. 'Coco Delaney. How tall are you?'

I'm never usually lost for words, anyone will tell you that, and I think people who say they're shy are just trying to draw attention to themselves, but I felt shy then for the first time that I can remember. 'F-five foot ten,' I stammered eventually, and Suzanne elbowed me in the ribs excitedly. She knew what was coming.

'Perfect. Have you ever thought about being a model? What did you say your name was?'

I opened my mouth. 'Sadie,' I said. And as I said it, I knew it was true. Sadie was my name. My *real* name.

'Sadie. Perfect. Well, Sadie, have you?'

I nodded. 'Yes. I'd love to. I'd love to be a model.'

When she asked me for my full name and address I only hesitated for a second before giving Suzanne's. I glanced at her as I did so, and she winked at me.

'Sadie what?' Coco asked.

I shrugged. 'Just Sadie.'

'Just Sadie, eh?' She grinned, and clicked her pen shut. 'You're a star already, aren't you? I'll be in touch, Just Sadie.'

And she got into her car, a dark green convertible, revved the engine and drove away.

Suzanne screamed and jumped up and down next to me, but I didn't move.

'OhmyGod, OhmyGod, Mary, you're going to be a model, I knew it, just like we always talked about. It's coming true. It's all coming true.'

I stayed still. I didn't feel excited, or even surprised really. I had known that something like this was going to happen. And now it had.

VELVET MODELS
13–15 Great Portland Street
London W1


*Dear Sadie,*

*It was lovely to meet you recently in St Albans. I wonder if you could come to see us at our office in London to discuss what steps we might take together next? Do bring a friend or parent with you if you'd like to. We can reimburse your expenses when you get here. Just bring your ticket.*

*So looking forward to seeing you again,*
*Best love*


*Coco xx*

So, there it is. The letter that changed everything. I wrote back and told her that I'd be there this afternoon, towards 6 p.m and that I'd be coming by myself.

This is it. This is the beginning of the rest of my life.

# Chapter Twelve

Downstairs I could hear Elfie watching *Shipwrecked* and Mark bumbling around in the kitchen. The sounds were comforting. Upstairs in my study, I stared at the screen. It was satisfyingly fuller than a couple of days ago. There was information there, real information that I could do something with, that I would have to do something with now. Leads to follow up, names and dates and places to research. Grandparents. Not very nice grandparents, by the sound of things. But my grandparents, albeit adoptive. I was uncovering a history, a family – one that I had never known I had. Roots. And it moved me far more than I could have imagined. My father's parents had died before I was born – cancer, both of them – and so in addition to my lack of a mother, I had lacked that extra layer of family that my classmates had had. Trips to toy shops, treats, ice creams – all the things grandparents bestowed on them had been absent from my childhood. I hadn't missed them, because they had never been there, but now I felt a small tug of regret.

I opened Google and typed their names into it. *Piotr Tomaszewski* first. A classical guitarist of around my age, a software architect, a Fulbright scholar ... no mention of a farming machinery manufacturer from 1950s St Albans. Unsurprisingly. Why would there be? He must be dead by now, anyhow, since he'd been in his forties when my mother was adopted. There was nothing that looked relevant for Anne either, just one or two namesakes on Facebook; she must be in her late eighties, early nineties, depending on how accurate Sadie's description of her age had been. And I doubted she'd be putting up photos of herself and poking people on the Internet if she were still alive.

'Mark says to tell you dinner's ready.' Elfie's voice was quiet and nervous and I turned towards her, shutting the laptop with one hand as I did so.

'Thanks. I didn't hear you. How was school? Get there from here OK?'

A single-shouldered shrug. 'Fine.'

Fine.

In the kitchen, Mark was cutting into a tray of lasagne. It was his speciality, and he made it carefully – even a touch obsessively. All the ingredients had to come from certain places; no quick trip around the supermarket would suffice. Italian pasta and Parmesan from the deli, special tomatoes, mince from a particular butcher . . . It was a high days and holidays thing usually.

'I thought I'd treat my girls,' he said, looking a little embarrassed, and I smiled.

'Lovely. You know I can never resist your lasagne.' I kissed his cheek and took the plate from him.

'How's the book going?' he asked.

I dipped my index finger into the sauce and sucked it. He'd made garlic bread to go with it, and I dropped a piece onto my plate.

'Bit slowly. OK.' It wasn't a lie. Not really. But, of course, it was.

* * *

99

I was distracted throughout dinner, and I knew Mark could feel it. He kept on glancing over at me as he made conversation, wanting and waiting for me to join in. I tried. I did. I asked Elfie about the history project she was doing, and promised to help her research it. I suggested that we go to the Imperial War Museum at the weekend, to find out more. I asked Mark about his practice and about one of the partners with whom he was always locking horns. But I was not 100 per cent present. My head was so full of everything that I had read, everything that I had discovered. It felt as though I had opened the door to another world, been given a glimpse of the past, of my mother's life, of the girl she had been and the woman she had been on the verge of becoming, and I couldn't wait to get back to it, to find out more.

As we ate and chatted, I made a mental list of what I would do next. Locate Suzanne. She would presumably be able to tell me more about Sadie's home life, about her parents, about their schooldays. I needed to find out what school they had been to – I must be able to do that, surely? I had my mother's name, her home address. Was there some sort of register? I didn't know. Maybe I could contact the adoptions agency? But what would they be able to tell me? Not much, I was sure. At best they might be able to confirm the date of an adoption and whether it had taken place, but I didn't even know if they'd do that much. Coco Delaney. Coco Delaney of Velvet Models . . . Now that was something that might be easier to track down. It had been a registered business, at the very least; it might even have been a famous agency – I wouldn't know. I had no idea about the world of fashion and modelling. But if they were still going, there would be records, and even if there weren't, there must be information about them somewhere.

I was restless, eager to get on, to read more of the diary, to delve deeper into what I had read already. Finally, I was getting to know my mother; although it was at a distance of decades, I was almost able to reach out and touch her. My long-lost mother.

www.companieshouse.gov.uk
Please search by company name or company number: Velvet Models
Name and registered office: Velvet Models
13–15 Great Portland Street
London W1
Company number 5938386

Status: Dissolved 1974
Date of incorporation: 1st February 1969
Company type: Private Limited Company
Nature of Business (SIC) – (7450) Labour recruitment

Then there were some details about accounting – the last set of accounts had been submitted in 1973 – and a previous name for the company: Floribunda Model Management and Odessa Models. No list of directors though, which was one of the things I had been hoping to find. I could register to get more information, but it seemed the full documents were only online for the past ten years or so. I could go there, but I wasn't sure what knowing who the directors of the agency had been would do to help anyhow.

*Coco Delaney.* I typed the name into Google and hit return.

That was more like it. A string of entries appeared, and I could see that the search had returned images as well. I clicked to them first.

I could see immediately why my mother had been so taken with her that day. To a suburban schoolgirl, Coco Delaney must have looked as though she had stepped straight out of a magazine. Maybe she had. She had that rock-and-roll look of insouciance. Dark-rimmed eyes, full lips, masses of dark wavy hair. There were modelling photos of her as a younger woman – from the Fifties, maybe. Elegant, wide-eyed, fresh-faced. But still with a look of mischief behind those big dark eyes. There was one photo of her dressed up in a rockabilly outfit, all puffy petticoats and carefully curled quiff, sitting astride a motorbike, winking at the camera. You could see it there, a hint of danger behind the perfect red lips. The rock-chick look had come later, probably around the time that she had scouted my mother. The photos of her from those years weren't modelling ones but reportage. She wasn't looking at the camera in most of them, but was usually on the arm of some man, often with tight trousers and hair almost as big as hers. In one she was in the background, behind Mick Jagger, one of a gaggle of giggling girls that he was herding into a waiting car. Coco Delaney had clearly been quite the girl about town.

I flicked back to the general search page.

*Coco Delaney, maybe one of the first MAWS (Model/ Actress/Whatever), has not passed into the popular consciousness. Unlike other models of her generation, such as Celia Hammond and Pattie Boyd, Twiggy and Jean Shrimpton, her memory has faded along with her looks. But there is no denying that at the time she was a big figure, in a small frame . . .*

The blog post was too badly written. I clicked on her Wikipedia entry.

*Coco Delaney, model and actress, born 21st December 1935, London, England.*

No death date. That was something.

*Nationality: British*
*Occupation: Fashion model, actress, interior designer,*
*model's agent, author*

She'd been to Lucie Clayton, along with others of her generation, according to the article, before getting her first modelling job at the age of twenty-one. She'd had quite a good few years when she was in demand, before things had tailed off and she'd started acting in slightly dubious-sounding film roles (credits included such delights as *Return of the Valley People* in which she had apparently played a 'swamp creature'; *Attack of the Giant Spiders* – her role in this was described simply as 'Virgin 2'; and *The Disappearing House*' in which she didn't even have a titled role. It seemed to be after this work had dried up that she had started working for Velvet Models, but the account of her career from there on was sparse. *Model's agent and scout with Velvet Models from 1969 till its closure a few years later* was all it said. She appeared to have set up an interior design company as well, and self-published a novel in the second half of the Seventies. And then she had simply faded from view. There was a reference to her working as a freelance model's agent, but nothing concrete.

What had started off feeling promising had fizzled out into another dead end.

The Imperial War Museum was rammed. Clearly half the schools in London were doing the same project as Elfie. We traipsed around the 1940s house, jostled by groups and too hot in our winter coats, and getting thoroughly fed up with not being able to see what we wanted to, until eventually I turned to Elfie and said, 'Shall we give it up as a bad job, and come back another day? We can go to the shop and get postcards and stuff if you like.' I gave a silent sigh of relief when she nodded gratefully.

'Don't tell Mark we didn't look around the whole thing,' I said as we left. 'He'll get all pompous.'

'I know. He'd say we should have gone first thing in the morning, to beat the crowds, instead of lying in bed for half the day,' and she giggled.

'Wouldn't he just. I'll take you to Topshop in Oxford Street instead, if you like. But I need to run an errand over there as well. It won't take long.'

Her face lit up.


I settled Elfie in the café on Great Portland Street with a magazine, a Danish pastry and a cup of tea, and promised her I'd be back soon. 'I'm just going to that building over there – see where the man is standing smoking?'

She craned her head, then nodded. 'It's fine, Klara. I'm OK by myself.'

I touched her cheek. 'I know you are. I just fret. Sorry.'

'It's fine. It's nice.' And she went back to her magazine.


The building was tall and fronted with grey stone, weather-beaten and solid. It was rather beautiful, if you bothered to look up from the pavement to examine it; there were ornate mouldings above the windows and it was topped with a sort of plaque, or ornamentation. Like a grand old dame in her family tiara.

The smoking man moved out of the way as I headed for the panel of buzzers.

*Sandpipe Recruitment*

*Fenson Office Supplies*
*Diva Designs*

No Velvet Models, and though I wasn't surprised I felt a little thud of disappointment. On impulse, I pressed the button that said *Diva Designs*.

'Yeah.' The voice at the other end of the buzzer was thick with boredom.

'Um. Is this Diva Designs?'

'Yeah. Delivery?'

The buzzer sounded in my ear. I waited until it had stopped.

'No, sorry, it's not a delivery. I was just wondering – you don't have anything to do with a modelling agency, do you?'

A pause. 'Nah.'

'Velvet Models? I think they were based here once.'

'Nah, we make the clothes, not model 'em. Wholesale, innit.'

'Right. And you don't happen to know . . .'

But the slight static at the other end had disappeared. The voice had clearly tired of the conversation.

The smoking man stared at me disinterestedly.

'I don't suppose *you*'ve ever heard of them, have you?'

'Modelling agency? I'd have noticed that, love.' He winked, snapping his gum and exhaling smoke all at the same time.

'It might have closed some time ago.'

'I've only been here six months, know what I mean?'

I nodded. 'Yes. It would have been longer ago than that, I think.'

He shrugged. 'Dunno then. You want a job in a call centre, we're your man – Sandpipe Recruitment. You want a job as a model, I can't help you, more's the pity.' The wink again.

'No, it's not for me, it's for . . . my sister.'

'Bit of a looker, isn't she?' He gestured with his head over to the window where Elfie sat, still engrossed in her magazine.

I bristled. 'She's *fifteen*.'

He sniffed, as though it made no odds to him. 'They start them young, these days, don't they? Good luck to her, anyhow. Maybe we'll be seeing her on the cover of one of those mags she's reading before too long.'

I bustled back across the road, suddenly filled with a righteous protectiveness, and ordered my own drink and pastry.

'All done?' Elfie asked.

'Yes. Just had to find something out for work. Thanks for waiting.'

'That's OK,' she said. Then: 'I'd like to see if they've got this in Topshop,' she added shyly, pointing to a picture of a striped dress, fresh and summery.

'It's sweet. Of course we can ask. I'm sure they will have it.'

I gazed at her, my heart still thudding with fury at the smoking man's comments. But as I gazed, I realised that she was beautiful, Elfie. Beautiful enough that a relative could fancy her chances as a model. After all, the man in the street had thought so. OK, he was hardly an expert, and neither was I, but she had something. Height, a willowy look to her limbs that made them appear pliable and soft, a light in her eyes that caught you and drew you in, high cheekbones and a neat chin. Maybe . . . And I had seen how she had devoured the fashion magazine I had left her with, studying the dresses and shoes, quickly flicking past ones that she decided were not up to scratch. She had a good eye, she always dressed well – quirkily, without looking weird.

I sowed the seed that night. It didn't need much. The idea was already there, I could tell, so it wasn't like I was pushing her into something. She leaped at it, when I suggested it.

'Elfie . . .' I was sitting on her bed as she tried on the dress I had bought her and showed me how she would wear it, dressing it up and down with scarves and bags and jackets.

'I was wondering. You looked amazing in those photos Serri took. Really special.'

She blushed, but waited before speaking. She knew there was a point to my compliment and half-suspected what it might be.

'I was thinking we could send them to a few people? It's not something I know much about, but it can't be that hard to find out. Only if you wanted to.'

The smile that covered her face told me that I had been right to suggest it. This was not a girl being coerced into anything.

'Really? Oh Klara, do you think – do you really think it's worth it? That they might like me?'

'I think they'll all love you.' And I did. Those big grey eyes, that smile . . . who could resist her?

She shrieked and threw her arms around my neck. 'Ohmygod. OhmyGOD.'

'Hey, hey, calm down! I'm not making any promises. It's a super-competitive industry, that much I do know.'

'Oh yes, I know it is. On *Britain's Next Top Model* they tell all the girls, "You should only be here if you're prepared to work hard, harder than everyone else. Because there'll always be someone willing to take your place if you're not." It's not really all about looks at all, you see.'

And she was off. Talking me through the industry, how it worked, what you had to do to be a success, the models she admired most and why. And it was done.

It took me a little while to track down Coco Delaney, but I did it in the end, via a circuitous and tedious series of phone calls and Internet searches. I finally had an address for her. No phone number, since she was ex-directory, but that was all right. The approach that I had planned didn't need one.

The photos that Seraphina emailed to me were perfect. She'd taken them before Elfie got in the water, so she hadn't yet gone blue around the lips, but she looked ethereal and fragile, her skin almost translucent in the watery winter light. I'd told her I wanted them for something to do with Mark's birthday, which was a couple of months away, not that I needed to have bothered with an excuse, really. Serri would have forgotten my request in a day, if that.

I had told Elfie that we should keep it a secret from Mark – 'just for now. I don't know whether he's going to be that enthusiastic, to be honest, and I think we need to decide how to tell him so he won't overreact. You know what he's like.' Elfie grinned at me conspiratorially and it took a second for the guilt to snap at my heels. 'We'll tell him when there's something concrete to tell. There's no point getting him in a tizz until then.'

'If,' she said, 'if there's something concrete to tell.' She bit her nail.

'When,' I insisted. And I sounded as confident as I felt. Somehow, I could feel it in my bones. Coco was going to bite.

# Chapter Thirteen

## 16th July 1970

When Suzanne gave me this diary, she told me that she was doing so because she knew that I would write 'some momentous things in it'. That it wouldn't be just full of little stories about boys and homework and complaints about being bored, like the diaries most teenage girls write, but that it would be a proper story. The story of my life.

And now it has begun. I have left home, I have arrived in London, I have started my new life. And oh, what a life it is going to be! I can already taste it. I should go back, back to how I left, because that's the beginning of the journey really, isn't it? Where you come from is important, I do know that. Even more importantly though, I have met the man who will change the course of my life. I know that sounds overly dramatic now, but it won't when I'm looking back, in the future. But more of that, later.

So, the day of my escape.

Anne had laid out my birthday tea as I had known she would (it feels wrong to call her Mum now, and Piotr, Dad – those names belong to a different person, a different life) – plates of crab-paste sandwiches even though she knew I hated them, and cheese and pineapple on sticks and all the things that she thought were celebratory. She doesn't understand me at all. Jeanette, my boss from the newsagent, was there, and stupid Trevor her son who I knew they were all hoping I'd get together with one day (no chance, not with those teeth and that BO), and some of the neighbours. The priest came along too, smelling of wet dog as usual, and there was Miss Brigham and Miss Manning from the WI, and Piotr had invited his friend Vlodek from the Polish Club: they were drinking beer. Father McBride looked as though he'd have liked a beer as well instead of the weak tea Anne had pressed into his hand, but of course he couldn't ask for one. And then there was Suzanne. The only way you could tell it was a party for me at all was because she was there, wearing her best dress and fidgeting because she was so excited – she can never sit still when she's excited. She had got stuck next to Trevor, poor thing, and he was staring at her bust, and I should have gone to rescue her but then I'd have ended up having to talk to him as well, and it was my birthday so I didn't see why I should. Anyhow, Miss Manning was telling me a long story about the day she turned eighteen, and God knows when that was, probably some time in the last century.

There was a cake, as well, once the sandwiches and everything had been cleared away, a chocolate one in honour of it being a special occasion (Anne didn't normally believe in chocolate cake, she thought it was indulgent) and it was iced and everything, with candles on the top. I wouldn't be able to have any, of course, because now I was going to be a model I had to watch everything I ate, but she brought it out with the candles lit and everyone sang 'Happy Birthday' and then as she was cutting it up and handing pieces round, it was time.

'I have something to say,' I said, and it was strange because my throat suddenly felt dry, so I had a sip of orange squash and carried on.

'I want to say thank you to my parents, to Mum and Dad,' and even then the words had started to feel odd in my mouth, but I could hardly have called them by their first names in front of everyone – imagine, 'for being such great parents. I'm sure I haven't always been an easy daughter . . .' When I said this, Anne waved her hand, and people tittered politely, 'but you've always been easy parents.' It was interesting how effortless it was to lie, when there was a reason to do so. The untruths tumbled from my mouth like kittens from a basket. 'You've always encouraged me to work hard, and try and be a good person, and luckily I've had you doing the same and setting me an example.' Mustn't lay it on too thick, I thought, but when I looked around, everyone was lapping it up. The priest was nodding approvingly and Miss Brigham was holding a little lacy handkerchief to her pink cheeks.

'Anyhow, I'm going to miss you very much, but of course I'll be taking everything you have taught me with me when I leave, and I'll carry it here in my heart.' I touched my hand to my chest then, and tried to look moved. After a second, I stole a glance at my parents. Their smiles were fading and being replaced by looks of confusion. There was a pause. I waited.

It was Trevor who asked in the end, clearing his throat awkwardly, staring at his big leather shoes. I was quite impressed. He had shown some spark for once in his life. 'Where are you going, Mary?' he asked, and then he snorted the phlegm up his nose and sat down on the pouffe as though he would be able to disappear.

'I'm going to London,' I said, and now I couldn't look at my parents. My heart was thudding and I wasn't sure whether it was because of excitement or terror or everything all at once, and I was doing it – it was like riding a bike and I could have screamed with exhilaration. 'I'm going to London, to be a model, and I'm leaving this afternoon. In fact, I'm going to have to go quite soon.' There was a silence. No one knew what to say or do. 'I've booked a taxi,' I added, as though that would explain it all.

They couldn't say anything, Anne and Piotr, of course; they had to pretend they knew all about it. 'Oh, a fashion model,' Miss Manning said. 'How exciting, you must be so proud,' and she patted my arm, and they just nodded.

'She always was a pretty one,' Father McBride said, and I shuddered.

I had booked the taxi to come at four o'clock, and it was five to. There were only five minutes to go – just five more minutes to get through. I had to fetch my things from my room, so I gave Suzanne the signal, saying, 'I must get my case,' and she leaped up and together we almost ran out of the room and up the stairs.

'Oh my God, oh my God, oh my God.' She couldn't stop saying it, and we were breathing as if we'd run ten miles, and giggling. 'You did it, you bloody did it, Mary. I can't believe it!'

'Did you think I wouldn't?'

'No, of course not, but – oh God!'

My suitcase was ready, I wasn't taking too much, because I didn't know where I was going to be staying after tonight, and I didn't want most of my things anyway. The only thing I wished I could take was my mirror, the one above the fireplace, because it was so pretty. I think it must have been there from when the house was built or something. It was engraved with flowers, sort of cut into the glass, and it had a swirly white frame with roses and vines all over it. It wasn't the sort of thing my parents would ever have bought, far too frilly and not very sensible. I loved it though. I looked into it and imagined the other girls who might have lived in this house before me, slept in this room, and looked into the same mirror. I stared into it now. It felt like I was saying goodbye, not to my family, but to the house, and to the girl that I had been. I reached out and touched it, and smiled.

That was Mary. That was the girl who had been Mary, and I was leaving her here. Now I was Sadie.

He cornered me in the hallway before I left. Most people had gone, but Suzanne was there, and Trevor and Jeanette. I had made Suzanne promise to stay and get them to stay as well, so that I wasn't left alone with my parents, but Piotr managed to find me when I was coming back from the bathroom. He grabbed my wrist hard and twisted it.

'What the bloody hell do you think you're playing at?' he hissed. 'Your mother is so upset. So embarrassed.'

I stared at him, right in the eye. I wasn't going to let him scare me, not any longer. 'I made it sound as though you knew,' I said. 'I did it on purpose.'

He laughed. 'Oh, so that's fine then, that's OK? Of

course they know we didn't know! Your mother looked as though someone had died.'

Someone had, of course. But she didn't know that. Or maybe she did. Maybe she wasn't as ignorant as she appeared.

'Don't be dramatic,' I said, but I wasn't as brave as I was trying to sound. He frightened me when he was angry, Piotr – he always had done. Maybe he always will. It won't matter though, because I'm never going back.

'What is this rubbish, Mary? You're going to be a model? Since when? You're going to live in London? You can't. I won't let you.'

'I can. I'm eighteen. You don't have to be twenty-one to be counted as an adult any more. I can vote, I can leave home, and that's exactly what I'm doing. I'm a grown-up.'

He laughed again, and shook his head. 'OK,' he said. 'You're a grown-up. You know everything. Fine. You go.' He held his hands up, and I took my wrist back and rubbed it. 'But you're never coming back,' he said quietly. 'You leave now, that's it. You are gone. For ever.'

I nodded. 'I know.' I almost started crying then, and I don't know why, because even now it wasn't as if I was sad or anything. It must have been the shock of finally having done what I had been planning for so long, I suppose.

She appeared in the hallway then, Anne, her face all wet, and she rushed up to me and took the hand that Piotr had just dropped. 'Mary,' she said, 'please ... I don't understand.'

I patted her on the shoulder. Of course she didn't

understand. How could she? Her world was this house, this street, this town. It was small, and safe, and she would never leave it. But it wasn't my world. It never had been, and now it never would be.

'It's what I have to do, Mum,' I said, and she whimpered. 'It's going to be fine. I'll write to you.' I leaned over and kissed her on the cheek, and she suddenly held her arms out and wrapped them tightly around me, kissing my hair. She didn't say anything to try and stop me. So she can't have been that upset.

'You are beautiful and clever and kind, Mary,' she said, and then she lowered her voice and whispered into my ear, 'You are better than this.'

I suppose she was trying to make me feel bad, feel guilty for leaving like this, but it wasn't going to work. She let go of me eventually, and then it all happened really quickly. There was a knock at the door and the taxi was there, and Suzanne came out with me and Trevor carried my suitcase, and Jeanette had a sour look on her face and said she supposed she was going to have to find someone else to work on Saturdays now, but I had already thought of that and told her Suzanne would be taking over the shifts and that I had already started to show her how the till worked, so as to save her trouble. She was surprised and a bit put out but also relieved that she wasn't going to have to place a card in the window, and Trevor looked very pleased about it too. Piotr wouldn't come outside, but I saw him looking out from the window in the front room as I got into the back of the car, and I ignored him. I wouldn't give him the satisfaction of waving goodbye. I took one last look at the house where I had spent the first part of my life: Anne was crying still in the doorway, holding her cardigan around herself, and she looked so small, but then the driver started the car and said, 'The station, right?' and I nodded and he began to drive away. And then before long it wasn't just Anne who looked small but all of them; the house and then the street shrank and disappeared, and I laughed, I couldn't help it. I sat in the back of the cab with my suitcase and my good coat and my handbag, and I laughed and laughed until I cried.

I went straight to Velvet in Great Portland Street when I got to London. I'd booked a room at a bed and breakfast off the Caledonian Road, but I didn't really know where it was, and I wanted to make sure I got to the agency before it closed, as I'd told Coco I'd be there today. She hadn't seemed that bothered. 'Come whenever, darling, there's always someone here – we're just going to be thrilled to see you,' she had said. But I still felt a bit nervous that I'd get there too late and would have to wait until tomorrow, and I wanted to get started right away.

I got a bus there from the station, not a taxi, it didn't take me too long to work out which one to get, and it wasn't too far, just three or four stops along the Euston Road. The bus driver was quite rude when I showed him the address and asked him if he could get me close to it though. 'We're not a bloody taxi service, love,' he said, which I thought was unnecessary, but then he did call out for me when it was my stop and wait for me to lug my case off, so it was all right in the end.

I feel a bit silly admitting this, but this is meant to be a record of everything, and an honest one, so I may as well – I felt quite nervous suddenly, when I was walking down Great Portland Street towards the agency's offices, counting the numbers on buildings as I went. London was huge and busy and everyone looked at the pavement as they walked; the place felt slippery and impossible to get a hold of. I had been here before, obviously, but never by myself. I had never been anywhere by myself, not really. I was going to have to get used to it.

The office was smaller, and less exciting-looking than I had imagined it. It was right at the top of the building, up five long flights of steps, and no one was at the reception desk when I got there. Eventually a girl came out after I'd rung the bell a few times, and she smiled at me sort of vaguely and asked if I was here for the casting.

'No,' I said. 'Well, I don't think so.'

She gave me an odd look. 'For the shampoo ad?'

'Oh. No. I'm here to see Coco Delaney. I have an appointment.' I had the letter ready to show her but she didn't look at it. I could smell Coco's cigarette smoke hanging in the air.

'She's not here.'

'Oh,' I said again, and then stopped. I didn't know what to say or do next. I had just assumed that Coco would be there, like she had said. The girl was chewing the end of a pen and staring at me blankly. She was obviously waiting for me to leave or something, and I almost did, almost just turned around with my suitcase and letter, but then I thought, No, that's what Mary would have done. Sadie wouldn't just wander off with her tail between her legs. How did I want this girl to remember me, in years to come, when they asked?

So I gave her my best smile – I'd been practising it – and nodded. 'That's fine. I can wait.'

The girl's face turned hard and a bit crisp and she put the pen down. 'I don't know when she'll be back. She could be hours. She might not be back today at all.'

I kept my nerve. 'Oh well.' I sat on the bench opposite her desk. 'I imagine she'll turn up at some point. Like I said, she's expecting me.'

I reached for the magazine that was in the side pocket of my suitcase, planning to sit and study it, looking casual, while she glared at me, but I'd only just started to get it out when the door of the office in the corner opened – and that was when things *really* changed for ever.

My first sight of him. It is important to record this. He took my breath away. I know it sounds like a teenage cliché and I know you'll think, whoever you are, that I have no idea about love or men or sex, but it's just a fact. As soon as I looked up and saw him standing there I started to fumble with the magazine and cough, as though my lungs had filled up with a thick smog. He smiled, a bit knowingly, as though he was aware of the effect he was having on me, which he probably was: he probably had girls choke and go red every day when he walked into the room.

He was tall, with dark hair starting to recede a little from his forehead – just a little, but the rest of it was thick and dark brown and almost wavy. His eyes were dark and his eyebrows were even darker – they were very thick, and very straight, and they nearly met in the middle, but not quite. He looked amused when he saw me, as well he might have, but I would learn before long that that was his usual expression. He wore a black polo-neck sweater and tweedy trousers with big turn-ups and brogues, and he strode across to where I had just managed to shove the magazine back in its pocket and stand up, pulling my coat down as I did so and then regretting it straight away because it made me look like a child, and that was the last thing I wanted. But he didn't seem to notice, and he reached out a long arm towards me – everything about him was long, and sort of elastic-looking – and he said, 'Archie Farrow. You must be Sadie. Coco's told me all about you.'

The girl at the desk looked daggers at me as he ushered me into his office, one big hand on the small of my back, and I gave her my sweetest smile and tried not to look as though I was saying *I told you so*, because you should be gracious when you win a point, shouldn't you? And then it was just me and him in his small, slightly musty-smelling office, and the feeling of not being able to breathe came back again.

Oh, I am taking so long to write all this down but it all has to be here, it all has to be right. I feel that, if I can capture it then I can hold it between the pages of this book, like a butterfly pinned to a piece of card or a pressed flower. Like that, it will never die. A memory cannot die.

He asked me all sorts of questions, about school and my parents and things – small talk – I can't really remember what now, because I was so overwhelmed by what had happened to me, by the whole day, by the party and leaving home and getting to London and now him. It was all too much, and suddenly I felt a bit weak and he jumped up and came round to me with a glass of water from the jug on his desk.

'Are you all right? You've gone very pale,' he said, and I wished that he would take his hand off my shoulder because it was making it worse.

'Sorry, I'm just a bit tired.'

'I bet you haven't eaten all day,' he said, his voice stern like a teacher's, and then he laughed. 'I know you all want to stay thin and I don't want you getting fat either, but you have to eat as well. Models are no good to me if they're keeling over in the middle of photo-shoots all the time.'

And despite my wooziness I felt a flash of excitement. He planned for me to be one of his models then, to do photo-shoots for him. It wasn't all a mirage.'

'Come on, it's six thirty already. Let's go and get you something to eat. We can carry on talking there.'

The restaurant he took me to was a few doors down from Velvet, underground, a little place with small wooden tables all jammed up close to one another and candles in wine bottles. The tablecloths were red and white checked and the waiter winked at me when he handed me the menu.

'You like Italian, I assume?' Archie said, not bothering to look at his, so I just nodded and put mine down on the table as well, even though I was desperate to look at all the things on it.

'Oh yes,' I said, 'you order for us both. I like every-thing,' and his eyebrows lifted an inch in what I hoped was an approving way.

And then he ordered octopus, though I didn't realise that until it came, because he asked for it in Italian, and red wine to go with it. When it came I knew it was going to be awful. I could hardly look at it, with its suckers, all purple and pink and with black bits, and I was glad the restaurant was dark so it wasn't staring at me as I swallowed as much of it as I could.

We talked about all sorts of things. It was such a relief to have a proper conversation with someone who *knows* about things, all sorts of things. He's had a terribly interesting life; he's worked all over the world and done so many things. He knows everyone in London, it seems; at least three times we had to stop talking because some friend of his came over to the table, and each time he introduced me as 'his newest discovery' – well, that is until the last person came to the table, a man in a business suit, and Archie was introducing me and then a voice came out from behind the man, saying, '*Whose* newest discovery, Archie Farrow?' And it was Coco, looking so so glamorous as usual, and she wagged her finger at Archie as if he was a naughty boy. The businessman grinned and looked at me and said, 'Good luck with these two, they're notorious,' and I smiled and said, 'Just the way I like it,' and they all laughed.

When Coco had sat down and poured some wine and refused to order anything, she reached over and took my hand. 'I'm so glad you're here, Sadie,' she said. 'We're going to have so much fun.'

I smiled, trying to look thrilled and as though it was all normal both at the same time, as though I was always in places like this with people like her and Archie, but the truth was that I was feeling a bit odd again now and my mouth was filling up with saliva.

'I'm going to send you to the hairdresser's tomorrow,' Coco was saying. 'Don't panic, we won't cut it all off, but it needs to look a bit more . . . London,' and I nodded, too nervous to open my mouth. 'We'll get Kato to do some photos, don't you think, Arch? And then we can start sending you out to go and wow people. Oh, I'm so excited – they're going to love you, everyone's going to love you!'

I smiled, but I could only smile for a second because then I knew for absolutely certain that I was going to be sick, and I stood up too quickly and everything went spinny and I grabbed onto the back of the chair which fell onto the floor with a clatter, and there wasn't time to say sorry or sort it out, I just ran to the door which I hoped led to the Ladies but there were three doors beyond that and I chose the wrong one, and ended up opening the door to the kitchen and being sick right there on the floor.

I know one day I'll laugh about it, and it'll be a funny story about my first day in London and I won't care a jot, but I don't mind admitting that right now I care a great deal and am still, a week later, very embarrassed about the whole thing and *I am never eating octopus again*.

A memory ambushed me then, as I read those words, of being on holiday with my parents when I was small, somewhere hot and sunny. Cyprus? Majorca? One of those week-long villa holidays that we would take sometimes back then. My mother would sit on the beach wearing an enormous hat and basting herself with baby oil until she turned the colour of a polished cocktail cabinet, gleaming and burnished, and my father would sit on one of those collapsible chairs, uncomfortable and bored, trying to read some enormous tome or mark up a set of proofs and getting them covered in sand. He wore a suit on the beach, I remembered, his two concessions to his location being an open-necked shirt, and a pair of brown woven sandals, worn with socks. I was too young to be ashamed of him on those holidays, thankfully, and later, once she had gone, we never went on those kinds of trips. Our breaks were city ones and far more improving in tone.

I had forgotten all about those holidays. My father would while away the time on the beach when he had been forced, by wind or my mother, to put his reading down, by eating ice creams, a particular sort of dark chocolate ice cream, one after the other, buying them from one of the boys with coolboxes who prowled the coves. My mother had the occasional lemon sorbet, served enticingly in a whole, hollowed-out lemon. I would have a Neopolitan, eating it in strict colour order (boring vanilla first, then chocolate, then strawberry), and he would eat . . . *Trufficonos*, that was it. He'd eat them until his beard was covered in speckles of dark chocolate, and then he'd wipe it off with a handkerchief and my mother would shudder as she thought hankies were unhygienic. She used to throw them away rather than wash them: it made him furious.

The memory ambushed me with its vivid colours and smells. Lemon and sea and salt and suncream and sticky fingers. How could I not have remembered it until now?

We would go to a little taverna in the evenings, where the waiters fussed over me and tucked huge white napkins into the collar of my dress and brought me special little titbits. I loved the salty cheese – it must have been halloumi, I realised now. It squeaked between my teeth.

'You can't order octopus, I can't have it on the table.'

'Why? You don't have to eat it.'

'I won't eat it. I won't touch it and I won't have it near me.'

'Don't be so unreasonable. I love octopus. It's one of my favourite things to eat on holiday and it's best fresh.'

'It's disgusting. I'll leave if you order it, I will.'

'Fine, leave. We'll stay here and eat, you go home and sulk. But I'm ordering the octopus.'

The conversation came back to me, fully formed; they might have been having the row right next to me. She hadn't left, but she had sat and glared at the offending octopus, making a sound of disgust every time my father put a forkful into his mouth, and only picking at her prawns. 'Prawns are just as bad,' he said mildly, and she jutted out her chin. 'Just don't talk to me about it,' she said, under her breath. 'Just stop talking and eat your revolting octopus.'

I hadn't understood why it offended her so much at the time, and I'd forgotten that the argument and, indeed, the holiday itself, had ever taken place. Now, of course, I understood. And now I wondered what other memories lay long buried in me. What else would reading the diary bring to the surface of my mind?

Coco was so kind to me that first night. She took me back to her house, off the Portobello Road, saying she couldn't have me going to some awful bed and breakfast by myself, and she'd got us a taxi and paid for it and told me that it didn't matter, that none of it mattered and that it would all seem fine in the morning after I'd had a good night's sleep and to stop crying.

Well, it hadn't seemed fine in the morning, but it had seemed better, when I woke up in her little spare room underneath a thick pile of quilts and looked around and realised I was in the most glamorous room I'd ever seen. She obviously used it as a dressing room, since there was a clothes rail in the corner, covered in beautiful things – silk dresses and capes and embroidered scarves – and there were piles and piles of shoe- and hat-boxes all stacked up, and bookshelves all along one wall full of not just books but magazines and records and necklaces on stands and ornaments and all kinds of things.

I found a bathroom next door where I washed my face and put my make-up on. I didn't dare use the bath, but I did open one of the glass bottles of bath oil next to it, just to have a sniff, and it smelled of everything decadent and exotic in the world.

She gave me breakfast, once she had found the bread, which was in the cupboard with the plates – I don't think she uses the kitchen much, she hardly eats anything and she's always out anyhow – and it was a bit stale but I didn't care, and she made me thick dark coffee that was strong and made me wince it was so bitter, and she smoked a cigarette while I ate my toast, and then she took me to the office with her. That day was amazing. No one said anything about the night before – though the girl on the desk, whose name I found out was Tanya, did smirk when I walked in, so she probably knew, but I ignored her, because she's just the receptionist and what does she know? Coco took me to the hairdresser's and they cut quite a lot off; they feathered it and set it in rollers and then blow-dried it so it puffed out in big curls away from my face, and Coco took my face in her hands and said, 'Perfect. Just perfect. You're going to be a star, Sadie, just like I told you,' and the hairdresser nodded and I tried to look mysterious.

Coco booked me into a different boarding house in Stockwell, one where she said the agency put lots of girls when they first came to Town. 'You won't be here for ever, darling. I know it's a bit bleak, but before long you'll be earning pots of money and living somewhere frightfully glam, but for now it's cheap and it's central and the landlady will keep an eye on you.' The landlady, Mrs Brindle, looks as though she certainly will keep an eye on me and not in the way I might want her to. She glares from her seat in the front room every time I come in or go out of the house, but I don't care, because I have my own room and all my things are there and most of all it's in London, and it's mine and it's not in Anne and Piotr's house in St Albans, and that's all I really care about for now. I won't describe it, it's small and boring and like Coco says, I won't be there for long.

I'd had my photos taken, and paid for them, which had been much dearer than I was expecting, but it's an investment, like Archie says, and the photographer and Archie, who came to pick me up at the end of the shoot (that's what you call it) both seemed really pleased with them, and with me. Archie said he'd take me out to celebrate. 'Don't worry, we won't go anywhere Italian,' he said, winking, and I blushed but he didn't seem to care so I pretended I didn't either and just laughed.

Instead we went to a bar near the photographer's studio. It was noisy and full of industry people, as Archie called them, many of them wanting to talk to him. He bought us Martinis and drank his quickly, and then turned around and said, 'It's been a long day, and this place is driving me crazy. Do you mind if we go somewhere else? I'm done in. Do stay if you'd rather, I can leave you with friends.' He looked so tired and so sorry to be a disappointment, which of course he wasn't – how could he be? He was the reason for it all.

'No, I don't mind at all, I'm tired as well,' I said, and he gave me a huge smile.

'You must be. It's harder work than it looks, having your picture taken, isn't it?'

I nodded. 'But I loved it. I felt . . . I felt as if I had come to life.'

'That's because you're a natural,' he said, and he took my hand and led me through the crowd of people, talking to me over his shoulder as we went. People moved out of our way and looked at him, obviously recognising him, and then at me, wondering who I was, who was this girl with Archie, but I didn't care about them. And all the way back to the boarding house, after he had seen me into a cab and kissed my hand like a medieval suitor, I floated.

# Chapter Fourteen

I had never been to St Albans before. The trains went from St Pancras, scores of them, it seemed, from looking at the time-table, so I didn't bother aiming for a particular one. I just made my way to the station on Friday morning, queued to buy a ticket then got on the first one I saw on the departures board.

I've always loved train journeys. They help you think clearly – it's something to do with the forward motion. And I love the fading away of London as it turns from city to suburbs to countryside, the tall tower blocks with their lines of washing and bikes on the balconies melting into squat semis with gardens with swings and then allotments, all in squares, full of lines of bean poles and sheds, and then fields and barns and cottages with proper driveways and even the odd tennis court.

Could I live in the countryside? I thought so sometimes, when I was driving through it mostly, dreaming of summer picnics and long walks ending at pubs and a small dog with an inquisitive face, or winters cosied up in front of log fires, autumns crunching through leaves, collecting blackberries from hedgerows to make jam ... the usual clichéd fantasies of a city girl who thinks she yearns for something else. As Mark always pointed out: 'You don't know how to make jam.'

'I could learn. How hard can it be?'

'You don't like long walks. You moan.'

'I do not!'

'Yes, you do. You think two miles is a long walk.'

'It is. In London.'

'You're scared of cows. You like being able to walk to the corner shop and buy chocolate at night because you didn't get any at the supermarket because you're on a diet but now you really, really want some. You hate being cold.'

He was right. All of these things were true. I'm sure I'd be rubbish at living in the country. But it's a nice fantasy to have bubbling away in the background.

I'd miss London though, I know I would. And Daddy, and Beth and the kids. Beth. She'd been trying to get hold of me. I had a voicemail from her that I hadn't replied to yet. *'Hi, Klar, it's me. Just checking in. Haven't heard from you for a few days. Sorry about the other day, I don't know what was wrong with me. I'm fine. Anyhow, call me. Love you, bye.'* I picked up my phone and texted her back. *Hey B, sorry for radio silence, work manic. Will call asap for catch up. xxxK.* It wasn't that I didn't want to see her. I just felt – focused. I didn't need the distraction.

I'd bought supplies, as usual, and I spread them out on the table in front of me. Hula Hoops; a big bottle of fizzy water; a bag of Maltesers. a smoked salmon and cream cheese sandwich from M&S. It was a weird assortment – children's food, not that I had ever had anything like it as a child, ready-made food that I never normally allowed myself and chocolate that I craved despite knowing that ten minutes after eating it I'd feel sick and jittery and regretful.

I slid a Hula Hoop onto the end of my tongue and let it dissolve there while I got the file that I had brought with me out of my bag. I'd put it in there the night before, ready, so I wouldn't have to find it in the morning and risk Mark noticing and asking what it was. I still hadn't told him. Nor had I told him what I was doing today. Well, I'd mentioned that I had no classes that day, which was true, but I didn't add that I was taking a day's holiday, nor did I explain where I was going. I was playing truant, and I had the food to go with the rebellion, I realised.

The house was as she had described it. A three-bedroom semi: an average house in an average street. Although the street probably wasn't that average if you were talking about the country as a whole. St Albans was a nice town, nicer than I had anticipated, especially in the older parts, like Laburnum Gardens. Sadie had been luckier than she had realised to grow up here.

I hovered outside for a while, wandering up and down the street, trying not to look suspicious and gathering up the courage to ring the bell. What would it have looked like forty odd years ago, when she left? Much the same, probably. Different models of car, fewer of them. No satellite dishes on the roofs. But otherwise, I couldn't imagine that a photo taken back then would have looked wildly different to one taken now.

I assumed that the area might have been an orchard once. At any rate, Laburnum Gardens was one of a cluster of streets named after plants or flowering trees. Acacia Street, Cherry Lane, Grove Road . . . The area was probably known locally by some collective term, but I wasn't sure what you'd call it. The Florals? The Orchard? The . . . *stop procrastinating, Klara. Get on with it.*

The house was nicely kept. A lavender bush in a large, squat pot sat in the centre of the paved front garden. A black and white chequerboard path led up to the navy-blue front door, which had little conical box trees either side of it. A heavy brass knocker sat solidly below the house number. 24. I lifted my hand to it, and knocked.

It took ages for someone to come, and I was about to turn

around and leave, part-cursing myself for assuming that anyone would be home on a Wednesday morning, part-relieved when I heard footsteps and a woman's voice saying, 'No, Wilf, don't open it. Wait for Mummy.'

Her face was open and friendly, she had blond hair pulled back into a ponytail and her natural reaction was to smile at the slightly nervous-looking stranger on her doorstep. Mine would have been to glower, and I tried to arrange my face so that it was a little more like hers, hoping that it didn't just make me look as though I were grimacing.

'Hello,' she said, and a small boy with sandy-coloured tufts of hair peered at me from between her legs.

'Hi.' I swallowed. I hadn't really thought this bit through. As the pause between my reply and any explanation as to what I was doing there lengthened, her expression turned to one of slight puzzlement. I didn't appear to be selling anything, or if I was I was doing a very bad job of it indeed. I hadn't shoved a leaflet or a Tupperware catalogue in her face, nor did I have a clipboard. As far as she could see, there was no reason at all for me to be standing in front of her. But she made no move to shut the door or try to get rid of me, simply waited.

'Sorry. I . . . this is going to sound strange.'

Her eyebrows lifted in her face. 'Go on.'

Once she had established that I wasn't some kind of con woman and I had managed to explain, sort of, what I was doing there, she asked me in. Her name was Casey Cartwright, and she and her husband had lived here for seven years.

'I don't know how much I'll be able to help,' she said, leading me through the hall, 'but I'm happy to try.'

'I'm sorry for not writing or anything, for just arriving here.'

She waved the kettle at me as we arrived in the kitchen. 'Tea?'

I nodded. 'Please. Thank you.'

'It's fine. As you can see, I'm here with this one.'

The little boy glanced shyly at me and then ran behind his mother's legs. 'It's not as if we have a frantic social schedule. Music and Movement at the church hall is about as exciting as it gets around here, isn't it?'

'How old are you, Wilf?'

A head appeared again for a second, and dark eyes flashed at me, then it disappeared.

She tutted. 'He'll get over it in a bit. He's two – three in a couple of months.'

They had bought the house from a single woman, Casey told me, when we were settled down in the living room with tea and chocolate Hob Nobs. It was light and airy, despite the dismal day, and the decor was modern but still comfortable. Mark would have liked it, I thought.

'She'd only been here a year or so – it was an awful thing. She had bought it with her fiancé, and they'd started doing it up, and then he'd left her, a week before they were due to get married. Just came home one day, said he couldn't go through with it, took his car and went. To Australia, I think.'

I tried not to smile. Mark would have had something to say about that. He was in my thoughts a lot. I pushed him gently aside so I could concentrate on what Casey was saying.

'I was a bit worried about buying the house when I found that out,' she continued, and smiled shyly. 'Stupid, isn't it? But I've always believed that houses retain something of their owners. Some – I don't know . . . atmosphere, energy, maybe? I'm sure it's what people are picking up on when they say they've seen a ghost, or felt something. A residual energy . . . Oh God, you must think I'm batty.' She blushed. It suited her.

'No. I know what you mean. I agree. Houses have personalities.'

'Yes! Exactly. And I was worried that this one was going to be tainted somehow, because of what had happened to her. But it isn't. You can feel it. This is a happy house.'

It hadn't been for Sadie, I thought.

'Well. If they take on energy, I guess you brought good energy with you.'

'Maybe. Anyhow, I wavered about buying it but it felt right, despite that, and Ant – my husband, he works in London – said I was being ridiculous. I'm so glad I gave in.'

I got the impression that despite Casey's sunny demeanour, giving in wasn't something she did that often.

'So she was here for a year. And you've been here for seven years. You don't happen to know . . .'

'Who she bought it from?' Casey's brow furrowed as she thought. 'She said it was from a woman who'd been here for years. They'd hardly done anything to the place, which was why she and her fiancé liked it so much. It was going to be a project for them. Hang on, let me get the file.'

'Oh – thank you.'

She left the room, and I found myself alone with Wilf. We stared at one another for a moment, before I thought I'd better say something friendly to him. 'What have you got there, Wilf?' He was holding a plastic sailing ship in one podgy hand.

'Pirates,' he muttered scornfully. Of course.

'Are they singing "yo ho ho and a bottle of rum"?' He looked up at me through long eyelashes, and did not answer, but he did hold the ship out to me and pointed at its plastic sail.

'Pirates,' he said again, more cheerfully this time. I took this as an encouraging sign and knelt on the floor next to him.

'Look, we could make the sea for them to sail on.' I took a cushion from the sofa and put it on the floor, then reached for the ship. Wilf held on tight to it. 'Look, here,' I tried to guide his hand and the ship to the cushion, making a rocking motion with my other hand. He stared at me, and began to yell.

'Oh God. No, it's OK, I wasn't trying to take it. There, there.' I patted his shoulder and he yelled even louder. Of course, Casey appeared in the doorway before he had had a chance to calm down. Not that that looked likely to happen any time soon, for his face had gone red and fat tears were threatening to spill from his eyes.

'Don't worry about it,' Casey said quickly, before I had a chance to apologise or explain. 'He's really unsettled at the moment. The Terrible Twos seem to be taking their time to disappear, don't they, poppet?' She scooped him up onto her lap as she sat back down on the sofa and he stared at me with what looked like a triumphant expression.

'I'm no good with children,' I said, getting back up off my knees.

'I'm sure you're fine. Don't have any of your own, then?'

'Not yet.'

She understood immediately – or so she thought. 'It's hard, isn't it? Our mothers had us when they were so much younger, and so all of their generation expects us to be popping babies out when we're twenty-five, but there's so much else we have to do now. All they had to do was find a man, get married. Maybe work in a nice office job for a couple of years. Then stay at home and keep house.' She shrugged. 'Though I suppose that's what I'm doing now, so maybe things haven't changed as much as I thought.' For a moment she looked distant and distracted.

'What did you do before you had him?' I couldn't stop staring at the file in her lap, but I couldn't very well ask for it.

'Oh, I'm a lawyer,' she said with a brief smile, visibly pulling herself back into the room. 'Corporation law, not very exciting, but I quite enjoyed it. I'll go back at some point, I expect, though we're trying for number two, so by the time I get around to it I'll probably have been taken over by a hundred young eager beavers champing at the bit and have to retrain. We'll see. Sorry, you don't want to know about all this.' She opened the file. For a moment we both felt awkward, I think, two women who had shared more than they had quite intended to and who were both wondering whether they would regret doing so.

'OK, here it is. I knew there was something in here.' She passed me a few sheets of paper. They were estate agents' particulars from the sale of the house, three sets of them.

'The first ones are from when we bought from her. So that would have been 2005.' The front of the house was a lot less smart in the photos than it was now. There was a ragged cream-coloured border of sorts around the front door, and instead of the white picket fence there was a tumbledown wall and a wrought-iron gate that was hanging off its hinges.

'We've done quite a bit, as you can see.'

I turned the page over. The photos of the house were almost unrecognisable. The front room was almost the same, though a much blander, shabbier version of its current self. But what was now the open-plan kitchen diner at the back was entirely different; previously, I could see, it had been two separate, far darker rooms.

'We knocked it all through and extended,' Casey said, pointing to the photo. 'Took us twice as long and cost twice as much as they said it would, like always, but I'm so glad we did it before he came along.' She hugged Wilf. 'Building works and small children really don't mix.'

'What about upstairs?' I asked, feeling as though I were pushing my luck.

She shrugged. 'I can show you, if you like. We didn't move

any rooms around on the first floor, but we did do a loft conversion. So now we're up there with an en suite and the three bedrooms are still there. One's a bit smaller than it was, because of having to add a staircase. Come on.'

'Which room would have been your mother's, do you know?' Casey asked as she unlatched the stair-gate at the top.

'I'm not sure,' I started to say, but then stopped short. I knew exactly which room had been hers; it would have been the one on whose threshold I was standing. It was Wilf's room now. Blue walls with clouds painted on them, those glow-in-the-dark stars on the ceiling. A big toy box in the corner, a lampshade shaped like a hot air balloon . . . a child's ideal room.

But it wasn't any of those things that I was looking at. It was the mirror above the original fireplace. I stepped inside the room and walked towards it.

'Oh,' I whispered. 'It was this room.'

I looked at my reflection in the mirror: white-painted, with roses and a vine climbing around the frame, and a floral pattern cut into the glass. It was screwed to the wall and looked as though it had been there for a very long time.

'It's too girly for a boy's room really, isn't it? But it was there when we bought the house, and it seemed like an awful shame to move it. I rather love it.'

I turned to Casey.

'She wrote about it,' I said to her. I couldn't help myself, I had to tell someone, and she was kind and she was there. 'In her diary. She wrote about this mirror. She wrote about leaving it here when she left home.'

'Wow. It must be like looking into the past.'

I looked back at the glass. That was exactly what it was like. For a moment, I imagined my face overlaid on hers. I saw her standing here, on this very spot, nervous and excited and full of life, on the day she left, looking into this mirror as though she would be able to see her future in it. Bidding farewell to her past.'

'I'd give it to you, if I could,' Casey said softly from behind me, and I turned back to her, feeling rude. 'It feels as though it should be yours.'

'Oh God, you're so kind. No, it's part of the house, isn't it? It's just . . . strange, seeing it. Makes it all feel a lot more real. Do you mind if I take a photo though?'

The particulars from when the previous owner, Martha Gall, had bought the house, were different again in terms of decor, but as Casey said, Martha and her runaway fiancé seemed to have done little or no structural work to 24 Laburnum Gardens during the time they had owned it. The layout was the same – a front room, a dining room and kitchen at the back, three bedrooms and a bathroom upstairs.

'Strange, looking at the pictures all together like this, isn't it?' Casey leaned over my shoulder as I stared at them spread out on the kitchen table. 'It's a bit like watching someone grow up.'

It was true. Like a young girl photographed in her school uniform, then her first grown-up party dress, then at her wedding, the house seemed to have grown into itself over the years, fulfilling its promise as different owners came and went, adding and changing and modifying as they did so.

Martha and the unnamed partner may not have got around to knocking any walls down, but the house they had bought had still looked very different to the one they had passed on to Casey and her husband. Then, the walls were covered in beige wallpaper downstairs and a faded floral one in two of the bedrooms, the carpets were swirls of brown and orange, and there was a little nylon skirt around the bathroom basin.

'They hadn't done the bathroom or kitchen – we did that. Well, the kitchen had to go when we did the extension, obviously, and we pulled the bathroom out as well. It was all Artex ceilings and soggy carpet – look, you can see.' She pointed to the relevant photo.

But my eyes had strayed from the pictures to the names written on the top of the particulars.

'Casey – is this who Martha bought the house from, then?'

'Yes, that's right. She said she'd written it down for us, when she gave us all of the paperwork – I'm not sure why. She was a real filer, Martha, kept all sorts of things.'

I looked up at her. 'What, to do with the house?'

'Mm, but nothing to do with the other owners, I'm afraid, nothing you'd be interested in. I thought when we pulled the walls down to replaster them that we might find something interesting – you know, like excavating the past. Letters or secret things hidden away or . . . oh, I don't know.' She looked embarrassed.

'But nothing?'

'No. Just some bits of old newspaper from the Seventies, nothing relevant.'

I was a bit disappointed, but it had been a long shot. And anyhow, I could hardly be too downcast, not when I looked at the names written in neat pencil handwriting above the estate agent's logo.

Casey pointed to it as I stared. 'They only live around the corner, in one of the newish flats overlooking the park. He's a bit disabled, so I think they wanted something without stairs. Suzanne and Trevor Barton.'

I hurried around to the block of flats, clutching the paperwork that Casey Cartwright had given me. 'Then she'll know I sent you. It's fine, take it.' She had waved her hands at me. 'Pop it in through the door or in the post some time. You know the address.' And I had left her, smiling on the doorstep, her small son still peering suspiciously at me from his position on her shoulder.

It was as she had described, a newish block of flats over-looking the park at the end of the street. Pale yellow brick with redbrick edging, five storeys, balconies that jutted out giving residents a view of dog-walkers and children playing. The balconies were a bit pretentious, I thought. It wasn't as though the block was a swish one by the river or anything, but they must have allowed the developers to extend the floorspace and charge a premium. 'All mod cons in the heart of St Alban's old town,' or something, they'd say, tempting buyers into thinking they'd got the best of both worlds.

There was a small car park next to the block and a Sainsbury's Local built into the bottom floor of it on the street side. 'Local shops nearby,' that would allow them to say, despite the fact that the only other shop I could see on the road was one selling carpets.

I waited a long time for someone to answer the door at this address as well, my fingers cold in my jacket pocket as I stood in the entrance hallway to the apartment block.

'They're on the ground floor, the side by the park,' Casey had told me. 'I think it's number 1B, but anyway, if you go in via the park it's that one.'

The hallway was lit with those striplights that give me a headache as soon as I look at them, and there were pastel watercolours of water lilies on the walls. The carpet was syn-thetic and static, and I stood on the doormat that sat in front of the door of 1B instead. *Home Sweet Home* it proclaimed in black block capitals. What a depressing place to move to after living in a nice little house like the one in Laburnum Gardens.

I had heard a man's voice inside the flat after I had rung the bell, so I knew someone was home. So I waited. Eventually, a woman of around sixty opened the door, chain still on, and said warily, 'Yes?'

My heart thudded with excitement and I could feel my hands begin to tremble. 'Are you . . . I'm sorry to disturb you like this, but are you Mrs Barton, Suzanne Barton?'

She inclined her head a little. 'Who are you?'

I reached my right hand out, hoping that the gesture would encourage her to take the chain off the door, but she made no move to do so.

'My name's Klara Mortimer. You don't—'

'We don't buy anything at the door. See?' She reached her hand around and jabbed a finger at the small sticker next to the bell. *NO junk mail, NO salesmen, NO charity collections* it said in emphatic red letters.

'I'm not—'

'And we don't need religion either.'

Her lips were pursed and the fine lines that threaded out from their edges were tightly knit. I could smell the cigarette smoke on her clothes, and seeping out from inside the house. She was not a tall woman, and she looked old for her years. She hadn't aged well.

Is this what Sadie would have looked like, if she had stayed, if she had lived? Bitter-faced, hair set in brassy blonde curls, full of disappointment and resentment, living in a soulless flat with a disabled husband. I stared at Suzanne and felt sure of one thing – this would not be what my mother would have wanted for her life. That was certain.

'I'm not anything like that. My name's Klara . . .'

'You said that already.'

I snapped at her then, in frustration. 'I'm Sadie's daughter. Or Mary's. Mary Tomaszewski.'

I'm not sure what I had been expecting. Not a warm welcome, exactly, not since she had half-opened the door with that look on her face, a look that said *go away, I'm not interested, I don't want the outside world to enter, it's done me enough harm already*. Or maybe that was giving her too much credit. Maybe she was just a miserable cow and always had been. But that can't have been the case. Sadie wouldn't have been friends with her, wouldn't have confided in her and trusted her as she clearly had. Once she had been a lively, sparky girl, excited by the prospect of her best friend leaving town and becoming a model, running away to the big city. Once she had wanted to be a writer, a journalist, working on fashion magazines and interviewing celebrities. And then she had married the son of a newsagent owner and never left town, had bought her best friend's parents' house where she had lived for more than thirty years, and even when she left there she hadn't made it further than a flat around the corner, where she would presumably stay until she was carried out.

'What happened to you, Suzanne?' I whispered to the door that had slammed shut in my face.

'Please, Mrs Barton', I called out. 'I'm sorry, I know it must be a shock, but I really need to talk to you. Or Trevor – maybe I could talk to Trevor?'

'Go away!' she cried. 'I don't want anything to do with that woman. Nothing, do you hear me? Not her, not her daughter, not anyone to do with her.'

There was silence after that, and I gave up in the end. What happened, Suzanne? What happened?

# Chapter Fifteen

It shook me up, the trip to St Albans. Absurd of me, to think that I could go rooting around in my mother's past like that without it leaving a mark on me.

The whole thing was absurd, I thought, as I got onto the train home. It was busier than the one on the way up here, Friday early evening and people going into London for the night. A gang of teenagers were taking up most of the aisle by the first seat I found. I shifted uncomfortably as they chatted and chucked sweet wrappers at one another, trying not to look disapproving, trying to be the sort of person who was completely unfazed by them. What would Sadie have done? Joined in, probably. Flashed them one of her wide smiles and charmed them into silence; but I had inherited none of my mother's easy charm.

I moved, in the end, sliding out of my seat and muttering, 'Excuse me,' as I tried not to knock them with my bag, hating myself for my awkwardness and my inhibitions. They didn't even look at me, and that was even worse than if they had jeered at me. I could command attention in my tutorials all right, I had no problem standing up in front of a group of students years younger than myself and connecting with them, laughing and joking when appropriate, reprimanding when necessary. But outside my work, it was different. These kids felt different. Dangerous.

Everything felt dangerous that day, however. It was as if I was a spy on some secret mission, and in a way I was. I was keeping secrets – from my best friend, from my father, from my husband – the three most important people in my life, the ones who knew me intimately. I had turned my back on them, and they didn't even know it.

I still cannot explain why, not really, not even now; it was as if something had overtaken me completely. It had become more important than everything else, this voracious hunger to find out who N.R. was and what had happened to my mother. There had been no mention of anyone with those initials in her diaries so far. I had been watching out for them, reading the entries with a pencil in my hand, ready to note down any names that might be relevant. I had been trying to dredge up more memories, thinking whether Sadie had ever mentioned a friend or acquaintance called Naomi Robert or Norman Reynolds or anything – but there was no one. No one I could remember, at least. I had been searching through magazines and newspapers in the archives at work, neglecting my marking, reading *Vogue* and *The Times* from the Seventies, poring over names, but nothing and no one seemed to fit.

Daddy was away still, so the questions that I had fizzing around my head after coming back from St Albans would have to fizz there for a while longer. It was no bad thing anyhow, since I could hardly just come out and ask him what he knew, could I? Where had my grandparents gone after they left 24 Laburnum Gardens, had he ever met them, and what had happened between Suzanne and Sadie to cause such a reaction in my mother's old friend? No, I could never ask him all that, outright. I'd have to come up with some kind of a plan.

I had time to think about it, since he wouldn't be back for a couple of days. My father was always best approached in an upfront way. He had always been happy to answer my questions when I was growing up, about anything that I could think of. What had he been like when he was a little boy? (Quiet, with big ears.) What did the tooth fairy *do* with all the teeth she collected? (Build castles that the angels lived in.) What is dark matter? (A mysterious type of energy that makes up the majority of the universe.) Why did Sally at number 23 always pat me on the head and look so sad? (Because you're so pretty it makes her sad that her daughters look like chimpanzees.)

All right, so the answers weren't always 100 per cent true. I realised when I was older that Sally's daughters were perfectly normal-looking, as was I, and that the reason she had always looked at me with such sympathy was because of my lack of a mother. However, my father never usually fudged or evaded, or made me feel as though I should not be asking. Apart from about Sadie, of course. So it seemed that the trick would be to make it appear as though I was asking a straight question, while really asking something else entirely.

A memory ambushed me then – suddenly, without warning – the one and only time I could remember my father losing his temper. And it had been because I was asking questions about my mother.

His reaction had put me off doing so for a long time after that. I had been bothering him for ages, question after question in the way that only children can do, dogged, unending. 'But why did she go away, Daddy? And where is she now? Why can't she come back and watch me do ballet? Beth's mummy is *always* there . . .' on and on until suddenly he turned and threw down the pile of proofs that he had been checking and I watched as they scattered and floated all over the floor as he yelled: '*Klara! Stop! Stop this godforsaken questioning I can't bear it any longer!*'

His face was red and I cowered.

He slammed his hand against the wall in frustration. 'She is gone. She isn't coming back. Ever. Understand? *Ever!*' He took my shoulders and his face was close to mine and I had been shocked before then, at the sheer volume of his voice, but then I was afraid, and I burst into tears and he let go suddenly, and his hands hung in mid-air as though he didn't know what to do with them. 'Oh God. Klara. I'm sorry.' He knelt and tried to pull me close to him but I jerked away and ran upstairs, and as I went I heard him begin to cry. And that frightened me more than anything.

It rolled round and round in my head, all weekend, that memory, in the same way that a bad dream stays with you sometimes long after you have woken up. On the Monday morning, I was making coffee and searching through the cupboards for something for us all to eat for breakfast. There wasn't much there, but in the end I found some cereal bars. It was better than nothing. The ugly images that would not stop coming. *My father shouting, how loud his voice had sounded how it had echoed all around the room*. I'd have to do a proper shop, I thought. We couldn't send Elfie off to school on cereal bars every day; she might as well be living with Maisie and Barney again. *The violence of his hand slamming against the wall*. Eggs, we needed eggs, and I should get bread for the freezer. I'd just have to avoid slipping back into the habit of having toast as soon as I got home, which was why I tried not to keep any bread in the house. I could also prepare a big jar of home-made granola so she could have that with fruit and yoghurt. *The fear I had felt as he grabbed my shoulders, the look of rage and pain and frustration in his face, which was all red and twisted.* Porridge, maybe? Would she eat porridge? I'd have to ask her. *Hiding under my covers upstairs, crying in big gulps, burrowed down under the sheets, wanting my mother, only my mother, knowing she was not going to come.* I blinked back tears. And then as though on cue, Elfie and Mark appeared in quick succession, both dressed and ready for the day and wearing the same expectant expression, distracting me. It made me laugh.

'What?' Mark waggled his eyebrows at me. 'Here, post.' He handed me the pile of letters. Somehow the junk mail, the pizza menus and charity appeals and Betterware catalogues always made it into my pile to be chucked away. And the bills, but that was fine. I liked to open them because Mark never added them to the spreadsheet when he did it. Nothing exciting today. Nothing from the person I was agitating to hear from.

'You two,' I said. 'I know what you're going to ask: what's for breakfast? And the answer is sod all. Elfie, take one of these to school and this,' I handed her a fiver, 'and get some fruit on the way as well. I'll do an Ocado order later.'

'It's OK, I've got money.'

'Take it.' I waved it at her. Did I want to appear generous, garner favour, keep her on side in case I needed her? She didn't seem bothered either way. Just shrugged, and took it.

'Thanks.' None of the Olivers cared about money. They'd never had to.

'I'll take you for a bacon and egg baguette on the way,' Mark said, wincing as he poured scalding coffee down his throat. He picked up his keys.

'Mark!'

'What?'

'Bacon and egg baguettes – come *on*.'

His shoulders shrugged his coat on and at me at the same

time. 'Nothing wrong with it once in a while. Who's the doctor around here, anyhow?'

'Pfffft. Elfie, make sure you buy some fruit.'

'Yes, Mum.' She rolled her eyes at me, and I blushed. Had I overstepped the mark? But she smiled shyly and waved goodbye. 'I'll see you later.'

'Yes. What time?'

'What time what?' She looked confused.

'What time will you be back? I won't get home till about six. I don't want you here for hours by yourself. You could always come to my work.'

'I won't make a mess.' She blinked at me, and I realised I'd got it wrong again.

'Oh no, that's not what I meant. I know you won't. I mean, it doesn't matter if you do. But that's ... Look, I just don't want you to be lonely.' I was embarrassed now, and so was she, and we stared at each other, neither of us knowing quite what to do or say next. She wasn't used to having anyone care what time she got home. Maisie and Barney wouldn't notice if she skipped school entirely or if she boarded, most of the time. 'And you know – dinner,' I blustered, trying to cover over our awkwardness with words.

Elfie smiled. 'I'll be back around four. I'll be fine, honestly.' She paused. 'Thank you.'

I don't know why I had assumed that Coco Delaney, if she was going to reply at all, would do so via the post. Something to do with a feeling that she was 'from the past', I guess. How patronising I had been, I realised, when I read the email from her later that morning, sent from her gmail account and with the tag *sent from my iPhone* at the bottom.

*Dear Klara*, it said. *Many thanks for your letter, which I was surprised and interested to receive.*

'Flattered', I hoped that meant.

*It's been a long time since anyone's sought my advice on the world of modelling, and I'm not sure how much help I can be to you, but I do have some contacts and knowledge in the area still.*

(It seemed that my ploy might have worked.)

*Elfie is certainly a beautiful girl, and I think she has potential. Do bring her to see me. Sincerely yours, Coco Delaney.*

She gave her address, somewhere in West London – Notting Hill it looked like. And then there was a p.s. *Am intrigued to hear how you came to seek me out, and assume there is a particular reason, obvious or otherwise.*

Of course I was going to have to explain myself – I'd known that from the start. I'd sort of put the issue to one side though, thinking that there was no point in deciding whether to tell the truth or make up some elaborate yet hopefully plausible tale until she actually replied. If she did ever reply.

And now she had. And not just that, she sounded like the sort of woman who would want to know specifics. She sounded sharp and savvy, not someone who would be fobbed off with some story about having read of her in a magazine story. She'd want to know which one, and when, and in what context, and though this might come as a surprise, I'm not a very good liar when I'm being questioned like that.

At work, I emailed Elfie. She'd check in throughout the day, I knew, they all did now. BlackBerries and iPhones meant that there was no such thing as having to wait for a teacher to go, in order to pass on a message. I remembered when a boy in the sixth form got a pager, and we all thought it was the height of cool. He would check it, ostentatiously, at every opportunity. And I'm not exactly ancient. Though I am to them, of course, and to half of my own students. They are a different generation, certainly as far as technology's concerned. I remember MS-DOS and the days of having an essay to write and No Such Thing As Google. 'What, no Google or Internet on your phone, you mean,' one of my younger first-year students had assumed, with a sympathetic face, when I had pointed this out during a research skills tutorial. No, none at all, I told him, and watched with amusement as his face gaped in horror.

'Well, it existed, an early form of it,' I went on, 'but it wasn't something we all had automatic access to like we do now. It wasn't until I was in my second year of university that I got an email address,' I announced.

The student shuddered. 'Dude,' he muttered, unable to comprehend such primitive times.

'And that's why you need research skills,' I segued triumphantly, 'because you shouldn't rely entirely on something that's younger than you are.'

*Finishing work early*, I typed. There was no point in using full sentences, but I refused to use text-speak. *Will pick you up from school. Have a surprise for you!*

I had debated going to see Coco alone, without Elfie, but decided against it in the end. I couldn't risk her refusing to see me, shutting the door in my face. She might do so eventually, even with Elfie, but at least this way I had a chance. It was still risky though. Elfie was going to have to go along with it, for a start, and although I thought she would – the girl had agreed to climb into the Serpentine in January, after all – there were no guarantees. I had to try, however. I had to try everything.

# Chapter Sixteen

Coco Delaney lived in a mews house, tucked away between Bayswater and Notting Hill. The mews was a pretty little cobbled street with houses painted in ice-cream colours. The perfect place to live if you wanted to be within easy reach of everything Central London had to offer, and yet still be secluded. In another life . . . I thought, as I walked down the street, ushering Elfie alongside me, one where I lived alone and had the sort of busy, glamorous job that meant I got in late and ate in restaurants every night. The life of a film producer, or . . . well, a model agent, I supposed.

An old Mercedes sports car was parked outside the final house, pale metallic green, and I checked the address in the email. It was hers. Was it the same car? The one in which she had driven to St Albans all those years ago, when she had discovered Sadie? It had pale, creamy leather seats, and a patterned silk scarf was chucked over the passenger seat. I tried to remember what I'd read in the diary, whether Sadie had described the car, but couldn't. I'd have to check when I got home. But that would have to wait, because while I was gazing at the car, Elfie had gone up and knocked on the door.

The woman who opened it was in her seventies but could have been a model still. She stood in front of us, tall and straight-backed, in knee-high boots over grey skinny jeans and a swingy black tunic, her hair thick and fringed and piled up messily on top of her head, and you could see instantly how beautiful she must have been in her time. She had that sort of soft, plump skin that almost looks better as it ages, and pale, pillowy lips. Flicky-lined eyes.

'So. You must be Elfie. And Klara.' She fixed her eyes on us, in turn, and we both gaped at her like idiots. She had that sort of effect on you, that mesmerising presence, and I couldn't help but wonder whether my mother had felt the same. Eventually I managed to pull myself together enough to speak.

'Yes. Hello, Coco. It's wonderful to meet you. I've . . .' I stopped myself. *I've been reading about when you were young*, was I going to say? *About how you discovered my mother and scooped her up from her dull small-town existence and swept her off to London. I've been imagining what you looked like now for days . . .*

'I've read so much about your career since I wrote to you. It was through one of my students that I heard of you. I work at a university. I know you were interested to know.'

My words crashed out awkwardly. I had decided to get the explanation in quickly, get it out of the way as I didn't want it hanging over me the whole time we were in there, didn't want to be wondering when she might ask, when I might have to arrange my face into the right expression. And I had decided to keep the story as close to the truth as I could.

She looked at me slightly strangely, then smiled politely. 'I'm astonished that any of your students have heard of me,' she said, standing aside and motioning for us to come in. 'What is it that you teach?'

'I lecture on European Cinema and Culture, mainly. It's part of the Media Studies course. But it involves quite a lot of discussion of other elements of culture, mostly popular, when you're putting everything into context.' True, all true.

'Anyhow, I've got a third-year student whose dissertation is on music videos, and he's really interested in those from London in the Sixties and Seventies. He's done masses of research on the home movies that maybe informed or inspired some of those videos as well – footage that the bands had recorded themselves, that sort of thing.' Almost true. I had once had a student who was into that period, though I'd made up the subject of his thesis after reading about some of the videos Coco had appeared in. And maybe slightly over-detailed. Was my mouth running away with me?

'*Anyway*, sorry, to cut a long story short, he came across you and mentioned something about your career as a model and a booker and I thought it was worth a shot. Better than picking some name out of the phone book, and I don't know anything about modelling. The worlds of academia and fashion don't really collide that much, as you can probably tell . . .' I gestured at my tunic and leggings combo in what I thought was a self-deprecatory manner, but she nodded, which shut me up. Which was probably for the best, because I had been gabbling.

'So,' I finished. 'Here we are!'

Coco nodded again, but said nothing. Waiting to see whether I was going to start up again, I assumed. I busied myself by looking around the room. It was beautiful, with whitewashed walls and floorboards that had been painted white and varnished till they gleamed. An enormous grey velvet sofa took up all of one side of the room, covered in Indian rugs embroidered with gold thread and mirrors, and a hotch-potch of cushions that should have looked mismatched but instead looked casually, artfully styled. A mirrored desk sat in one corner, with a big orange-shaded lamp overhanging it. The room led into a kitchen, floored with the same white boards, the walls covered in those rectangular tiles that you got in subway stations. And all over the walls were photos, of Coco when she was younger, on beaches and at parties, of Moroccan tiles and Balinese temples, of rock stars and actors and men who looked as if they might be gangsters. Memories of a life well and exotically lived, all lined up in elegant black frames.

Elfie's eyes were wide, as she gazed at a photo of Coco leaning over the shoulder of a Beatle at what looked like an awards ceremony. I went up to her, put my hands on her shoulders, pretending to look at the same photo, but really scanning the wall for pictures of my mother. I felt like a spy.

'Nineteen sixty-seven,' Coco said. She had perched on the arm of the sofa and was regarding us with faint amusement. 'That was a good night. You must think I'm terribly vain for keeping all these images of myself on display.'

We both shook our heads. 'If I'd done so many exciting things I think I'd spend all day looking at pictures of them, when I was—' Elfie stopped herself and blushed. *When I was old*, she had been going to say; we all knew it, and she looked so mortified that I could have cried for her.

'When you were old?'

We kept quiet.

But Coco simply laughed, throaty and rich. 'It's all right, I am old. Fucking ancient, in fact. But I don't care. It's one of the advantages of being as old as me. You stop giving a toss about most things.'

She made us mint tea, with leaves fresh from her garden, in a glass pot and served it in little emerald-coloured glasses with silver filigree on the sides. It was all very beautiful, very bohemian. And yet I had the impression that it was all carefully choreographed, that nothing happened in Coco Delaney's life that was not styled and stage-managed with as much thought and planning as a *Vogue* cover-shoot.

'So,' she said eventually, after we had chatted about the area and Elfie had shyly admired her boots and Coco had told us a story involving a famous actress and a swimming pool and a bottle of rum that made our eyebrows shoot up in the air with shock before we tried to look totally blasé about it all.

'You want to be a model, Elfie.' It wasn't a question. I held my breath. I hadn't really briefed Elfie, not as such, had decided that it would be best to tell her the minimum necessary, rather than getting her to lie. And all teenage girls want to be models, don't they? I mean OK, I didn't, but then I was – me.

'Yes. I'd love to more than anything. Well, I'd love to be an actress as well. Or a fashion designer.' She smiled timidly, and I was filled with affection for her that overwhelmed the guilt I had been feeling. She did want this.

'You're very pretty. But it hasn't really got much to do with that.'

Elfie looked uncertain. 'OK.'

'What do you think is the most important quality that a model should possess, Elfie, if it's not beauty?'

'Adaptability,' she said quickly. 'I mean, not just having one look. And also professionalism, a good attitude, that sort of thing.'

Coco smiled. 'Not bad. But I'd say it goes further than being adaptable. I mean, some great models could only ever look like themselves, couldn't they? You'd never mistake Kate Moss for anyone else. Those cheekbones, those teeth . . . But she has what all the great models have. The ability to inhabit the essence of a shoot entirely. Great actresses have it as well, in a way. They take on the essence of a character, don't they? It's not easy. Especially not when you *are* beautiful. You have to know how to let that beauty, that natural beauty – go.' She clicked her fingers. She was enjoying her role as wise woman. 'Become the photographer's vision. Become the woman they need to sense, to smell, to touch.' Her voice had lowered to a whisper. Elfie was transfixed. I was more cynical. She was playing on the drama. But I said nothing.

She sat back, pleased with the effect her words seemed to have had on Elfie. 'I never had it,' she said in her normal voice, and laughed, and I liked her again.

'But you were a wonderful model,' I said, and hated myself as soon as the sycophantic syllables had escaped my lips. She shrugged, and hardly glanced at me. Coco Delaney was no fool.

'I was capable. I could get by well enough. Nothing more. I was better at other things. And others were better at modelling.' I hoped that she would say more. More about the women who were better models than she – was Sadie one of them? More, too, about the 'other things' that she was better at. What were they? But she fell silent.

'So, what will we do for you, little Elfie?' she said, turning to her and smiling. Her manner changed as she did so, softened. I didn't think that she liked me much.

'I will talk to a couple of people. Show your photos to them. See what we can see. I make you no promises. The industry's not what it was when I was working. There are so many girls, now. It's like a factory. Think about whether it's what you really want.'

Elfie bit her lip. She wanted it. I could see it in her eyes.

'There's no pressure,' I said cheerfully. 'If she decides she doesn't want to take it any further, then that's fine. No one's committed to anything, are they? Let's just see how we go.' I touched Elfie's arm. I wanted to reassure her, and also to show that she wasn't being pushed into anything by me. But I was desperate not to let Coco Delaney slip through my fingers just as I had found her. She had told me nothing of Sadie yet. I had had no opportunity to delve deeper into her past or to winkle out information that might lead me forward, and added to this she didn't really seem to like me much, whereas she had taken a definite shine to Elfie, and vice versa. I had to do whatever I could to keep her in my sights.

When we reached the door, I turned for one last look at the walls, desperately scanning the photos for a glimpse of Sadie.

'You must have so many stories about those days,' I said, trying to sound casual. You worked with Archie Farrow, didn't you?'

A shadow passed across her face, I thought, though I might have been imagining it. She hid it quickly. 'Yes. How do you know of Archie?'

'Oh, I read something that mentioned him when I was looking into your career before we came. I don't know anything about him, really. Just that you worked for his modelling agency.'

'You have done your research on me,' she said, a touch sharply.

I faltered, but decided not to let her make me feel nervous. 'Well, Elfie's precious. Like I said, I don't know anything about the industry. I wanted to make sure I was taking advice from someone who knew what they were talking about.'

She raised an eyebrow, and looked pleased, if not a little impressed. That was better. She liked direct. I could relate to that. I pushed it.

'What happened to him? Is he still working? I suppose probably not.'

She paused, her hand on the door handle. 'Ah, so you haven't read everything about that time, then.'

I waited for her to continue.

'He died,' she said, and I could tell that the conversation was over.

# Chapter Seventeen

*23 September, 1970*

He likes me. I really think he likes me. More than the other girls, more than just as one of his models, I mean. Does he – does he like me *like that*? I don't know. I think he might, but it's hard to say with Archie. His face is hard to understand sometimes. He gives these little smiles and stares at you and they could mean 'I like you, I can't help but smile when I look at you' (I hope they mean that, oh how I hope they mean that) or they could be polite, 'thank you, Sadie, now please go away' smiles, which would devastate me because I'm sure we understand each other better than that. I can feel it, I know I can, there's this – energy. Or it could mean any number of other things that I am not imagining, because all I can really think about is whether he likes me or not, whether he is thinking the same thing as me, whether he can feel this feeling in the pit of his stomach like I can or whether I'm making the whole thing up like a stupid teenager.

Oh, my head is everywhere and in a million pieces, and if he doesn't like me then my heart will be too.

I must stop obsessing about it. But he is in my mind

and my heart and my soul all of the time, all day, all night. It's as though he has possessed me, like an evil spirit but he's not evil; he could never be evil.

*Stop it, Sadie.* There is so much else to tell. I made a list so I didn't forget anything. *Concentrate.*

So, what else. Archie is at the centre of it all but around him swirls my life in London, full of movement and bubbles and I am swept up in it and it carries me along.

My life. For the record, I am living in the boarding house still, with the witch of a landlady, Mrs Brindle, who looks at me as if I am Jezebel herself, whenever I come in or go out. I have started playing with her now, to amuse myself. Every time she is there, sitting in her armchair all fat and old like a spider in her web, I make a point of saying something outrageous to one of the other girls, if they are nearby, or to her, or even to myself. 'I must go and get a new pack of the pill,' I shouted the other day to Annie, whose room is along the corridor from mine. 'My last one's almost run out and I'm planning on having an awful lot of sex in the next four weeks.' Annie gave me a funny look, then she realised what I was doing and sniggered. Mrs Brindle glowered. The next day was a Sunday and so I muttered (loudly) to myself as I was walking out of the door, 'Now, have I got my whisky? I simply mustn't forget it. Father Joseph does bang on so during his sermons.' I thought she was going to die right then and there, she made such a noise – a huge wheezing choke of disgust. I had to stick my fist in my mouth until I was out of the front door so she didn't hear me laugh, and I carried on all the way down the street. People think models are just dim, pretty faces. But we know better, don't we?

The other models. I don't see much of them, thank goodness as they're mostly awful, stuck-up and no fun at all. Some of them are OK though, and I have made one or two friends, or they might be friends soon. Niamh, she's Irish and has these amazing blue eyes and is always laughing at everything. She's not the best model, and I know Coco doesn't think she's got what it takes. She's a 'catalogue girl', Coco says, which she means as an insult, but Niamh doesn't care. 'I make a living in catalogues and I'm going to save up and buy a nice house, so what do I care if Coco Chanel over there doesn't think I'm the next Shrimp?' She's got a point, and good for her, but I can't ever bring myself to completely agree with her, because I *do* want to be the next Jean Shrimpton, or bigger, even. Anyhow, she's fun and if we ever get sent on castings together we always go and share a bottle of wine afterwards, and don't count the calories.

She's probably the best friend I've made here, though I wouldn't call her a real best friend, not like Suzanne (I'll come back to her in a moment). The girls in the boarding house are mostly secretaries or typing pool girls, and they think I'm exotic and a bit racy, I can tell. Between you and me I don't make any attempt to change their minds.

What next? Oh yes, Suzanne. She's been writing to me, and I've been writing back, but it's a bit difficult, to be honest. I mean, it's not like we have much in common any more, is it? I don't think anyone could blame me for finding it all a little awkward. She talks about St Albans (I almost wrote 'home' then, but it isn't, not any more Force of habit, I suppose) and people we know and places we used to go to as if I'm still there, or just around the corner, and maybe that's how it feels to her, but to me it feels like another country. Another world. So distant. I can't even remember some of the things she seems to think I should. But it is nice to be in touch – comforting somehow – so I write back and tell her things about London without rubbing it in her face that I'm doing all the things we said we would do together, without her. *Maybe you'll come and visit one day*, I wrote in my last letter, but even as I wrote it I felt treacherous because part of me – no, most of me – hopes she won't. I know. I'm like one of those girls who dump their friends as soon as they get a new boyfriend. But in this case, my new love is London and a new life.

Well, my new love is Archie, of course. But that's different.

Did I say that? That he's my new love? Premature, you're thinking. Silly girl, jumping the gun. Well, we'll see.

So, we've done the boarding house, the girls, Suzanne. Those are the important things. Now I can tell the rest about Archie. I have saved it till last, like the best chocolate in the box. See, there's a reason I think he likes me back, that I don't think I'm just pie in the sky about him. When we were in his office the other day and he was telling me about a shoot he wanted to put me up for, he stopped suddenly in the middle of his sentence. I hadn't been listening to what he was saying, not really. I had just been staring at his eyes, his amazing eyes, and trying to look interested and keen rather than all moony. I don't know whether it worked and he hadn't noticed, or he had noticed and wanted me to know it, but either way he paused, and looked at me, and him stopping talking made me wake up and I looked at him and he was giving me the strangest look, as if he was really *seeing* me. I'm not sure anyone's ever looked at me like that before. It felt as though – oh, it sounds stupid but I have to say it – it felt as though he had taken my soul out of my body and was turning it over in his mind, examining every inch of it. I said it sounded stupid. Maybe though, just maybe, you'll have felt the same thing, and then you'll know. You'll know what it felt like there, in that room, in that moment.

Reading my mother's diary was mostly like looking into a cloudy mirror, one that obscured more than it revealed. But every now and again, I caught glimpses of myself in Sadie. Like the list she made to remind herself what she wanted to write in her diary – that was the sort of thing I did all the time. Was that where my list-making, cataloguing side came from? If she had been a slightly different sort of person, less beautiful, less desperate to escape, might she have ended up a bit like me, with the sort of job I had, using that side of herself?

If, if, if. Sadie's short life had left a trail of them hanging, like an unfinished daisy chain. If she had stayed in St Albans, if she had never met Coco or Archie, if she had never married my father, if I had never been born. If she had not left. If she had lived.

So many paths not travelled, so many words unspoken. And now so many questions for me to answer.

# Chapter Eighteen

Questions. My whole life was full of them now. They were everywhere, like when you spill a pot of those silver balls that decorate cakes and they race all over the floor, treacherously waiting for you to skid on them or sliding down cracks in the floorboard ready to be discovered covered in dust a few months later. But that wouldn't happen to my questions. I was determined to get them all answered now.

I should have done it a long time ago, of course. It's not as if I never tried. I asked Daddy, every now and then. Well, I say every now and then, but in reality there was a pattern to it, like there is with everything. I asked him every year, on the same day. A random day, not the anniversary of her leaving or anything. Not that we ever marked that day. Or …

A memory flashed before my eyes, triggered by the thought of dates and anniversaries. Daddy booking flights somewhere a couple of months before the anniversary, when I was – how old would I have been? Twelve, thirteen, maybe? Old enough to be sure that the memory was real, but young, still. I dug deeper. Him sitting on the old settee, talking on the phone. I could hear him speaking, his voice unusually urgent, agitated. 'No, no, it has to be next week, it'll have to be a different airline. There must be. Look again. No, I need to be away over—' Stopping himself, glancing at me, thinking I was deep in my book. 'I need to be there between those exact dates. Yes.'

Now, however, I thought I knew what that feeling had been. It hadn't just been the amorphous sadness that was so often present, but something more. Something disturbing. Because it wasn't the first time that he had made sure he was away from home on that particular date.

I went up into the loft. It's big and has proper flooring and lighting, and a solid ladder that I can pull down easily myself, so I never need to wait for Mark to come home to get in and out of there. We use it to store all sorts of things, camping gear and suitcases and old paperwork, a set of curtains that are too big for any of the windows but that we don't quite want to throw away, the weights Mark pretended to use for a few years before admitting defeat, boxes that laptops and TVs came in in case we ever get burgled.

And my old diaries, neatly packed away in a box. Oh, they're not like Sadie's diary. I was never one for impassioned outpourings. No, these are records – archives, more like. A note made of everything I have done, every lunch meeting or cup of coffee with a friend, every essay handed in, exam taken, doctor's appointment attended. Every single thing that could be of note, written down. I like to know where I was and what I was doing on any given date, and it's more for looking back than planning forward. I'd be a brilliant witness, I often think, when I'm watching some crime drama on TV. Most people would never be able to tell you what they were doing on 13 July 1994, say; they'd have no clue. I would though.

I started when I was ten, so I have twenty-two years' worth of my life catalogued in these boxes. Twenty-two plain black books, neatly stacked in date order. Twenty-two years. Two hundred and sixty-four months. Eight thousand and thirty days. The same number of entries. I have a format, you see.

Otherwise each day would have a different number of things written in it, depending on how much I had on, and it would look all uneven and then I might be tempted to leave things out so that the pattern wasn't disturbed and then it wouldn't be accurate. Dominos. But you can avoid it if you plan ahead. So, I write one paragraph only, containing all the necessary information. If I've seen a friend I write their name and where and at what time we met; if I haven't, I write NONE. Same with doctor's appointments and the like. I use abbreviations – GP, or DN for the dentist or GR for the garage. It doesn't sound as if it would work, but it does – for me – and I've refined it over the years, so now it only takes me a few seconds to write up each day. It has the added bonus that it wouldn't be that easy for other people to read, should they happen to try. It's not a code, I'm not mad. But it would just take them a while, and they probably wouldn't bother, and I find that reassuring. And it niggled away at me, this memory, this image of Daddy being away, by himself, every year. Not over the anniversary of my mother leaving us; he was always at home for that, even though we never talked about it. But a couple of weeks or months earlier . . . Was it coincidence? He travelled a lot, after all. No, there was a pattern to it, I was certain.

I searched back through the pages. 1992, when I would have been twelve. There it was. *Daddy to Hungary, 12 p.m. Klara to Mrs Brown's.* This was on 2nd of June. I stayed with Mrs Brown the local childminder sometimes, when he was away, until I could persuade him that I was old enough to be left alone in the house overnight. Was that the year I had remembered? Or was it another? I pulled 1993's book out of the box and flicked to the same month. Yes it had been a longer trip that year, a whole week in June this time. *Daddy to Washington, 6.50 a.m., Klara to Beth.* That was right. I had been excited to stay with my best friend for the week; we had spent hours in the run-up planning all the things we were going to do . . .

Something thudded in my chest. This was no time to reminisce. I pulled more books out of the box, flipping quickly through them until I found what I was looking for. And I did, in each and every one. *Daddy away . . . Daddy in London. Henry at a conference* (that was when I was fifteen and going through a brief phase of insisting I call Daddy by his first name). *Daddy Beijing 5.31. Daddy to Glasgow.* The dates differed slightly, but every year, every June, he was away over the third. At conferences, meetings, giving papers, on research trips. Or so he had claimed. Now though, I suspected otherwise. It could not be coincidence, these trips, all taking place over that date without fail. So either he really had been at those places, and had just made sure that they fell over the necessary days, or he had been somewhere else. But where?

I set him a trap, later that day. I felt treacherous doing so, but I had no choice. He had left me no choice.

'I know it's a while away, but do you have any idea of your schedule for June, Daddy?' I asked casually as I poured him a glass of red wine. He was having dinner at ours. Mark was marinading chicken to go under the grill, and the kitchen was full of good smells and warmth. We were all relaxed, and happily chatting about books and holidays and food in the way that we did when we were together. The three of us had a nice, easy pattern that we fell into. Elfie sat in the corner, headphones on, a magazine in her hand, looking over at us every so often, smiling a little. I think it was reassuring for her, to be surrounded with gentle activity and to know that she had a place within it.

I watched him carefully while trying not to appear as though I was doing so, and I caught the flash of panic cross his face. It lasted only for a brief moment, less than a second, but it was there, like a candle flaring in the dark before fizzling out. 'What for, my child? I'll have to check, where's my . . .' He rummaged in his breast pocket for the small diary that he always carried with him, full of scrawled dates and crossings-out and random notes to himself. The lack of a system made my fingers itch and I couldn't look at the book's pages, covered in blots of ink and drops of lunchtime soup, without wincing.

'I've got a pair of tickets to *The Marriage of Figaro*,' I lied. 'It's coming on at the ENO. I thought we could go together.'

I kept my eyes on him as he let his run down the relevant page in his diary. He didn't flinch as he shook his head and began to speak. It was impressive really, or it would have been had it not been so disconcerting, his ability to lie so smoothly, after the initial start my question had given him.

'Ah, no, no, what a shame. I have to go to Wales, to this meeting.'

'What's that?'

He raised his head and our eyes met, and for a moment I thought that a flicker of understanding passed between us, as though he knew that I knew and it was simply necessary for us both to keep pretending in order to make sure that the whole house of cards did not flutter and fall . . . but then it was gone again, and I thought that I had most likely imagined it, and it was just me standing in my kitchen listening to my father lie to me. Mark touched me on the shoulder as he passed by and I reached for his hand and squeezed it. 'Sorry, just pass me the spatula . . . thanks.' He carried on poking the chicken in that way men do, as though somehow it will make things happen quicker, and I felt a rush of affection for him.

'Oh, a Board of Trustees thing for the university. It'll be all minutes and ham sandwiches, but I'll be there for a couple of days I'm afraid. How annoying, I'd have loved to have seen

*Figaro* again. I don't suppose you can persuade Mark to go with you instead?'

The three of us smiled. Mark's lack of patience for any kind of theatre was a running joke between us. He found it impossible to sit there for more than five minutes without starting to fidget and look cross. 'How can they DO it,' he had ranted at me, the first time I had taken him to see something. 'Stand up there on stage and make such fools of themselves, pretending that they can't hear what someone else is saying a few feet away? It's ridiculous. It's not the Middle Ages. We all KNOW they can see him behind the bloody arras.' I had tried a few more times after that, before giving up.

'Don't worry. Maybe I'll ask Beth. Plenty of time.'

He smiled vaguely at me and nodded, and if I hadn't known any better, I would have thought there was nothing more to it than that.

I did know better though.

I stayed up late again that night, after Daddy had gone home and Mark and Elfie had gone to bed, and this time I sat on the sofa and instead of reading I wrote. Everything I could remember, everything I could think of that didn't sit right or didn't ring true, all the times I had wondered about my mother and tried to find out about her. It all came out onto the pages of my notebook in a big scrawl and I wrote and wrote until my hand ached in a way it hadn't done since the end of my A-levels.

Because of course this wasn't the first time that I had tried to discover more about Sadie. There had been plenty of occasions over the years that I had asked Daddy about her, asked him where he thought she had gone and what exactly she had done after she had left and before she had died. He had never answered, not in a straight way, I realised as I wrote. It was always, 'Oh, I don't know, Klara, she was a law unto herself, your mother,' or, 'You can bet that whatever she was doing, she did it with gusto,' laughing fondly, or just a change of subject. I recorded the time he had lost his temper, the suddenness of it, how quickly it came upon him and how guilty he looked afterwards. How he tiptoed around me for days, trying to make it up to me, to get me to trust him again.

I may not have continued to ask him, but that didn't mean that my interest in Sadie had disappeared. I had searched the house, hoping to find clues as to her whereabouts, or simply something of hers that I had not previously known about, but with no luck. Other than the few bits that I had always had, it was as though she had never existed. As though my father had removed all traces of her from our lives, I thought now, as my pen continued to fly across the page, as though he had been determined not to be reminded of her. Again, I had always assumed that this was simply due to his grief. Now I thought that his grief had been more than a little tinged with guilt. Guilt at what though? That was the question.

My mother had lived in a world where the Internet didn't exist; she had briefly been someone with potential, but she had never really had a chance to turn into that person, the woman she had so confidently claimed she would become in her diaries, before she had disappeared. And anyhow, I knew now that she had changed her name once, so she might have done so again. I had no way of knowing.

It wasn't just stuff about Sadie that I wrote that night, in my frenzy. I dredged up all sorts of memories about Daddy, ones that had nothing to do with my mother, or so I had thought, but just things that I had forgotten about until now because they were unpleasant or unpalatable. They ambushed me now; I could not ignore them any longer. I couldn't afford to, not when they might be evidence, might help me to build up the picture that had started, very slowly, to take shape.

Daddy had been kind and patient and loving and understanding, all this is true. But there had also been times when this had not been the case. When I had come home from school early after there was a fire alarm and found him drunk, not that I had realised this at the time, but as an adult the evidence was clear; he had been asleep at his desk and had been unable to focus on me when I had woken him and then he had shouted at me, asking what I was doing home, before shoving some papers from his desk into his briefcase and storming out. The time when I had got up in the night to go to the loo and had walked past his bedroom door, silent and afraid as I listened to him weeping and saying over and over again, 'I'm sorry, forgive me, forgive me. I had to do it, my darling, my dearest girl.' The time I had drawn a picture of my mother, I could only have been eight or so, it was not that long after she had left and I still remembered what she looked like, her presence was still a clear enough memory for me to miss her, and he had stared at it for ages, not saying anything, and then had begun to cry. And I had been sure that I had broken his heart, and I had been so sorry, and I had vowed never to do anything like that again, never to remind him of her in that way, never to make him so sad, and I had taken the picture away and torn it into little pieces and buried them deep in the garden where they could not hurt anyone again.

The paper was wet with my tears by the time I had finished writing down all of these stories, and I stared at it for ages, my eyes sore and my wrist aching, not quite knowing where all of these words had come from, not sure what to do with them, until in the end I fell asleep over it, and dreamed of nothing at all.

# Chapter Nineteen

*30th October, 1970*

There is no doubt in my mind any more that Archie feels the same way as I do. It's just a matter of time before he makes his intentions clear. Before he feels able to show his true feelings. I do understand that he can't make some kind of move straight away, it would be ungentlemanly, not very honourable, and Archie is an honourable man, whatever some of the girls say when they whisper in the loos. I don't listen to the gossip. People love to talk, love to make up stories, especially about people of influence, people who matter. They're jealous, they can't bear that people like Archie (and yes, like me, I know what it's like to have people gossip behind your back, it's something else we have in common) have something that they don't, and that they never will have. It's not something you can learn, or buy, charisma, is it? It's a gift.

How do I know that he feels the same way? Well. There have been two occasions where it has been impossible for me to ignore what has been going on. I'll be brief. Firstly, last week, when I was having a coffee with Coco and talking about the jobs that she wanted to send me for (Coco likes to have these strategy meetings with all of the girls, and actually I think it's a very good thing too), he came to find us, saying that he needed to talk to Coco about something later. She gave him a strange look and said OK, she'd talk to him later then, and he put his hand on my shoulder and asked, 'So, how's our rising star getting on?' And as he spoke he rubbed his thumb over my shoulderblade. She couldn't see him do it, but she could see my face and I think she could tell something was going on because she narrowed her eyes and snapped at him, 'Very good. She'll be doing even better if you let us get on with our meeting.' And he grinned and his thumb strayed to the nape of my neck and touched my bare skin just for the briefest of most delicious, most wonderful moments, and it only lasted for a tiny fragment of a second, so short a time that if you had made him swear he could have said it was an accident, but I knew it wasn't, I felt the intent in that touch. And I can still feel it now, as though his thumbprint was tattooed onto me with it.

So that was number one. Number two was yesterday, and thinking about it still makes my heart race and my wrists start to tremble. This was bigger, more – I couldn't have ignored it even if I tried. I was at the boarding house. I had been to a casting and I didn't think I had got it and so I was feeling blue, eating chocolate that I shouldn't have bought and reading a novel about true love, and dreaming, as always, of him. And then, as though I had brought him into being like the genie in the lamp, Annie knocked on my door and said, all breathless, that there was 'a MAN' on the phone for me and that he sounded 'very masterful and said he had to speak to you *right away*,' and I knew it was him, I just knew it. I opened the door and she was standing there all nervous and she obviously wanted to ask who it was and I thanked her and then waited for a minute, because I didn't want him to think I was just sitting around doing nothing, and then I walked slowly down the stairs in case he could hear and picked up the phone and said, 'Hello?' as if I didn't have a clue who might be on the other end.

'Sadie,' he said, and his voice was soft and strong.

'Yes?' Still keeping up the pretence that it might be any number of men calling me on a Monday night.

'It's Archie.' I could hear his smile and I bit my lip and clenched my fists.

'Oh, hello. How are you?' Polite, friendly, distant. I modelled my tone on Coco's, just a little. Just that edge of cool.

'I'm very well, thank you. I . . .'

I waited. Held my breath. Why was he calling? What couldn't wait?

'I just wanted to see how the casting went.'

I couldn't stop the smile from breaking out over my face. He didn't need to ring to find that out. Coco had been there, he could have just asked her. Or waited until he saw me. Or asked the casting director. Anything. But ringing me? It was an excuse. I gave a little laugh.

'You are sweet. It was great, thank you.' It hadn't been great, but why tell him that? Confidence was attractive; putting yourself down wasn't.

'Of course it was. You always are.'

'Oh.'

'I've embarrassed you. I'm sorry. I shouldn't have said anything.'

'No. No, thank you. You just took me by surprise.'

There was a pause.

'Yes. I know the feeling.'

I swallowed. Did he mean what I thought he meant?

'Sorry. I should . . . I should go.'

I nodded, overwhelmed, and forgot to speak, forgot that he couldn't see me.

'Sadie?'

'Yes! Sorry. Yes, I should go too. I'm – you know.'

'Yes, I know. Well. I'll see you in the office, I suppose.'

'You will. You most certainly will!' I sounded stupidly perky, but I couldn't help myself. I didn't know what to say. Neither of us did. In the end, he laughed, and I wanted to reach down the phone line and hug his voice, it was so warm and comforting.

'All right, sweet Sadie. Until then.' And he had hung up before I could say goodbye, which was probably a good thing because I wasn't sure I could speak over the lump in my throat. *Sweet Sadie*. I went up to bed and let the words run around my brain all night long.

I have big news, the biggest, the best, the most amazing. When Suzanne gave me this diary, she told me that she was doing so because she knew that I 'would write some momentous things in it', that it wouldn't be just full of little stories about boys and homework and complaints about being bored, like the diaries most teenage girls write, but that it would be a proper story, an important story. The story of my life.

And now it has begun. I will never forget the kiss that was bestowed upon me yesterday by someone of real significance. A man, not a boy, a lover, a man of experience and stature, a man who knows what it is to touch a woman's heart with his lips. Because that is what I am now – a woman. There is no going back. I wish I could tell Suzanne about this transformation, but we agreed not to write to one another, not until everything had settled down at least. Well, I will write it here and one day I will tell her. Maybe one day when we are old and are sitting around together looking back on our youth, I will tell her about the day that it happened to me.

(Speaking of Suzanne, before I tell this most amazing news, I should write an update from the home front. She writes to me regularly. Things are going well with her and Trevor. I'm happy for her. But last time she wrote she told me that Mary and Piotr have been looking for me, asking her where I am, turning up at her house and things. She's sure that they know she knows my address, and she's worried that they'll find it out somehow. What should she do? she asked. I didn't know what to say to her. What can she do? I suppose if they're determined enough they'll find out, but I really don't want them to. The thought of them turning up here makes me feel all panicky. I never told them which modelling agency I was going to, of course, so it's not as though they're likely to turn up at the offices, thank God. But you never know. Piotr is determined and I don't want them here. I don't, I can't.)

Anyhow. All will be well, I hope. I pray.

Now to the happy part, the best part, the best thing ever. I went back to the office late, after my shoot for Deloir had finished, because I had agreed to drop some stills off for the photographer (doing them favours is always a Good Thing, I have decided; they're the ones who have the power to make you look good, or not, after all; ditto the make-up girls – always make friends with the make-up girls), and he was working late. He often did. There was no one else there, I could tell as soon as I walked in the door. The rooms had that empty feeling, I could feel the distance between me and the walls.

'Hello?' he called out, and I nearly hopped with pleasure at the sound of his voice. He emerged from his office, his hair ruffled, his eyes tired, and smiled at the sight of me.

'Oh good, it's you.'

Oh good. Oh God.

'Yes. Philippe sent these back.' I waved the folder of images at him, but his eyes remained on my face.

'Thanks. It go well?'

'Very.'

We watched one another for a moment.

'I'm finished here. Have you eaten?'

I shook my head. I couldn't speak, it might have broken the spell.

'Good.' He pulled his jacket over his shoulders and ushered me out of the door.

As we drove through London in a cab I asked him how he had come to start the modelling agency. 'I've done lots of things over the years,' he told me. 'I ran a politics magazine for a while, I worked in Asia as a journalist, I managed a gallery in New York for a bit, but I've got a butterfly mind. I get bored easily, and . . . it seemed like a good idea. Coco and I had worked together before, and she decided she wanted to stop modelling herself and do something new, so we were both looking for a project and we came up with Velvet.'

'But had you worked in the industry before?'

He shook his head. 'No. But when you've been around for as long as I have, you learn that you don't need as much direct experience as some people would have you believe. You just fake it till you make it.'

He was right, of course, why wouldn't he be able to run a modelling agency? He was clever and worldly and successful, and it was just another business. But I was still impressed.

'Well, you're obviously making it.'

'We're doing all right. Coco and I work well together.'

I wanted to ask more about Coco and about how he knew her, but then the cab pulled over and he leaned forward to pay the driver from a wodge of notes that he pulled from his pocket, and we were outside a mansion block.

'There's wine in the fridge and other stuff in the drinks cabinet, and I make a damn good omelette. I know it's not the fabulous London evening that you might have been expecting, but I think we can make a pretty good fist of things.'

I couldn't have asked for anything more. To be with Archie, listening as he talked, watching as he poured me a glass of white wine and beat eggs and chopped a pile of herbs with a big knife, standing in his tiny kitchen, close enough to feel the scratchiness of his jumper when he reached across me for something, was the most fabulous thing I could ever have imagined – more so.

And then it got better than I could have hoped for.

'Sorry,' he said suddenly, putting the knife down and wiping his hands on a tea towel, and then before I knew what was happening, he put his arm around my waist and pulled me towards him and kissed me, for a long time, hard, and I sort of gasped because I was so surprised, and then I just stayed completely still because I thought that if I moved he might change his mind and stop and I wanted it to go on forever.

It didn't, obviously. He stopped after a while, and I held my breath until he spoke. 'I'm sorry. That's really inappropriate. But I couldn't help myself. You're so beautiful.' He brushed my hair away from my cheek. 'So beautiful.' He was whispering.

'It's fine. It's not . . .'

'No, it's not fine. It's a bad idea.' But he didn't move. 'I don't seem to be able to move though.'

I giggled, and then stopped myself. I didn't want to sound like a silly schoolgirl, but he laughed as well, and rested his head on my forehead. 'Oh dear. Bad Archie.'

'No.' I lifted my hand and sort of rubbed the back of his head. Maybe it would encourage him to lean forward and kiss me again, I thought, but instead he pulled back and took a deep breath.

'I had better get myself under control, otherwise we are both going to be in trouble. Don't go anywhere.'

He winked at me as he walked out of the kitchen, and I smiled at him over the brim of my wineglass, and I hoped I looked sophisticated and grown-up rather than girlish. I had to make him realise that I was old enough for this, that I was not some silly child, but that I was a woman. Well, I was now, at any rate.

My cheeks were burning and it was probably a good thing that he had left the room because I could get myself under control as well. There was a hot feeling around my lips where his stubble had rubbed against my skin, and I touched it with my finger and felt tiny raised bumps there.

I put my glass of wine down and went to the small window in the corner of the kitchen. The street glowed under the lamps, and the road was wet. A line of trees ran down one side of it, dripping rain onto parked cars below them. I craned my neck so I could see the street sign. There it was. *King's Court*. My first one. My first proper kiss.

Her excitement leaped off the page. I could almost touch it. I could feel it in my own heart, racing through my veins. And it wasn't just her excitement, it was my own. Because Sadie's words reminded me of how I had felt, with Mark, that first time. His skin on mine, the realisation that yes, it was going to happen, he was going to kiss me and mean it, the knowledge that came from I knew not where that this would not be like the others. The smell of him as he moved his face nearer to mine, the sense of the space between us getting smaller and smaller . . . But it was not just the memory that jolted me and made my blood quicken. It was the similarity. We had felt the same things, Sadie and I: I might have described that first kiss with Mark using the same words.

For the first time, I could feel the silken thread between us tauten and tug at me. My mother. Her daughter. An invisible bond. It was there, after all.

# Chapter Twenty

*5th November, 1970*

I floated on air for the rest of the week after that night, actually floated, or that's what it felt like. Now I understood what all the songs and poems were about. I'd thought I had got it before, what they were all talking about when they mentioned rushes of blood to the head and feeling bowled over by love and love hitting you like a hurricane and all of those things; after all, I'd been in love with Tommy Jones and sort of in love with Steve Hill, hadn't I? Well, I can tell you now – and I'm sorry, Tommy and Steve, if you ever read this – but the answer is no, 100 per cent no. Maybe I was in love with the idea of being in love, maybe it was just lust or infatuation – but whatever it was, it was not love. And this is. This is it.

I feel like a different person, as though I have been transformed. Reborn. Maybe if you have experienced something like this then you will understand what I'm talking about. Part of me doesn't believe that you could have though. Part of me thinks that no one has ever experienced anything quite like this, not in the history of the world. Because how could they have done? How could they have felt the touch of his hand, or the intensity of him looking straight at them as though they were the only person who had ever mattered, or the strength of his arms wrapped around them so tightly they thought they might burst with love?

That night, the first night, I went home not long after he kissed me. I couldn't bear for anything to spoil the magic of it. Most of me wanted to stay, all night, just staring at him, I could have stared at him for ever, but I knew that I had to retain some mystery. Archie was a real man, used to real women, he was not some schoolboy who wanted a girl mooning over him as though she had never been kissed before, so I pulled myself together and I made myself ask him to call me a taxi when I had finished my wine. That was the other thing. I was so nervous that I was glugging it down again, and I didn't want to embarrass myself like before. It was the right thing to do, but it was the hardest thing I have ever done, I think. In fact, it was harder to put my coat on and walk out of Archie's door than it had been to leave my parents' house. What sort of a person does that make me? you might be wondering. A woman in love, that's all. Just a woman in love.

He looked a bit confused when I said I was going, but I tried not to let that throw me and instead I just stood on tiptoe and kissed his cheek and whispered into his ear in what I hoped was a sultry sort of a way that I would see him in the morning. Oh I know, it's not exactly a great line, but there we go. I suppose he was expecting me to stay the night, to sleep with him. But somehow I knew that if I did that tonight, something would be broken, and it would be something that I might not be able to get back again. Also, I needed some more time to psych myself up for that and I was wearing my worst pair of knickers, my period ones, and there was no way I was letting him see *them*.

All the lights were off when I got back to the boarding house, thank God. I had been dreading that old witch sitting in her chair in the front room, staring at me as I walked past. I was thankful that I did not have to deal with her, but at the same time I wished for a friend, someone I could confide in as I used to with Suzanne. I wished that I could get ready for bed and take my make-up off and climb under the covers and all the while have someone to talk to, to relive the whole night with, giggling and whispering like girls in films. Instead I crept up the stairs being careful not to make the boards creak as I went, and cold creamed my face and got my things ready for the next day so I could lie in bed as long as possible in the morning, and then I climbed under the covers and started writing this. You'll just have to be my friend, for now.

I still felt different when I woke up the next day, and the feeling lasted all through the morning as I got dressed and travelled to the office where I was going to get my schedule for the day and, more importantly, see my love again. Of course it wasn't just the kiss that had changed me, I knew that. That was like a trigger, like pulling the curtains back on a brand new stage-set for a play. I had changed even before the kiss, I just hadn't really seen it yet. But I had transformed myself. I was no longer Mary Tomaszewski, a schoolgirl from St Albans. I was Sadie, a model from London who was in love, and it felt as though everyone could see it written all over my face. I felt different inside. I moved differently, I thought. As I walked from the bus stop to the office that morning I could have laughed out loud with the joy of it. I almost did – I couldn't help the smile creeping across my face, and I hugged my bag to myself as I buzzed and waited to be let in. I had done it. I had really done it.

I didn't see him all morning, he was in meetings, shut away inside his office, and I was sent straight out again to a casting that had come in, for a new fashion designer who wanted faces no one had used before. 'This is an incredible opportunity,' Coco told me as she wrote down the address I was to go to. 'You're exactly right for it, Sadie.' She looked really excited, and so I hid the fact that I was a bit disappointed that it was for someone no one had ever heard of, rather than one of the big designers. I didn't want to seem unprofessional or like a know-it-all, and it was the job of Velvet Models to build my career and I trusted them, but surely it would be better to make a big splash and start off as you meant to go on. 'He's doing some amazing things with appliqué,' she continued, and then: 'I know, I know, it sounds mad, maybe it is, but wait till you see the clothes. You'll be fabulous in them – he'll love you – go, go, go.' And she hurried me out of the door and shut it behind me.

I didn't have much time to get there, and on the way I got a bit lost, and so I was late arriving at the place where they were doing the casting, and I tried to look as though I was relaxed about it as I told the girl at the desk my name even though my heart was thumping in my chest and I could hardly speak the words, 'Sadie, just Sadie,' because my breath was all uneven from running up the stairs.

I got the job, despite being so late and the last one to

be seen. Of course Coco had been right, the clothes *were* amazing. Appliqué didn't really cover it: he made these weird and wonderful dresses that consisted of hundreds of layers of fabric cut in different shapes, so that everywhere you looked you saw a different pattern. It was like staring at clouds: every time you let your eyes wander you saw a face or a castle or a flower emerge from what had looked totally random. The designer was short and wore big glasses that almost covered his whole face and he didn't smile once when I was there, hardly even looked at me really, but later when I got back to the office Coco said that he had 'loved me, couldn't get enough of me, I had made his week when I walked into that room,' and she was so proud of me, and I just thanked God that no one seemed to have told her how late I had been.

I should have felt surprised and proud to have got the job – certainly everyone else was reacting as though it was a big deal, not just Coco but the other girls in the office; even Tanya gave me a sour, jealous sort of smile and said, 'Well done.' But that was what I was there for, wasn't it? This was my job now, and if they were so surprised that I was doing it, then what did that say about everything? Surely they expected me to be a success? Because I certainly did. To be honest, I would have been more surprised if I *hadn't* got the job, especially after I saw some of the other girls leaving the casting. But it didn't matter. None of it mattered, because there was only one person whose opinion I really cared about.

'Is Archie around?' I asked casually, but maybe not casually enough because Coco's head jerked up and she gave me a look.

'He's busy,' she said, and I was a bit taken aback at how sharp she sounded.

'Oh. I just thought he'd want to know.' My eyes went to the door of his office which was still firmly shut. He would want to know, I knew he would.

'He'll be told, don't worry,' Coco said, and she moved so she was standing between me and the door, so I couldn't see it properly. Her voice was softer now but I could tell that she was just trying to get me to stop asking about Archie.

'Well,' I said, making sure I sounded more confident than I felt, 'I'll probably be seeing him myself later, I'll just tell him then.' Who did she think she was, standing in front of his door like that, like some kind of gatekeeper? I liked Coco, and I was grateful to her, but I loved Archie, and I was sure that if he didn't feel the same way already, he soon would. I could feel it.

She just nodded. 'OK,' she said, and smiled.

I didn't know what to say then. My confidence disappeared and I wasn't sure what to do next. She knew it as well – she could tell, because she kept smiling, and it was then that I realised, she was trying to keep me from him on purpose, because she was in love with him too. Of course. She can see that I'm a threat to the cosy little set-up she has and she's worried.

I'm back in my room now, writing this. I left the offices without seeing him. I didn't want to give her the satisfaction of thinking that I was hanging around waiting for him. So I swept out trying to look as though I didn't care. Of course I did care, a lot. But it's all right, because like I told her, I am going to see him later. Before I left, I managed to look at the diary that Tanya keeps on her desk and which has all of the appointments in it – Coco's and Archie's and the different castings and who's going to them. It's more like a battle-plan than a diary, and I saw where he was going to be later. Bertie's Bar, 6 p.m. He has a meeting with someone called Rupert and the diary says it's *re: financing*. It can't go on for too long, I'm sure. I plan to arrive there at 7, and surprise him.

The next page was almost empty. Halfway down the page, there was an indentation in the paper, from something that had been written with a pen pressed hard against the page and then removed. I held it up to the light. *Finished* had been written in small letters and then crossed out lots of times. It took me a few minutes to decipher what it said, but I was sure that was what it was. *Finished*. I peered more closely. It looked as though a page or two had been torn out of the diary. Yes, they definitely had. I ran my finger down the rough edge, deep in the folds of the book. What else had she written on those missing pages? And what had she done with them?

*10th November, 1970*

Well, it's been a few days, so I need to catch you up. Life in London is like a whirlwind of exciting things. Honestly, I'm hardly getting a minute to myself, which is why I haven't had a chance to write it all down. I've been to a couple more castings and I got both of them. Coco is very pleased. Everything is fine between us, now. She and Archie had a big row, and he put her straight on a few matters. He told me all about it afterwards.

'Coco and I have known each other for a long time,' he said, over dinner two nights ago, holding my hands between his. 'Old friends fall out. Especially when you add business into the mix.'

'I understand,' I said. I couldn't stop staring at his face, I wanted to never have to tear my eyes away.

'I knew you would,' he said, and he kissed my fingers. 'The thing is, it's not just friendship and work, with Coco.' He paused. I waited. I trusted him. 'She's always been . . . well, a bit in love with me, I suppose.'

He looked almost embarrassed to admit this, and his shyness only made me love him more. He is not an arrogant man. Of course he didn't want to go around shouting to everyone – to anyone, even to me – that Coco was in love with him. It might make him sound up himself, he would think. He was a thinker, Archie. Always looking at things from every angle.

'I can see that.'

He smiled. 'I thought so. You're very intuitive, aren't you? Very sensitive.'

He's right, I *am* extremely intuitive, I always have been. But I love that he can see that about me, that he just *knows* that. He knows me inside out, he always has done. Always will do. My Archie.

Anyhow, we talked it all over and he told me about the row. She was jealous, he said. She had got like this before – I assumed he meant when he had got a new girlfriend in the past but he was tactful enough not to say that – but never this badly, obviously because she could see that this was different, me and Archie, what we have. He would deal with her, he said, keep her under control, the important thing was that she and I didn't fall out, that I didn't let her get to me and spoil things for me. 'She has her moments, our Coco, but she's bloody good at what she does.'

I nodded, though my face must have shown something of what I was feeling, because he rubbed my chin with his finger and thumb and said, 'Hey, she's the one who found you and brought you to me, isn't she?'

I laughed then, I couldn't help it, and leaned across the table and kissed him, and he kissed me back for a minute and then he stopped and said, 'We mustn't, not here. I won't be able to control myself,' and I laughed again. 'So, you promise?' he said. 'You'll play nicely with her? Leave all the other stuff to me, and just concentrate on work?'

I promised him, of course. But we'll see. She'd better play nicely as well, otherwise she'll find out that Sadie isn't the walkover she might have thought.

I don't know why she still has her claws into Archie though, because it's not as though she's single and pining for a man; she's going out with Rupert, Archie says. I didn't much like him, but Archie says he's a good chap, so I'm sure he's all right. Maybe we'll end up on double dates, maybe even a double wedding???! Don't dare to hope, Sadie, don't dare to dream.

# Chapter Twenty-One

Something about the diary felt different. The second part. I read it again. It was touching, reading the outpourings of my mother as a teenager in love for the first time. Full of hope and excitement and the certainty that this was it, that Archie was The One. True love – or so she thought. *Had* what she felt for Archie Farrow been true love? Maybe. But what about what he felt for her? I was less sure.

Were Sadie's emotions the real thing? There was no reason why they shouldn't be. People did fall in love when they were young, after all. It wasn't all mooning over inappropriate men and snogging in the back seat of Ford Sierras. Some people married their first loves. What must that be like? But Sadie hadn't married Archie. And from the way she had written about the beginning of their affair I thought it unlikely that it would turn out to be she who ended it.

Something was missing. There were pages missing, for a start. *Finished*, she had written on one of them, and then crossed it out and torn it out and thrown it away, presumably. But it looked as though more than one page had been removed. I looked again at the words she had written – hurriedly, I thought, her pen flying over the pages in her rush to get them down. 'A woman in love,' she had called herself. But she had only been a girl.

Not that much older than Elfie, I thought later, as I wrestled to get the front door key into the lock without dropping the stack of files and marking that I was carrying under my arm. Was I doing the right thing even considering sending Elfie into that environment? How had Coco described it? As a factory, a meat market – something like that. I had been busier looking for evidence of Sadie than listening to what she said, but now it played on my mind. I swallowed the lump of guilt that threatened to choke me. I wasn't making Elfie do anything, she was desperate to be a model. *Remember her face when you suggested it*, I told myself. *It lit up. That was real*. And Elfie was a bright girl, she knew what she was doing, and she could look after herself. She had had to, being brought up by Maisie and Barney. I didn't have to worry about her. I didn't.

The key to our front door in Hamilton Road always stuck, and every time Mark and I came into the house together one of us would say, 'We must get that lock sorted out,' and then we'd forget about it until the next time. It was one of those jobs that always seemed to be someone else's responsibility. I bent down and picked up the post from the doormat, cursing the fact that I seemed to be the only one who ever did this, and hung my coat up on the hook next to the door. My shoulders released as soon as I had done so. I might moan about picking the post up, just like I moaned about the sticky lock, and the fact that whenever Mark emptied the bin he forgot to put a new liner in, and any number of other minor domestic irritations, but the truth of it was that it was precisely these things that made me know that I was home. The ritual of it soothed and reassured me, had become part of the pattern of my life.

I had not had the same security when I was growing up. A psychotherapist might draw a clear line between the two in confident black ink: *childhood marked by loneliness and lack of routine = a need for security and regular habits as an adult*. It was the same for Mark – far more so, for him. Whereas my home life as a child had been quiet and lonely, yes, his had been actively full of neglect. I had never once felt that Daddy didn't care about what happened to me or where I was, just that sometimes he wasn't really aware of where I was or what I was doing. His head was full of other things, of the practicalities of caring for a small girl alone, for one thing, and of his work, always of his work. And it was fine, I was self-sufficient and didn't need lots of looking after, or attention, and when we spent time together he was attentive and interesting and I was glad that he was my father.

But there were those days when I got home from school and let myself in and didn't know whether he would be there or not, and often it would turn out to be not, and I would make myself bread and jam for tea and curl up on the sofa under a blanket and wish that there was someone there to tell me to do my homework, and to make a snack for me; that I knew as I was walking along the street towards home that the lights would be on and there would be someone waiting for me. I could always go to Mrs Brown's, but her house was noisy and full of children, her own and those that she minded, and I would end up with a toddler stuffing honey-covered toast into my ear as I tried to watch TV, and being there among the chatter and chaos would remind me that I was different, and I would feel lonelier than before.

Sometimes on those days, the lonely days, I would talk to my mother. I had forgotten that I used to do that. I dumped my files on the side in the kitchen and went to flick the kettle on. I would turn the lights on in the kitchen, just as I was doing now, to make it feel warm and lived-in, and I would chatter away to her, about my day, about the things that had happened and the things I wished had happened, as though she were standing there, resting her chin in her hands, asking me questions. 'Yes, maths was fine, though I hate it and my teacher always picks on me' – I would adopt an injured tone for this bit – 'but sport was a disaster. I got made centre-forward in netball and you know I can only play defence,' as though this were a conversation we had had many times before. As though with words I could somehow conjure her into being.

The kettle was almost boiling. I stared into the cupboard and opened the freezer, wondering about dinner. I wanted to have it on by the time Elfie got in. She could walk in through the door and the lights would be on and there would be sounds coming from the kitchen as I worked and pottered, and something would smell nice, and even if she chose to go straight upstairs she would know that there was someone there, someone who cared enough to make her dinner and make sure that it had vegetables. And for Mark, too. Like I said, my childhood had been unusual, but his had been downright weird, and not in the benignly eccentric way that Maisie and Barney liked to portray. He didn't talk about it much, these days. But sometimes I saw the shadow of it in the way he talked to them, or about them, and it made me want to give him something better, now.

And now, for Elfie, as well. I wanted to create something different for her. She'd only been living with us for a few days, but I liked having her there, and I thought that I could do something to make her life easier, make it feel more settled. OK, she was hardly a small child, but she still needed something that she had not been getting at Gironde Road with Maisie and Barney. This was her home now, and the thought of making it a happy one for her was strangely exciting.

The thought also made me sad, however. That was what I

wanted to do for a child of my own. Elfie was Elfie. She was lovely, funny and good company and I was enjoying her. But she was someone else's daughter. I wanted my own. Or a son. But a baby, a child that was mine, for whom I could create a home, one in which they felt safe, knowing that I would always be there, me and Mark, whenever they needed us.

I know, I know. I don't need any amateur psychologists analysing my need to build a home and fill it with children, thanks very much. I know exactly where it comes from. But that doesn't make it any the less keen.

I poured myself a glass of wine now, and looked at the letter I held in my hand. I hadn't read Coco's handwriting before, as she had emailed me to arrange our first meeting, but somehow I knew that this was from her. It was confident, slanting, it had flair. I scoured it with my eyes to see if I could spot any similarities between this hand and the note that I had received with the key, but they looked different. It didn't seem to be Coco who had written the note to me. Though I supposed that if she had done she wouldn't have been so stupid as to write this envelope in the same handwriting. And I would have guessed, surely, when we had met, if she had been drawing me to her. She would have given something away, wouldn't she? Or maybe not. But I felt it in my gut that Coco Delaney was not N.R.

Elfie Oliver, and then our address, the envelope read. I held it up to the light but it gave nothing away. Really, it was a bit off that she'd written directly to Elfie, and not to me, or at least not to me as well. I was Elfie's guardian, as far as Coco was concerned. Starting up a private correspondence with a starstruck teenage girl was hardly appropriate, was it? Actually, the more I thought about it, the more I decided it was downright irresponsible. And that it would be irresponsible of me in turn to simply let Elfie open the letter herself. I needed to know what was going on – what, if anything, was being proposed by Coco.

*Elfie will tell you*, a voice said inside my head. *You should trust her to tell you.* Yes, she probably would. But this wasn't just about Elfie. It was about Coco. It was typical of the woman – she obviously hadn't changed at all since the old days. Keeping Sadie from Archie, keeping him all to herself despite the fact that she had a boyfriend already . . . trying to push me out of the equation with Elfie, probably trying to influence her in some way . . . it all added up to a picture of the same sort of someone who wanted to keep everything under her own control, to be the Queen Bee, sitting proudly at the centre of the hive. Well, she wouldn't manage it with me. I was my mother's daughter, I was beginning to realise. I would deal with her, just as Sadie had. Better.

And so as I heard Elfie's key stick in the lock and then give, knowing that what I was doing was wrong but telling myself that I had been given no choice, and that what would result would make it all right, I slipped the letter into the file that held my marking and put the whole lot away in my bag.

# Chapter Twenty-Two

*Dear Elfie,*

*I have made some enquiries of a couple of friends, who agree with me that you could certainly have some success modelling if you decide that is what you wish to do. I would suggest that the following is the best course of action.*

*1) You take some time to think about whether this is definitely the road you want to go down. Modelling is not easy – it will take a lot of your time and energy, and I would not blame you if you felt you would rather spend that time and energy on other things. Indeed, you might be better advised to do so – study hard, go to the cinema with friends, kiss boys, that sort of thing.*

*2) If you are sure this is for you, then ring me, or write, or whatever you prefer. I will arrange for you to have some professional photographs taken. Nothing complicated, just some simple headshots. They need not be expensive, indeed, they should not be, but you will have to pay for them. Presumably this will not be a problem, but I suggest that you talk it over with your aunt to make sure.*

*3) When we have these, I can use them to introduce*

*you to some friends and contacts who could help you further. I would offer to manage you myself, and if it were twenty years ago I might have done so, but I fear that these days I would not be your best representative in a world that has moved on beyond the one I once knew so well. I will, should we get to the stage of you being offered representation by someone to whom I have introduced you, discuss the issue of a finder's fee with them, and with your aunt. But there is no need for you to worry about that for now.*

*So, lovely Elfie, take your time, and let me know when you have made a decision. There is no rush. Modelling will be here for a long time, and time is something you have plenty of – you are so very young.*

*With best regards,*

*Coco Delaney*

I read the letter three times, each time bristling at being referred to as 'your aunt'. As though I were no one, of no importance to Coco other than in relation to Elfie. I was her sister-in-law, not her aunt; had she not paid attention to what I told her? Did I look so old, so matronly, in comparison to Elfie's fresh-faced youth? Probably, yes. Or was it an intentional slight? And 'lovely Elfie' – who did this woman think she was? She was talking to her as though they were old friends, intimate confidants. I was beginning to regret the path I had chosen and the way that I had decided to make contact with Coco Delaney. But I had to stick with it. And at least I had time. She was not expecting to hear from Elfie immediately, or from myself, presumably, so I could wait a while and decide what to do. I was tempted to simply get rid of the letter and pretend that it had never arrived, tell Elfie that Coco must have changed her mind and let the whole thing fade into the background. But that would not help me, and now that I had started this whole thing off, I didn't feel as though I could just abandon it. I could email Coco as though from Elfie . . . No. That way madness lay. Madness and trouble. I had learned that much, at least.

I folded the letter up and returned it to its envelope before putting it back in my file, swapping it for a pile of marking that I began to plough my way through instead. *Good point* I wrote, over and over again; *try to go deeper with your argument. Why? Expand on this . . . Be more concise . . . Too many points in this paragraph, separate them out.* And so on. Stock phrases that I scribbled almost without thinking, because my mind was not in my study with my students' work, it was not on the differences between the representation of men and women in French cinema, or how the First World War had influenced and inspired directors, or on the symbolism of mobile phones in American blockbuster films from 1990 to the present day (niche). It was on Sadie, and Coco Delaney, and everything that I had read and discovered in the last few days, and everything that I was yet to discover, whatever that might be. It was in the 1970s, in London and St Albans and in modelling studios and tatty boarding houses. And most of all, at that moment, it was on Archie Farrow.

'Klar?' The door opened.

Over and over again I had typed names, places, my fingers hitting the keys ever more furiously. I had come up with nothing, nothing of any use. A few mentions of him, but nothing substantial. No obvious revelations, no explanations. Still, I had printed everything that I had found, and it lay in a slim sheaf in the printer tray next to me.

As Mark opened the door I shut down the Internet browser

and looked up at him. 'Sorry. Got caught up in my marking.'

I waved my hand at the pile of essays that I had left next to my elbow.

He shrugged, and perched on the edge of my desk. I tried not to look as though I wanted him to leave.

'Anything good?' he asked.

'What?' Panic, panic. What did he know, what did he mean?

'Your marking. Anything good?'

'Oh.' *Get a grip, Klara.* 'Average, I'd say. Bit early to tell.' I wanted to pick up the print-outs and hide them away safely, but I didn't want to draw attention to them.

'So. Thai or Indian? I'm afraid Elfie and I ate all the spag bol.'

'Oh – you choose. Sorry. I had good intentions.'

He stood up and smiled. 'It doesn't matter, darling. I'll get you something.' His car keys were already in his hand. 'Any requests?'

'Pad Thai?'

'Finish up. See you in a bit.'

If only he wouldn't be so reasonable. So considerate. I'd feel much better about the whole thing if he were a bit grumpier about his inattentive wife. I almost wished for something to rail against.

I reckoned I had half an hour. I grabbed the pile of print-outs and began to read.

Archie's Wikipedia entry was frustratingly brief.

*Archie Farrow, founder of Velvet Models, born 1st June 1932, died 3rd June 1985. Previously Farrow had been a financier, and had worked abroad before returning to London to start his agency in the late*

*1960s. Velvet Models was dissolved in 1974. See also business partners Coco Delaney and Rupert James.*

Coco and Rupert's two-line biographies gave no more information than I knew already. Actually, that wasn't true, since I now had Rupert's surname. Not that I thought it would do me much good. A money man and Coco's boyfriend. What useful role could he have played in Sadie's story?

*Archie Farrow, founder of Velvet Models, said: 'She was a beautiful woman and an inspiring one. I feel privileged to have worked with her.'*

That was a quote about some actress who had died in 1969 and who had apparently been represented by Velvet for a while.

There were a couple of mentions of Archie in relation to Coco.

*Coco Delaney, who worked with the disgraced Archie Farrow for a number of years . . .*

*The disgraced Archie Farrow.* That was interesting. Why had he been disgraced? I looked at the print-out. It was from a blog site about the Seventies; the entry was about forgotten models of the era, and Coco was one of the main focuses of the piece. A series of photos of her, both posed and candid, aimed to remind readers that she could have been 'as big a star as Twiggy', had things gone better for her. I went back to the site, and scoured it again, but there were no more mentions of Archie. *Disgraced.* I filed the word away for entry in my dossier.

And that was it. It was a thin selection. My sympathy with

the student who had expressed such dismay at the lack of Internet during my own student years had increased a hundred times over. What I would give now for the web to have been invented a few decades earlier, for Archie Farrow and Coco Delaney and Sadie to have left the same digital trail that people of our generation would leave. What a strange thought. Had the Internet been around then, I would be overwhelmed with information; my problem would be how to work my way through it, not how to winkle out some tiny scraps. I would be combing through Facebook pages and Twitter accounts and CVs on LinkedIn, they'd all have had their own websites and there would be hundreds of photos of them on Flickr and Instagram, scattered around the Internet. I couldn't stop thinking about it. Snapshots taken with mobile phones turned towards themselves, recording every moment of their relationship. *Me and Archie – so in love!* the caption might say. Sadie would have had no need for a diary, she'd have had a blog or just tweeted her thoughts to the world. Building her brand. I wanted to scour the Internet to see what you might be able to tell about *me*, Klara Mortimer from the trail I had left, what picture you could build up. It wouldn't be too much, not as bad as some – I didn't tweet and I wasn't a big photo-taker, and I had no time or desire to blog about any aspect of my not very interesting life, but there was probably enough to form a fuller dossier on me than I would like, if you were so inclined. The thought made me shiver.

Mark's feet stamped on the doormat and the bags of takeaway rustled as he and Elfie returned.

'Come on, you! All work and no play . . .' he called up the stairs. I slid the print-outs into the file, along with Coco's letter, and went downstairs feeling fidgety and frustrated. I had got no further forward, and all I was doing was neglecting my husband and sister-in-law, as well as my work, in the process.

I tried not to seem distracted while I ate, but I couldn't concentrate on the conversation Mark was having with his sister about the ethics of treating a mentally ill patient. However, I heard enough of it to think how intelligent she was, how bright a future she could have if she got over the hurdles of her parents' distrust of ambition, as Mark had done. She could do anything she set her mind to, really.

'Eat up,' Mark said.

I smiled at him. 'Sorry. Not that hungry.'

'Stop thinking about work. You have to leave it there,' he admonished gently. 'They get enough out of you as it is.'

I nodded. 'I know. Hard to switch off sometimes, you know.'

'I do.'

'Sorry. It's harder to leave patients behind than students, I know.'

And then he squeezed my knee, and got up and refilled my glass of wine, and the memory of his touch and every drop that I drank drove the stake of guilt further into my heart. I did not deserve this. I did not deserve his love, did not deserve any of it.

I went to bed soon after I had eaten, pleading a headache, and turned the light out straightaway and tried to force myself to sleep. I was punishing myself, sending myself to bed early without my pudding, the sweet treat of Sadie's diary that I was getting hooked on.

In the end I got up again, after a couple of hours, and went back downstairs and necked another large glass of wine, furtively, without Mark noticing. He was dozing on the sofa. I hoped that it would knock me out.

'Wake up, sleepyhead.' I nudged his leg with my own and watched as he came to.

'Guhurgh.'

'Come on. Bed.'

He shut his eyes again.

'I'll leave you there, and you'll wake up in the middle of the night and be cold and feel grim,' I warned, and he grinned and held his hands out to me to be pulled up from where he sat, like a child, and we padded upstairs together, hand-in-hand, me leading him, his fingers hot in mine, and for a moment I forgot all about Sadie and her diary and everything inside it. Right now, it was just him and me, and that was all that I needed once more.

And then, around four o'clock in the morning, I woke up with a dry-mouthed start. And it came to me. Archie's death date. The third of June, 1985. The third of June. The date on which, I had worked out from my own diaries, Daddy was always away. What did it mean? Why would my father avoid being at home on the anniversary of Archie's death, a date which surely meant little to him? There was somewhere I had not yet looked. *The other boxes.* I had been so quick to search through them that I hadn't looked properly at their contents, and when I had found the diary I had shoved them to one side. But there had been some files in there, folders full of what seemed to be magazine cuttings. Could there be something else as well? I lay absolutely still, trying not to let my breathing change – sometimes even that shift was enough to wake Mark up – knowing that I could not do the one thing I was desperate to do – to get up and go and rifle through them, right this minute. It would have to wait until morning – and so would I.

# Chapter Twenty-Three

*1970*, the file said, in black handwriting on the outside. It was one of a few inside the box, some fuller than others, some labelled by date – 1970, 1974, 1971. But the first was the fullest and looked as though it would contain the most bounty. I had brought them all to work, stashing them in the battered old satchel that I used to carry all my paperwork around in. I'd had it since school. Mark was always trying to buy me a new, smarter bag, but I resisted. I loved the rough patches on the leather, the faded and ink-stained lining. It reminded me that life could be as simple as the difference between an A and a B for your essay.

My office. It was tiny, no more than a cubby-hole, really. More ambitious lecturers would have – and had – baulked at being put in here. But Film Studies was not a prestigious course, the office was near the archives and the rooms where I taught, and its out-of-the-way location suited me. I had never had any desire to take part in the corner office game that academics played just as keenly as Manhattan lawyers – more so, maybe. At least the lawyers were honest about their desire for obvious signs of their status, whereas my colleagues couched their requests in reasonable-sounding explanations and excuses. '*I really am running out of space for my books*,' they'd say. '*If I had the space to hold tutorials in my office, it would free up room 2B for Mrs Hampshire's class.*' All so calm, all so library quiet, all the while jockeying for position. But here, I was not disturbed, whether holding a study session with a student or simply getting on with my work over lunch. Or, as I was doing now, opening the document on my laptop called 'ST' and preparing to list the contents of the battered folders.

The fattest was from 1970. I set that aside for a moment, prolonging the anticipation. Some of the others were unlabelled. One contained nothing save for a tube ticket from Kings Cross to Oxford Street. I checked the date. It was from May, 1970. The day she had first arrived in London?

The folder labelled 1971 was quite full – here were adverts for fashion brands, some appearances in gossip columns, a few head shots. By the back of the folder, though, and the end of the year, presumably, the jobs had started to thin out and become less prestigious.

By 1972 and 1973 there were one or two images only – one for a small chain of chemists, one for a local authority brochure. It seemed that Sadie's career had been short-lived and less illustrious than I had imagined. Or been led to believe? Daddy had always let me think she had been successful, working throughout my early childhood; after all. All those work trips she was supposed to have taken . . . But the contents of these files told a different story.

I put the others to one side, and opened, the folder labelled 1970.

To be suddenly confronted by so many images of my mother all at once was more shocking than I had anticipated, and I had to put the pile down on my desk and fix my gaze on the memo board for a moment in order to gather myself, before picking them up again. There she was, the woman whose ghost I was chasing through the past – her past and my own – staring out at me in a variety of poses. Younger than I had ever seen her – of course, she would have been just 18 in 1970. She had just arrived in London and clearly Archie Farrow and Coco Delaney had been doing something right in the management of her career, because the photos from that year were good ones, for campaigns that must have been prominent at the time.

An advert for face cream showed her touching a perfect meringue blob of lotion to a perfect cheek, the tag line proclaiming that *Skin this soft only happens with Only*. A gin company had her dolled up as though at a cocktail party, Martini glass in hand, her eyes twinkling at the camera, the perfect advertisement for a good time. She gazed lovingly into the eyes of a fake fiancé to sell engagement rings, she supervised a rainbow-jumpered and dungareed child as he stirred pancake batter, she posed with cigarettes, fruit, tampons and with new-fangled kitchen aids, she ran through daisy-filled meadows and frolicked on beaches and strode across London streets. It was as though she had hundreds of different lives, that she walked in and out of as she pleased, changing her appearance and demeanour as it suited for each.

In all of the images she looked different: she was flicky-haired, smooth-haired, had hair tied back into a pony tail, piled up into a chignon. Red-lipped, frosted-lipped, natural-lipped. Smiling, laughing, gazing, eyes closed, eyes open, eyes letting a single tear fall. Her face seemed elastic, changing completely with each new expression, and if you put some of the images side by side you could only just see that it was the same woman in both.

It didn't make any sense to me. How she could be so much one person, or seem to be, in one image. The personification of calm motherhood, cradling a tiny baby wrapped in a fluffy white towel to her breast, glowing and blushing and perfect. And then, in another, a party girl on roller skates, carefree, grabbing onto the hands of her friends, looking ten years younger and ten times *less* serene. Someone completely different. I realised something that day, looking at those pictures. I realised that the little I thought I knew about her might not be true at all.

Because while I'd known all along that my mother had been a model, what I hadn't known was just how much acting was involved.

I began to type a list of the cuttings. *Kitchen appliance advertisement, date unknown.* But the words became fuzzy and wavered in front of me and I had to close my eyes to regain my balance. When my eyes were closed I could shut out the world. I could almost shut out the guilt I felt but could not quite pin down. It followed me like a wisp of smoke, invisible and yet utterly present.

1970. The year Sadie moved to London in search of fame and excitement and adventure. The year she signed up with Velvet Models and kissed Archie Farrow in King's Court. The year she had been polished and buffed, transformed from a St Alban's schoolgirl into the glossy, slick model turning all sorts of poses. I thumbed through the pile once more, and as I did so, the reason for my guilty feelings stared back at me.

It was not guilt at the secret I was keeping from Mark, though no doubt it should have been. I'd never been very good at feeling the things I was meant to feel. Nor was it guilt at the steps I was taking and the questions I was asking behind my father's back – though again, I probably should have felt at least some discomfort about that.

Finally, I placed the feeling: I felt as if I was trespassing.

* * *

It wasn't just modelling cuttings that the file contained. At the back of the folder, tucked into an envelope, was a smaller stash of cuttings. They weren't from the same year as the rest of the material. These were from much later. And they were carefully kept – neatly cut out, slid into the envelope, with a piece of card behind them, to make sure the envelope didn't get crumpled and its cargo damaged, presumably.

And they were about Archie Farrow.

*'Archibald McAllister Farrow, b Jan 1st 1932, d June 3rd 1985. Archibald "Archie" Farrow was the co-founder and co-owner of Velvet Models, a small but briefly successful modelling agency active in the early Seventies, until his death. Velvet Models notably launched the career of Mimi Lane, but although Farrow's partner Coco Delaney attempted to continue the business following his death, the company went bankrupt and was dissolved in 1974. Farrow was a well-known figure in London society during his heyday and counted fellow socialites such as Hugh Rathbone and Lady Violet Montague as his friends. Following his arrest in 1976 for tax evasion and on fraud charges, however, he mostly disappeared from view. Rumours of drug addiction and financial problems dogged him for the remainder of his life. He died in a house fire caused by a cigarette.'*

The cutting was from a magazine, rather than a newspaper, since it was printed on slightly thicker paper. Whoever had cut the paragraph out had not been interested in anything that surrounded it. I turned the paper over, but its reverse provided no clue either. It was simply a portion of an advert, a black and white photograph, but it was small and badly printed and impossible to tell what the image was of or what it was attempting to sell. I laid it carefully down on the desk in front of me.

Reading about Archie gave me no clues as to what the link between the date he died and my father's absences might be, but it sparked something off inside me. It all felt much more real now. I was no longer just reading the musings of a teenage girl – these were real people whose pasts I was shuffling around in. Or, in the case of Archie and Sadie, they had once been real people, with families and secrets and hopes and dreams. My mother. Her friends, her lovers, her past. My father, too. I hadn't yet come across him in the diary – she wouldn't have met him yet – but I would, soon. I would read about how they met, about how she felt about him, what her first impressions of him had been. My father said it had been love at first sight when they met at a Christmas party. I would find out.

At first, the whole thing had felt vague, like a treasure hunt. Disconnected from my life and that of my mother. A near anonymous note, a key to a lock-up garage . . . it was the stuff of storybooks. Now though, now it was real, now it was important, and urgent and I had to know. I had to know what had happened with Sadie and Archie and Coco, how it had all played out and how they had ended up where they had – two dead, one alive and seemingly thriving. How had Coco come out on top while Archie's life had ended in a house fire? Thus far, I had tiptoed around Coco, worried that she might find out who I was and why I had really written to her, but I didn't care any longer. I needed to know.

Archie had died in 1985. Sadie had left home – had left *me* – in the same year. Was it coincidence? Or was his death linked to Sadie leaving? It seemed both likely and unlikely at the same time. It wasn't as though Archie had disappeared; if that had been the case, I might have wondered whether she and he had run off together. But he had died – in a house fire caused by a cigarette, so that article said. Might he not have died at all? But no, things like that didn't happen in real life. Archie was long dead and buried. But the date, the date could not just be meaningless: if I was learning anything, it was that everything meant something. Everything was a potential clue.

And she had cut the out article and kept it. Grief-stricken, I imagined. The loss must have hit her hard, despite the fact that by that time she was married – I almost said happily married, but caught myself, because how happy can it really have been? Not happy enough to stay, after all. Even married with a child, hearing about Archie's death must have been devastating. I wonder how she had found out. Had they been in touch? Had someone told her – Coco, maybe? Or, worst of all, had she read about it, as I had done – had the very words I had just read been the ones that had told her of his death? Had she sat somewhere, in our house even, curled up on her bed, reading about how he had died, disgraced and alone? The thought of it made me wince, and try to imagine how I would feel, if I found out that someone I had loved like that had died. It would break a part of me, I think. And maybe that's what had happened to Sadie. Maybe his death had broken something in her. Maybe that's what had made her leave me.

I didn't know. But I knew that I couldn't rest until I did.

# Chapter Twenty-Four

Mark had a late surgery that night, and I knew that afterwards he'd stay on to catch up with paperwork, so I made Elfie and I a quick supper from what I could find in the fridge, which turned out to be a sort of Spanish omlette, and parked her in front of a couple of rom-coms that I'd rented, and disappeared off to my study. 'I'll just be upstairs if you need me,' I told her, and she smiled, all curled up like a cat on the sofa.

'I'm fine,' she said, and, of course she was fine; she was a teenager, for goodness sake, not a baby that needed watching constantly, but still I felt a spike of guilt. She was here so that she could have more attention, more normality, not less. I should have been budging her up on the sofa and sitting with her, making popcorn and giggling over the boys in the films, letting her choose which one we watched first and saying she could stay up past her bedtime. I should be making a better job of this.

But the diary called me. Sadie and her stories called me. My mother was weaving her spell.

Sadie had not been a diligent, once-a-day-without-fail sort of a diary-keeper. She only wrote in it when she had something to say, something to report. If someone really had been using the entries to form the basis of a book about her life, as she had hoped and dreamed, then they would have been sorely disappointed, for this was no carefully kept record of her daily routine. I had read plenty of volumes of diaries of the great and the good, and the minutiae of what people ate for dinner and saw at the cinema and who they bumped into or rang up for some inconsequential reason was as fascinating as the big set pieces, sometimes more so. You couldn't always know what would appeal or be interesting decades later until time had passed and the players in your story had become famous, or infamous, had lived longer or died sooner. Sadie had had no understanding of that. How could she have been expected to, really? She was young, and in love, and in London.

I lay in bed reading for hours that night, absorbing her account of how she and Archie became closer as though I was making it part of myself. In a way I was. It was as though I were taking Communion, almost – what a strange thing to say, I know. It had that sense to it though. *This is My body, this is My blood. Do this in memory of Me.* Oh, I wasn't experiencing an hysterical vision in which Sadie had become some kind of religious icon, don't worry, but reading the diary continued to bring her to life, summoning her into being in a way that I had never known and could not have anticipated, and her voice swirled around me like droplets of perfume suspended in the air and I breathed them in.

She wrote of dates with Archie where he took her to smart restaurants and to the theatre. He opened up London to her, it seemed, showing her a world that she had known existed but of which she had only ever dreamed of being a part. He took her to Harrods and bought her her first proper handbag, a red leather one with a long strap and a gold zip that she described in breathless detail as being *so much better quality than most, you can tell it's Italian.* He took her away for the weekend, to a country-house hotel where they signed in as Mr and Mrs Smith and made love thirteen times in thirty-six hours. He introduced her to the joys of oysters, opera, oral sex and Opium, the scent that she would wear from that moment on (*he took me to a wonderful department store called Liberty's to choose it, and the assistant selected it especially for me, she wrote, she told me all about the base notes and the top notes and all sorts of other things, but all I know is that as soon as I put it on I smelled me and Archie and sex and love and I knew it was the one for me*). And as I read, I realised how much of Archie Farrow had remained with my mother long after he had faded out of her life. The scent she wore and which I remembered her spraying on herself when I was tiny, that I used to close my eyes and breathe in and that I thought all beautiful women smelled of – that had been Archie's scent. Did she think of him every time she put it on, even all those years later? The thought was an unsettling one.

There were letters from Suzanne mentioned in the diaries, alluding to her and Trevor getting married. Sadie sounded pleased for them, but at a distance. It wasn't her life any more, they were from another part of her story, one that she had left behind. But still she cared enough to note it down. Was this just for show, for the readers who she imagined would one day be reading her diary, looking for evidence of the delightful, the beautiful Sadie? Or because she had not quite left that part of her life behind as fully as she made out, had not completely forgotten how important her old friend had been to her. *I'm so happy for Suzanne*, she wrote, *though of course I can't understand her choices, not really. We had so much in front of us, both of us, and she's chosen not to follow it. To stay there. But she must be happy! She's in love, and that's enough for her, and so I am happy for her.* The wedding came and went, without Sadie's presence: *Of course I couldn't go, such a shame, was working my socks off, but I sent them a lovely present, an antique Samovar set with all the little glasses, it's beautiful, she'll love it* – and the image made me smile, because I couldn't think of anything less fitting for the woman I had glimpsed in St Albans than an antique Samovar set. Whatever would she have done with such a thing, other than stare at it and wonder about the life her friend must be leading, so far removed from her own?

And then the mentions got briefer, and sadder. *Terrible for Suzanne and Trevor, so much hope, but another loss. I sent her some flowers, yellow ones for the spring, and got them to put a card in, but she hasn't replied. She must be grieving too much.* She never said what the losses were but I could guess well enough, and I could guess at how Suzanne felt about her oldest and supposedly closest friend sending an impersonal card written by a florist along with some flowers. Maybe that explained her reaction when I had visited, although it had seemed more violent than for that.

Coco appeared in the tales of Sadie and Archie's blossoming relationship too, naturally. Sadie's wariness of Coco seemed to have softened, and she wrote of evenings spent at parties, she and Archie, Coco and Rupert, though she never seemed to regain the trust in her that had been there when she had first moved to London. Coco and Rupert split up, though from what Sadie said, it didn't seem to cause much disruption or even change things: *We went out for dinner last night, the four of us, and Coco and Rupert went home together again. I wonder if he knows she's seeing two other men? I'm obviously not going to be the one to tell him, though someone will eventually, and then what will she do?*

She sounded as though she almost relished the thought of Coco having to deal with a tricky situation. There was a new sense of distance in the way she wrote about her scout and early mentor. *Coco was there, of course,* she would drop in now and then, or, *Coco and I went shopping while Archie and Rupert discussed the company, though I could tell Coco was furious not to be involved in the meeting*, and I could imagine her pleasure at Coco's apparent struggle to remain involved in the running of Velvet Models and not be relegated to babysitter status, as Archie appeared determined to do. Secretly, I wondered whether this had really been the case. I had met Coco, after all, and seen the steel in her eyes, and I suspected that she would not be easily shoved out of a company that she had helped to build, by Archie Farrow or by anyone else. Was Sadie missing something? It would hardly be surprising if she were, since all the events that she wrote about were viewed through the haze of a young girl in love, not one keeping a sharp eye on the machinations of men and women who were, after all, much older than her. She was playing with the grown-ups now, and I wasn't at all sure that she had been as able to keep up as she had believed.

And then, of course, there was Sadie's work. Modelling jobs seemed to be coming in thick and fast. She took this for granted, I thought; the sense of thrilled disbelief that had emanated from her when Coco had first approached her, had been transferred to her relationship with Archie, and her attitude to her career as a model seemed – a little entitled, actually, if I am honest. *Of course I got the gin campaign*, she threw in casually. *Archie was pleased and rather relieved, I think, as it's worth quite a bit of money and no one else seems to be doing that well at the moment.* Or, *Another job for Pablo in the morning. This one is shooting in the Michelin Building which should be fun, though I'm not sure about the frocks he wants me to wear. I might have to put my foot down about one or two of them.* This smacked of diva-ish tendencies that I couldn't imagine Coco tolerating.

Still, she was pulling the jobs in, and making enough

money to have moved out of the shabby boarding house she had been in when she first moved to London and into a whole flat of her own off the King's Road, near enough to Archie to just about satisfy her, though I got the feeling that nothing less than actually moving in with him would have made her truly happy about her accommodation. *He needs his space, of course he does, he's a man, and I know men have their ways and their needs, but I can't help thinking that he'd be much happier with someone to take care of him a little more,* she wrote in one entry shortly before she moved, and then: *Archie found me the flat, and took me to view it as a surprise, and it really* was *a wonderful surprise. I'm so grateful to him, for taking the time to help me, and it really is lovely – everything I might have wanted. I've decided that it is best this way. I came to London so that I could be independent, and I'm doing it, I'm doing everything I said I would, so THERE, St Albans and everyone in it.* And I could have wept for her as I imagined the disappointment that she must have concealed when she realised that the surprise was not the key to his own flat that she had so obviously been hoping for, but a place of her own with a lease of months and months that she would have to get through before things might conceivably change.

But the sympathy that I felt for Sadie then was nothing compared to my feelings when I read about her first Christmas spent in London, and the party she attended at Rupert, Coco's boyfriend's apartment. I had that creeping sense of familiarity when she first mentioned it:

I'm writing quickly to say that we're going to a party tomorrow night, me and Archie, and I can't decide what to wear, the red Gucci or the black YSL. I'm definitely wearing the silver sandals Archie bought me. I love them. They're the most beautiful things I've ever seen. Honestly, they're more like a work of art than a pair of shoes. Anyhow. The red is more festive, obviously, but the black shows off my shoulders and Archie's always saying how elegant they are. And it's going to be a very elegant party, at Rupert's house. Everyone's going to be there, and Rupert really doesn't ever do things by halves.

I can't wait to see his place. I've never been there but Archie says it's quite something, and he's not that easily impressed. Anyhow, that's not really why I'm writing. I just wanted to record how I feel and remind myself to write about the party afterwards. It's my first Christmas in London and I can't wait. No more dull Christmases in St Albans going to Mass and then sitting around pretending to be happy about the Queen's speech with my parents. No more awful dried-out turkey. Archie and I are going to go OUT for Christmas dinner, just the two of us, and then we're going to walk home through London and do presents in the evening.

I've been saving up for ages for his. I don't even want to say what it is in here in case it spoils the surprise, isn't that silly? OK, I'll say – it's a watch, a really old one from an antique place in one of the arcades off Piccadilly. It's called a Jaeger LeCoultre, and it's got a rectangular face that flips around, so you can sort of shut it. It's terribly sophisticated and was terribly expensive. It cost me all the money I earned from the last five jobs I did and a bit more, and I've been eating cereal all month because of it, but I don't care, of course I don't. Archie's worth it. I can't wait to see what he'll give me.

* * *

A party at Rupert's house, a Christmas party . . . I held my breath. Shut my eyes for a moment, before I allowed myself to open them and read on. Because this was what I had been waiting for, waiting and hoping for. This was where Sadie's words were going to overlap with what I already knew.

It had been at Rupert's Christmas party that my parents had met and fallen in love. The story was one of the few that Daddy had told me. It had been part of my armoury of tales about my mother, part of the suitcase full of images that I carried around with me and peeked into when I needed to remind myself that she had been a real person, that she had existed.

*We met at a party. It was Christmas*, his story began. And every time I heard those words I shivered with excitement, knowing what was coming, knowing every word he was about to say off by heart. I closed my eyes, and remembered the story he had told me so many times, when I was growing up, that I had held close to me like a talisman. I knew it off by heart. I let my father's words return to me one more time.

'We met at a party. It was Christmas,' Daddy would say. 'Everyone was having parties. I hadn't wanted to go to this one. I was tired and grumpy. I'd been working hard and I'd been to a few too many parties already.' *(A smile, a wink that the seven-year-old me didn't understand but returned nonetheless.)* 'But something made me drag myself out of my armchair at home – the very one that still sits downstairs' *(this always thrilled me)* 'and have a shower and put on a clean shirt.

'The party was being held by the friend of a friend; we'd met a couple of times but I didn't know them well. But some other people I knew and liked were going, so I bought a bottle of wine to take with me, and didn't plan to stay for long. It was being held in this chap's flat, a very grand place in a smart bit of London ...' (*'Where?' I would always ask at this point. 'Where was it?'*) 'Oh, near Hyde Park – you could see the park from his window even.' (*'Terribly exclusive,' he would joke. 'Far too posh for the likes of me.'*)

'Anyhow, I got there, and straight away I realised that this wasn't the sort of party I was used to. Everyone there was glamorous, and dressed up, and there were waiters serving cocktails on silver trays' (*this detail made me shiver with excitement. Imagine!)* 'and canapés. I was just a teacher. I was used to going to the sorts of parties where people sat around talking about a clever chap called Kierkegaard and drinking cheap red wine, where you might get a block of cheese to eat if you were lucky' (*I would nod at this part, as though I understood well the subtle social differences between the two types of gathering, and I suppose, in a way, I did – enough to know that I wanted to attend the former party far more than the latter, at least.*) 'There was a huge Christmas tree, and candles everywhere, and I was worried that I'd knock them over and start a fire, or do something clumsy and embarrass myself and the friend who had invited me, so I found a spot near the window and positioned myself there.' (*This was true, my father was hideously clumsy. I had spent my childhood warding off attacks from bollards and roller blinds and other inanimate objects.*)

'The chap whose party it was, Rupert, came over and chatted to me for a while, and then he got dragged away to dance by his girlfriend. He waved at me as he went, and then he was gone, and the room was noisy and drunken and I was out of place. And I was just about to leave, thinking that I still had time to catch the news on the radio, when *she* appeared next to me.'

'"You look like I feel," she said. "You're just trying to

work out whether it's too early to make a discreet exit, and whether everyone's drunk enough yet not to notice. You just want to go home and get into bed with a brandy? A cup of cocoa? I like them both together. You're bored of Christmas already and there's another week to go before it's even here."

'I smiled. It was as though she had lifted up the lid of my brain and scooped out my thoughts from inside it before presenting them to me.' *(As a child, I would wrinkle my nose up when he said this. Yuk.)* 'And as I turned my face towards hers it was as though the whole world changed, in a way that no one else but us noticed. Everything was the same, and yet everything was different. I was the same person I had been a few moments ago, wearing the same clothes, with the same slightly scruffy haircut and the same awkward way of holding my glass as if it was a hammer, but nothing was as it had been. We both felt it. She reached out her hand, and I took it. I felt as though I was dreaming.

' "I'm Sadie," she said. "Come on. Come with me."

'She didn't wait for me to tell her my name, just led me through the room by the hand.

' "I'm Henry," I said, in a fluster, as I tried to find somewhere to put my glass as we went, "Henry Mortimer."

' "I know," she replied, and I blinked. We had reached the little kitchen at the back of the apartment. She turned to me, smiling. She must have read the confusion on my face. "Rupert told me your name," she explained. "I asked him who you were. You looked more interesting than anyone else here. Come *along*."

'She pushed me gently through the door at the back of the kitchen, past a waiter who was reloading his tray, and then we were outside on the fire escape, and the dark and the cold hit me in the face and made me gasp. She just laughed, and took a huge gulp of air, saying, "Isn't it wonderful? It's like stepping into a secret world."

'And then she was on the move again, pulling me up the spiral metal staircase, laughing when her shoes got stuck in the rungs and she pulled them off, and we climbed higher and higher until we were on top of the building and on top of the world itself.

'We sat there for hours. I sneaked back downstairs for blankets and a bottle of wine and we wrapped ourselves up and stared down at the partygoers as they stumbled down the street, at the lights, and the shadows of the trees in the park beyond. We talked about everything you can think of. About her life, and mine, and what we wanted from the future; what we were scared of and what we loved and what we thought about politics and art and people who were rude to waiters and what we would rescue from our flats if they were burning down. I told her things I have never told a single soul before or since. And then, in the dead of the night, when the band downstairs had stopped playing and our fingers and lips had turned blue and we knew we were going to have to go inside or freeze, she worked her fingers between mine so that they were interlaced, and then turned her face to mine and kissed me. And I knew that I had met Her. The person who would change everything. Make everything OK. And I was right.'

The story thrilled me, every time. How could it not? It was a tale of love at first sight, of two people brought together by fate, at a glamorous party. It had fairy lights and music and dancing and adventure. Everything little girls dreamed of. And it was about my mother and father. But also, more than that, it had reassured me. Made me feel as though the world were a safer, better place. Because true love did exist, and it did happen to ordinary people. Like my father. Like me. And

I had believed in that. Relied on it. When I met Mark I had counted on it. He had fallen in love with me, and I had told myself that it was real, and true, and that I could count on it. And as I had counted on it so it had become truer, and more real. I had willed it into existence, within myself, and I had fallen in love with him, as well.

In a way, my father's story was the reason why Mark and I were together, why I had allowed myself to believe that he could love me. It was more than the story of how my parents had met, it was the story that enabled me to believe in possibility.

I could not wait to read Sadie's version.

# Chapter Twenty-Five

What a night. What a strange, magical, unsettling night. And what a party. We didn't get there until nine, though the invitation said seven. Archie said no one would be there then and he was right; it was obvious when we arrived that seven really meant nine, because everyone was getting there around then as well. Oh, there were a few people who had been there for hours, embarrassingly, but they weren't our lot at all, just some friends of an old schoolfriend of Rupert's that he'd obviously felt he had to invite. He is good at things like that, Rupert, I'll say that for him – he knows how to behave. I suppose going to a school like Eton teaches you proper manners, or maybe it's just the sort of family he comes from, the sort where you just know how everything works without having to be taught at all. If I have sons I'd like them to go to that sort of school, Eton or Harrow, one that will mean all those doors are opened to them and they never have to wonder whether they're going to say or do the wrong thing.

Anyhow, my goodness, but Rupert's flat is spectacular. You can see Hyde Park from his living-room windows, which go right up to the ceiling, six of them in a row. It's huge, the living room, and he's got such wonderful furniture, and beautiful things everywhere – paintings and silk hangings from India and sculptures and a big glass coffee table shaped like a curve, and a thick rug that your shoes sink into so you feel as if you're standing on a cloud. He's travelled all over the world, like Archie, but whereas Archie has stories and memories to show for his experiences, Rupert has things. 'Always was an acquisitive little bugger,' Archie says about him, 'even when we were at school. He liked proof. Souvenirs.' Archie doesn't even really like taking photographs when he visits places; he thinks it interrupts the quality of your experiencing a place, and I do agree with him. You can't live life from behind a lens, after all, but I do think sometimes it would be nice to have a memento of things you've done. After all, you never know when you're going to get old and forget, do you?

It's not just the living room, there's a big dining room behind, all dark and Oriental, and even a library, with bookcases covering all the walls and one of those funny little ladders to reach the ones at the top. Actually, it was in the library that the slightly strange thing happened. I had been dancing, dancing and dancing for what felt like hours, with Archie first and then with Teddy and Ralph and Rocky, and the band was playing my favourite songs, and I was so happy. It was Christmas and I was a model, an actual working model, with a boyfriend I was in love with and who loved me, and I was at the sort of party that once upon a time I had only ever read about in magazines and dreamed of going to, and here I was, all of those dreams had come true.

I had a flash of guilt about Suzanne, then. I hadn't written to her for an age, and promised myself that tomorrow, I would go out and buy her a Christmas present, a special one, and send it to her to show that I had not forgotten her as she must have thought I had, that I was still her friend, still thinking of her. And then I got spun around by someone and whirled into the middle of the dance floor by Rupert again and I realised that I was a little drunk, that the champagne the waiters had been topping me up with and the dancing had made me light-headed, and so I managed to disentangle myself from him and shoved him towards another girl so he could carry on dancing and I went off to the side of the room to catch my breath. Then I realised that the heel of one of my shoes had come loose and I didn't want to start fiddling with it there so I went off into the library to sort it out. It was quiet and calm in there and I was glad that I had come in. I felt damp from the dancing and my feet were killing me so I took both my shoes off, and sat on the little ladder stool thing to try and fix my heel. 'Damn,' I think I said, because I saw that it was hanging off, and it looked like it would need glueing back on, so I glanced around for something heavy to slam it back in place until I could take it to the mender's. I could use a book, I thought, and I turned to the shelves to try and find a hardback one that didn't look too precious to be used for shoe-mending purposes . . . and it was then that I saw him.

'Oh,' I said, and I took a step back. He was standing in the corner, just staring at me from behind thick glasses, not moving. It was as if he had hoped to disappear into the shelves. He almost had; if I hadn't turned I probably wouldn't have noticed him at all. He hadn't made any noise, hadn't moved. Just – stood.

When he heard me exclaim though, he sort of jerked into action and leaped forward, sticking his hand out at me and smiling or trying to smile. It was more of a sort of grimace really.

'Henry,' he said, 'Henry Mortimer,' and I was so surprised that I just nodded at first.

'I know,' I managed to say in the end. 'Rupert told me your name.' It was true. He'd pointed him out to me earlier, when Archie and I had first arrived. 'That's Henry Mortimer,' he'd said, 'one of the bores who arrived bang on time, clutching some ghastly bottle of plonk like a student. He's a friend of Ned's. He's terribly clever, but a bit odd. Ned thinks he's fascinating, but then he's into all that science stuff. I wouldn't have thought you'd have anything in common with him.' I'd pretended to be cross, because really what Rupert was saying was that I was too stupid to talk to someone like this clever man, but then he wasn't exactly wrong. Science was hardly my forte, and this man did look as dull as anything.

He looked thrilled though, when I said this about Rupert telling me his name, as if I'd given him a wonderful present, and he grabbed my hand and shook it for too long, until it was sticky and limp. I didn't know what to say after that, and obviously nor did he, so we just sort of stood there staring at each other, and then he said, 'Can I help you with that?' and waved at the shoe in my hand.

I didn't want him touching it. There was something a bit dusty-looking about him, and the way he had been silently staring at me made me feel uneasy, so I shook my head. 'No, thank you. I'm just going to leave them off – they're horribly uncomfortable anyhow,' I said, and I laughed. 'You know, we women suffer for beauty,' and he didn't laugh, just carried on staring. I thought it was a bit rude, actually. I was only trying to be polite, and he was the one who had been lurking in the library like a weirdo.

'I'm going to go and find Archie, my boyfriend,' I said. 'He'll be wondering where I've got to. It was nice to meet you, Henry.'

'We haven't really met,' he said quickly, in a rush, as I was about to go out of the door. 'I mean, of course we have, but I hope we can meet again properly, soon. So we can talk. I'd like that.'

'I'm sure we will,' I said, and I was trying to be polite but really I just wanted to get out of there. He was giving me the creeps, this strange silent scientist. 'Have a very Happy Christmas,' I added, and I went back to the party and the noise and the dancing and I found Archie and kissed him in the middle of the dance floor so everyone could see, and I forgot all about odd little Henry Mortimer until this morning when I woke up. It's the sort of encounter that I thought I should put in here. One day he might be a terribly famous Nobel Prize-winning scientist, mightn't he? You never know.


I looked away from the page. I couldn't focus on the words any more; it was as though I was seeing everything through a child's kaleidoscope. The world was refracted and fragmented and broken.

The stories he had told me rushed to the front of my mind, from their hiding place at the back of my memory, jostling for attention. All the words, all the images, competing.

*She glittered when she came into a room.*

*Like the froth on a wave when it catches the sunshine at the seaside. She was all of those things and more . . .*

*She was a model. Everyone wanted to be seen with her.*

*And then when she went away, she went to America. She didn't want to leave you. But it was hard for her . . .*

*Like a princess in a fairy-tale . . . Like a fairy at the top of a Christmas tree.*

*Like the very one at the Christmas party where I met her.*

Because the story that I had just read wasn't the story I had grown up hearing. It was the same event, there was no doubt about that. The facts matched up, or some of them, at least. That was my father she was describing. But it was not my father as he had portrayed himself. The strange silent scientist lurking in the library. That was him. Of course it was.

And now that memory was shattered like a bauble knocked from the tree. The lines that I had known by heart might as well have been those from a storybook, because they were all made up. I hardly even noticed the mention of a man called Ned, a friend of my father's, though I must have registered it somewhere, because later on, I found that I had made a note of it. I didn't think about it then though, I couldn't. Instead I just closed the diary and let it fall onto the floor.

# Chapter Twenty-Six

I didn't sleep at all that night, after discovering the gaping lie that lay at the heart of my father's story, my father's life. My life. Just lay, eyes wide against the soft darkness, listening to the words, hers and his, his and hers, play over and over again in my head. The conversation between their words formed an unstoppable circle that raced around the inside of my mind like the early moving images of a horse cantering around the circumference of a zoopraxiscope. Trapped.

What would you do, on discovering such a lie? What would normal people, with normal families, do? Should I confront my father? Pretend I knew nothing and try to catch him out? Ask him outright? Ignore the whole thing and hope it would go away? Choose some other, unknown option that would provide the perfect answer and which had not yet occurred to me? I chased after the question through two, three, four o'clock in the morning, but found no answers. Maybe I don't have the imagination to conjure up such scenarios.

What would you do if you had been brought up by two parents, who had conversations, confrontations, rows. Who bickered over whose turn it was to load the dishwasher and who it was that had insisted they take that last right turn that had led them down this dead end by a plumbing warehouse, who had a gin and tonic too many on a Sunday lunchtime and fell asleep in front of the James Bond film, who giggled over private jokes from before you were even thought of and spoke to one another in Franglais when they didn't want you to know their plans. Who bestowed siblings upon you, siblings who stole your toys and scribbled over your favourite storybooks and followed you around the house wanting to play, whose snores you went to sleep listening to in the bunk below, whose toes you wiggled yours against in the sand on family holidays to the beach house where you went every year. Who built traditions for Christmas, Easter, birthdays, so that those ritual celebrations became yours and yours alone and you could turn your nose up at how 'other' families did things, because it was all wrong, because it was not the Family Way.

The feeling that I thought I had shaken off since marrying Mark and finding a place to slot myself into had returned. The sense of being other, of being different, on the outside of things. I had never known it was a thing really – had just assumed that everyone felt a bit like that, when I was growing up. Of course I had wondered how, if they did feel the same way, they managed to hide it so well. How they shrugged it off and got on and made friends anyhow, throwing themselves into games where they looked stupid without caring, chatting to other children they didn't know without fear of saying the wrong thing and being thought odd; how they faked that easy confidence that they all seemed to possess and which I could never imagine even coming close to having. It wasn't until later, until I was older, that I realised there was no subterfuge involved in their behaviour; they just didn't have anything to hide. They had probably never, or only rarely, felt that crushing awkwardness that creeps over you when you realise everyone else is paired up and chatting and you have no one to talk to and no way of knowing what to say. You can only watch and hope that someone rescues you soon – a kindly teacher who will find someone who will let you into their game, another oddball to be paired up with, both of you somewhat resentful to be stuck with one another, yet still grateful that there is another. Another like you.

With the arrival of Mark in my life, all that had begun to disappear. I had a partner, an ally. I was part of a team. There was always someone to glance over at and confirm that yes, that man sitting opposite me at dinner was a terrible boor with extremely suspect views on the welfare state, or to seek out the hand of at a dutiful yet dull work do, or simply to sit next to on the sofa, in silence, and know that you were not alone.

But now it was four o'clock in the morning, and I *was* alone, wrapped up like a silk worm in my secrets.

In the end, I did nothing for a few days. I felt suspended in a sort of limbo, soggy and slow, and the thought of making any definite move one way or another was quite beyond me. I just carried on with my normal life, as much as possible, going to work, talking to my students, colleagues, coming home, making dinner, asking Elfie about her day, nudging Mark to tell us about his over dinner, acting like a family. I saw Beth, took the kids to the park with her, bought them ice creams and got sticky fingers.

I tried not to think about my father. I ignored an email from him, from Berlin where he was giving a lecture, and then a phone call when he returned. I felt guilty for doing so, as I knew he would be wondering why I had not been in touch, but the thought of speaking to him was too difficult and complicated to face. I would not be able to remain silent about what I had discovered, and yet the thought of saying anything was so fraught with decisions and questions that keeping my mouth shut seemed like the only option. So I pressed *reject* on my phone and *delete* on my email and tried to do the same with my mind. To no avail, of course. Blocking out things you don't want to think about never really works, does it? Oh, you can get on and pretend it's not there much of the time, go about your business, think of other things. But it's always seeping in around the edges, the not thinking of it weighing heavy. '*Don't touch it, don't look at it,*' I would cry when I hurt myself as a child, and I knew that I was doing the same now, and it was about as effective a pain-relieving strategy as it had been then.

And then, on the Thursday night, I was jerked out of my torpor, suddenly and unexpectedly, and had no time to fret about my father, or read more of the diary, because Mark discovered that I had taken Elfie to see Coco, and all hell broke loose.

Of course he was going to find out at some point. I knew that, in my rational mind. But like so much else, I had pushed it to one side while I focused on Sadie, and the diaries, and the truth. The truth had a lot to answer for, it seemed.

I had forgotten how terrible it was when Mark was this angry. I had only seen him like it once before, and I had done my best to forget it ever since, so it was almost as though I was seeing him lose his temper for the first time. It was a shocking, violent, visceral thing, one's temper, I thought, as I watched him raging. More physical than psychological, almost. And yet I felt as if I was watching him from a distance. Observing, like a natural scientist might observe animals in the wild. This was not my life that was falling apart at the seams, this was an interesting event to be recorded and analysed later, quantitatively and qualitatively, picked over then filed away. I knew that doing this was not normal. That my detachment was probably only increasing Mark's anger. But it was the only thing I knew how to do. Separate.

'What the fuck did you think you were doing, Klara? We took Elfie in here to protect her, to give her some stability, because God knows she's had precious little of that in her life. And you of all people should have known better. You know what it was like for me. You *know* how it all affected me. We agreed that we'd—'

'I know. I KNOW. I'm sorry. I got distracted, I thought it was for the best.'

'For the best. Klara, seriously, what the fuck? This isn't you. This is not like you.'

He stared at me, uncomprehending, and it hurt me, because he was looking at me as if I was a stranger, and because he was right. I was behaving like one.

Elfie wasn't in the house. Mark had sent her to the cinema, or shopping or something. She had gone, with a look on her face that might have been guilt, might have been satisfaction. Had she done it on purpose? Broken the promise that she had never made but which I had thought was implicit in our joint actions – in order to hurt me? I couldn't tell, couldn't be sure. I had no idea of the reliability of my instincts any more, whether or not to trust what I felt or thought. I was swimming through uncertain waters and the things I knew were clinging to my limbs and dragging me down just as deeply as those which I did not know. Swirling around me. Confusing me. My father was not who I thought, my mother was someone I had thought didn't exist. But she existed now, more than ever, as though I were willing her into life like some kind of a phantom from a legend, rising up from the ashes, while my father was fading, or at least the man I had thought he was. The man with whom she had fallen in love at that glittering Christmas party and had taken up to the roof and kissed – he did not exist. *So who did? Who was real?* I put a hand to my forehead. It felt strangely cold.

Elfie had told Mark about Coco, and I couldn't understand why. I felt betrayed by her, even though I knew that *I* was the one who had started the daisy chain of betrayal, by lying to Mark by omission (the same thing as lying outright, he would feel, I knew from past experience) and then by hiding Coco's letter from her. It was my fault. But I had felt that we had an understanding, a bond, that she knew I was doing the best thing for her, that I was just trying to . . . I let my thoughts trail off. The truth was, I had not been trying to help her.

'And it's not as though your own teenage years were so fucking idyllic, is it?' Mark was yelling. 'If you'd had some sort of golden childhood, never known what it was like to be lonely or scared, to feel as though you were all by yourself in the world, then this might actually be easier to understand. Because I'd know you couldn't understand, you couldn't imagine. But you *can* imagine, Klara, you can more than fucking well imagine! You KNOW, and you still can't seem to make that little leap, can you, to transfer what it was like for you to what it must be like for her. I thought that we'd got past this, years ago. I thought you'd learned that you have to tell the truth, that you have to not keep things from me. I thought I'd managed to get that through to you. But I was wrong, wasn't I? Nothing's bloody well changed. Nothing's different.'

The thing was, he was right. More right than he could know, even. Because of course it wasn't just the modelling plan that I had been hiding from him, it was everything else of which he was still unaware. And as well as the slightly sore feeling of having been turned on by Mark, I felt relief, relief that Elfie seemed not to have discovered everything else in the folder where Coco's letter had been, or that if she had, she had not thought it interesting or relevant enough to mention. So it was only one secret that had been told, only one lie that had been uncovered. The less important one. I told myself that this made it OK. That I was off the hook.

Not with Mark though. He had been talking all the time I had been thinking, ranting more than talking.

'How many more secrets, Klara? Because that's the thing, isn't it? It's not just about Elfie, and this stupid fucking plan you've somehow come up with to turn her into an anorexic clothes-rail. God knows where you got the idea from, by the way, though that's hardly the point.' (It was entirely the point.) 'It's about everything else. This is one lie, one little plan you've come up with all by yourself, that you've been squirrelling away at. What else is there? What else am I going to find out about?'

I stared at him, wondering at the possibilities that were no doubt ratcheting through his brain at that moment. That I was having an affair, that I was going mad, that I was stealing from him or someone else . . . Mark was a scientist; he would be examining all the possibilities, as unpalatable as they might be, and searching for evidence to either substantiate or disprove each individual theory before discarding it. Working his way through methodically. I knew though, that however long he flicked through the options, he would never guess the truth.

And then I had an awful thought. What if Elfie had found and gone through all of the paperwork relating to Sadie and Archie, all of the cuttings and my printed-out archival sheets and the notes I had made. What if she had read them all, running her slim, pale fingers over them, taking it all in, following my steps back, back, through the streets of St Albans and London and into my parents' past, soaking it all up, knowing everything . . . and had simply elected to say nothing, to keep the knowledge to herself, wrapping it up in her chest like a parcel, biding her time. It was, after all, what I might have done in her position.

'It's not such a big deal. I wanted to do something for Elfie, I saw an opportunity, and I took it. Maybe you should be asking why she was looking through my papers? Searching my study.'

'Because she's a teenager? Because you were hiding things from her, and she knew it? In which case, she's obviously a lot smarter than me, isn't she?' Dangerous ground. There was a lot more I was hiding from him than this.

'Okay. It doesn't matter, I suppose. It's not like I keep the secrets of the realm in there.'

Mark sighed. 'No, she shouldn't have done it. I'll talk to her. But Klara – why didn't you just talk to me about it? Why did you just go ahead?'

'I thought you might be happy that she and I were doing this together.'

The wrong path, the wrong door.

'You thought I'd be happy for her to stop focusing on her schoolwork and start trying to be a model? Worrying about being too fat when she weighs seven stone, comparing herself to six foot freaks with dead eyes? You thought that would make me happy? Klara – do you even know me at all?'

I stood, accused.

'But what if it made *her* happy, Mark? Despite what you think of it, plenty of people are happy doing things that you don't like or understand. You know? Just because you don't get something doesn't mean it has no place in the world, that no one else should do it.'

I was trying a new tactic, playing offensive, not defensive. But I was no sportswoman, and I had no coach cheering me on from the sidelines telling me when to change tack, when to abandon one strategy and pick up a new one, and I had chosen the wrong one. Mark's hand slammed down on the side and he winced in frustration. Maybe he was right. Maybe I really didn't know him at all.

'Jesus. I thought my family were the ones who used logic like that. I thought you'd be cleverer than that, Klara. I expected more.'

He shook his head. His disappointment nudged at my conscience. How acute would it be if he knew the whole truth? How deeply would it cut him?

'Be honest with yourself, Klara, even if you can't bring yourself to be honest with me. Did you really think you were doing the right thing here? Really?'

His voice was quiet now and that was worse; it was so much worse than the shouting. I could not observe his quiet hurt, could not detach myself from it. I wanted to protect him from that feeling but I had caused it and could not undo it, could not go backwards, only forwards into something worse.

I couldn't speak. I wanted to, but I couldn't. It was like being paralysed. I was trying to make my mouth and throat form the words, but they wouldn't come. My body betrayed me.

He shrugged. 'I didn't think so.' He turned away from me.

'Mark,' I managed to whisper.

There was a long silence. 'Yes?' he said eventually, and it almost made me weep. Even in his hurt and disappointment he could not bear to be impolite or coldly cruel to me.

'I'm sorry.'

And I was sorry – so sorry – for his pain, for everything he was feeling, for being who I was and for the fact that I also knew that he loved me, as I loved him. Because by rights, I did not deserve it.

# Chapter Twenty-Seven

I was upset and shaken by my row with Mark. I hated fighting with him. It made the world seem less safe. So to comfort myself I did what I always did, these days, and reached for the diary. Disappearing back into Sadie's world was an escape, and I sank into it as into a deep, thick duvet. Or that was what usually happened, but not that day, however. That day I read something that shook me deeper still.

*I am shaking still*, she wrote, and I was struck by the coincidence. I could feel her reaching out to me through the pages of the book. I could almost feel her hand on my head, stroking my hair. '*Go to sleep, Puffin*,' I heard her whisper. '*Go to sleep now . . .*' But of course she was not there, and I could not sleep.

*February 19th, 1971*

Thank goodness Henry was there, thank goodness he is so calm and thinks so quickly. All right, I'm sorry, I am making no sense. I'll start at the beginning. I'm just in such a state. Deep breaths . . . Here we go.

I've been seeing Henry a bit, you see, the strange man from Rupert's party. He phoned up and asked me to go out with him, saying that Rupert had given him my number. And I thought all right – just as friends, I told him, and he said of course, he quite understood. I didn't want to lead him on or anything, but Archie's often busy and I do get lonely sometimes, and he seemed so eager to take me out. I thought it might be fun. And it was, in a strange way. He's an odd sort of a man but he's terribly clever and he takes me to interesting places that I would never have bothered to go to on my own – like a museum all about the history of medicine, and he actually understood the exhibits and why they're there and told me all sorts of stories about them. Anyhow, we went there, and then the other day he took me to the cinema, and then we went walking in Richmond Park. Archie doesn't mind, he thinks it's funny. Which is a bit annoying, as why isn't he more jealous, more possessive?

Then today we were going to go and see a show. Henry had got last-minute tickets to this ballet at Covent Garden, after I told him that I'd never been to one. His eyebrows went all wrinkly and waggly and he said that I must go, I would love it. When he came to pick me up, he was wearing a new tie, well, new to him, he'd have bought it from a charity shop, of course, like he does everything. I opened the front door before he had a chance to ring my bell, and was just about to go down the steps when I saw it, propped up on the side, where all the residents' mail was put each day. I recognised the handwriting at once. My blood ran cold and I pulled Henry inside and slammed the door shut. I didn't know what to do.

'What's the matter?' he asked. 'Sadie? Are you unwell?'

My face was hot and my breath was all gasping and I didn't know if I could speak but I knew I had to.

'Henry, you have to help me. You *have* to . . .'

I couldn't get the words out, and he put his hand on my shoulder and his kind eyes looked into mine and he just said, 'Sadie. Breathe. And again . . . That's good. And now, tell me what the matter is and what you want me to do.'

His voice calmed me, and I was able to do so.

The letter had been from her parents, who had managed to track her down. She wasn't sure how – they didn't say in the letter, and it didn't matter anyway. All that Sadie cared about was that she had been found.

Henry, of course, was keen to do anything he could to help, anything Sadie wanted. And what she wanted was for him to lie.

He wrote a letter then and there. We went to a café around the corner and he bought writing paper and envelopes from the late-opening newsagent and sat there, thinking carefully, a pot of coffee in front of him, until it was done. I watched, and waited, and then when he had finished and he handed me the piece of paper for my approval, I read:

*Dear Mr and Mrs Tomaszewski,*

*Your letter arrived today. At first I was unsure what to do with it, since I did not want to open mail addressed to one of my former tenants. In the end, however, I decided that it was for the best that I did so, given the circumstances, and having read it, I am glad that I made that decision.*

*I am the landlady of number 32 Walpole Road where, until recently, your daughter Mary was living. I am sorry to have to inform you that Mary moved out more than a fortnight ago now. She left no forwarding address, unfortunately, but she did mention to me that she had a possibility of a job in Manchester, and had talked of friends in that area before also.*

*I am so sorry that I cannot be of more help, and I wish you every success in tracking Mary down.*

*Sincerely,*
*Agatha Carter*

No mention of Mary's new name, of course, in his letter – a letter that was so brazen it took my breath away. Oh, I was no stranger to the things that love could make you do, the extremes to which it could drive you. But the ease with which he had lied, and to her parents, who must have been in such distress, shocked me. I had never thought that my father was the sort of man who could lie. And yet in the last twenty-four hours I had uncovered, without even trying, two instances of him doing so, and not minor lies either, but big, important ones that made a difference to things, to people. To life. To *my* life.

Everything was fragmenting. And yet, like a driver slowing as they passed a car crash, I kept reading. The trip Henry and Sadie had taken to the ballet after he wrote the letter for her; the letter that came a few days later from her parents addressed to her 'former landlady', thanking the woman for her reply, must have given Sadie some small pause for thought – for guilt, maybe?

*We will not write again*, the letter said, *as we do not wish to bother you, but if you should hear anything of our beloved Mary we ask that you contact us at 24 Laburnum Gardens, St Albans*. They would be waiting for a long time for that letter, I thought.

I felt a pang of sympathy for poor Piotr and Anne, and wondered what had happened – whether they had carried on searching for Mary, whether they had seen pictures of Sadie in magazines, and if they had eventually tracked her down.

I could not keep the letter but I didn't want to throw it away, so Henry kept it for me. I know I can trust him. He said he would put it in his safe place, where he keeps everything important. 'What, do you have a secret hide-away or something?' I asked. I always make stupid remarks when I'm nervous; it's one of my worst traits. He smiled kindly. 'No. Just a favourite book.'

I knew straight away where he would have put the letter. I hadn't lived with my father for all those years for nothing. What I didn't know – couldn't know then – was whether the letter would still be there.

I sat outside my father's house that evening for more than an hour, waiting for him to come home. I could have let myself in, I had a key. But it felt wrong to do so. Too familiar, too normal. Nothing was normal, not any longer. There was no point in pretending.

I had spoken to Elfie before I left. Mark had stalked out, muttering something about going for a run, though he was still in the clothes he had worn to work. He didn't seem to notice and I didn't point it out to him. Everything was upside down; what difference did small lies and excuses make now?

Mark's anger reverberated around my head, mingling with my own guilt, my recriminations, my relief, until I couldn't bear it any longer and I had to get out of the house as well. I grabbed my keys and my bag and pulled a scarf around my neck and headed down the hall – and as I did so, came face to face with Elfie on her way back in.

We stood, silent, staring at one another for maybe a minute. She had a magazine and a bag of the mouth-clenchingly sour sweets that she loved in her hand, and as we looked at one another she lowered them, like a child caught stealing the cake mix. I didn't care what she'd been buying – it could have been cigarettes and vodka for all I was bothered just then – and she seemed to realise this because she shrugged and took a sweet out of the bag and ate it. I could have slapped her then; for a dangerous moment my fingers trembled and I felt my cheeks flood with rage as I watched her, defiant, defensive, so young-looking, so innocent-looking. To look at her, you might think she was entirely unaware of the damage she had caused. But I knew better. She wasn't innocent of any of it. Her eyes betrayed her; their search for my reaction told me that she knew exactly what effect her words had had, and that she had known this before she had spoken them – had wanted it, maybe. My mind stumbled over itself as I started to wonder how far back this all went. Had she planned the whole thing? Maybe she had intended this, all of it, from when she had first moved in here, had sat and plotted and worked out exactly how she could drive a wedge between her brother and me. Teenage girls were devious and sly, after all. I should know that better than anyone. She could have done it, she could have . . .

And then the cellophane of her sweet bag rustled as she held on to it more tightly in her fist, and I started, and caught myself. None of this was her doing. It was my folly and mine alone that had brought me – *us* here. She was just reacting to the path I had set her on.

'I was going to tell you about the letter,' I said eventually, and as the words formed they became true.

Elfie blushed. She had obviously been hoping to get past me without having to discuss what had happened. 'I was just upset,' she said quietly, and she looked guilty, as though suddenly regretting what she had done, and her shame made mine flow deeper still. I had caused this.

'I thought she would have written. I just wanted to check.'

'You should have asked me.'

Neither of us acknowledged that I might have lied to her if she had done.

She nodded, and gave me a quarter-smile. My bag was still hanging heavily and uselessly from my hand and my scarf was all scrumpled up around my shoulders from where I hadn't finished putting it on properly.

'I know,' she said, and she rolled the magazine in her hands into a tighter tube. 'It's OK,' she carried on.

'I was going to tell you, Elfie, I promise.'

'Why didn't you just leave it for me to open?' She felt let down, betrayed. I could hear it. I couldn't blame her.

I cleared my throat. 'I was impatient, and impulsive, and nosy.' This was true. 'I wanted to see what she'd said, and I didn't really think about what I was doing.' This was not quite so true. A bit true. Just not entirely. 'And once I'd done it, I didn't know what to do. I didn't want to admit to having opened it, so I put it away while I decided what to do. I had decided to just come clean.' This bit was not true, not even a bit. 'But then you found it before I had a chance to.'

'And I told on you.' Her phrasing made her sound even younger than her years. 'Is he very angry?'

'No.' A lie not even I could quite pull off. She grimaced. 'Well, OK, yes, he's pretty angry. Not with you though. He's angry that I didn't tell him we were going in the first place.'

'Shall I talk to him? Tell him I didn't want you to?' Her face was pinched with anxiety. She was trying to make amends, and my heart contracted. I reached over and squeezed her arm.

'No. It's fine, Elfie. It'll be fine. It's . . . it's complicated. It's not just about the letter.' Elfie looked worried. Oh God. I was meant to be reassuring her, not panicking her that she had left a madhouse only to land in a war zone. 'Look, I don't want you to worry about it. Mark will be fine. You know what he's like. Grumpy. He's just annoyed he was left out.' I grinned at her, hoping that my face looked relaxed and confident rather than rictus-like. She seemed satisfied enough. Life was simple, when you were fifteen.

He was whistling as he got out of his car and went around to the other side of it to get his briefcase and coat out. I didn't have to look over at him to know that he would be walking unevenly around the car, lumbering a little as he reached in for the case that would be overflowing with papers, one buckle coming undone as it always was, something threatening to spill out. A book, or an academic journal. He would be wearing a jacket and his hair would be sticking up as it always was at the end of the day. It would start off tamed with a comb and water, but it would spring up again gradually throughout the day so by now, at six o'clock, it was at its fully uncoiled height. It made him look surprised, and energetic. Although these days, his energy was definitely waning. I could hear it now, as he puffed and panted a little on his way up the garden path. I would have to cut down on the ginger cakes, I thought.

'Klara!' I tried not to feel irritated by his obvious pleasure at seeing me. It had always been the same. It might only have been the two of us, but he had always made me feel as though there was no one else in the world he would rather be with. Maybe it had been true. But right now, there were a thousand places I could think of where I would rather be.

'Hello, Daddy.' I let him kiss me and pat my hand as he rummaged for his door keys.

'Aren't you freezing? You look freezing. Why didn't you go inside? I tried to call you the other day . . . maybe you were busy.'

I followed him into the hall, where I nearly abandoned the whole thing. How easy it would be to just start chatting. Say, 'Yes, sorry, I was working,' or 'I was with Mark, and I didn't get a chance to call back so I just thought I'd drop in. How was your trip? How are you?' I could still do that. I could forget about all the rest, and just let things slide back to normal. Except, of course, I could not.

'Tell me again how you and . . . how you and Mummy met.' I almost said Sadie, but stopped myself in time.

He paused, then carried on walking down the hall. Dumped his briefcase on the small half-moon table near the door to the kitchen. It belched out papers onto the floor.

'Klara. What's the matter? What's wrong?'

'Nothing.' I spoke too quickly. He could tell something was upsetting me. He might be a scientist but he was still my father. 'Oh, Mark and I had a row. I just . . . I just wanted to hear the story.'

He put his arm around my shoulder and gripped me tight. I held my breath. 'What about?'

'The row? Oh. Nothing important. You know. Stupid stuff.' I wanted to cry. I wanted to flop onto the worn leather sofa and pull the old crocheted granny square blanket over myself and cry my heart out, and tell him everything that had happened, what I had been doing, all of my questions and fears and worries and guilts. Let him soak it all up with ginger cake and tea that was too strong and the smell of his old tweed jacket. But he was the one person I could not tell. Not yet.

'I'll make tea,' he said, as I had known he would. 'I think there might be some of that ginger cake left,' and I almost laughed. He might have kept secrets from me, for years – and there were more to come, I was sure – but in some ways still, I knew my father. Everything could be cured with tea and a piece of cake.

He told me the story again, when he had served up the ritual. And I listened to him tell it, and wept inside with every word that I knew was untrue. I had needed to hear it again. To know that my memory had not been playing tricks on me, that his version had been as I remembered it. His expression was the same as it had always been, wistful, sad, yet happy to be in the memory of the most important moment of his life. His words sounded the same, his voice emphasised the same cadences and he smiled at the same turning points in the story – the bit where she first came up to him, and said, 'You look like I feel,' the bit where she knew his name already. All the same, the same as it ever was. And every word a lie, every smile a betrayal.

I don't know what made me ask him about Coco. She must have been in the forefront of my mind, I suppose, with everything that had just happened at home.

'Did Mummy ever talk about someone called Coco Delaney?'

He stopped eating his cake when I spoke, slowly lowering it to the plate so as not to drop any crumbs. He wiped his mouth carefully before replying, and folded his square of kitchen towel into four, tucking it under the plate rim.

It must have been a big decision for him to take. Whether to deny outright, or to tell the truth – whatever that might be – or maybe come up with some approximation of the two, some smudgily grey middle ground. I was remembering that there was much of that.

'Why do you ask, my love?'

So the decision was not quite made yet. He wanted to see how much he could get away with not saying. Gauge where my interest had come from and how much I knew.

'I came across her recently. One of my students . . . It occurred to me that Coco and Sadie would have been working in the industry around the same time. I don't know. I just thought I'd ask.'

'A lot of people were working in modelling and fashion around then. You know it's not really my area.'

'Yes. But if she'd worked with her you might remember.'

'Why do you think she did?'

It was like fencing. We were dancing around one another.

'I'm not sure. Her name sounded a bit familiar. I thought maybe I'd half-remembered something.'

I looked at him, and waited. He sighed. 'Klara.'

'Yes?' I bit the corner of my thumbnail.

'There are probably many things you half-remember from that time. There are many things *I* half-remember. It becomes hard, doesn't it, as the years pass, to know what was real and what fantasy?'

I nodded. I didn't dare say anything, in case he was about to make some sort of confession, some statement. I didn't want to interrupt it.

'I miss her as well, you know. She was my first love, your mother. And I hers. That never goes away, you know? It never really leaves you, your first love. And for us – well, our first love was our last, of course.'

His words took me by surprise. *Our first love was our last.* It sounded like something from a Jacobean tragedy. But it was true – for him, at least, or as far as I knew. He had never remarried, nor had he had girlfriends, either when I was growing up or more recently. As a child I had never questioned it – the thought of my father loving anyone other than me was quite out of the question, quite preposterous. What would he need with a girlfriend? And by the time I was an adult and might have wondered, it had simply become the norm. Stupid of me, not to look deeper. But then you don't, do you? Not when it's your own family. *Our first love was our last.* No, it wasn't true for my mother. Her first love had been Archie Farrow, that much I knew. She had loved him deeply, madly, wildly.

But it wasn't just my father's words that took me by surprise, it was the expression on his face when he raised his head and looked at me. His eyes were full of tears, but his face? It was full of guilt. Unmistakable. Sorrow was there as well, yes, but mostly? He looked guilty. His next words confirmed it. 'I'm sorry,' he said quietly. 'I'm so sorry.'

I didn't ask any more questions after that. How could I? My curiosity, my suspicions, were half-formed, vague and liable to disappear when held up to the light, certainly not enough to push him with, to increase his distress. So I patted his hand and said that no, *I* was the one who should be sorry. I shouldn't have brought it up, I went on. It was just a silly thing – I'd got caught up in wondering after reading some of my students' work. It was like that sometimes; I would get an idea into my head and not be able to shake it.

All that was true, and my father nodded and laughed a little and said I had been like that – tenacious – ever since I was small. That I had once spent three weeks keeping a detailed log of Mr Samson next door's movements, as I had become convinced that he was a spy. The memory made me feel a twinge of disquiet in case I was doing the same thing now, but I shook it off and told myself that this was entirely different.

We moved on and chatted about other things – work and his trip and a book we had both been reading. Of course, I told myself, while he was wrong to say that he was Sadie's first love, it did not necessarily mean that he was lying. Just that he was unaware. I had access to her diary, I reminded myself, could read her private thoughts. She might well have told my father that he was her first, her true, her one and only love. Might even have promised him that there had been no others, that she was a virgin when they met, for all I knew. But . . . I thought not. It didn't match up. Nothing matched up. As I sat on the sofa I made a mental list of the possibilities. What was he sorry for? What was he trying to say?

1. He felt guilty simply because he knew that my childhood had not been easy, without a mother. The guilt was the same that any parent would feel when their child's life was less than perfect.
2. He was sorry for lying to me. Or for avoiding my questions. This option had various sub-categories. Lying to me about *what*, exactly?
   a) Lying by omission about Coco.
   b) Lying about how he and my mother had met, both now and when I was a child.
   c) Going back further and deeper – lying about something more, something I had not discovered yet. Something to do with why Sadie had left?
   d) Lying about where he was going every year in June. And this led me on to:
3. Maybe he was sorry for something that I had not yet

uncovered or considered. Maybe he was sorry for being the reason that Sadie had left?

'Do you mind if I stay here tonight?' I asked him.

He looked quizzically at me. 'Of course not.'

I had to offer an explanation. The lie tripped easily off my tongue. Like father, like daughter?

'Mark's taken Elfie to his parents' for the night, and I just feel like some company. I thought we could get fish and chips.'

That had always been the big treat when I was younger. Fish and chips and mushy peas, all drenched in vinegar and sprinkled with crunchy salt. He looked pleased, as I had thought he would.

'That would be lovely. I'll put some white wine in the fridge.'

I smiled sweetly and felt like a traitor.

We had a lovely evening. That's the thing, we always have a nice time together, me and Daddy. We have lots in common, we make each other laugh, we genuinely enjoy one another's company. I know I'm lucky in that respect. I almost forgot the reason why I was there. Until he went to bed, and I sat up saying I wanted to watch a movie on my laptop for work, and I sat there in the half-light, listening, waiting.

By half past one everything was silent, and when I was sure he was completely asleep, I tiptoed upstairs to his study. As I opened the door I faltered – it was the smell of it, again, that hit me. Books and old records and cologne and dust. The particular smell of that room that would always be the same, always specific to that house and to him.

I trod carefully, softly over the patterned rug that covered the bare floorboards to the bookshelf. *Tender is the Night*. My fingers found it straight away. He had more than one edition, of course – collecting them was something of a hobby – but I knew the one Sadie would have been referring to in her diary. It was a beautiful hardback volume bound in forest-green leather. He had always loved the book, and I had come to love it too, and all of Fitzgerald's work – had caught his enthusiasm for the writer over the years. '*Gatsby* may be the better known, easier work,' he would expound, 'but *Tender*? *Tender* has something special. You might have to work a bit harder with it, but it is well worth the effort.'

I slid it out from the shelf. Paused for a moment before opening it. I wasn't sure I could bear the disappointment of finding it empty, just a book, just the pages laid bare.

I needn't have worried. My subterfuge was richly rewarded, if you count the confirmation that your father is a liar and quite possibly responsible for your mother's disappearance as a reward.

# Chapter Twenty-Eight

Mark was there when I got home, early in the morning, the city just starting to wake up. He was sitting at the kitchen table, drinking coffee, waiting for me.

'Henry emailed me,' he said, 'to let me know you were staying there.'

'Oh. Good.'

'He seemed to think I'd taken Elfie to Maisie and Barney's.'

I shrugged resentfully. I felt like a teenager who had been caught in a lie, and the worst of it was that that was exactly how I had been behaving so I could hardly complain. I sighed. 'I'm sorry, Mark. I just needed a bit of space.'

'I understand, K. But just tell me, you know?' He frowned, and I felt terrible. I don't find it easy to say sorry, not the big sorries, at least. *Sorry I spilled the sugar* or *sorry I forgot to post your letter* is fine, but *sorry about that thing I said earlier, sorry for hurting you, sorry for behaving badly*? I find it – embarrassing.

Instead I went over to him and stood next to him, my body close to his, and rubbed his hair. He reached up and slid his arm around my waist, and kissed the bit of me nearest to him, a spot on the side of my ribcage. 'I love you,' he said, and I squeezed him. It would be all right.

It would be all right with Mark. With my father, with

everything else – I had no such faith. I hadn't known what to expect when I opened the book, had been half-wondering whether the old letter from Sadie's parents – I found it impossible to think of them as my grandparents – might still be there, but not really expecting it to be. It had been decades, after all, and I had no way of knowing whether Sadie had asked him for it back, whether he had destroyed it, whether it had got lost . . .

But it was there, slid between pages twenty-eight and twenty-nine, written on thin, lined paper in a faltering, uneven hand. Piotr Tomaszewski had been no scribe. I had read it, in the lamp light of Daddy's study – I hadn't turned the main light on, not wanting to disrupt things any more than absolutely necessary. It was as Sadie had described it in her diary, a brief letter, no chat or other details, though why would there be? I photographed it with my phone anyhow, both sides, so I could examine it more closely later if I needed to.

There was something else inside the book as well. Something thicker than just a letter. I could feel it through the pages – and I had already guessed what it was.

I shook the book gently and it fell out onto the floor. I picked it up and opened it, flicked to the back page, though there was no need. I knew that it could only be hers. It was Sadie's passport.


Mark and Elfie did go to visit his parents later on and decided to spend the night there, encouraged by me. I said I hadn't slept well at Daddy's and wanted to go to bed early. Elfie seemed happy enough to be going there – I did check before sending them off, I'm not heartless. 'I'd like to see them,' she said, 'and Serri.' It was important that Elfie didn't feel that by moving in with us she was shutting the door on the rest of her family. Mark had explained that to me and I agreed.

When they had left and the house was quiet again, I went up to my little office and took out my phone. I hadn't taken the passport away with me, of course, but I had photographed every page so I had a copy of it to look over in my own time.

She hadn't been to many places, my mother. She hadn't got the passport until she was eighteen. Hadn't needed one, I suppose. The Tomaszewskis had obviously not been ones for holidays abroad, which would have been expensive in those days. It was a little surprising that Piotr had never taken her to Poland, but maybe he had been waiting until she was older. Waiting for a trip that would never come, because before he had a chance to take it with her she took a trip of her own. Her first excursion abroad had been a weekend in Paris for her honeymoon. How excited she must have been, packing for the trip, choosing the right dresses and shoes, selecting her jewellery, accessories. Imagine how she must have felt, stepping out of the temperature-controlled environment of the plane and breathing in the French air and knowing that she had made it, she had escaped drab St Albans and become the sort of woman who takes trips Abroad, with her new Husband.

It made me weep to think how brief that life she had made for herself had been.

I flicked through the rest of the pages. Greece, Spain, other holidays in Europe from when I was small. A two-day trip to Budapest, presumably with my father for one of his conferences, from before I was born.

But what was far more interesting and far more relevant, was not where she had been, but where she *hadn't*. The passport confirmed what had been clear from the sparse collection of modelling photos in the folders after 1971. There were no trips to Milan, New York, and only that one visit to Paris. None of the high-octane fashion destinations that I had anticipated. The work trips for modelling jobs that had punctuated my childhood had not taken place, not one of them. I checked – more than once, of course. Pored over the pages in case I had missed something. Because I remembered, you see, I remembered her coming back from them, the presents she would bring me, the stories she would tell. So many stories. Little handbags made from shiny Italian leather, a snowglobe with the Empire State Building inside it, a pastel-pink box containing a single chocolate éclair that she had carefully transported all the way back from Venice for me. Or, as I now realised must have been the case, had carried all the way back from a patisserie in Town.

I sat at my desk and drank hot chocolate, staring at the pages until my sight blurred, and then I cried, for the mother I had lost before I had ever known her, for the father I was losing too, for the life that was crumbling before my eyes. Because everything had shifted now; everything had become wobbly and uncertain and fragile. I am someone who needs solid things to hold onto. Mark knows it, and provides me with that firm base. I thought my father knew it too, but he doesn't care – how can he care? My whole life he has been lying to me, again and again, smiling and lying, and . . . I couldn't bear it. I couldn't bear the thought of what I was losing and what he had taken away from me. My family. My faith.

It took a while, but I pulled myself together. You have to, at some point, don't you? However badly you hurt, eventually the tears stop flowing and the burning in your chest diminishes a little and you can breathe easier again, and each time it gets slightly less painful. I almost didn't want that to happen; like a child in the throes of a tantrum I wanted to hold on to my hurt. I didn't want to feel better, I didn't want to get used to it, to this new truth, if that's what it was.

Because it wasn't just the work trips that hadn't happened, was it? It was the final trip that my mother was meant to have taken. The biggest, most important piece of the puzzle so far, the one that sat in the pit of my stomach like a ball of acid, gnawing away at me. The proof that Daddy had lied, not in a small way, not in a way that I could write off as trying to spare my feelings, or stretching the truth, or evading a question. A big, inescapable roadblock of a lie. My mother left, or she had disappeared, at least. But she had never gone to America. Not on a work trip or any other kind of a trip. She had not lived there, and she had not died there.

So where *had* she gone?

# Chapter Twenty-Nine

The conversation with my father kept coming back to me in a jumble. I replayed it, over and over, and then I started imagining other conversations with him – ones that I had not yet had; ones in which he lied, ones where I knew he was lying but couldn't prove it, and ones where he was telling the truth and still I could not believe it.

It was like sitting through a nightmare. I knew that I must stop, pull myself out of it, but I couldn't. I kept on returning to these scenarios as though I were working my way through every possible outcome in order to prepare myself. If you do this, run through the things that might happen, the discussions you might have, the advantage is that not much in life tends to come as a surprise, or a shock. Whatever happens, you are likely to have rehearsed it at least once in your mind already. The downside – well, I suppose the downside is the same, good or bad. Not much comes as a surprise. No, there is a bigger downside. It's that you risk completely losing track of what's real and what's not – or not yet real.

I went over my notes again, running through everything that I had found out, and all the questions that remained unanswered, and it was then that I came across the note I had made a few nights previously, when I had read about the Christmas party and what had really happened that night.

*Ned?* I had scribbled in sloping, messy letters. A friend of my father's, the reason he had been at Rupert's party. Could *he* be N.R.? I made another note, to try and look him up, to find out the rest of his name. I couldn't ask Daddy, who was going to start wondering why I was suddenly asking all these questions, and he might hide some crucial bit of evidence that I was yet to find . . . God, I almost laughed as I heard myself think that. It sounded so preposterous – and yet I couldn't let it go, couldn't shake off the suspicions that had rooted themselves deep inside my brain.

I realised, when I opened the diary at the page I had been on last, that I was no longer simply reading through it for pleasure, or interest, or to get to know my mother. I was not just reading it, but searching for evidence of the truth, or a lie, or a betrayal.

I found it, that night, listening to the house creak quietly. What you might call buried treasure. But it wasn't at all what I had been expecting.


*13th March 1971*


There's no point in pretending here in this diary, despite all the acting I might be doing in real life. After all, if you're reading this then you'll know the truth. Either because I went on to do something amazing and it turns out that this period of my life was just an unfortunate blip (obviously this is my hope and my plan) or because I just turned into a loser and you're reading this diary because – oh, I don't know why. Because you found it in a jumble sale or something, or maybe in a dustbin. Maybe I've forgotten all about the time I spent in London, and am back in bloody St Albans, a housewife.

Maybe I'm dead. Who knows?

(This bit made me swallow. It was written with such a blithe, throwaway tone. She didn't really believe that she would be dead. She was far too young to be able to. Death was not in her plan. And yet it had happened to her.)

Anyhow, the point is, I am no longer represented by Velvet Models. Coco and I had a terrible row, and I left. Resigned. It's the most impulsive thing I've ever done, and I can't believe I had the nerve to do it. But I'm not sorry. I don't know who she thinks she is, but I won't be spoken to or treated like that.

I've made the right decision. I mean, it's not as though I don't have other options. I've been working since I got here, doing better than any of the other girls in the agency by a mile, and everyone knows it. It wouldn't surprise me if that was part of the reason – I mean, for her pushing me out. It's obvious that was what she was trying to do, has been for ages. Well, she might think she's won, but she's wrong. I'm the one who's won. Because I'm going on to something bigger, and much, much better.

I'm not going to say what the row was about. It doesn't seem dignified to pick over the bones of it. Unfair to her, when she doesn't have the chance to speak here. I'm able to be the bigger person, you know? It's something I've learned recently. It's more dignified to remain silent sometimes, hard as it might be.

So, I'm just going to trust that I know the truth, and so do the people who matter. One day, maybe everyone else will know as well, and maybe they won't, and I'll just have to accept it however it turns out. Meanwhile, I need a new plan.

It's not as though Velvet is the be-all and end-all of everything, is it? There are other modelling agencies, lots of them. And I know they'd want me. I just have to pick where I want to go, and make it happen. It'll be fine. It'll all be fine.

There were more pages missing after that. I rifled through the diary in the hope that the missing leaves might suddenly fall out, or magically appear in some way. Of course they did not.

But my eye was caught by something else, further on.

He's given me some wonderful presents, and not just when we row. Not just making-up gifts. Like I always tell him, it's not the gifts I like about making up ... though they're a bonus, of course. What girl doesn't like to be spoiled? And Archie knows how to spoil a girl.

He just has this sense of what the right thing is, what I'd most like. It's as if he knows me inside out. Before I even know I want something, he's got it for me. Before I know I feel something, he's letting me know he understands. He knew me before I knew myself.

I'm keeping all of them. I'm never going to give them away or let them get lost, not ever. And not just the gifts he's given me either. Some of the gifts he hasn't. I've been a bit naughty. I took his jumper, one of his favourites, before he got on the plane. Hid it and didn't tell him. I knew he wanted to take it with him, but he can get something else to keep him warm. I need it here, to keep him with me. It's the cream Aran one, big and a bit scratchy, like when he hasn't shaved for a few days. It smells of him. I'm sleeping with it. That way, he's here.

The sweater . . . It was reminding me of something . . . *the boxes*. I had seen the sweater in one of the boxes. And not just the sweater. There were other things she had mentioned in the diary that I had glimpsed when I had first rifled through her possessions, impatient and baffled. I thought through the items of clothing that she had mentioned. The dress that she wore to the Christmas party, the one at Rupert's flat where she met Daddy – hadn't I seen a flash of red fabric at the bottom of the box of frocks? And the earrings that Archie had given her, they must be there too: I had seen jewellery boxes tucked in amongst the slips of satin and silk.

I turned out the contents of the clothes box, searching through it slowly and methodically this time. I sat on the floor, my legs crossed, dressed in leggings and a nightshirt, and took every single item out. Some of them I remembered seeing described in the diary as soon as I lifted them out of the box. Some I didn't recognise. So I went trawling through the diary for those items, searching for mention of silver sandals and gold earrings. I found almost everything. And, of course, I logged every single one on my spreadsheet.

## Box 1: Unlabelled

1 silk Flamenco-style scarf, black with scarlet fringing, embroidered with a pattern of birds and tropical flowers. Label reads Fortuna, Paris.

1 dress, pleated chiffon, full-length, red, with plain red sash belt around waist. Frayed/somewhat torn

around hem. Label reads Gucci, Milan. Size 38. Wrapped in tissue paper.

1 pair silver snakeskin platform sandals, strappy front with long ankle straps. Well worn, some fraying to stitching around buckles. Label reads Gucci, Milan. Size 40. In box.

I × Paisley print handkerchief.

3 × bracelets, 1 gold link, appears to be solid gold, heavy, no engraving or other markings. 1 silver bangle, inlaid with circular turquoise stones, no engraving or other marking. 1 fine gold chain, small in size, possibly designed for a child? Comprises chain plus small gold cross attached by a link. Bracelets inside small velvet drawstring pouch, no markings.

1 × satin drawstring pouch, no markings, containing 5 × pairs of earrings. 1 × pearl studs, butterfly-backed. 1 × diamanté chandelier-drop earrings. 1 × gold hoop earrings, approx 3 cm diameter. 1 × silver rose studs, with small pink stone in the centre of the flower. 1 × plain gold studs.

1 × pair of women's leather gloves, maroon-coloured, elbow-length. Label inside reads *Cornelia James*, size 6½.

1 cashmere wrap or blanket, white, no label or other identifying characteristics. Small stain/mark in one corner.

1 × newborn baby outfit, comprising white long-sleeved cardigan, white leggings, white socks with ruffled edging, white hat. Perfect condition, wrapped in tissue paper.

1 × man's jumper, cream Aran knit, wool, no label. Appears hand-knitted. Approximate size – extra large.

1 × cream trouser suit, Ossie Clark. Size 10.

The dress and the shoes were easy – the Christmas party. I found the passage where she had written about them and re-read it. She had chosen to wear the red dress, in the end. She must have looked beautiful. Resplendent, scarlet, glowing.

The jewellery, too, I found most of that. The diamanté earrings Archie had given her when she had got her first magazine modelling job. The pearl studs she bought herself, from a shop in Chelsea. *I think pearl studs are something every woman should own, don't you? Classy, understated, the sort of thing one can wear to anything and never feel over- or under-dressed. Archie approves, he thinks they're 'very becoming'. He likes me in things that aren't too flashy.*

There were the gloves, I found those a bit later in the diary. *I shouldn't have bought them, I can't afford them at all, but sometimes you have to throw caution to the wind and look on purchases as an investment, don't you? An investment for the future.*

There was the jumper, Archie's jumper; that was easy, that was what had led me back to the diary. I put it on. It felt comforting, in the way that something far too big for you does. And it felt as though it was connecting me to her. To him. Completing the circle.

And then there was the cream trouser suit and the beautiful embroidered scarf, which must have been expensive. I could find no mention of it as a gift Archie had given her, or of something she had bought when with him. Eventually I had to force myself to stick to the task I had set myself, and not get distracted by reading the diary. I was only going to unravel the tale if I was methodical, if I stuck to the right way to do things. Before, I had ignored the boxes, jumped straight into the diary. And look what had happened. Chaos. What had I been thinking? I was a structured person, a person who made lists and who spreadsheets and who catalogued information, a person who had order in the way they went about things. I would not ignore that again. But I did notice one thing I couldn't help it. The diary only went up to 1972. She had only kept it for a couple of years. And the last entry of all told of her marriage to my father.

Finally, I touched the corner of the little baby hat. Had I worn this once? Was it the first thing to touch my skin, as a fresh, new baby, other than a hospital blanket? Was this the outfit I had been brought home in, carried reverently over the threshold, precious cargo wrapped in these delicate layers of cotton and wool? Yet they seemed brand new, unworn. There was no mention of it in the diary. Unsurprisingly, really. The diary only went up to 1972, and I hadn't been born until 1979. I was touched that she had kept the items. It was the only real evidence I had that I had meant something to her, I realised. That I had been important in her life, too – as important as the gifts Archie Farrow had given her, as important as the shoes she had danced in on the night she had met my father.

What I still could not figure out was the importance of some of the items in the other boxes.

Box 2: Unlabelled

1 × set of 6 linen napkins, white. Two slightly stained, folded and ironed.

1 × set of 6 napkin rings, silver-coloured metal, tarnished.

1 × cream or milk jug, in the shape of a cow, white china, small chip on rim.

1 × set of Babycham glasses, in original box, good condition.

1 × cheese-grater, appears old, somewhat rusted on

one corner.

1 × Le Creuset round casserole, burnt orange in colour, used but clean.

Once again, everything in the box was packed and arranged with care, the lightest and most delicate items on the top. The napkins and rings were wrapped in brown paper bags, the jug in a piece of soft muslin cloth. The Babycham glasses, fragile and twinkling, had been packed with newspaper to keep them from knocking against one another. When I took one out and held it up to the light I could almost hear the laughter and music and chatter of a cocktail party from years gone by flowing out from its shallow bowl.

I unscrunched a piece of newspaper from the box. *Evening Standard*, 8th July 1985. Boris Becker had become the youngest person ever to win Wimbledon the day before, at just seventeen. A photograph of him posing with the trophy balanced on his head took up much of the page. *1985*. The year my mother had left.

Also, like the first box, it appeared to be a collection of favourite or treasured items, this time household objects rather than clothes and jewellery. It could have been a trousseau, a pile of wedding presents chosen for a young bride and groom setting up home. Things chosen for their longevity, their beauty as well as their usefulness. Things that Sadie had bought before she married Daddy, or when she moved in with him? Was this her setting up their marital home? They weren't in the diary, of course, that all happened after she had stopped writing it. But whereas I had thought this box contained just a random collection of junk; I now realised I had been wrong. Everything was here for a reason, every item was precious, treasured.

All apart from the cheese-grater. I turned it over in my

hands, wondering at its significance. It wasn't an especially nice grater, not a smart designer brand or anything; it seemed to be the sort of thing that you'd pick up for a couple of pounds and throw away once it got a bit bent out of shape and rusted, as this one had done. But no one had thrown this one away. On the contrary, they had kept it, wrapped in paper, safely stowed away, for years and years. Maybe it had just got forgotten, packed into the box with everything else by mistake. But I didn't think so.

## Box 4: Unlabelled

1 × large stuffed rabbit made from pink and white fabric, holding a fabric carrot.

This was the box that had contained the diary. In with it was the rabbit, the kind of toy you might win as a prize at a fairground or on a seaside pier. I held it to my nose and inhaled, hoping for some clue as to why it was there. It did not smell of her. It did not smell of anything. As I lifted it to my face, I squeezed its belly and felt something hard inside. A square lump. The rabbit had obviously made a noise at some point, played a tune when you pressed it or something. Not any longer though. I had no idea why it had been included in the box.

The sun was rising, just the beginnings of it, changing the colour of the light that oozed in from the edges of the blinds in my bedroom from the metallic orange of the street-lamps to a greyer-toned glow. I could hear the street starting to stir; the neighbour who lived two doors down shutting his front door on his way to work – he was a policeman and worked shifts – the rumble of a van somewhere nearby. The feeling of the house had shifted almost imperceptibly from night to morning, and I moved my stiff legs out in front of me, stretching them and wiggling my toes to try and get the blood moving through them once more. I felt the ache and thick head of my sleepless night, but no desire to get back into bed and rest. I just wanted to keep moving. Keep going. I was getting closer, I could feel it, I could almost touch it.

And I knew what I had to do next. There was one person who I knew could help me, if I could convince her to do so. It wasn't going to be easy; it was going to involve more truth-telling than I had been prepared to do. But it was the only way. I had to come clean. I had to go back to Coco.

# Chapter Thirty

I didn't mess around with letters or emails or stories about modelling aspirations, this time. What would have been the point? I just showered and dressed and gathered together the things that I would need, and then left for her house. I wrote a note for Elfie and Mark, telling them that I'd gone to run some errands, and would be back later. Before I went, I put things out for their breakfast: juice, in a jug, croissants from the freezer that I kept for unexpected guests, a teapot with bags already in it, the coffee pot ready for Mark, and two pretty mugs. It looked nice, sitting there on the side, the little spread. Welcoming. If I couldn't manage to be normal, at least I could make things *look* normal – though what was normal for Elfie? Not this. A bag of ancient muesli somewhere in the back of a cupboard, more like.

It wasn't until I was in the car, sitting at a set of traffic-lights and well on my way over there that I realised it was still only a quarter to seven in the morning. 'Oh God,' I said out loud, and I started to laugh. 'Oh fucking hell.' This whole thing was sending me crazy. I carried on laughing, unable to stop, almost crying with laughter at the ridiculous-ness of myself, fired up, behind the wheel of my car, wearing, as I now realised, a dead man's jumper, heading to the house of a woman I had met once, with no appointment, to persuade her to tell me the story of what she knew about my mother.

'And that's as far as I've got,' I told Coco. 'My mother left Velvet Models. She had a meeting with Rupert about some kind of business plan. There's more in the diary, about her and Archie, that I haven't read, but flicked through it when I was searching the boxes. It's all quite brief. I mean, some of it goes on quite a bit, but it doesn't seem to say much. It ends when she marries my father.'

I was in Coco's kitchen once more, sitting at her table, all of my paperwork spread out in front of us. The diary, the folder, the print-outs of the spreadsheets detailing what had been in Sadie's boxes. My journey. And Sadie's story. To Coco's credit, she hadn't turned a hair when she had opened the door to find me standing there, wild-eyed, in jeans and Mark's jacket, my satchel overflowing with papers. At least I had had the presence of mind to leave Archie's jumper in the car.

I still don't know how I told her who I was. How I managed to get the actual words out, I mean. I'd been so fixed on keeping the secret, not telling anyone what I was doing, hiding it all away, that telling felt – shocking. She didn't look shocked though.

'I knew that there was more to you than you were saying,' was all she said, before standing to one side and letting me in. She smiled, but it was knowing rather than warm, and I felt embarrassed.

'I'm sorry for lying to you,' I said, once I was inside, because I felt that I should. I had to say something, anyhow.

She just shrugged, and went to make tea.

'I haven't read about their wedding, yet. It feels . . . like I'm intruding, a bit.'

Coco raised an eyebrow. 'Only now?'

I took her point. But she carried on before I could think of justifying myself.

'She didn't leave, Klara.'

I stared. 'She did. Here, look.' I held open the diary, and handed it to her. Coco read it slowly, her eyes not moving from the page until she was done.

'Yes. But Klara, it's not true. I know she was your mother – but it's still not true. Sadie didn't leave because of a row with me: she was fired. Archie got rid of her.'

'But it was her diary. Why would she lie in her own diary? *You're* lying to me.'

'I promise you I'm not. What reason do I have to lie, now?'

I couldn't think of anything. I couldn't think at all. Apart from, 'But there was the row. She said something about having learned the value of a dignified silence.'

Coco laughed at that, only briefly, because she quickly realised that I didn't see the humour.

'Your mother was amazing in all sorts of ways. But one thing she was no good at was dignified silence. She was too impulsive, too fiery. It was one of her most appealing traits, as well as one of the worst. She couldn't hold back, even when she wanted to. It drove Archie mad.' She smiled. 'It was good to see, as a matter of fact. He'd met his match, because he couldn't control her, not that side of her.'

'You said he *did* control her.'

Her eyes acceded the point. 'In a way. He controlled everyone. And maybe he controlled her the most because she, out of all of us, loved him the most.'

'Even you?'

She didn't look at me then, didn't answer that. Simply said: 'The point is, she wasn't someone who would have held back about me if there had been something to tell. She would have been shouting it from the rooftops. She didn't write about the row in any detail, didn't say what it was about, because there *was* no row.' She sighed. 'Archie was cruel, Klara. He was a cruel man. Sadie should never have been with him.'

'But you loved him too.'

'Yes. And that was my downfall. I never wanted it to become Sadie's as well. I tried to protect her from it, right from the start. You know this. It's all in there, isn't it? If you look.'

I bristled. Don't tell me what's in the diary, I thought. You haven't read it. And you're lying. Lying to me, just like you lied to my mother. Even what you're saying now doesn't add up. First you say you and Archie had this special relationship, that you were the only one he couldn't walk away from, then you claim she was the one he couldn't control, then you say he controlled her the most. It *was* all in the diary: how Sadie had felt that Coco was pushing her out, standing between her and Archie.

'I knew he would discard her, you see,' Coco continued. 'He did it to all of us.'

'How many were there?'

She shrugged. 'Other women? I don't know. A lot. He and I were different. We were together for a long time. On and off, interspersed with others. There were always others. But he could not just get rid of me like he could them.'

'Why not?'

She looked away. 'Because I knew him. We understood each other. We'd – we'd met a long time before. It was just different.'

There was something she wasn't telling me. 'He still could have walked away though. From you. He moved countries.'

'With me.'

'You knew him abroad?'

'I told you. We'd met a long time before.'

'So you met him travelling?' I was trying to get to the bottom of it. Of what bound Coco and Archie together; what formed the ties that had proved strong enough to keep her by his side if he was as unkind as she claimed.

She sighed, and lit a cigarette. 'No, not travelling. Not how you mean, at least. Oh, I may as well tell you. I don't know why I'm hiding it any longer.'

I waited.

'We met on the streets, when we were sixteen and seventeen. We had both run away from home. He was from a good family, had been to a good school.'

'Eton. Where he met Rupert,' I murmured.

'Yes. I wasn't from the same kind of background at all.'

'So why had you run away? Why had he?'

She still didn't meet my eyes. 'I thought I was going to have to stay there forever. Stuck in that hellhole.'

'Where? Where did you live?'

'Near Sheffield. Small town, no jobs, no prospects. Unless you counted marrying the local landlord and running the pub. That was about the best I could have hoped for up there. It was a grey place. No hope, no joy.'

'And you wanted more, so you ran away to London.'

She shook her head. 'It wasn't as simple as that. Or maybe it was simpler. It wasn't about thinking the streets of London were paved with gold. Even at sixteen I knew that wasn't true – they're lined with preverts and predators.' Hard-won cynicism showed in her face.

'I was just trying to get away,' she went on. 'Trying to survive. I would be dead now, if I had stayed there.' There was no emotion in her voice when she said this. It was simply a fact.

'Why?' My voice was almost a whisper.

'Oh, it's one of the oldest stories in the book, mine. Mother a drunk, father dead, step-father drunk and violent. But I was beautiful. Oh, not like some of them – I was never going to be the next big thing. Just enough to make my life at home hell.'

She put her cup down and began to roll another cigarette, saying nothing for a minute or two. Once again, I waited. The ritual of it seemed to soothe her enough to continue.

'You're not a child. I'm sure you can imagine the sordid details.'

I could.

'I signed up with a modelling agency as soon as I could – an awful one, but it didn't matter. It was enough to convince my mother that I was going to become a star and make them their fortunes. Enough to mean that they paid for the first set of photos I needed and my train ticket down here. Enough that I could disappear.'

'What did you do when you got here?'

'Got away from the man who owned the agency as soon as I could. It took a while, but I did it. I worked for him for a few months – long enough to realise that I was never going to pay off the debt he claimed I owed him, despite the fact I knew that my mother had already given him money for the pictures. Long enough to meet Archie.'

'Why had he left home? He wasn't from a bad background, you said.'

'No, not at all. Though I suppose it's all relative, isn't it? What we can cope with. What we're prepared to live with, and what we're not. If you're going to understand Archie, you have to understand that he never fitted in anywhere. Nor did he want to. There was nothing in him that wanted to conform: it was like a badge of honour for him, to swim against the stream, no matter what it cost him to do so. Whatever his home-life was like, he would have hated it, on principle. However idyllic. He went forward, he ran towards something, and then he found that he couldn't find his way back, I think.'

'But why?'

She lit the cigarette that she had finished rolling. 'Why is anyone the way they are? He was hard enough to understand when he was alive.' A half-smile. 'I think there was a part of him that just wanted to do the most shocking thing – something that no one would have expected. He had been to Eton, his parents were happily married and there was no shortage of money; he could have got a university place easily, gone into the City, something like that. But that would have been too predictable. He would just have been another upper-middle-class boy from Surrey at Oxford or Durham or Edinburgh. Another man in a suit. And that would never have been enough for him. So he did what no one would have thought. He just left. And then ... then he could be anyone he wanted to be.'

'And he chose to be Archie Farrow.'

'Yes. I suppose you could put it like that, though that was his real name. I don't want you to think he lied.'

You both lied, I thought. You still lie. Everyone does.

'So why did he tell you – where he came from, I mean. Why he had run away. Surely it would have been easier for him to make something up?'

If she was going to keep on claiming that Archie Farrow had been such a paragon of honesty then I was going to call her on it, get her to explain.

'He was a strange man. I've told you. He could be very cruel.'

'So he just cut them off. Never went home again, never saw his parents again?'

'No, he saw them. But not until much later. He didn't seem to have any need for them.'

'And you didn't think that was odd?' I raised my eyebrows in question.

Coco shrugged. 'I of all people could understand that someone might not want to go home, and imagine why.'

'But you said Archie's home was fine.'

'It was. To me, Christ, it would have been heaven. But he left. On a whim, an impulse, whatever. And once he'd left, he changed. Don't you see? He became a different person. He could never just have slotted back into that world again. He'd gone beyond that.'

'I still don't get why you stayed together for so long. What it was that made it stick.'

'There was something about Archie . . . we clicked, I suppose.'

'You fell in love?'

'No, it wasn't like that. I loved him, yes. And he loved me.'

'And you were sleeping together.'

'On and off. But it was never . . . we were never like a normal couple. We were more than that. It was more important.'

'I don't understand.'

'I don't expect you to.'

I bristled. She didn't notice.

'We were the same sort of age, and everyone else we hung out with was much older. It was a strange scene back then. Dangerous, I guess, though it didn't feel so at the time. It felt exciting. And it felt safer than what I'd left behind, anyway.'

And then I understood, or thought I did. 'He protected you.' A young teenage girl, beautiful, on the streets of London. She'd already fallen victim to one unscrupulous modelling 'agent'. She teamed up with Archie, he felt responsible for her. And so later, he carried on this feeling of obligation. It made sense.

She smiled. 'Almost right. But *I* protected *him*.'

I blinked. Coco looked pleased to be able to turn my assumption on its head. 'I told you where he came from. A nice family. Not like mine.'

'Yes, you said.' The words came out more sharply than I intended. But I was tiring of her tales of woe.

'He wasn't prepared for the life he'd thrown himself into. Didn't know how to handle it. Whereas by the time we met I'd been in London for a few months.' She tapped ash off her cigarette. 'I stopped Archie from getting sucked into something he would never have been able to get out of. When I met him he was on the verge of becoming a full-time rent boy, and getting hooked on smack.'

She watched my face for a reaction. I refused to give her one.

'Did Sadie know about this?'

She let out a stream of smoke. 'I doubt it. He might have told her, but I wouldn't have thought so. It's not something he liked to shout about.'

'I suppose not.'

'But that's why – well, not why we stayed together, but why we were more than just boyfriend and girlfriend. He trusted me. And more importantly to him, he owed me. He may have been the big-shot businessman coming back from the Far East and setting up Velvet, but it was my money that started it. Mine and Rupert's. Archie was a talented man, but in business? He was a failure.'

I was shocked.

'You think I'm a bitch, don't you?' Coco said. 'I'm not. I did love Archie, and I respected him. But I was also clear-eyed about the sort of man he was.'

'So why did you give him the money, and stay with him, if you knew he was such a bad lot? A crap businessman, a cheat, a junkie . . .'

She bit her lip. 'That was all other people though. How can I explain it? He was never like that with me. And he always came back to me.'

And then, finally, I understood. She didn't care about the other women, Sadie or any of the others. She didn't care about the money. Like Sadie, she cared only about Archie. About keeping him close.

As I was leaving, a sudden thought came to me.

'Did you know Ned?' I asked her casually, throwaway.

'Ned Davidson?'

My heart sank, but I clung on. 'I don't know his surname. A friend of my father's, another scientist.'

She nodded and looked amused. 'That's him. Clever man. I never took much notice of him, but he was always around. One of Rupe's hangers-on – he sort of collected them, these strange guys. He found them interesting, I think.'

Ned Davidson, not N.R. then. I almost told her why I was asking. She might have been able to guess at who N.R. was, after all, might have been able to help. But something stopped me, some kind of loyalty to Sadie, to my mother. I had been set on a mission, and it was up to me to find out the truth now. No one else could do it for her. I would do this by myself.

# Chapter Thirty-One

It was the cheese-grater that did it, in the end. The battered cheese-grater that had been so carefully packed in with all the fragile china and glass. I had known from the start that there had to be something more to it, some special reason why it was in the box with all of her other precious things.

*1st July, 1972*

> Today I got married. The merry-go-round continues to whirl and I don't want to get off. It was beautiful and wonderful and everything your wedding day should be. It was small, and intimate, just the two of us and witnesses – Henry's dear friends Ned and Ruth. My parents couldn't have made the trip, it wouldn't be fair, poor things, and his are all the way up North, and anyhow we decided that one and not the other wouldn't be right, and how romantic to be just us, like something out of a movie. Who wants lots of guests clogging things up and demanding poached salmon and chocolate mousse?! Not me. Weddings like that are so conventional, anyhow. Old-fashioned.
>
> We did some things the traditional way though. He

wore a suit, and a flower in his lapel, and he looked very handsome, and I wore a cream trouser suit with a floppy hat and an embroidered scarf, and he told me I looked beautiful and gave me flowers to carry, and we had our photo taken on the steps and Ned and Ruth had even brought confetti.

We had a few gifts, as well. Some lovely napkins and silver rings from Henry's colleagues, and some Babycham glasses from Rupert – such fun! And a cheese-grater from Archie, the silly boy. He sent it in a huge box, tied up with a bow as though it were a silver salver to be carried into a ballroom by butlers in dickie bows. Henry looked confused by it.

Archie always used to tease me about my love of cheese, saying that models shouldn't eat as much of the stuff as I did. I said what did it matter if I didn't put weight on? He warned me that I would turn into a truckle of cheddar if I wasn't careful, and I said that would be fine by me. 'You'd eat yourself all up though, and then there'd be nothing left for me.' Such a sweet gift, so thoughtful.

The cheese-grater. So it had been a wedding present from Archie – that was why she had kept it, wrapped so carefully. Such a small thing – and yet not, to her. I could hear it in her words. I knew her a little better by now. *Archie always used to tease me about my love of cheese.* A throwaway sentence, you'd think, but I heard the memories in it, I heard how wistful she was. And I knew that she was not telling her diary the whole truth.

I flicked back, turning the pages to read again about Sadie's relationship with my father. There was lots about how she admired him, how she thought he was so clever, so kind, so considerate. Nothing about how she loved him. No, that wasn't true. *Henry told me he loved me tonight,* she wrote, a few weeks after they had started dating. *He knows it's fast, but it's how he feels, and of course I feel the same way – what's the point in spending lots of time talking around the subject when you might as well just get on and say it?* Henry told me he loved me tonight. I imagined my father summoning up all of his courage to do that. Or maybe he hadn't needed to, maybe he had been buoyed along with confidence and passion and emotion and had just blurted it out. Daddy had never been much of a blurter, but if I had learned anything through this process so far it was that you never really knew your parents. You couldn't.

I read it all again. The courtship she described with Henry made sense if you thought you were reading the diary of a much older woman. It was restrained, measured. It had none of the bare-knuckle passion from her earlier entries, the ones about Archie. And which I could still hear in Daddy's voice when he talked about her.

But you never knew, did you? Maybe those feelings had been there, but she was afraid to voice them again. Maybe she had learned lessons, whatever Coco said, and was living them. Maybe she had just grown up.

No. There was more. There had to be more.

I searched through the boxes, not carefully cataloguing this time, but pulling everything out, taking it all to pieces. There had to be something else. Everything in here was here for a reason. It was not random, it was ordered, selected, chosen.

The diary had fallen short of what I wanted from it, and I felt resentful of it. It sat on the floor before me, its hard black edges mean and intractable. *Sadie* had fallen short of what I wanted from her, I might have thought, but I did not. She had told me of the wedding, but not really, not of what was behind it. Not of what had led to it. Not the truth. I may have questioned that that was what I wanted when I had left Coco's, but now that the truth was slipping out of my grasp once more, I wanted nothing else. I had to know, had to see everything that had happened. I had to be able to touch it.

The contents of the boxes were strewn in front of me, scattered all over the floor, and the sight made me panic. I should order it. Sort it, somehow. How? Height order, order of importance, order in which I had found it? There had to be a key, a clue, a way to unlock its secrets. Linen napkins, napkin rings, a milk jug. Decorated glasses, a casserole, the cheese-grater. What did they mean? I picked up the grater and ran my finger down its edges, feeling it rasp against my skin. Clothes, dresses, leather gloves, fancies and fripperies. I might have been a child, surrounded by dressing-up clothes purloined from her mother's wardrobe, lipstick-faced, small feet in shoes too big . . . and it was all blurred in together, Sadie and the woman that I remembered or thought I did, and the woman my father had told me about, and the one that Coco described.

Who was she? Who was the real one, the true Sadie Mortimer *née* Tomaszewski, from St Albans or London or simply my imagination? And I was all questions and no answers and the clothes were going to strangle me, suffocate me, and I pushed them away, kneeling and keening until eventually I had no breath left to sob with and became aware of myself once more, and felt ashamed.

The rabbit was sitting in front of me all by itself. I picked it up and held it to my chest. The last few angry tears fell on to the top of its head and I squeezed it, hard, as a small child might squeeze a beloved but infuriatingly unresponsive pet hamster before realising that it had squeezed too hard.

And then I felt it: the lump that I had noticed before and had assumed was some kind of squeaker. This time, however, my fingers found it from a different angle and I discovered that it was not box-shaped after all, but cylindrical, with a ridge around it. A roll of money, maybe? Hidden from sight, tucked away safely . . .

I turned the toy over and searched for an opening. There was none. It felt wrong to just rip it open, and its eyes stared at me accusingly as I went to the bathroom and found a pair of nail scissors in the medicine cabinet. A few small snips and it was open, its spine unfolded in front of me. A memory of doing the same with my soft toys when I was small floated up at me from the floor. Playing surgeon. *And here's the kidneys, yes, we'd better take those out. Oh dear, nurse, what a lot of blood . . .* Children are gruesome, aren't they?

My childhood surgeries had only ever yielded synthetic stuffing and a sense of sadness that I had done something that could not be undone. This operation gave up far greater rewards. For in the bowels of the rabbit, tucked deep inside the stuffing and bound with a disintegrating rubber band, was a thick roll of paper.

The missing pages of Sadie's diary.

# Chapter Thirty-Two

It was Sadie's diary still. The paper was the same, the handwriting the same. But the story?

The story was different.

*5th November, 1970*

> I should never have gone to the bar. I'm so humiliated. I'm going to write this down here because if I don't I think I shall explode, but then I'm going to tear it out and burn it and never, ever think about it again.
>
> I got there at just past seven o'clock. I'd spent ages doing my hair and make-up, blow-drying and curling my hair and choosing the right outfit and everything. I wanted to make a good impression, to make sure that the girl on Archie Farrow's arm was the most beautiful girl in town. I bought a new red lipstick specially, a posh one, from Chanel. I wanted to look perfect.
>
> Bertie's Bar is near Charing Cross station. It's sort of underground, built into the arches of the bridge there, and it's big and has lots of tables all crammed in close to one another. It took me a while to find them, as they were sitting right at the back half-hidden behind a

pillar. But I spotted them eventually. I could see Archie's thick dark hair and it made my heart thud. My hands were all trembly. I stood up straight and put a smile on my face and imagined I was at a modelling job, playing the part of a confident woman off to meet her husband for dinner. Gliding across the floor, waiting for him to see me, to stand up, pull the chair out, kiss me tenderly . . .

I can't, I can't, I can't bear to write it. But I have to write it. It'll poison me otherwise.

The look on his face when he saw me was awful. I had been hoping for and expecting delight, and what I got was – disgust. He looked appalled that I was there – embarrassed even. I faltered; my legs felt too long and too bare and my dress felt wrong and my make-up too sticky on my skin, but I kept on walking. I was wrong, I told myself, I was misreading his expression. *Keep walking, confident woman, elegant, gliding* . . . but as I got closer to the table I knew that I was not wrong, I was not misreading anything.

When I was a couple of yards away from them, he seemed to leap into action whereas before he had been frozen. 'What the fucking hell are *you* doing here?' he asked, and I stared at him. Sitting at the table behind him were Coco and another man – Rupert, it must be. There was a bottle of wine in front of them and a pile of papers and they were trying not to look at us, but I could tell that Coco, at least, was watching out of the corner of her crocodile eye.

'I wanted to surprise you,' I whispered – I couldn't bear for them to hear me. Archie took my elbow and led me away from them. He obviously didn't want them to hear or see me either.

'Jesus, Sadie, why are you here? You've got a shoot tomorrow, no? You should be back at home, in bed.' He stared at me, waiting for an answer, but I couldn't speak. I knew that if I opened my mouth, hot tears would spill out from everywhere, not just my eyes but my lips and nose and brain and everywhere, so I kept it shut and just nodded.

'So why . . .' He looked genuinely confused for a moment, and then he said, 'Oh, I see. Right. You think that last night – you think we're together now, is that it?'

A tear had escaped and slid down my cheek and he could see that what he had guessed was the truth.

'Jesus. It's my fault. This is all my fault.' He closed his eyes for a second. Then he opened them again and grasped my wrist in his hand. It was not gentle. 'Listen to me, Sadie. Last night was great. You're a beautiful girl. We could have some fun together – if you don't mess things up. But pull a stunt like this again, and you won't just drive me away for good, you'll make sure your career is dead in the water, because I'll bin you from Velvet and send you back to wherever it is you came from faster than you can imagine. We're *not* a fucking couple,' he finished. 'Do you understand?'

I was too shocked to do anything other than nod. Too shocked to cry, even.

'Do you?' he said again, and his hand was gripping my wrist too tightly, so I nodded again. 'Yes,' I managed to whisper. 'Yes, I understand. I'm sorry, Archie.'

He let go of me. 'OK. It's all right. Go home, get some beauty sleep and I'll see you tomorrow. We'll forget all about it. Start again. All right? Good night, Sadie.'

And he turned away from me and went back to Coco and Rupert and none of them looked at me again as I left the bar, my best gold handbag shaking in my hands as I tried not to drop it, and my mascara running down my cheeks and onto my jaw. It was as if I was invisible. I wished that I was.

Now I'm sitting on my bed, still wearing my dress with a jumper over the top and I'm freezing cold and I can't stop crying. My make-up's all over my face but I don't care. I bought a bottle of brandy on the way back here and I've had some of it already. I poured it into my tooth glass, and I'm going to sit here and I'm going to drink brandy until I pass out or until something happens to stop this terrible pain, and when I wake up in the morning, if I wake up at all, well – I'll deal with tomorrow then.

### 10th November, 1970

OK. I should finish this, even though these pages are coming out of the diary. I feel that I need to tell the whole story somewhere. And maybe I won't burn them after all. Maybe I'll just put them somewhere else. I want the diary to be clean, neat, perfect. It's not a lie to miss out bits of the story that make you flinch every time you see the words on the page. It's just protecting yourself.

I didn't go to the shoot. I know. It's awful and I'm ashamed of myself and I'm never going to do it again. I'm never going to drink again, not like that. I drank brandy all night, it felt like, until I was just sitting there crying and feeling sick and forcing it down. In the end I did pass out. And I didn't wake up again until it was too late to get there, even allowing for it all being late and everything. I felt totally sick when I woke up and realised that the dusty blue light coming in through my window was the sun setting, not rising, and that I had missed the entire day, but then that nausea was overtaken by a much more urgent feeling and I had to rush to my basin and throw up, a lot. I couldn't stop for ages. I just kept on being sick until it felt as though my stomach was going to turn inside out and my throat was raw, and I was so weak I couldn't even get back into bed. I just sort of sat down and leaned my head against the base of the sink, waiting until I could move again and wondering whether I would die before that happened. I didn't really care either way.

Obviously I didn't die. It did take me a good few hours to move though. It was properly dark by the time I pulled myself up and just about managed to brush my teeth, take the dress off and crawl back beneath the sheets. I didn't sleep again for a while, as my mind was racing even though my body was still exhausted, and my head was pounding, pounding. All I wanted was for someone to come and bring me some orange juice and aspirin and tell me everything was going to be all right, but there wasn't anyone. That was the worst bit. There was no one there.

I slept and woke and dozed all night, and every time I woke up it was awful, all over again. I remembered the bar, and Archie's face, and coming back here on the bus crying and pretending I wasn't crying, and drinking the brandy and throwing up and all of it, all at once, and every time I closed my eyes again and prayed to go back to sleep and not wake up this time. No doubt I should have gone to the hospital, had my stomach pumped or something, but I think the vomiting helped; it's a good job I bought such cheap brandy, as my body got rid of it by itself.

Eventually I woke up as the sun was rising on the second day, and knew that I had sweated and puked all the alcohol out. I still felt terrible, but not as though I was actually dripping poison any more. I got up and crept down the landing and had a bath, then came back to my room and got dressed and sat on my bed wondering what I should do next.

And then he rang. 'Hello, Sadie,' he said, As soon as I heard his voice, it felt as though all of the last forty-eight hours had been erased, and we were back in his flat without phone lines and streets and buildings between us, just me and him and the us that we created.

We were both quiet for a few seconds and I could hear him breathing.

'I'm sorry,' he carried on. 'I was too harsh the other night.'

'I'm sorry too. I shouldn't have turned up like that. It was inappropriate.'

'Will you come now? I need to see you. I can't do this over the phone.'

It was then that I looked in the mirror. 'I can come in a couple of hours.'

He laughed, a bark. 'Really? After all this you're going to keep me waiting? Fuck.' But he didn't sound angry. He sounded – almost impressed. 'You're something else, Sadie.'

And I knew, then, that it would be all right.

\* \* \*

It was more than all right. It was – sacred, I want to say. Oh, I can't burn this, I can never burn this. This is the truth of our love. I arrived at his flat and he was waiting for me, and as soon as he opened the door he pulled me inside and kissed me, hard, and I could feel every bit of his body moving towards mine and mine towards his, and I knew that it was going to happen.

'I'm sorry about the shoot,' I started to say, because despite all of this he was still my boss and I had behaved badly, but he shook his head and undid the buttons of my coat with one hand.

'I don't care about the shoot. Do them good to think you're in demand. I told them you'd been booked on something else.'

I blinked. 'What about Coco?'

'I told her I'd changed the plan.' My coat was on the floor and so was my carefully chosen jumper, a thin-knit red one that made my skin glow. But it didn't matter now because my skin was exposed. I was standing there in just my bra and jeans. He rubbed his hand over my bra and moaned. 'Sadie.'

'But she saw me . . . at the bar . . .'

Archie stopped touching me then and stood back from me, looking at my body and then at my face.

'Sadie.' His expression was serious.

'Yes.' Oh God, I thought, had I ruined it all again?

'Do you really want to talk about Coco and the modelling job? Because I fixed it. Look, I'm sorry about the bar, but you caught me off-guard. Don't do it again and we'll be all right. I knew you'd be upset, I knew that's why you didn't show yesterday. So I covered for you.'

He reached out and put his fingers down inside the top of my jeans and I shivered.

'That's what people do when they care about each other. That's what people do when they love each other.' I couldn't breathe, but – it didn't matter. He was oxygen and water and everything that I needed. I swallowed, and took a step towards him.

'Good girl.' His hand went lower. 'We understand each other, don't we? We understand.'

And I did. As he lifted me up and carried me into his bedroom, I understood everything. It was him. *He* was everything.

I'm stopping outside the bedroom door. Now that I'm not going to burn these pages, I'll keep them somewhere safe. But I'm not the sort of girl that kisses and tells. I know what happened, how it happened. How I became a woman. And that's enough. Everything about Archie is enough.

I was beginning to understand. There were two diaries – or rather, there was one, but it contained two truths, two Sadies. Like pulling away bark from a tree, I had reached the smooth inner core, the heart of things. She had written the truth, and then she had covered it up, carefully brushing leaves and soil over it to conceal it from the world that she was so sure would be watching her – and then she had buried it deep inside – a toy rabbit. Why this?

# Chapter Thirty-Three

*19th January, 1971*

He's thrown me out. Archie's thrown me out of Velvet. I'm writing this sitting in the café around the corner from my flat. I can't bear to be at home by myself. It feels all wrong. As if I'm an imposter in my own life. So I have come here, and I'm writing this and crying onto the page and the old man who runs the café has just given me a free piece of cake because he feels sorry for me. I'm going to eat it, as well. It's not like I've got some campaign to slim for. Not any more.

I'm going to take these pages out of my diary when I've written them. Again. It's important that I keep that record clean. That I portray myself in the best possible light. It sounds mad, doesn't it? Even so, I know in my heart of hearts that it's important. That one day someone will read it, and that person will matter. And it will matter that they don't see all the – mess. But I have to write it down otherwise I'll go insane. I have to tell the truth somewhere, and if I can't do it in my own diary then I'm really screwed, aren't I? It doesn't change the fact that my diary will be true. It will tell the truth. Just – not all of it. Not about everything. There's nothing wrong with that.

*Oh, stop justifying yourself and tell what's happened.*

Truth is, I'm not really sure. I don't know how it's all fallen apart so badly. Oh God, now I'm crying again and it's going on the paper and I've already turned my napkin into a soggy shredded mess. I'm wiping my nose on my sleeve like a child.

We had this awful row. I hadn't turned up to the shoot he'd booked me on. I meant to, I really did. But I was getting ready and it was all taking me ages and I messed my hair up so I had to wash it and start again, I couldn't leave with it looking as bad as it did. And then I got into a bit of a state, because it still wasn't going right, and I started crying, so stupid – so, so stupid – so then I had to wait until my face stopped being all red. I phoned them, I really did, or I thought I had, but Archie said I hadn't rung, hadn't even bothered to tell them I wasn't going to show up, and I'm not sure how that happened, but maybe I forgot. Maybe I just practised ringing them, in my head. I do that sometimes, if I'm nervous about something; I have the conversation in my own head before I have to have it out loud. Not just with phone calls. Sometimes I just do it before things happen. I'm not making any sense. I know what I mean though. It helps me feel prepared. So I thought I'd rung but it turns out maybe I just did it in my head, and when I said I definitely had, Archie called me a lying little tramp, and I cried and cried, and begged him to be nice to me, and then he just walked away.

Rupert was in the office when I went back there, having some meeting with Coco, and he was so kind, he drove me back to my flat. 'We're finished, aren't we, darling?' he said to Coco, and when she nodded, he took me by the shoulders and steered me outside. I had tried hard not to cry in front of her, but as soon as I got into the street it all fell apart. He was being so nice to me and that always makes me cry. He just put me into the car and let me sniffle away and passed me his beautiful Paisley handkerchief and didn't care that I got snot all over it. He drove me back to Walpole Street and didn't tell me I was stupid or anything, just made sure I got home safely, and then when I was getting out of the car, he said, 'It'll be all right, you know. Coco will look after you.' Well, Coco hasn't done much looking after me so far, has she?

I said before that I had this great plan – but it was a lie. I don't have any sort of a plan. I don't have any money. No savings at all. Oh, I kept meaning to put money aside out of each pay cheque, but I never did. There's always something more fun to spend it on, isn't there? I was sure Archie would cover me, if I needed him to, but after today I don't think that's going to happen. So unless I do something drastic, I'm going to be homeless in a couple of weeks. I don't think things can get any worse. I don't see how they can.

I was right. Things didn't get worse. They got better. Oh God, they got better! I never thought I'd be writing this, not now, not like this, but – I'm pregnant.

I found out yesterday and I haven't been able to stop smiling. Oh, it's all wrong. I'm not married, I can't pay my rent, I haven't even spoken to Archie for three days and five hours. My parents would disown me if they knew, I haven't a clue how to look after a baby and I don't even know how far gone I am. The doctor told me, but I didn't take it in, so I'll have to ask when I go back. But I am happy, happy, happy.

I plan to go and see Archie tonight and tell him. Don't worry, I'm not going to surprise him again! I rang earlier and said I had to talk to him about something to do with the lease on my flat. He co-signed it, so he had to agree to see me really. I could tell that he wasn't keen, but he agreed. It hurt me, hearing that. Hearing him sounding as if it was a trial that I was going to visit him, as if he was worried I was going to cause him problems. Of course I'm not. He'll be so pleased when I tell him, we'll be able to forget everything else. And I've got an idea for how to tell him. I want to make it really special, not just blurt it out. He's going to love it.

My stomach sank. He wasn't going to love it. I knew Archie Farrow well enough by now to be sure that he was not going to react like a thrilled father-to-be at the news he was to receive from Sadie. I picked up the baby's shawl, my eyes still fixed on the pages, and rested it over my knees. Was this me? Was it me that she was talking about, the beginnings of the thing inside her? I had a sudden flash of guilt for disembowelling the rabbit that she had chosen with such care. Then no, it couldn't be me. The dates didn't add up. Archie Farrow couldn't be my father. *Could he?*

This was the real Sadie, the raw, unedited version. She had written her story in these pages and then torn them out, even in her darkest moments unable to bear the thought of presenting a less than shiny picture to the world. She was Sadie, who had left home in such a puff of exultant smoke, this was Sadie who was going to set the world on fire. This was Sadie who clung on to the prospect of fame and fortune, of future generations reading her diary, so she had pulled the darkness from the heart of it and hidden it deep inside a stuffed bunny. It was pathetic, and touching, and I loved her for it. This was the real woman, this was the woman I had been waiting to meet.

## 26th January, 1971

He didn't love it. He hated it. Hates me, hates the baby, hates, hates, hates. I've never felt more stupid in my life. I turned up at his apartment with the stuffed rabbit that I bought for him at the smart little gift shop around the corner. Not that I can afford it, but I didn't flinch when I handed over the money, even though it was a week's gas or a lot of meals. The lady in the shop put it in a thick paper bag tied with a bow and smiled at me when she handed it to me, as though the two of us had a secret. I suppose we did.

'I'm pregnant,' I told her, for no reason other than it just came out, and she smiled at me again and said, 'Congratulations.'

It felt odd to say it, as if I was playing a part; I might have been at work, being a pregnant woman in an advertisement for baby clothes or something. It didn't feel like me, as if I had the right to say it, though I wasn't at work, of course. There was no work, not any longer. There was just me, and this thing inside me, the beginnings of this thing, and there was Archie – or there would be again, soon.

I cried as I read Sadie's account of how she told Archie about her pregnancy, her heart filled with hope, seeing how sharply that hope was shattered. 'I can't have a child with you, Sadie,' he told her. 'It's out of the question.' *Out of the question.* No room for discussion, negotiation, tenderness, regret. Just a straightforward decision, made by him for both of them – for all three of them.

She begged, and pleaded. She humiliated herself in front of him.

But Archie didn't care.

'Please, Archie,' I said, 'you'll love it when it's here, can't you see? It'll be like the best of you and the best of me, in a whole new person.'

He shook his head. 'No, it won't be, Sadie. It won't be, because it won't get to that point. It can't. Do you understand?'

No, I didn't understand. How could I? He loved me, I knew he loved me, whatever he said now. I could see it in his eyes, in the way he wouldn't look at me. He did care, he did.

'I'll pay whatever you need me to,' he told me, 'don't worry about that. And don't worry about the rent for a while either. I'll cover you for six months – I owe you that much.'

Six months' rent and some money for the bills. Is that all I am worth to him, then? Oh, and the money for an abortion, of course – mustn't forget that. Pay her off, the stupid model from out of town who's got herself into trouble, give her enough cash to satisfy your conscience and she'll fade away, fade back into nothing-ness and you can carry on as you did before. Archie

295

Farrow, big man about town, nothing can touch you.

I was so angry then I couldn't look at him. I felt as if I was a big ball of pain and fire and everything bad, and I couldn't contain it any more, so I didn't say anything else. I knew that I couldn't, the words wouldn't come out right, so I just nodded and he looked relieved and came over to guide me to the door. 'It'll be fine, honey,' he said. 'You'll see. It's for the best. Trust me.'

I heard a noise coming from the other room just then and I turned my head. Stared at him. He stopped. I knew that look on his face. I knew every one of his expressions. Happiness, excitement, frustration, disappointment. *Guilt.* 'There's someone else here, isn't there?' I whispered. He didn't answer – and that was all the answer I needed. I just ran, then. Out of the door, down the front stairs, into the street, listening all the while to my blood thudding in my ears and the silence, the silence, as he did not call out after me.

It had been Coco in the other room, I was sure. Hiding herself away, hustling into the bedroom or bathroom when they heard Sadie's knock at the door. Listening, hovering quietly, but not quite quietly enough, to those most private and intimate exchanges. Making herself heard on purpose, making her presence felt, sending Sadie a message? One that said: *I am here now, in your place, in his arms, with him. There is no room for you, not any longer.*

I expected to read about the abortion next, to get confirmation that this baby was not me. Even though I knew rationally that it could not be, I still wanted to read it. But that wasn't what happened.

It was exactly the same as I remembered it. I don't know what I'd been expecting, but of course it was *me* that was different, not St Albans. I had left here in a taxi, aged eighteen, not looking back, not planning to ever come back – and now here I was, back again but changed. Unmistakably changed. Then I had been Mary still, just trying on Sadie for size, really. Now I would never be anyone other than Sadie. Then I had been full of hope and excitement and plans and promises to myself. Now? Now I was full of another sort of hope.

I had been given a chance, I told myself, to do a good thing. To change someone else's life. To make someone else as happy as I had been when I had first found out about the baby, when I had still thought that I could make it work, make Archie love us. I had been wrong, so wrong, but that didn't mean that I couldn't put things right; it would just be in a different way to how I had thought.

St Albans might look exactly the same as when I had left, but Suzanne didn't. She stood in the doorway of the little terraced house that she shared with Trevor – her husband, now – and we stared at each other. It hadn't been that long since we had last been together, but it felt like a decade. She was a grown-up now, I realised as I looked at her. A married woman, not a girl. She had a grown-up hair cut and sensible shoes, and she was wearing a cardigan and a pinny over it. A pinny. She held her hands out to the side and I noticed that they had flour on them.

'Look what happened,' she said, and I laughed. 'Not quite the career journalist I talked about, am I? At least one of us is living it though. Look at you. Mary Tomaszeswki.'

'Sadie,' I corrected her gently. 'I really did change it.'

She nodded. 'Of course. I remember.' And she reached out her arms and hugged me, and it was as if I had never been away.

We sat at her kitchen table, with big mugs of tea and hunks of Victoria sponge still a bit warm in the middle from the oven. It was like being at home, but not one that I had ever known. The sort of home you imagine other people have: warm and welcoming, with a mum always there in the kitchen, dispensing tea and cake, smelling of flowers and flour and everything familiar. There was a fire in the front room and the buzz of the racing on the TV that Trevor sat watching. He was polite and friendly, but as awkward as ever with me, and once he'd shaken my hand, he retreated.

'He used to have the most awful crush on you, you know,' Suzanne said. I was glad she had, because then we could both pretend that I hadn't noticed, that she knew him better than I did, and I said, 'Oh God, did he?' and we laughed about men in a way that made us both feel better and worse all at once, I think.

'So,' she said, after a while, after I had told her about parties and being a model and living in London and all the things she wanted to know. I didn't tell her I wasn't with Velvet any more. Didn't want to shatter her illusions. I could still be impressive, sort of, here. Still be the success story.

'So. I don't really know . . .'

'I can't thank you enough.'

We spoke at the same time and then stopped and

laughed, nervous around each other. 'This is silly,' I said. 'How long have we been friends?'

'A long time. Long enough that . . . Look, I wouldn't be able to even think about this if it was anyone else. It wouldn't feel right,' Suzanne said.

'I wouldn't think of doing it if you *were* anyone else.'

'But you're like family.'

'Yes.'

She took my hand. 'Sadie. Are you sure?'

I stared down at the table, at our hands linked over it. It was scrubbed pine and the whorls and ridges blurred while I tried to pull myself together. I wasn't sure, and at the same time I was. I didn't know how it was going to work, or what the next few months would be like, or how I was going to feel, or any of those things. I didn't know anything, really. But the only way out of the situation I had found myself in, was to give Suzanne my baby. My mother sort of did it for a stranger, didn't she, so I could do it for a friend. My best friend. My only friend.

I had been sitting on our bedroom floor, resting my back against the side of our bed. I stretched, and let my head fall back until it touched the mattress. Sadie's plan made sense, in a strange, warped way. Suzanne was desperate for a baby; Sadie was having a baby she knew she could not keep. She hoped that giving it away would bring Archie back to her, bring her career back to her, I could tell. I wanted her to be right. Wanted to read that she had got her happy ending, but I knew that she had not. I knew how Sadie's story ended – or, at least, I thought I did.

# Chapter Thirty-Four

*10th February, 1971*

Nothing ever happens the way you plan it. Or maybe it's just me. Nothing ever happens the way *I* plan it. It all falls apart, sooner or later, usually sooner. I'm a failure. At everything. I thought this would be my one chance to do something right, to make something good come out of something I got wrong – but that was never going to happen. I was stupid to think it would.

It's *her* fault. Everything's her fault. If I sit and stare at the window for long enough, I can see the truth there. There are raindrops on the glass but they don't stop me seeing it. She got me here in the first place, she led me to him, she pushed me away from him, she took him – and now she's taken this child from me. Not because she wants it for herself. I could understand that, almost. But she doesn't want me to have it, doesn't want me to do a good thing: she doesn't want anyone to be happy other than herself. She's full of hate and it seeps out of her and infects everything. She's infected Archie. Stopped him seeing the truth, the truth in the glass, even with the raindrops.

It's all muddled in my head. But there's something

that she can't control, and that's Archie. As it turns out. Because her plan hasn't worked, has it? She told him about my plan, and that was her plan too, but now her plan has become a better one for me, and a worse one, all at once, because I don't have a choice any more, so it doesn't matter whether it's better or worse, it just is, it will just be. Will be, will be, will be. What will be and what won't be.

Well, I know what there *won't* be. There won't be a baby, for me or for Suzanne. There won't be me getting fat and her waiting and me giving her a bundle and a happy day and a knowing that I can see it sometimes and that I did a good thing, that I made a life and saved a life and gave a life. There won't be a child growing inside and up outside.

But there will be me, and there will be a job, a contract, a career to go back to, and a life, not its life but my life. I am saving my life, you could say, taking it back, taking it back from her, not losing a life but regaining one, but most of all regaining him. That's all that matters really, in the end. There will be him, again. Him.

It felt as if the contents of my mother's mind had been tipped onto the page, straight from the source. And her mind was obviously disturbed. I read the lines again. It was Coco that she was talking about, of course. I read beneath as well as between the lines. Coco had found out about her plan somehow, her decision to go through with having the baby, Archie's baby, and give it to Suzanne. And then she had told Archie, and Archie had put a stop to it. Sadie might have wanted to do something different, something that she thought was right, but there was nothing she wouldn't do for Archie. So she had given up her plan for him. For the promise that they would be together again? That everything would go back to normal, that she would have it all back, her career, her London life with her King's Road flat and her nights out and her figure? That she would have *him* back? I felt a fierce rush of protectiveness for her. She had been weak, vulnerable, lost. And Coco and Archie had fastened on that, bent her to their will, taken advantage of her in almost every possible way. Coco.

It made sense, the conclusion I had come to, that Coco was at the heart of this. Suzanne's reaction when I had tracked her down in St Albans contained the sort of bitterness, I saw now, that grows from years of nurturing a deep hurt, a devastating disappointment. The blame had been turned back on Sadie, naturally. She had offered Suzanne the one thing she wanted – yearned for – and had then taken it away again. Taken away hope. Without explanation? I didn't know, had no way of knowing. Sadie's resentment of Coco had seeped in through her words even in the edited, 'public' version of her diary. She had not been able to suppress it. And I did not blame her.

I didn't know what had happened after that. But whatever it was, it wasn't the happy ending that Sadie had hoped for. She had expected Archie to take her back, into Velvet, into his arms, into his life. But Velvet had disintegrated, as had Sadie's career. There had been no resurrection from the ashes for her. She had transformed herself into someone else entirely, into Mrs Henry Mortimer. Into a wife.

*I'm ready for this*, she had written. *I have found someone who can make me happy – properly happy, in a real way, not in the superficial way that I thought was happiness before. Someone who takes my happiness seriously, takes me seriously. Who will look after me and care for me and who I can care for. This is what I was meant to do. Maybe this is why I was meant to come to London after all – to be led here, to this place, on this path. And I am lucky, and grateful that I have found it.*

Controlled, serene, happy. The perfect bride. Or so you might think. So she *wanted* you to think. She was whitewashing her life. She still thought, somewhere in her mind, that she was creating this document, recording her life for posterity. And she was determined to be in control of the image she was creating.

And in a way she was. She had moved in with my father, and had me, and that had been it. There had been a few jobs, as evidenced by the pictures in the folders, but no modelling trips to London, or Paris, or America. No glamorous friends inviting her to parties that she simply couldn't miss. Her modelling career had been a brief flash in time for her, one that illuminated everything else around it, but one which did not last. More of the stories from my childhood evaporating between my fingers as I tried to catch them.

So what had she been doing, all those times when she went away?

I found the answer on the next pages. The final ones.

### 3rd April, 1981

I am afraid of what Henry will do when he finds out. Because he's sure to find out, isn't he? People do. You can't keep these things covered up forever. And anyhow, when we are together he'll have to know. Obviously. Even I can't manage two husbands! Oh it's a mess, a mess, my head is a mess.

I never thought he would come back to me. I thought that when he said, 'No, it isn't going to be like it was,' that that was it. All over, for ever, everything gone. And it was. Everything *had* gone. Me, and him, and the baby, and modelling, and Suzanne, and – all of it. There wasn't anything left. Apart from Henry. And so I married him. And it was the right thing to do – for me and for him – because he loved me and wanted me and could look after me, and I needed him and he was all there was and that's love, isn't it, when there is no one else for you? You are everything to each other and that's what we were and so there it was.

I thought that I would die, when it happened – when he rang me, after all these years. Saying he couldn't stay away; couldn't stop thinking about me. I told him that he must never, ever do that again because it would break me into tiny pieces, pieces of nothing. I had done it all for him, you see, all for him – and then to have nothing . . .

But he won't do it again. I could hear how he missed me, how he needed me to come back to him, and so of course I went. I got the bus and I went into central London, for the first time in a long time, and it was bigger and brighter and louder than ever, and it made me feel small and grey and transparent, not like before. But then I was there, and he was there, and it was exactly like before – his smell, his skin, his hair – and I buried myself in him and would not could not did not come up for air until the sun rose, and I rose with it like the dawn.

And since then, every time has been everything, and I cannot keep it contained within my heart any longer. I cannot stop, but I cannot go back – and so I am stuck, torn in two, in more than two – in three – because there is Klara now, and I cannot take her with me, cannot leave her behind. And so forever I am here, floating in limbo, like dust in the sunshine . . .

*I am afraid of what Henry will do when he finds out . . . Torn in two, in more than two – in three – because there is Klara now . . .*

Her fear transmitted itself to me through the pages, through the years, like a tremor. The first, tentative signs of an earthquake, growing in strength and power. Unstoppable. And she hadn't been able to stop it, had she? Henry, my father, had discovered her secret, her passion, and – and then what?

She had disappeared, that was what. I couldn't voice the words that were forming in my mind, not yet. But they were there. She had disappeared, and he had told everyone she had left, and then he had told everyone that she was dead. He had erased her from our lives with calm, cool efficiency, and he had managed to convince me that this was not that unusual. He had conned me, all my life, and now the scales had fallen from my eyes and I saw him for what he was, a . . .

No. Not yet, not yet. Something superstitious deep in my soul told me that once I let that word slip out, there would be no going back, there would be no return, and I had to make sure I was ready, first. I would be ready, though the thought scared me.

*There's nothing to fear*, I told myself. *He cannot do to you what he did to her. He cannot make you disappear. Mark would not allow it.* And yet still, the fear lingered.

If you had told me a few weeks ago that my mother had been terrified of my father, at any point in her life, I would have laughed. He was gentle, kind, patient. These were the words I used to describe him. But now? Now I had remembered that long-forgotten day when he had shouted at me with such unexpected rage. Now I had uncovered so many lies. Now I knew that he had been keeping her passport, secretly, telling me the same story over and over again, for years, knowing it was untrue. Now my father was a man I did not know at all.

I glanced back at the final paragraph. It was the first time I had read mention of me, and it would be the last. There was no more diary. No more pages in her hand. At least she had written my name, somewhere. It made me feel as though I existed, for her, for the first time. I had not invented her.

I sat on the floor and smoothed the pages out in front of me. Their edges curled stubbornly back together, like two lovers, two swan's necks, intertwined. The rubber band had long disintegrated but the roll had stayed intact, as Sadie had left it.

There was something else at the heart of the roll of papers; a cutting, neatly edged. It looked as though it had been taken from a glossy magazine. The paper was smooth and shiny.

*Archie Farrow with Coco Delaney, pictured at the launch of the Tindara Photographers exhibition, The Photographers' Gallery, July 1970.*

I stared at the image. It was, as the caption described, a photograph of Coco and Archie, taken in the street outside a London gallery. Black and white, a shot from a paparazzo waiting for celebrity guests. Coco wore a pale trouser suit, with big lapels, almost gangster in its style, but cut for a woman's shape. A big hat with a floppy brim that almost covered her face, but not quite, just enough to tease and to cause her to lift her chin in a coquettish way. She carried no bag, but in one hand she held a pair of gloves, and a scarf was thrown over the crook of her arm. It looked as though it were fine silk, embroidered with something, maybe, or somehow patterned.

And next to her was Archie.

Instantly I could see why Sadie had been so taken with him. He was tall, with the springy dark hair she had described in her diary, and the thick eyebrows. It felt odd looking at his image after absorbing her words – as though a character in a novel had stepped off the page and come to life. He was good-looking, well dressed in a shirt and slightly flared trousers, a jacket slung over one shoulder. He was smiling at someone or something just to one side of the camera, whereas Coco was looking straight into the lens. I wanted to step into the photo, to call to him from the photographer's viewpoint, 'Over here, Archie, if you don't mind?' and see him look directly at me. I wanted to look into his eyes.

It wasn't so much his looks that were striking though, it was something less tangible. Even in this old photo he had a presence, a charisma that practically crackled. An energy surrounding him.

But I was also struck by Coco. Or more specifically, what Coco was wearing. The pale suit, the hat, the embroidered scarf. It was all familiar. And of course, when I turned to the box of clothes it was all there. Sadie's wedding outfit.

# Chapter Thirty-Five

It took me ages to arrange it all. Seraphina and her photos and strange projects had inspired me though, and I didn't notice the time passing. I would invite her to come and look, when it was finished – she would appreciate it, I knew. For more than just the story. She would see that I had created something here. And after all, it was Seraphina who had given me the idea. As I was sitting in my room, surrounded by half-answered questions and evidence and notes and documentation, I thought how like some kind of modern art installation it looked. And then I remembered Elfie, and the photos of her taken in the Serpentine, and how in a strange way they had started this whole journey off . . . and I knew I had the answer, the way to reach and represent the end of it and to do what I had to do at the same time – to force out the truth. Smoke it out, once and for all.

I texted them all, before I had finished. *9 am tomorrow, Sunday, number 17, 31 Founthill Way, London SW21 3NG. Please come. I have something very important to show you.*

It was all starting to become clearer, as I worked. The things I couldn't forget, the little bits of truth that floated around behind my eyes, stopping me from sleeping as they jabbed and tickled at my subconscious, all were adding up. I had tried to ignore them, hoping that if I did so, they would fade like an old memory. But they had not. They were persistent: they would not let me be. So I was going to have to drag them into the light.

The lock-up was cold and my fingers prickled and burned as I worked. I tried to make as little noise as possible, although there had been no sign of anyone around when I had arrived. The other garages and units had been shut, and there were no lights on in the main building on the other side of the yard. And anyhow, I had a key. I had every right to be here, I told myself. But still, I did not want to be disturbed. This was a private task, a silent, reverent one: the creation of this tableau that would provide the final proof, the final piece of the puzzle. It felt ritualistic.

Once, when I was younger, I had been to Russia with my father. He had been visiting some colleagues in Moscow, attending some conference. I don't recall what the point of the trip was now. It doesn't matter. I was fifteen and had accompanied him. One day, when he was busy, I had taken myself off to walk around, map in hand, pretending that I wasn't phased by the street signs being written in the Cyrillic alphabet so I couldn't even read them out loud. It was a strange feeling, one of total alienation, but I found it exciting rather than frightening. I could disappear here, I remember thinking. I could melt away, into the frozen canals and the snow, and no one would know.

It had been the churches that I loved the most, and it was the churches that I was reminded of now. I had walked into one on a whim, having stumbled across it in a back street, and pushed the door open with nervous fingers, unsure of what I would find behind it. And what I found was darkness. Darkness studded with candlelight, like an orange full of cloves at Christmas. It was a soft darkness though, not a cold, unwelcoming one, and I stood silent at the back of the interior and let my eyes widen to it. And when they did, I found that I was standing in the most awe-inspiring place I had ever seen. It wasn't grand or opulent, but simply full of reverence and worship. The walls were unplastered, and I could see the dusty crumbling edges of the stones they were made from, and they were covered with icons, embellished with burnished bronze and gold, lacquered and layered in red and blue and green – images of the Virgin Mary and Christ and the prophets, an array of saints and sinners, and in front of almost every icon was a candle, lit or unlit, flickering in the dark or waiting to be ignited by someone's faith and coins in the jars that sat on wooden pedestals every few metres or so.

I watched as a woman, dressed in layers of wool, her hair encased in a headscarf, lowered herself on unsteady legs to knees that I could almost hear creak to say her prayers, hands wrapped around a cross, and I was suddenly aware of my hair flowing down over my shoulders, disrespectfully, and quickly covered it with my scarf. I stayed there for more than an hour, not moving, not speaking. A priest came and said prayers in Russian, quiet and soft; the same priest disappeared into a confession box and a few men and women filed in and out, not looking any lighter of heart or conscience, to my eyes, when they left than when they entered; a child came in with his mother and chattered until she gently covered his lips with her finger and they both knelt to pray. And all the while, the Virgins looked down on Her flock.

And that was what this felt like. As though my own mother were here, looking down on me, her image becoming stronger and her presence more powerful, the longer I worked. I was bringing her back to life here, I thought. Resurrecting her.

By 7 a.m. I was done.

\* \* \*

They began to arrive a couple of hours later. I was twitchy, on edge, waiting for them. The man who had the carpentry workshop next door arrived at half past eight exactly and the sound of his car parking and doors shutting and opening pulled me out of the sleep-deprived trance that I had slid into, sitting on the crate in the centre of the lock-up. From then on I listened out for every sign.

Elfie and Mark arrived first, and I was happy to see them, even though Mark looked at me strangely, with worried eyes that searched my face. I made them wait outside, naturally. They couldn't come in until everyone else was here. I needed them all to see together.

'What is this, Klara? What are you doing?' Mark hovered around my shoulders like a pet parrot. 'You look exhausted. You need to sleep. You need to get some rest.'

'I know. I will. When I've done this. This is the last thing, Mark. This is it.' I patted his cheek with light, flickering fingers, and he did not flinch, but he did begin to say, 'Klara—' I shushed him. Another car was arriving.

Coco stepped out of her convertible and I could feel Elfie tense next to me. 'Hi,' she whispered nervously. That fucking woman had worked her dark magic on Elfie as well as Sadie. I moved so that my body was between the two of them.

'Hello there,' Coco said, as nonchalant as anything; she might have been arriving at a coffee morning, though of course she wasn't the sort of woman who would ever have been to one of those. 'Isn't it a lovely day?'

I looked up at the sky. She was right. It was clear and blue and cloudless. I couldn't decide whether it was appropriate or not. If I had been staging the scene in its entirety, directing it in a film, would I have made it a day like this, or would I have brought in the wind machines and sheets of fake rain, waiting for glowering skies and dramatic light?

'Who else are we waiting for?' she asked lightly, and I directed my eyes to her for the first time.

'Just one more.'

She nodded. It was as though she knew exactly why we were here, as though she had all the answers tucked away in her head – and I wanted to push her to the ground and wrest them from her. I wanted to open her up, slice open her skull and drag out what was inside . . .

And then he arrived, carefully driving through the gates, his face wary. He did not know where he was going or why, and it wasn't until he saw the cluster of us standing outside the lock-up that his eyes seemed to focus and he raised a hand to me. I felt everything then, at that moment, and I almost changed my mind and locked the garage up again, led everyone away from it and told them no, it was a mistake, it was nothing, I was sorry. Looking at my father brought it all into focus. Everything I had been through. Every emotion that I had felt over the last few weeks, they all came rushing to the surface. Guilt that I was doing this to him. Anger that he had done this to me. Regret, regret that I had ever found any of this out, that I had been sent the letter and key, that I had pursued it, that this door that I could not shut had ever been opened. Love. Love for him and the life he had given me. Anger that it had been taken away. Fury, blind, red-hot fury, for what he had taken away.

'Klara?' he said, as he got out of the car, and I couldn't speak, couldn't say a word to him, for I knew I would fragment if I did and it would all be over. Instead I just stood as he walked towards me, towards us, and greeted the others, the car keys in his hand, his face uncertain.

I almost broke again then, but I took his hand and turned away from him, leading him and the others to the door, which I unlocked with shaking hands. I had locked it up while I waited; it had felt necessary, and now I knew why. It was because I had to unlock it in front of them, had to show them the secret I had been preparing – and as I did so, I heard more footsteps coming up behind me. I turned and saw a man standing a few feet away, with thinning sandy-coloured hair, dressed in a simple striped shirt and trousers, and I thought that maybe I recognised him.

Elfie was the first to speak, when she said, 'Who's that?' Asking what we were all wondering, expecting me to have the answer.

However, it was not me who gave it, but Coco, when she said, 'This is Rupert Montgomery. Or, as your mother used to call him, Naughty Rupert.'

# Chapter Thirty-Six

I stared. Naughty Rupert. N.R. The man who had showed me to the lock-up garage, the first time I came here. The man in front of whom my mother had humiliated herself in Bertie's Bar with Archie. The man who had started off this whole daisy-chain. Who had written me the note, sent me the key. Who had kept safe the boxes of my mother's belongings, everything that was now displayed in front of us, for more than two decades.

We stared at one another and he smiled, almost apologetically. 'Hello, Klara. I'm Rupert.'

I couldn't speak. I could feel Mark to my left, his presence, his breath. His silence. The silence of everyone in the room as they stared at what I had made. What we had made. Sadie and I. But I was staring only at Rupert.

'Sorry,' he continued softly. 'This must be a shock. It is for me as well. Seeing you . . . you look like her. The eyes. You move your hands in the same way.' He gestured. 'I saw you coming in last night, Klara, and then the others arriving this morning – and I thought I'd see what was going on. Thought that it was probably time to show my face and explain things a bit. Though it seems as though you're going to do some explaining of your own.'

He looked around the room. Nodded. 'God, she was so

beautiful,' he said quietly, almost to himself. 'You forget, don't you? And then something happens and it hits you all over again.'

The penny dropped then, finally. He had been in love with her as well. That was why he and Coco hadn't lasted, because his heart had never really been free. I should have worked it out before then, but I had been so focused on Daddy, and Archie, and Coco, that I had paid little attention to the references to Rupert in the story. I suppose it had been the same for my mother, too. She just hadn't really noticed him.

'I shouldn't have put N.R. on the end of the letter I sent you about this place,' he said. 'It's just – it's what she always called me. It's hard to think of being anything else, in relation to her.'

There were so many things I wanted to say. But I couldn't say any of them.

Mark's hand rested on the small of my back. I looked round at the others: Elfie, Coco, my father.

It felt as though Sadie was in the room with us. I had felt that way ever since I had got to the lock-up. She had been here with me, watching as I worked, guiding my hand, whispering to me. She was there, in my head. In my heart.

When I say it felt as though she was in the room, it is true: she was everywhere. All of her modelling pictures, from the first campaign that she had shot, to the last image I had found of her, were mounted on white card and displayed around the garage. Her face looked down on us with a hundred different expressions. Playful, seductive, carefree, thoughtful. Every emotion she had ever felt was there, it seemed; Sadie in her infinite variety.

'Oh Klara.' My father's voice was a sigh. He was standing in the centre of the room, gazing up at the walls. Overwhelmed. It wasn't just the photographs. It was everything. I had made a room of her life, a cocoon, and brought everyone into it. And it was all for this moment, really. To see what he did. I had photocopied all the pages of her diary before coming here, and I had mounted them on white card as well, all of it with that sticky spray stuff. My hands still smelled of it, and I could feel it on my fingers.

I had managed to nail some hooks into the walls, and her dresses and shoes hung from them. The door was ajar, and a breeze caught the hem of her scarlet dress, lifting it up so it fluttered. Her shoes hung from strings over one of the hooks. The baby clothes from another. The hat she had worn for her wedding hooked over a third. Her jewellery I had placed on a small table in the centre of the room, laid out. And then, on another table, there was the pink rabbit, surrounded by all of her domestic things. Her trousseau. The napkin-holders, the glasses, still carefully packed. The cheese-grater.

It niggled at me that Suzanne and Trevor were not here, because they were part of the story as well. I had asked her, of course, had rung and tried to explain what I was doing, offered to pay their train fare, but she had put the phone down as soon as she had realised who I was talking about, and I was not surprised. But still, they were missing and they were missed.

'Klara,' he said again, and this time he was a step closer to me. I held my breath. No one else spoke. 'What have you done? What have you done this for?'

I closed my eyes for a second. 'How does it make you feel?' I said, when I turned to him.

My father raised his hands and then let them fall again. His face was blank. I could not read it. 'Confused,' he said. 'It makes me feel confused. What is all of this? Where has it come from? Klara, my child, what have you been doing?'

I looked around the garage, at my guests, at faces covered

in concern and bewilderment, and I knew this was the moment.

'This is my evidence.'

'Evidence?' my father repeated. 'I don't understand.'

I felt Mark's hand take mine and I shook it off. He and my father exchanged a look: I saw it and ignored it. I knew what they were thinking. But they were wrong.

'It's all here,' I said, moving so that I was in the centre of the room and everyone was in front of me. I was surrounded by Sadie, protected by her. 'Everything I have found out, it's all here, in this room. You'd all see it, if you looked for long enough, like I have been. But you can't, you don't have time, you won't see it, so I'm going to tell you a story. Sadie's story.'

And I did. I told them everything that I had found out. I showed them my dossier, my spreadsheets, all of my notes, the diary and the torn-out pages. I explained about Suzanne and how Sadie had been going to give her her baby. How she had met Archie, how he had betrayed her, how she had covered up her hurt and tried to carry on. How she had been let down. Of course, some of them knew this story better than I did – Coco, and my father. But they could listen. I wanted them to listen.

I told them how my father had lied. How he had talked of a great romance, how he had reinvented the story of their meeting and told it to me as though it were the truth, and how I had discovered the real truth from her diary and knew now what he had been hiding from me for years.

When I had finished, there was silence again. My father was leaning against the wall now, not looking at me, not looking at anyone.

'Oh Klara,' he said eventually. 'Why? Why would you believe everything she wrote over what I told you?'

'It's a diary,' I said. 'People don't lie in diaries.' But as I spoke the words they suddenly felt hollow. Laying out my case like this had not felt how I had expected it to. Their reaction had not been what I had been expecting. They were all staring at me, but they didn't look impressed or enthralled. They looked – worried. For me.

'Don't they? She did though, didn't she? She hid the truth. You found her real diary, the pages she had torn out. They weren't the same as the others. You could tell that when you read them, couldn't you, my darling? You could see the difference.'

'Of course I could. But that's not the point. She was scared of you. Scared of you finding out that she was seeing Archie again.'

'She didn't need to be.'

'Well, that's what you would say. It's not true though, is it?'

'Why do you say that?' He looked genuinely confused, and his demeanour chilled me. He was more cold than I had suspected. He was not who I had known.

'She didn't just leave, did she?' I demanded.

He cocked his head.

'Sadie. *My mother*. She didn't just leave, the way you said.'

He lowered his head. 'No. I suppose she didn't.'

I inhaled sharply. There it was. What I had been waiting for and all the while hoping never to hear. This admission.

'Oh no.' The words slipped out and tears began to flood down my face. It was all crumbing in front of me. Mark stepped forward and put one hand on each of my shoulders.

'Klara, you must stop this. I'm taking you home.'

'No, no, I have to hear. I have to know. *Now*.' I looked at Daddy, and his face was sad. In fact, he looked as if his own heart was breaking. I didn't know whether I felt sorry or angry or pleased. This had been waiting for him, for me – for all of us. This truth.

'Klara, I'm so sorry,' he said eventually. 'I never wanted you to find out. I thought – I thought I was doing the right thing.'

'The right thing?'

'Yes. The right thing. For you, but for her as well. I had to protect her. I promised to, you see. To keep her safe from harm. She had no one else to do it.'

I couldn't breathe. It took me hours, it felt like, to be able to open my mouth and force the air out in a way that would form the words I needed to say.

'So you killed her.'

He gaped. Mark's hands dropped from my shoulders, as though he had given up.

'Klara. Of course I didn't kill her.'

'You did. You found out she was seeing Archie again, that it was him who she really loved – that she was going to leave you – and you killed him, and then you killed her.'

'I didn't kill your mother, Klara. How could I kill Sadie? I loved her. I still love her. It doesn't matter what her diary says, what Sadie says. I can prove it to you.'

I began to cry then, proper childlike sobs, because I knew that he could not do that, that I could never trust him again, or anyone, that the touchstone of my life had come loose and I was on my own. Daddy stepped forward, and I was stuck between him and Mark, and though I wanted to shrink from him, I could not. He took my hands and his felt big and rough, and I was reminded of so many things that I could not remember, and still I cried. In the end he took my face and held it, and made me look at him, made me calm down enough to hear him as he told me how he could convince me of his truth.

'I can prove it to you, my darling, darling girl, because Sadie is alive. Your mother's alive.'

# Chapter Thirty-Seven

I don't remember much else of that day. After the lock-up, after what Daddy told me, everything changed. I thought I had found the answers. I was so sure. So sure. I had gathered all the evidence, had assembled my case; it all interlocked neatly, tidily in my mind. And then it didn't. Then nothing was neat or tidy or could be put into spreadsheets or boxes, because the one thing that I had known to be true my whole life, the single inescapable fact about myself – that I was Klara Mortimer whose mother had left and then died – was a lie. That truth had simply floated away, like a dandelion puffball into the air, and had left nothing in its place but a void.

Mark and Elfie took me home. Mark with his caring face and his strong arms and his taking charge, Elfie unsure of what had really happened or what to do but trying to be grown up, trying to comfort me as I simply stared ahead. And Daddy followed. Mark told me later that I would not look at him, that I behaved as if he was not there. But that was how it felt. It was as he though he had disappeared. Sadie was gone – or the image of Sadie that I had created was gone – and the real Sadie was alive. She had been dead and I had felt as if I had resurrected her – and then I actually had. Or he had. Someone had. And all along she had been . . . where?

* * *

Here.

The building was large and white, turreted at the top. It had been a private home until the middle of the twentieth century, when the family who owned it had run out of money and had been forced to sell. They had done so to a holiday camp initially, who had quickly gone bust when it turned out that no one wanted to go and stay in this particular bit of Norfolk, which was too far from the coast to be a seaside break and not near enough to anything else to be a country-side holiday. They had made a half-hearted attempt at keeping it going, but had been forced to give up, and by 1962 it was bought by the Arbour Group, who had quickly transformed it into what it was today – a somewhat shabby but relatively genteel mental hospital.

I found all this out the morning before arriving there. I liked to be prepared.

Nothing could have prepared me for the reality of it, however. How could it?

The building was impressive from a distance. As the car pulled in through the gates I looked up at the windows, at the bevelled edge that ran around the roof, at the line of tall, thin chimneys that ran down its centre. This was where she had been, all this time. This had been her home. It was fitting, in a way. Dramatic, unusual, isolated. All the things Sadie was. Or had been, once.

As we drew closer, however, it became less lovely a setting. The arched windows were covered with bars, not decorative ironwork but thin, solid bars designed to keep hands and limbs inside. No one wanted lawsuits arising from patients throwing themselves out onto the sweeping gravel drive, did they? There were other signs now that this was no ordinary country house as well. The men and women dotted around the garden might, at first glance, have been guests at a weekend house party; however, they moved with the characteristic shuffle of those heavily sedated, their elbows supported by the staff who accompanied them. The sound, as we pulled up to the front door, was of a woman wailing – a long, keening howl that lasted far longer than you would think a breath could go on for. The smell of cooking that could be nothing other than institutional wafted from the kitchens at the back of the building as I opened the taxi door.

'Visiting?' the driver had said, when we got into the cab at the station and gave him the address, and I had said yes. He looked at me suspiciously now, as I got out, as though he was having second thoughts about whether to believe me or not. I ignored him.

'Thank you,' Daddy said to him, holding the door open for me. *We do not want to talk*, his words said. *We are not going to gossip with you about where we are going or why.* Now he pulled his wallet from his pocket and took a fold of notes from it, handing them to the driver. He didn't need to ask how much. This was a journey he had made many times before.

'I don't want you to have – expectations,' he had said, at home in London. His home. It was the day after my exhibition, as I thought of it, and we trod around one another like strangers. Scuttling. 'She is not what you think. Not any more.'

'I don't think anything,' I said, knowing it was not true. 'How can I? I don't *know* anything.' Not any more, I thought.

He nodded, accepting the silent rebuke. What else could he do?

'She's fragile,' he continued. He was determined to tell me about her, though I didn't really want him to. The image I had built of her had gone, and I did not want to replace it with a new one until I could do so with the real person. But it appeared that I was to be given little choice. 'Her memory is not good. She wavers. She changes from one visit to the next. Sometimes she is pleased to see me.' He smiled at this. 'Grateful that I've come. Sometimes she won't look at me, not because she's angry with me, but because she just doesn't see me. Can't see me. Sometimes she thinks I'm someone else.'

He paused here and I felt the hurt that he was trying to cover, and I knew who it was that Sadie sometimes mistook him for. The name hung thick and silent in the air. *Archie.*

Her room was on the ground floor. 'She was upstairs,' he said, as we walked down the corridor, 'but she didn't like being so far from the gardens. She's very specific about what she likes and doesn't like, as you might see – if she says anything. That's something that hasn't changed.' He grinned then, raising his eyebrows as though to say, 'difficult woman, your mother,' like a normal father in a normal family might, and for a moment everything felt just that – normal. Him, talking about and remembering her. Her, alive in his memory and almost in mine once more. Her, with habits and foibles and irrational elements to her personality that were just that, personality, not a symptom or a part of her illness. It was only a flicker, but I held on to it.

As we got closer, I listened out for her voice. Would I recognise it? Would she even say anything? Behind other doors a nurse soothed, a man muttered, a trolley clattered. Nothing that I could match up to her though.

'She will not recognise you,' Daddy said, and he stopped walking and put his hand on my arm to stop me.

'She might.'

'She will not.' His voice was firm, certain. 'I just want you to know. I want you to – I want you to not blame me.'

I took a deep breath. The sadness of decades filled his throat and my eyes pricked. *How can I not blame you?* I wanted to say. *You are the only one I have to blame. You are the only one left.*

'I wanted to come,' I said instead. 'It was my choice. I'm ready.'

We both knew that it was not true, could not be true, and yet we both knew that I had to try and believe it. Maybe I *was* ready. Maybe she *would* recognise me. Maybe she *would* be everything that I needed and wanted her to be. Maybe. Maybe.

What is it they say about *maybe? If wishes were horses, beggars would ride.* Something like that.

She was sitting next to the window when I went into the room. Daddy had knocked first, but there had been no answer, and his face told me that this was not uncommon. He opened the door gently.

What had I been expecting? A crazed woman, a madwoman in the attic, like something from a nineteenth-century novel? Or the beautiful model from the photos, preserved, or simply a little faded? The woman that I remembered, in soft focus, from my childhood.

She was none of those things. It is wrong to say that she was a disappointment because of it, but it is fair to admit that the reality of her could never have lived up to the images in my head. She was a sad, middle-aged woman now. Not the bright, shining light her words had painted for me in her diary. Not the woman with sparkling eyes smelling of Opium that I remembered.

She was pale, and her hair was sapped of colour, as though the years spent inside had drained her of life. Her skin was thin, I could see veins beneath it. She wore a soft, pink dressing-gown that looked like something an old lady would wear, and I wished that I had brought something beautiful for her, a silk robe or something that befitted her. But of course it would not have befitted her. Not any more. The soft pink dressing-gown was who she was.

'Mama?'

She didn't turn. Daddy squeezed my hand. He would have been hoping against hope that she would respond to me, even more than I was, I sensed. He wanted so badly for me to get what I needed, what I had been looking for, even though he knew that there was no chance of me finding it here.

I took a few steps closer. She did not move. 'Mama, it's me. Klara. I . . . I'm sorry I haven't visited for so long, but I know Daddy's been coming. I'm sure he's been telling you what I've been up to. I'm a teacher now, at a university.'

I hadn't planned any of what I was going to say to her. But the words came, more easily than I could have imagined. I told her everything. Daddy melted away, and I sat there, looking out at the gardens and the trees, the view that had been hers for so many years, and I told her about my life. Everything. I told her of my childhood, teens and twenties, of the years that she had missed, of boyfriends and friends and parties, ill-conceived travel plans and unconceived children, of my regrets and hopes and wishes and dreams.

I talked to her as though she could hear every word and at the same time as though she was almost not there, as though she were simply a mirror reflecting myself back at me, and as I talked I realised how true this was, how much I had in common with this woman, how deeply her life echoed and resonated through mine, and I understood for the first time the fear that Mark had felt when I had pushed to have children, to have a family. Maybe he could see it in my eyes, the ability to slip over the edge; Maybe he feared that he would be the one visiting me in a place like this, going home to our children, keeping secrets from them, and he would have been right to, because I saw myself in her face, my future within in her eyes, and I nearly shrank away because of it.

Instead though, I kept talking, until I had told her everything, as if by filling the room with my own words I could make up for the lack of hers, as if my story might replace hers, as if she could feel my presence and somehow know me even though I wasn't sure that she had even registered I was in the room at all.

When I had finished, I waited, suddenly feeling awkward, suddenly aware of all the secrets I had spilled to her. And then she did turn to me and looked me straight in the eyes, and I bit my lip and said nothing. *Say nothing*, I told myself.

She lifted her hand to my cheek and I remembered, I remembered her doing the same when she put me to bed, and when she woke me up, that touch of her finger on my skin. I remembered how I had missed it, how I had longed for her to be there, and I wet her finger with my tears but she didn't seem to notice, or if she did, she didn't move. 'Klara,' she said, just once, and I nodded. She did remember. She did know.

And then she turned from me. 'No,' she sighed. 'No, I gave her away.' It was as if she were reminding herself. 'Of course. I gave her away.'

She shut her eyes, and I leaned forward. 'No, Mama, you didn't give me away. I'm Klara. I'm right here.' I tried to take her hand again and bring it to my face so that she might remember once more, but it sat, limp, between my own. And she was not there any more. She was – who knew where? Somewhere grey, somewhere floating, somewhere none of us could reach her. I just hoped it was somewhere she could be at peace.

We walked through the gardens, he and I, neither of us ready to set off for home yet. I could not yet leave her behind. He had been doing it for years.

'The stories you told me about her.'

'Yes.' His hands were folded behind his back. He seemed more himself here, in this place, than he ever had done before. Was it being close to her?

'How many of them were true?'

He shrugged. His shoulders were rounded and pathetic-looking. He didn't answer my question. 'I wanted you to have what other children had,' he said simply. 'To have the stories. To have a mother. Even if it was just my version of one.'

'So you just – made them up?'

'You couldn't have the real ones, Klara. You didn't need to know that your mother was a failure. A model who could not model because no one would have her, because she couldn't turn up and do the job, because she was losing her mind, slowly, surely.'

'Even then?'

'Always. Since I first knew her. *He* was in her heart, and her mind, and her soul, and she could not bear the weight of the love she had for him.'

'But what about you?'

'What about me? I loved her. That was enough for me.'

'You didn't need her to love you back?'

'She did, in her own way. I promised to keep her safe, and that's what I did.'

'What about when you found out she was still seeing him?'

He shook his head. 'You still don't understand. I never "found out." I always knew.'

'But in her diary . . .' I trailed off. I kept on returning to the words that I had read, believed, absorbed as truth. And I kept on remembering that they were fragile as cobwebs.

Daddy smiled. 'That's what I mean. She was secretive, furtive – and utterly transparent. I knew she loved him. I knew she was still seeing him. I knew I would never have her heart.

But I had enough. I had her, and I had you, and I could help her – I could make her happy. He would never have been able to do that. There was too much darkness in him.' There was bitterness in my father's voice for the first time, and I saw what it had cost him to do what he did for so long, and also what he had gained.

'But why couldn't you have just told me the truth?' I asked. 'When I was older, at least. Life isn't a romantic film, a black and white movie like the ones we used to watch together. I didn't need to think that it was.'

He smiled sadly. 'But maybe I did.'

And then I understood. He hadn't created the myth of Sadie for me, but for himself. Whatever he claimed – that what he had had of her was enough – he had needed to believe in the version of their love that he had made up, to remember a love that had never really existed, at least not in the way he had wanted it to. He needed to do this if he was going to be able to carry on protecting her.

He had given his life for her, in a way. Had never remarried, had remained faithful to her. Had kept her memory alive for me. *Our first love was our last.* I had written those words off, when my father had first spoken them, as being untrue. But now I realised that they were as true for Sadie as they had been for Henry. His first love was her – his first and only love. And hers? Hers was Archie.

'You married her.'

'Yes.'

'Because you loved her. Whether or not you could have her properly, whether or not she loved you. I can understand it, sort of. I can see why it was better than not having her, not being close to her. She had that power over people, didn't she? So I can see it. But I don't understand why she married you.'

'Neither did I,' he replied, and he was not offended. 'Not

at first. We had not been courting long. I was amazed that she agreed to go out with me at all. She could have had anyone in London. Anyone other than the man she really wanted, that is. Anyone other than Archie. But she chose me. A slightly balding, badly dressed academic, who might one day make some big discovery but who never did, who didn't have much money, who couldn't offer her a big house or an exciting life or anything that you'd think she wanted. But I think that was why.'

He scratched his ear. 'I didn't ask anything of her. She knew I would look after her, as I promised. And she knew that there was no threat from me, with regard to Archie. I was never going to throw her out because I discovered that she was still in touch with him.'

'She would always have the upper hand.'

'In a way, yes. There weren't many people she could have been sure of that with. They would always have wanted something more from her, in the end. And she couldn't have given it. She knew herself well enough to know that, at least.' He sighed. 'It sounds pathetic, doesn't it?'

'No,' I said. 'You loved her. You gave her what she needed. You saved her.'

He looked up at the building before us. 'Not really. Not in the end.'

'She married you in Coco's suit – did you know that?'

'Yes. I knew. It was her way of saying she had beaten her,' my father said. 'Of course she hadn't. But she thought she was sending a message to her, to him. It meant something to her.'

'And you didn't mind? On your wedding day, even? You didn't care that you were . . .'

'Second best? On the day when I should have been first, just for once? Of course I cared, Klara. I never said I didn't.'

I saw the sadness in his eyes and I saw just how much he had cared.

'But I was not willing to risk losing her over it. Over something small like that. And the thing is, all the small things become big, but only over time. At first they're just small things. It's only when you look back that you see how big they have become.'

'All those times she was modelling in London . . .'

'She was with him,' he confirmed. 'Or sometimes here, with her doctors. It was breaking her, even then.'

'And then when she left? I mean . . . what happened? How did she end up here?'

He exhaled. This was the part of the story I still did not know. How Sadie went from living with us, seeing Archie, living this strange part-life, a life full of lies but functioning within it, with my father's help, to living here. A patient in a mental hospital, with no life behind her eyes, no life to live any longer.

'I told you that she died,' he said eventually. We were sitting now, on the edge of a stone wall. The building that contained my mother was before us, and my eyes were drawn to the area where her room was. I could not help but imagine her life here, what it must have been like. Day after day, week after week, month after month. Was she even aware of the passing of time, the slipping away of the years?

'It wasn't a lie, you see – not entirely. The Sadie I knew, the mother you knew, did die. She disappeared. You saw it for yourself. The woman here? That's not her. That's not the girl who wrote those diaries, is it? The mother you remember?'

I shook my head. It was not.

His voice was choked now. 'I'm sorry that I lied, that you found out. I'm sorry that your life has been as hard as it has been because of this. But I'm not sorry for what I did, Klara.

330

She might not be the woman I fell in love with any more, but she's the one that is here. I promised to look after her and I have done so. And if I've done nothing else with my life?' He shrugged. 'Then at least I achieved that one thing.'

It was my turn to apologise now. 'I'm sorry, Daddy. I should have known you could never have . . .' I couldn't even say the words any longer. He squeezed my hand. 'I should have remembered how much you loved her,' I said. 'And I should have been able to see the truth.'

'Ah, but that's what Sadie did, my darling. Beguiled, misled.' *Lied?* The word remained unspoken.

'Anyhow,' he continued, 'I gave you reason to doubt me. The evidence you uncovered – well, you drew the wrong conclusions from it, but you were right to be suspicious. I had been keeping secrets from you, and I should not have.'

His generosity made me feel like even more of a heel for doubting him.

'Where did you go every year?' He smiled, sadly. 'To her. To Sadie.'

'But why on that date? Why not your wedding anniversary? A date that meant something to both of you?'

'Because it wasn't about me, or us. Just about her. I couldn't leave her alone every year on that day, on the day he died.'

That generosity again. His selflessness pierced my heart. But still I had one more question. 'That day ... what really happened?'

He stopped. Sighed. Spoke again. 'She went to see him – as she often did. But this time was different. He died. And she was never the same again.'

I shoved my hands deep into my pockets. What was he telling me?

'What . . .'

'I can't tell you, Klara. It's the part of the story I don't know. No one knows what happened.'

'But there must have been—'

'An investigation? Yes. Police reports, all of that. But she never spoke of it. She couldn't. Sadie was gone. Whatever happened in London, whatever happened with Archie, the truth of it – it's locked in her mind somewhere. It haunts her, I think. Sometimes you can see it in her eyes, this fear . . .'

I had glimpsed it, I thought, back in her room. A flash of something had passed across her face while I was talking, something unconnected to anything I was saying. What has she been reliving?

'We don't know what she saw,' he continued heavily. 'What happened. All we know is that Archie died in a house fire, they think started by a cigarette. She was in London that day, but I don't know whether she was with him or not. It doesn't matter, not really, because it doesn't make any difference. In every way that matters, she died with him that day.'

# Chapter Thirty-Eight

Information is so important. Sadie and I both knew the value of information. I have spent my life gathering it, organising it, as has Daddy. He instilled the importance of learning in me when I was very small. 'Stories are more than stories,' he would say to me. 'They are everything. They can contain whole worlds. If you have knowledge, if you have learning, you can own the world.' And I wanted that. Who doesn't? I wanted to know everything, to understand everything. I believed him when he said that I could own the world. Well, children do believe their parents, don't they? That has been my problem all along.

So I spent my life trying to learn, trying to gain the knowledge that he told me I should and could have, trying to understand it all. And I did well. I got a degree, another degree – a Masters, a PhD – I got a job where I could not only spread learning but gain more for myself, and with every mouthful of it I became stronger, richer, wiser. I could feel it feeding me like a sunflower.

But information about myself, I had none. So those links that I began to see in Sadie's story became more important than ever. As I recognised shadows of myself in her, in her words, in the images that she painted, I became hooked. I had finally found what I had been looking for, yearning for, for so many years. A way of learning about myself. She was the key that might allow me to unlock myself, she was the mirror in which my image finally started to become clear.

I don't feel the need to fill in every single gap, but I do feel the need for something solid, something I can call myself, my family, my home. I'm pregnant, you see. After three years of trying, suddenly, in the midst of the aftermath of all this, I woke up one morning with a sharp pain in one side and I knew, somehow I just knew. I took five tests, all different brands, before I told Mark, laying them out in front of him on the kitchen table. Proof, again, but of a different kind.

He cried. I have never seen him cry before. And that made me cry. And then Elfie came down and started crying without even knowing why, and then we told her and she cried some more. She's staying here, with us. We've all decided it's for the best. Serri comes and visits her sometimes. Mark's just about forgiven her for the whole thing in the Serpentine, but he won't leave Elfie alone with her, and I don't really blame him.

We see Maisie and Barney when they aren't too busy meditating or realigning their chakras. They drive me mad but I want this baby to know them, even so. I want it to have a sense of family, of where it comes from. It. He? She? Elfie's sure it'll be a girl, and I think she might be right. I don't know why. Call it mother's intuition. (Now that's something I never thought I'd say.) Beth is thrilled, she's already started giving me huge piles of maternity clothes and baby clothes and mysterious things like squares of muslin. 'Trust me,' she says, and I do. She's still with Steve. They seem happy enough most of the time, and maybe that's enough.

I went to see Coco. I had questions remaining for her. And, as it turned out, she had some for me.

'Why didn't you just ask me who N. R. might be, Klara? I would have told you.'

'Would you?'

She gazed at me. 'Yes. I'm not the sort of witch you think I am. I would have liked you to know your mother. Truly.'

I believed her.

'What about the baby? That's what I can't . . . I can't get that out of my head. She couldn't, and Suzanne couldn't, either. My mother had a chance to do something good, to turn things around for Suzanne, at least, and you stopped her. Why? Why would you do that?'

Coco's eyes dipped. 'Why do you think?' she said eventually.

'You were jealous?' It was the only reason I could think of.

'No. I wasn't jealous. Archie was.'

I stayed silent. She lit another cigarette.

'He didn't want a baby. That can't surprise you. He didn't want the responsibility, nor to be tied to Sadie. But he couldn't bear the thought of someone else bringing up his child either. A macho thing? Or maybe he was more sentimental than he would have admitted to. I don't know.'

'I thought you knew him the best?'

'I did. But in lots of ways he was unknowable. I told you that before.'

She had.

'Anyhow, it doesn't really matter why, does it? He was insistent that the adoption must not be allowed to go ahead, that we must put a stop to it. And so we did.'

'You did.'

'If you like.'

'How?'

'It wasn't my finest moment, Klara, I'll admit that.' She spoke quickly now, as though by spitting the words out fast

335

they would not leave a bad taste in her mouth. 'I took her to my flat and told her she had to get rid of it. That if she did, everything would go back to normal; she would be able to start working again, she and Archie would be together again and everything would be how it was.'

'But you knew it wouldn't.'

Coco exhaled a long plume of smoke. 'I knew he wouldn't take her back, not after that. She had become – unstable. Honestly, Klara, I'm not making this up. She was obsessed with Archie, with me. She had lost weight, too much, even for then, she was drinking . . . she would leave strange notes for him and turn up at odd times of day. I felt sorry for her. He probably did as well. But it turned him off.'

'He was meant to LOVE her!' I yelped. 'She was carrying his child and he had made all those promises to her and he just turned it off, just like that? Because she was unhappy, because he had made her that unhappy?'

Coco nodded. 'You see now, don't you? You under-stand what I said to you when we met before? Archie was cruel. I told you, just like I warned her – and neither of you listened.'

She was right. Neither of us had listened. The awful thing was that Archie *had* taken Sadie back eventually.

'He didn't talk to me about her, when they started seeing each other again. I didn't know until later,' Coco said. 'He was aware that staying away from her would have been the kinder thing to do. I suspect that he knew what I'd say, knew that I'd do something to try and stop it. Because I would have tried, Klara. Believe me. She was married to Henry, she had you – she could have had a chance at a normal life. But she couldn't stay away from him.'

'Nor he from her.'

'It seems not,' Coco said sadly.

We were quiet then, for a moment, both in our individual sorrows.

'Did you know Rupert was in love with her? When you were together, I mean.'

She laughed, and I saw a flash of the beautiful woman she had once been. 'Of course I knew. Everyone loved her. And Rupert is transparent.'

'Didn't you care? Archie, then Rupert . . .'

She nodded. 'I cared. Not enough to try and destroy her though. God, Klara, what must you have been thinking of me?'

I couldn't answer. I felt too ashamed.

'Rupert and I were never going to last. And it wasn't because of Sadie that we broke up. He knew he couldn't have her, was too late. We stopped seeing each other because he cheated on me with one of the models. And I wasn't having *that*.'

One eyebrow arched, and I grinned. No, I imagined she wasn't.

I had one last thing to ask her.

'She got married in your clothes,' I said.

Coco nodded. 'I saw the photos. She stole them, naturally. I don't know when – one of the times she was at my flat. They weren't the only things she took. I noticed various things going missing – earrings, scarves, that sort of thing. I think maybe she thought . . .'

She paused. I finished the thought for her.

'That she could slide into Archie's life? Replace and erase you?'

She gave me a small smile. 'It sounded too mad for me to say.'

I sighed. 'No. It's the kind of thing I can see her thinking, now.' Now I knew her.

Coco looked at me then, and her face was beautiful and lined and so, so sad. And it seemed ridiculous that I had put so much hatred onto her, had allowed Sadie's bitterness to seep out from the pages of the diary and into my own heart, clouding my vision.

'I'm sorry,' I said. 'I'm sorry for coming into your life, for bringing all this up again, for raking up old memories. I'll leave you alone now.'

She stubbed out her cigarette. 'You haven't brought anything up, Klara, not really. There are some things you can just never forget.'

And then I went to see Rupert – N.R., as I can't help but think of him. Naughty Rupert, as my mother called him. He told me why that was, when he came to see me, two days later, bearing a bouquet of lilies. Apparently it was because he would turn up at her shoots, bringing her flowers, and offer to walk her home. 'Even when I was with Coco,' he said and smiled ruefully. 'I couldn't resist.'

'I bet Sadie loved it,' I said, and he nodded.

'Yes. It pleased her, I think, that I couldn't stay away. There was a rivalry between them.'

'You could say that.'

He grinned sheepishly. 'I know. I was there.'

Of course. I had spent so long reading her diaries that sometimes I forgot that I myself had not been there, it all felt so real.

'She liked lilies in particular,' he said, gesturing to them. 'And she would always say, "Oh Rupert, you're naughty, Naughty Rupert". So sometimes when I sent her flowers I would sign myself as that. N.R. It started to be how I thought of myself, with regard to her. N.R. So when I came to write to you, it's just what came out. I almost changed it, ripped it up and started over. But it seemed fitting to leave it. I hope it didn't confuse.'

Of course it had confused. But it didn't matter now. His hand was soft when I shook it, but not weak. I didn't know what to say to him, so I just led him into the kitchen and put the kettle on. It's what we do, isn't it? Make tea. It gives our hands something to do while our minds try and decide what to say next.

I didn't need to think of what to say though, as Rupert did it for me. It was as though the weight of the knowledge he had carried with him for years and the burden of holding the key for me had been lifted by what I had done, and he was able to speak of it and let it run from his mouth and his life, and he did just that, standing there in my kitchen as the kettle boiled and the tea steeped and then went cold.

He admitted that he had been in love with her. 'So in love. I was far from the only one – well, you know that. There was your father . . . and then Archie, in his own way. And there were others, others who never even got close.'

'Did you get close?'

He blushed a little. 'I like to think I did. We all flatter ourselves like that, don't we? "If it weren't for him, if it weren't for her, if things were different, it could have been me . . ." I don't think it ever could have been me, not really. But we were friends. She trusted me, I think.'

'Which is why she gave you the key.'

'Yes.'

'She didn't tell you why?'

'Not then. She was . . .'

'Not herself?'

He shook his head. 'No. She came to me after Archie died.'

'Ah, so *you* were who she was with. My father didn't know where she was.'

Rupert nodded. 'I know. It was only for a couple of days. She made me promise not to tell. Anyone. I did as she asked. I always did as she asked. She was . . .'

'Persuasive.'

'Yes. And I loved her. I would have done anything for her. Anything she asked. And that was what she asked.'

'And she didn't say why?'

'Why she wanted me to keep the key for her? No. She was distressed – utterly distraught. She wouldn't tell me what had happened. I wasn't even sure if she knew what had happened. She just kept on saying over and over again that I must keep the key, keep her things safe. That the boxes were her story, that they would keep her safe.'

He sighed. 'Honestly? I thought she was delusional. I loved her, yes, very much, but not blindly. I could see the state she was in and I thought that it was just going to be a collection of rubbish, or something. But I agreed to do what she asked, because I wanted her to feel as though she could count on me. To know she had one person she could rely on.'

I bristled a little at that. 'She had my father.'

'I didn't know him though, not well. I didn't know how things were between them. And she was ranting in her sleep, incoherent. "*If Henry finds out, if Archie comes back . . . no one will forgive me.*" A lot of things that made no sense – nonsense talk. But these fragments . . . I didn't know how seriously to take them.'

'You knew she was mad.' It was the first time I had spoken the words, and they shocked me.

'So I shouldn't have trusted her? Love doesn't work like that though, does it?'

He was right, of course. And he had been right. To take her things and the key, and lock them away for her and keep them safe, because by doing so he was in some strange way keeping *her* safe. Playing his part.

'Why now?' It was what I had been wondering for days. What had moved him to send the key, to unlock the past now, when it had lain dormant for so many years?

Rupert paused, as though he was unsure whether or not to continue.

'When your mother brought me the boxes, he said eventually, 'she was . . . fairly unstable.'

I waited. It had taken me this long to uncover the truth, what were a few more seconds?

He carried on. 'She always had this idea that she was going to be famous, you see. Renowned. She told me that she was giving me the diary and the other things so that they would provide a record. People would want to know, one day, she said, about her life, and this would tell them the truth. I've got to say, Klara, much as I loved Sadie, I didn't think much of it at the time.'

'But you did as she asked.'

'I did.'

Because he loved her. Even in her madness, that Sadie had inspired such love was a measure of her power.

'Right up to . . .'

'Right up to now. You asked me why now, why write to you now? It's because I've run out of time.'

I stared at him.

'I'm dying, Klara. Pancreatic cancer. One of the quick ones, which I suppose is a blessing.'

'I'm sorry.'

'Thanks. But don't be. It's not your problem.' He shrugged his shoulders. He had come to terms with his fate.

'Look, when I found out how bad it was, that we were talking months – if I was lucky – I knew I had to do something with all of her stuff. I'd put it off. Told myself it was best left.

341

Really though, it was because I wanted to hold on to it.'

'I see.' It made sense. Everyone had wanted a piece of Sadie.

'I'm sorry. I should have got in touch before. But I loved her. Having her things, keeping them for her – it . . .' He looked ashamed, and I saw a flash of the young man my mother had once known, and why she had trusted him. 'God, it's so stupid.'

I helped him out. 'It let you feel as though she wasn't really gone?' He looked relieved. 'Yes. I suppose it did.' He sighed. 'Anyhow, after the diagnosis I knew I couldn't carry on doing that. I had to do what I'd promised.'

'Give them to me.' It was the natural assumption. And it was almost correct.

'Sort of. Like I told you, when she came to see me she was distraught, all over the place. And she was still fixated on this idea that she would be remembered. She was terrified of being forgotten. So I promised her I wouldn't let that happen. 'You'll know when the time's right,' she kept saying, 'you'll know'. She was gripping onto my wrist and repeating herself, over and over again. 'Promise me. Promise me, Rupert.' So I promised, that when the time was right, I would pass her things on to someone who would tell her story.'

I was beginning to understand. The biographer or historian Sadie who had always imagined would be interested in her story had never quite materialised, just as her planned fame and fortune had never quite come to anything. But there was someone who was interested, someone who cared enough to pick their way through the past and unravel the threads of her life. Me.

I wrapped my fingers around my mug, as though to eke out the last vestiges of warmth from the rapidly cooling tea inside it.

'How did you find me?'

'I'd kept tabs on you, a bit, over the years. Not in a creepy way,' he added, hurriedly, 'I don't want you to think I've been lurking in the shadows or anything. Just making sure I knew where you were living. I'd been changing my mind about whether to send you the key or not. Part of me thought it was best to leave well alone – after all, you'd never have known any different, and nor would she. But then I saw that you were a lecturer, a writer. And I'd promised to give her things to someone who could tell her story. Who better to do that than her own daughter?'

And so that's what I have done; what she always wanted. It's taken me a while, and it's been the hardest thing I've ever done, but here it is, the truth of it, at long last. Sadie's story.

# Epilogue

Sadie walked down the street towards Archie's flat. It was a beautiful, bright day. The sun blazed in the sky, and she should have felt joyous, young and vital. But instead she felt like a husk of herself, as though Sadie had been scooped out from inside her body and left her with just this gossamer-thin shell. Like one of the dresses she had modelled, back when people had still wanted her to wear their clothes. Back when she had been wanted. Been somebody. It felt like a lifetime ago. She hadn't known then. Hadn't seen. Now, though? Now, she knew.

It was thanks to Coco, this lesson she had learned, Thanks to Coco, she thought, and laughed to herself. Nothing had turned out as she had planned – but had it turned out as Coco had planned? Was this what she had wanted all along? Sadie thought maybe yes. Though she couldn't think why. Why she would have found her, in St Albans, why she would have picked her, out of all the girls . . . but then women like Coco couldn't be pinned down to 'whys'. They were like vultures, devouring those who got in their way and those who didn't. They didn't need a reason.

Sadie was different. Sadie had a reason for what she was

doing now. The best reason, the only reason. Love. That was all there was. All that mattered. All that would remain.

She had watched as Archie left, hidden behind a tree in the park across the road. Lurking in the shadows, feeling like a shadow herself. Careful not to be seen. Careful not to move, not to let herself rush forward as she saw him kiss Coco goodbye. The couple exchanged a few final words, then Archie raised a hand in farewell as he got into the taxi. It was one of the hardest moments of her life, that holding back, that restraint. Every instinct she possessed prompted Sadie to race across the road, to put her arms around him, to tell Archie, 'Hello, it's me, I'm here, you don't need to be with her any more. I've come for you, I've come *to* you – we can be together now. It's just us, you and me, and nothing else matters.' Coco would fade away into the background forever, and allow Sadie to finally be where she should be, where she had wanted to be for so long.

She would miss Klara. Of course she would miss her little daughter. It was going to be hard. But she would see her, every so often. Henry was a reasonable man, a kind man; he would not keep her daughter from her out of spite, she trusted that. And you had to make sacrifices sometimes, in life. You had to let things go, in order to let other things come to you. It was part of the circle. She understood that. She would not be letting Klara go for ever; she would come back to her, and by then she would have Archie, and it would all have worked out.

*She* would have worked it out. She had been planning it for a long time. Knew what she was doing. Coco had to disappear – that was all there was to it. She was the one thing standing in the way.

She waited, across the street, in those gardens, until it was dark. Until the light went on in the flat she had under surveillance. Until she saw the silhouette at the window, drawing the curtains. Until hours had passed, and the lights behind the curtains had been extinguished, and she was sure. Absolutely sure.

She still had her key. A spare one that she had had cut, that she had never told Archie about and had kept long after she had given his back to him. She had kept it in her jewellery box, this most precious of objects, nestled amongst her diamonds and cut glass and trinkets. Every so often over the past few years she had taken it out, run her thumb along its edge, imagined sliding it into the lock and turning it. And then she would put it back in the box, and take comfort in just knowing it was there.

Now, she did what she had imagined so many times. Silently slid the oiled key into the lock, waited a moment, holding her breath, listening for any small sign that she had been overheard. But there was nothing. She crept in through the door. It was useful that she was such a husk of herself, she thought as she did so. It enabled her to move like a ghost, unheard, undetected, unnoticed. She was light and invisible and this would be her triumph.

She had the right sort of cigarette, the black Sobranies that Coco had smoked since she had known her, that Sadie had so coveted once, seen as the epitome of sophistication. Now they seemed to stand for everything bad. But there was still an appealing elegance to them. And they were essential to her plan. They would make it look like a tragic accident. Everyone knew Coco smoked the cigarettes – they had become her trademark, associated with her. And now they would be part of her memorial.

In the indigo light of the hall she paused and held the one she had out and ready to her lips for a second, pouting with an approximation of Coco's bee-sting lips into the mirror. Was that part of the appeal? she wondered. Coco's sexiness, her posed and perfect expressions. Was it her hair, or her laugh, was it the way she said 'chocolate' or any of those other strange things that people cited as reasons for loving someone? If she could just have done one thing, or done one thing differently, would he have loved her more?

Quickly. She must do it quickly now. She didn't know how much time she had.

She tiptoed to the living room and found the ashtray. It was half-full, as she had known it would be, of black cigarette ends. It made no noise when she tipped them out onto the cream carpet, nearer the door, as though the ashtray had been knocked off the arm of the sofa. They were light and the ashes scattered easily.

It made no noise when she took the lit cigarette between her lips and positioned it on the rug, near the sofa. The shagpile rug, with its long cream strands, made no noise as she ruffled it, so as to better direct the flames.

This was the riskiest bit. The part where she was most likely to be discovered. The noise, the smell – either might alert Coco to her presence, and then what would happen? She wasn't sure. There might be a fight, Coco might call the police. Sadie would be taken away and who knew what would happen after that. But that was all right. She had made her peace with that chance. Klara would be fine. Henry would look after her, that was the important thing. She would have failed in what she had set out to do, but at least she would have tried. And *he* would know. He would see the depth of her love and it would turn him back to her. Coco would never have done that for him.

She waited, despite the risk. She needed to make sure. And when she *was* sure, she silently slipped out of the flat and back downstairs, took up her place in the gardens opposite once more, and waited, and watched.

She had never known anything like the emotion she felt when they brought him out of the flat. Had never even known that such a feeling existed. He looked so frail on the stretcher, his body so insubstantial – not solid enough to be Archie's. Her heart leaped: *maybe it wasn't him. Maybe it was someone else*. But the look on Coco's face, Coco who was standing next to him, and staring down at his shrouded body, shaking and unable to move, told her that it was Archie. Archie who was not meant to be there, who had left that flat, whom she had seen with her own eyes walk down the steps and get into a cab, a cab that had taken him away. And now there he was, like some horrible reverse-magic trick, where the girl really is sawn in half and can never be mended, can never be stuck back together.

She was close enough to hear what the ambulancemen were saying, that was the worst of it. The words would haunt her forever. 'It was sheer bad luck that the fire caught in the way it did. If you'd planned it you couldn't have known it would go up like that. Just bad luck.'

The magician's assistant could never be mended, and nor, from that moment on, could Sadie.

And then it happened. Coco's eyes moved away from the body and towards where Sadie was standing, as though some magnetic force drew them there. Their eyes met, just for a second, and Sadie's breath stopped in terror. They stared at one another, both shocked, both unable to react.

And then Coco moved, breaking the spell, and with a flick of her wrist seemed to gesture to Sadie to leave, and Sadie did so, disappearing into the trees and running until she could run no longer and somehow she found herself at home, at her front door, repeating the phrase over and over again. *'If you'd planned it you couldn't have known . . . just bad luck.'*

\* \* \*

Henry pushed himself out of the chair where he had been sitting in the corner of her room, watching as she stared out of the window, her lips moving slowly. Some days she would relive it just once or twice. Other times it lasted all day, the words becoming jumbled as she tripped over them, unable to stop the record turning and turning in her head. He was grateful that, by pure chance, she had not done it when Klara was here earlier. Their daughter would have asked what she was saying, what she was trying to say, and there would have had to be more lies, more stories, and he was done with all of that.

As he stood up, her lips continued to move, as she went over and over and over the moments before she had died, before Sadie had ceased to exist. '*It was sheer bad luck that the fire caught in the way it did. If you'd planned it you couldn't have known it would go up like that. Just bad luck. Just bad luck. Just bad luck.*'

Always the same words. Her mind held on to them, grasping them. It would not let her forget. That was her punishment. Memory.

He had known, of course. He had always known. The final lie that he had told Klara – the one that he would never, ever admit to – was that he had no knowledge of what had happened to Sadie that day. That she had never told him, that no one knew. He knew. And Coco knew. And they had agreed never to tell. It was the last way he could care for his wife, could keep her safe from harm.

'The memory will not be Klara's,' he promised Sadie, as he went to the window and pushed the curtain aside to look out to the gardens beyond. Klara sat on a bench, her thin frame bundled up in a thick jacket. She looked fragile, and he felt fiercely, painfully protective of her, just as he had when she was a newborn baby, a squalling scrap of a thing. No. No more of Sadie's memories would be Klara's. He would save her from that, as he had tried to save her from it all, but had failed. This one last secret – that it was not he who was a murderer, but her mother – was one that he would keep.

He kissed Sadie on the forehead, and slowly walked away.

Read on to delve deeper into the world of
*The Lies You Told Me . . .*

# Reading Group Questions

- When Klara receives the note and key from 'NR' she doesn't mention it to her husband. Why do you think she doesn't tell him about her search?

- In the diary entries by Klara's mother we only get her version of events. Is Sadie an unreliable narrator?

- Do you feel Sadie's experience of the modelling world is related to the era in which she enters it, or more universal than that?

- Why do you think Sadie finds herself so attracted to Archie?

- Do you admire Henry for sticking by Sadie, even though he knows she pines for Archie?

- Coco is an ambivalent presence in the novel. How do you feel about her?

- Do you feel Klara's father is justified in keeping the truth secret from Klara? And why do you think 'Naughty Rupert' feels that Klara should know what really happened?

- If the truth is painful, is it sometimes better that we never know it?

- Discuss the importance of the parent–child bond in the novel, and the different ways in which it appears.

- What, for you, is the central theme of the book?

- How did you feel at the end of the novel? Is there a sense of redemption for Klara?

# Author Q&A

**Q: Where did the idea for *The Lies You Told Me* come from?**

The original seed of the idea actually came from one of my favourite poems, 'Autumn Journal' by Louis MacNiece. The line 'And all of London littered with remembered kisses' is one that I've always found hugely evocative – the image of all these kisses left lying around London by lovers, stored as memories, ready to be tripped over one day in the future . . . It built from there really, around the themes of memory and different versions of memories and the truth. I had wanted to write an unreliable narrator for some time, and have always been interested in epistolary novels and the use of ephemera, so combining the two formed the basis for Sadie's strand of the novel. And I loved the idea of a character delving into the past through those diary entries, winkling out the truth behind them, uncovering the layers of mystery . . .

**Q: Did you do much research into 1970s fashion and popular culture? How did you go about it?**

I find visual imagery really useful when I'm researching time periods. I spend hours on the Internet, doing Google image searches – it throws up all sorts of stuff I would never have found otherwise. Family photographs, fashion photography, old newspaper images – they all feed into the visual map I hold in my head and help me create the world I'm writing about. YouTube is also fantastic – a real treasure box for writers.

**Q: Do you think there is hope at the end of the novel?**

Yes, absolutely. I never really write traditional 'happy endings' as they tend to feel false to me, but there's usually an element of looking forward. In this novel, Klara is looking forward to the birth of her first child, and she's able to do so having reached a sense of resolution regarding her mother. She spent her whole life up to this point not knowing what had happened to her, with this huge, silent presence looming over her. Now she's able to rebuild her relationship with her father and also to build the foundations of her own family. Of course, there's still a little bit of a twist in the tale, as in the Epilogue we realise Klara doesn't know everything . . .

**Q: Where do you find inspiration for your novels?**

Everywhere and anywhere . . . I get ideas from articles and books, films, music, images . . . Almost anything can spark off a thought, which builds into a character, or a question, or a setting.

**Q: Where do your characters come from? How do they develop?**

I don't know where they come from really. They tend to emerge pretty fully formed – I don't do lots of those character building exercises. Their name is absolutely key, though – until I've got that right, I don't have a proper sense of them. Once I know that, and their place in the story, they're usually there, ready.

**Q: How did you first get into writing fiction?**

I had always been a reader and I come from a family where books are very important. I started off writing screenplays, then moved on to writing non-fiction and some journalism. I was editing and working for a small publishing company, and eventually I realised that what I really wanted to do was to write a novel. It had been in the back of my mind for ages but I hadn't felt the right idea. Then I started thinking about the idea which would eventually become my first novel, *Luxury*, and from that point on I knew I had to write the book. I wrote it over about two years while studying for a degree and working freelance, and it was published in 2009.

## Q: What advice would you give to an aspiring novelist?

Get it written. It's all very well having hundreds of great ideas, but what really counts is being able to sit down and write it, from beginning to end. It's not until you've done that that you can know whether your idea is really any good or not. And read, read, read.

# Jessica Ruston's Top Ten Themed Reads

Mothers and daughters, family mysteries, obsessive love and secret diaries . . . here are ten of my favourite books with themes that echo those in *The Lies You Told Me*.

### *Asylum* by Patrick McGrath
Probably my all time favourite book, this novel contains the best depiction of sexual obsession I've ever read.

### *The Hand That First Held Mine* by Maggie Farrell
This has various elements in common with my book – a dual narrative, family secrets, a London past and present setting and a moving portrayal of motherhood.

### *The Last Letter From Your Lover* by Jojo Moyes
A beautiful love story, more mingling of past and present and an inspired use of real-life love letters.

### *Engleby* by Sebastian Faulks
One of the best unreliable narrators in any recent novel. Deliciously creepy and, psychologically, incredibly astute.

**Gone Girl by Gillian Flynn**
This fantastic psychological thriller is utterly compelling and uses the diary of one of the main characters in a genuinely original and disturbing way.

*Rebecca* **by Daphne du Maurier**
Ghosts and memories and a lost love whose influence pervades the lives of all the players in this classic novel.

*House of Leaves* **by Mark Z. Danielewski**
The most original epistolary novel I've ever read, Danielewski uses letters, footnotes, interview typescripts and all sorts of other documents to tell a terrifying tale.

*The Thirteenth Tale* **by Diane Setterfield**
A big, juicy, family mystery. Gothic and gripping.

*Divine secrets of the Ya-Ya Sisterhood* **by Rebecca Wells**
A glamorous mother, a daughter trying to understand her and a scrapbook stuffed full of the past, this book is Southern women at their worst – and best.

*White Oleander* **by Janet Fitch**
The dark, difficult, intense mother–daughter relationship at the centre of this book is explored intimately and depicted unflinchingly.

JESSICA RUSTON

# The Darker Side of Love

Lies: we all tell them. To protect those we love, to disguise failure, to hide disappointment. To mask betrayal, or deceit. But what happens when they start to catch up with us? When our lives begin to be shaped by the lies of others?

The late 'noughties'. A global recession looms. A group of old friends, all leading outwardly successful, interesting lives. All in apparently loving, secure relationships. Yet all, in some way, lying to those closest to them, concealing secret worries, jealousies, desires. This group of friends is about to discover that the truth won't stay buried for ever . . .

Welcome to the darker side of love.

Praise for Jessica Ruston:

'It's the sort of book you want never to end. Intriguing, atmospheric and utterly mesmerising' Penny Vincenzi

'Deeply moving and emotional, full of twists and knockbacks, it's an addictive tale that you won't want to put down' *Heat*

'It's what long-haul flights were made for' *Elle*

978 0 7553 8360 3

headline
review

Now you can buy any of these other bestselling titles from your bookshop or *direct from the publisher*.

FREE P&P AND UK DELIVERY
(Overseas and Ireland £3.50 per book)

| | | |
|---|---|---|
| The Darker Side of Love | Jessica Ruston | £6.99 |
| Cuckoo | Julia Crouch | £6.99 |
| The Fall | Claire McGowan | £6.99 |
| The Other Half of Me | Morgan McCarthy | £7.99 |
| Stranded | Emily Barr | £7.99 |
| Heart-Shaped Bruise | Tanya Byrne | £6.99 |

TO ORDER SIMPLY CALL THIS NUMBER

**01235 400 414**

or visit our website: www.headline.co.uk

Prices and availability subject to change without notice